"Shelly, I do...

"No? You sure fooled me."

He took a step closer so she had to look up. "What do you think that display of lust by the river was about? It certainly wasn't hate."

Shelly raised her chin. "Maybe you hate me because you lust after me."

Dillon shook his head. Her pained, tear-soaked face was irresistible to him. He lifted a finger and stroked her wet cheek. "I have to be mean to you," he whispered, "to keep us apart. I have to get rid of you," he said, his fingers slipping over her jawline and down around her neck, "so I'll stop wanting you so badly. Every time I'm nice to you, I start kissing you." He moved so his body was flush against hers. Shelly's gaze was locked on his mouth as he spoke. "I don't hate you, I don't," he said softly. "I want you like you wouldn't believe."

Dear Reader,

December is a busy time for most of you, and we at Harlequin Historicals would like to thank you for taking a moment to find out what we have to offer this month.

From author Marianne Willman, we bring you *Thomasina,* the continuing story of a character from *Vixen,* Ms. Willman's first book for Harlequin Historicals. Set in the Mexican countryside, the heroine lives out her dream of becoming a doctor and discovers love along the way.

In *A Corner of Heaven,* newcomer Theresa Michaels has written the touching story of a woman reunited with the father of her child amidst the danger and hardships of the Civil War.

Isabel Whitfield's *Silver Fury* takes place in a California silver town where a stubborn washerwoman and a rebellious blue blood manage to overcome their differences and find happiness. Caryn Cameron's *King's Man* takes the reader to Tudor England where a lady smuggler and a loyal soldier outwit their common enemies.

We hope that you will enjoy our December titles. From all of us at Harlequin Historicals, our best wishes for the holidays and the year ahead.

Sincerely,

The Editors

Silver Fury

Isabel Whitfield

Harlequin Books

TORONTO • NEW YORK • LONDON
AMSTERDAM • PARIS • SYDNEY • HAMBURG
STOCKHOLM • ATHENS • TOKYO • MILAN

Harlequin Historicals first edition December 1991

ISBN 0-373-28705-4

SILVER FURY

ISABEL WHITFIELD

lives in a small town surrounded by mountains, with her husband and young daughter, one neurotic dog, two finches and two fat cats. Her favorite jobs of many tried are writing and working in bookstores. She dreams of having a garden, fruit trees and more time to read.

To the seven-year-old who played in bamboo
and wanted to be a movie star.
To Angela, who read the original and uncut story.
To the man who bowed for many, many years.

Prologue

⟲~~~~~~~⟳

The small cabin sat in the nightly darkness of the woods outside the town of Santa Cruz. Light stole from the edges of the shuttered windows, illuminating with a diffuse glow the branches of nearby trees thrashing in the wind. Grady Allen stopped in the dirt road and stared at the cabin. His upper body swayed forward, then back, and he concentrated on steadying himself before raising his bottle to take a long drink. He was not aware of the whiskey that trickled down his chin. Then he stumbled forward, as if wading in water.

A shutter flew open and banged against the wall, letting a square of light spill onto the forest floor. She was alone now that the mother was dead. He should stop...say he wanted the rent money now...not let her take advantage of him. And then he could look at her. He drained the almost empty bottle and tossed it into the darkness.

Inside the cabin, the crack of the shutter startled Shelly Young and she dropped the teacup she'd been washing. She stared down at the three pieces of pink pottery, chips and shards that had once been her mother's favorite cup.

The shutter slammed again and again, relentless and staccato, causing Shelly's neck muscles to tighten until her shoulders were three inches higher than they should be. She stepped over the broken cup and moved to the window, her jaw clenched against the repeated gusts of wind attacking the outer cabin walls. A cold, damp rush of air pressed against Shelly's back as she closed the shutter. She turned in puzzlement and saw her door wide open and Grady Allen standing grinning and swaying in the doorway.

Shelly instinctively took one step back. "What do you want?"

Grady's bloodshot eyes blinked. "The rent money." He smiled.

Shelly stiffened. "You said this afternoon you'd wait another week."

Grady stepped farther into the dirt-floored, two-room cabin. "Maybe that's not such a good idea." He closed the door behind him. "You must be scared in this storm."

"I'm fine."

"I have a good idea. You come up and clean and cook for me instead of Mr. Hill and I'll pay you the same wage he's payin' and give you your rent free." He grinned wide. "Sounds good, huh?" He moved closer to her until he stood three feet from her.

"I'll think about it, but it's late, and I'd like you to leave."

"Don't be tellin' me nothin' with your uppity mouth. Your ma raised you to be nothin' but trouble, not makin' you go to church and with that talk 'bout your daddy bein' such a fine man."

Shelly backed slowly to the fireplace as Grady's mood got nastier. Grady pursued her step for step. "Well, your ma is cold in the grave now, and you ain't got nothin' and nobody. I'll set you up real nice—hell, I'll even marry you if you're sweet to me!"

Shelly rolled her eyes and Grady grabbed her by the bodice of her dress and shook her. "Don't you be rollin' your eyes at me, girl!"

"Get your hands off me!" she yelled.

"Shuddup." He yanked her against him and grabbed her bottom with his other hand. He mashed his mouth down on Shelly's, the alcohol fumes almost making her vomit. She struggled just enough to keep his hands busy holding her tight. Then, reaching behind her, she grasped the fire poker and raised her knee into his male parts. Grady gasped and backed off, holding himself with one hand, but since her leverage had not been good and he was partially anesthetized with drink, he was not incapacitated.

"You goddamn bitch. I'm really gonna give it to you now." He lunged for her and Shelly swung the poker with a strength born of carrying water buckets and hefting sick animals. The iron caught him across the cheek and he screamed and fell backward, then crawled toward the door, blood streaming from his open cheek. Shelly stood unmoving while he rose to his knees and fumbled with the door latch. She moved across the room when he'd crossed her threshold and slammed the door on his heels.

Shaking and sweating she sat down on her cot, still holding the poker. "Drunken bastard," she muttered. She set the poker on the floor and lifted her feet onto the cot. Crossing her arms under her breasts, she slouched against the rough wood wall and stared down at the broken teacup.

It seemed fitting that the last pretty dish in the house was gone now that her mother was dead. The fire burned low, then out, but the oil lamp burned steady and bright on the table in front of her. Shelly's eyes, like two gray orbs, were fastened on the flame as she plotted her life from what had been to what would be.

Her mother had died four nights ago, her fingers wrapped around Shelly's wrist, her mouth and eyes open. Shelly had wakened, panicked, jumped from bed and realized her mother still held her. She had pried herself free, almost feeling revulsion at the cold, still form that had been Sarah Young.

She buried her mother the next day and hadn't left the inside of her cabin until this afternoon. The day of the funeral the sun had hurt her eyes and she'd wanted to throw rocks at the singing birds. Today she'd ventured outside and walked to her landlord's house to ask for an extension on her rent money, which Grady Allen had gladly given, along with a slow rub over her breasts as she'd raised the hood of her cloak. She'd thought that would content him, but obviously not.

She could stay in this place, replace her mother as housekeeper and cook for Mr. Hill. She'd been doing the work anyway the last few months of her mother's illness. Mr. Hill was a gentlemanly sort, not grasping and drunk like Grady Allen, but Shelly knew as sure as there were trees outside her cabin door that there was something beyond Santa Cruz for her. Besides, she'd have to find a new place to live. There was no way she was going to stay here and let Grady think she welcomed another attack.

She held up the pearl-and-diamond ring that had been her mother's engagement ring, which Shelly now wore on her hand. The diamond glittered and Shelly was dazzled.

San Francisco. She had enough money to get there and not a penny more. Domestic help was always needed there. Somehow, some way, she'd get together enough money to take her to New York, where her mother's family lived. She knew she belonged somewhere, and it certainly wasn't here in this small, isolated town.

Shelly sat up straight, tossed her long, thick braid of mahogany hair over her shoulder and decided which blanket to fill with her things. She threw in a few clothes and personal items and then wedged in her precious sketchbooks and drawing pencils. She changed her dress, leaving the one speckled with Grady's blood across a chair; she took a short nap, woke when dawn began to light the sky and stepped out her door.

Shelly screamed when she tripped over legs. She stifled herself, clutched her bulging blanket and gaped down at Grady Allen. Was he dead or just passed out? She relaxed when she heard deep breathing. He was going to want to lynch her when he woke. She stepped around his body and started running.

Chapter One

Shelly's eyes flew open to the darkness of her new room. She jumped out of bed and ran quietly through the silent kitchen to the tall case clock in the sitting room of the San Francisco boardinghouse. The black hands pointed to four-thirty, and Shelly smiled at her ability to wake early. She padded quietly back to her room, her bare feet freezing on the cold floor.

She had arrived in San Francisco more than a week ago and had landed a better position then she had hoped for. The Faulding boardinghouse was on the tenth street she'd walked down looking for work. Aggie Thornton's four-year-old daughter had opened the door at her knock, and Shelly had been met with the confusion of Tom Thornton saying goodbye to his wife as he prepared to leave with three of his boarders for the mines of Virginia City. Shelly pieced together that he'd decided to leave only the night before. She stood out of the way until the men departed and in the ensuing silence asked, "Will you be needing help now, ma'am? I can do just about anything and I can do it fast."

Tall, blond Aggie Thornton, eyes still snapping with anger at her husband, had looked Shelly up and down, staring at the dingy, bulging wool blanket tied over her shoulder.

"Can you cook?"

"Yes, ma'am."

"Can you sew? Can you use a hammer and nails? Can you bargain a fair price?"

Shelly nodded and kept nodding.

Silver Fury

"I won't allow any male visitors in your room."

"I'm not interested in men."

"Fine!"

Here she was now, cooking and cleaning and mending and shopping in return for her room—her very own room!—and board and a decent wage besides. But this wasn't the job she was up at four-thirty for. One of the boarders, a quiet man named Karl Booker, had confided to her about the robberies happening at his silver mine in Virginia City. He knew who the robbers were, but he couldn't prove it. Shelly had accepted his offer to clean the office building where the robbers met. A Mr. Snelling, the building owner, paid her to clean; Karl paid her to spy. At the rate she was earning, she'd be in New York by fall!

When Shelly quietly left the Faulding hours before dawn, the streets were deserted except for an occasional stumbling drunk, singing lustily and often incoherently. Shelly kept crossing the street to avoid all such personages. Now she hurried down a narrow alley to reach the back door of Snelling's Shipping. She groped in the darkness to find the still unfamiliar doorknob and did not feel safe until she shut and locked the door behind her and lighted the lamp.

She walked down the hallway to the front office of Snelling's Shipping. In the glowing rays of the lamp, she saw that yesterday's dusting and straightening had barely made a difference. She succumbed to a huge yawn, which made her eyes water, and decided she'd try sweeping and mopping today. A shiver of apprehension shot through her at the thought that she'd be eavesdropping for the first time this morning.

She threw off her cloak and patted her cap, making sure all her hair was tucked away according to Karl's instructions. She ran outside to fill her pail with water and then set it out of the way, at the back of the front office, in the middle of the doorway to the hall. While her chilled arms swept the broom across the floor, she thought of Aggie, who said she was crazy for venturing out, practically in the middle of the night, for extra money. What if she was a terrible failure at this spying? She didn't want to let Karl down or lose this extra income, but she was only an eighteen-year-old girl against a group of experienced crooks. Sometimes she forgot her age and her "position," as one of the Santa Cruz biddies had once told her. She certainly had not been raised with the rules and conventions of the other girls her age. She always felt she could do more than they felt capable of. Her pondering ceased when she heard the low rumble of male voices outside. She concentrated on the dust balls she was sweeping into the center of the room.

A key rattled in the back door and two men entered. Their eyes flicked from the pail up the hall to the girl busy sweeping in front of it in the wide front office.

"'Bout time this place was gettin' cleaned," said the smaller of the two men, smiling at Shelly. She nodded civilly in response. "Let's take a look, Parker," he said to the big man at his side. They both quickly opened the office doors that bordered the hallway in the back of the building, illuminating each office with a lamp.

Shelly kept sweeping as they made their way upstairs. Karl had said there would be four. She'd wait. She was still chilled in the drafty room, but her hands were perspiring profusely around the broom handle.

The back door swung open again while Shelly was on her hands and knees under one of the massive desks, trying to dislodge a crumpled paper. She twisted her upper body around, but all she could see beneath the obstruction of the desktop was a pair of legs in light gray trousers. The well-muscled thighs and black leather boots remained poised in front of her pail. The room crackled with silence. Shelly felt foolish when she realized her behind was wagging in this man's face. She returned to her efforts with the paper. When she turned back, the legs were gone and she breathed easier. She'd felt the wearer of those boots studying her. She crawled backward to get out from under the desk, but in the process of standing up she banged her head into the hard wood.

"Ouch!"

"You okay?"

She spun around to see a Mexican with a black, drooping mustache standing by her pail. Why did she have to leave it there? she cried silently.

"I'll be fine, thank you," she answered curtly, and picked up her broom. The Mexican shrugged and made his way up the stairs, also.

She gripped the broom tightly and furiously swept the floor, stirring more dust and dirt into the air than into her pile. Here she was downstairs, while the men she was supposed to be listening to were upstairs. Was this some kind of joke Karl had staged? No, Karl was not the humorous sort. She concentrated on the growing pile of dirt. At least she was doing the cleaning Mr. Snelling was paying her for.

Shelly considered leaving, but as she scooped the dust and debris into the pan a pure, clear drop of an idea fell in her mind. She froze. Yes, she could leave and there would be nothing strange in that to anyone. She would have finished her morning's work. The men didn't know what time she'd arrived. She smiled. To all appearances she'd be gone. Aware of the time she was wasting, she threw the pail of water out the back door and returned her supplies to the closet. She slammed the closet door shut and then did the same with the back door. A nervous grin flickered on her face.

Tiptoeing like a thief, she crept up the stairs. She congratulated herself for checking out the building the day before. And she felt like punching herself for not planning how she was going to overhear their conversation. She already knew that the portion of step closest to the wall did not creak. Halfway up, at the landing, she could hear voices. Her heart crawled into her throat as she took each step slower than the last.

They were behind the first door on the right. She pressed herself against the far wall and inched along it. Carefully, gently, she pushed open the door of the office next to the occupied one and disappeared inside. The moonlight trailed in dimly through the window, enough for Shelly to see her way around the small, cluttered room. She sidled up alongside the wall of cabinets that bordered the room where the men were.

"...keep our eyes open...it will get...it's just so damn frustrating...don't have that much...." Shelly rolled her eyes. To be able to hear snatches was worse than hearing nothing. Frustrated, she walked to the window that was ajar. She quietly swung it open and leaned out for some fresh air. The cool air and the sounds reached her simultaneously. She heard the measured steps of someone pacing, and two male voices were arguing about transportation to Virginia City in the cold and muddy month of April. Shelly saw that the window next door was open, also. She wanted to jump up and down with satisfied joy.

She carried a chair to the window to kneel on and leaned far out the opening so that her nose was almost buried in the mildew-plagued blooms of the window's flower box. A light drizzle fell on her head and neck, soaking down into her dress, but she didn't care. She could hear every word, even smell the savory aroma of pipe tobacco. A deep, rich voice was speaking.

"The winter snows have halted the robberies from the Avalon, but it's March now, and the snow will melt soon. I want to be prepared."

"Why do we have to meet so damn early, Dillon?"

"Winter has made you fat and lazy."

"Maybe, but you should know by now, *amigo,* that I would join you on any venture, even to that hellish place. No need to make me rise before the sun."

"I want these meetings before the building fills up with workers and clients." Then the man named Dillon began talking about guns, and an involved discussion ensued that bored Shelly. After about forty more minutes of guns, silver and stage routes, he drew the meeting to a close. Two of the men left and clumped down the stairs.

"How about some breakfast?" asked the Mexican.

"No thanks, Diego. I have to work on Ryder Shipping. I've been so distracted by the mine I'm lucky I still have a shipping business."

No, go for breakfast, pleaded Shelly. Diego left alone. Shelly raised her gaze to heaven as she contemplated leaving the building unnoticed. She scooted off the chair and rubbed her cramped legs and bruised knees. She put the chair back, shut the window and waited until her legs felt normal, then slipped down the stairs and outside. A black carriage waited on Battery Street at the end of the alley. The door opened and she climbed inside. Sinking back into the plush seat in relief, Shelly greeted the thin man across from her.

Karl was pleased with the information Shelly poured out to him. He had the driver of their carriage take a leisurely course around the city while Shelly talked. She told him that some of the ore in the Avalon was promising one thousand dollars to the ton. The man named Dillon was concerned that some of his employees in Virginia City were really working for someone else. The piece of information that made Karl's pale blue eyes glow was to hear that a shipment of ore was going to come down the mountain by a different route, a trail even more difficult than the popular Old Emigrant Trail with its rock-strewn path, which often twisted high on the edge of a ravine. Shelly took a deep breath when she finished.

"Well done." He tossed a small purse heavy with coins into her lap and her hand automatically closed over the velvet cloth. "I knew you were a bright girl."

Shelly nodded in agreement without thinking. Every syllable that fell from his lips was of interest to her, dusted as it was with a New York accent. She'd already asked him if he'd heard of a Young family or an Exeter, her mother's folks, but he hadn't.

The carriage stopped and Karl opened the door from his seat. The morning light had about as much color to it as the pale blue of his eyes. The hair of his head, mustache and beard was black, even darker than his black hat and such a contrast with his white face. He nodded, no expression ever marring the surface of his sharp-featured face. "I'll pick you up again next Wednesday and I'll see you at supper."

Shelly hopped out and found herself a block from the Faulding. Aggie had just started the coffee when she came running in. Shelly made straight for her room behind the kitchen, where she threw down her cloak and changed out of her damp clothes.

In the kitchen she helped Aggie, who was quiet and slow. Shelly was thankful, for it gave her time to review the events of the morning. As she set a fresh slab of butter in a dish she wondered who these men were besides the crooks Karl knew them for. She shouldn't worry or care—that was Karl's problem. She absently toyed with a button on her bodice as she wondered which name went with the man whose thighs she had stared at.

"I hate breakfast," muttered Aggie. "Tom always made it."

"Well, now I will," said Shelly. "Go see what Mary's doing." She set the bacon on to fry and cracked two dozen eggs into a large white bowl. Their deep yellow yolks bobbed in the sea of egg white. Shelly loved to cook. She liked the colors and textures of food; assembling it into different forms was like making a painting.

The table that morning was full of boisterous men. One timid woman sat quietly next to her husband. One man Shelly tried to ignore. He had a bushy yellow mustache, and his eyes followed her every move around the table. They lingered on the bodice of her dress, where her breasts strained against the rust-colored wool. Shelly frowned at him and he smiled at her unabashedly. She couldn't smash the butter into his face since it wasn't her boardinghouse, but one day she'd live in a house among respectful, loving relatives and she wouldn't have to serve, cook or clean for strangers again.

That evening after the dishes were washed and put away, Shelly, her sketchbook open in front of her, sat in the kitchen drinking tea with Aggie. The tea smelled like sweet,

night-blooming jasmine. Shelly knew her mother would
have appreciated the fragrance.

"Oh, Shelly!" exclaimed Aggie with a laugh, glancing at
the sketch Shelly had made of the leering man at the breakfast table.

Shelly studied the picture. "He does look ridiculous with
his tongue hanging out." She flipped the book shut and
watched Aggie mend one of Mary's frocks, though her fingers itched to make another drawing.

"I guess you'd tell me if you'd heard from Tom?"

Aggie stopped plying her needle. "It's too soon to expect
a letter, but I do have such a bad feeling. What will I do if
something happens to him?"

"Nothing will."

Aggie smiled sadly. "That's how I can tell how much
younger you are than me, Miss Shelly Young. You still believe you'll get everything you want when you want it, but
bad things happen every day."

Shelly crossed her arms under her chest and leaned back
in her chair.

"Mama, come keep me company," a little voice interrupted.

"All right, sweetheart, for a little while."

Shelly watched Aggie walk away with the little girl with
copper curls and brown eyes just like her father's.

"I better get what I want," she mumbled to herself. "I
don't want that much." She dumped out the cold tea and
washed their dishes. Later, ensconced in her little room, she
lighted a lamp and plopped her sketchbook in front of her
crossed legs on the bed. She flipped past pages of her
mother, her mother's animals, the flowers and vegetables
she had grown, Karl and other boarders, until she came to
a blank page. Eyes fixed on the page, she recreated two
thighs, knees and a pair of black boots. At the bottom of the
page she wrote *"Dillon?"* in her bold, slanted print.

Chapter Two

This was the thirteenth morning that Shelly had cleaned Snelling's building, but it would be only the sixth time she'd eavesdropped on the gathering of men. The other times in the past four weeks, only the man named Dillon Ryder had come. He stayed in his office at the top of the stairs and worked. Shelly arrived first and did her cleaning, and on the days the men met, she hid in the office next door and eavesdropped. The days only Dillon Ryder came she left after cleaning. Something in his dark visage warned her to stay out of his way, not to mention, of course, that he was a thief.

Her work at the Faulding and getting up early three mornings a week for this job was taking its toll on her. She had light blue shadows beneath her eyes and often fell asleep at night in the midst of sketching, but her funds were increasing and she was much closer to getting to New York.

The pail of soapy water she lugged across the office floor felt pounds heavier to her than it had the first week. This morning she was washing windows. The muscles of her shoulders and the back of her neck protested as she raised her arm and began scrubbing.

The men had met twice last week instead of once, due to the worsening state of their affairs. When they talked she tried to make her mind like a blank piece of paper that they filled with their words. She had restrained herself from bothering Karl with questions until last week, when she asked him why this Dillon Ryder spoke as if he were the owner of the mine.

"Ryder has a few shares in the mine," Karl had explained, "but he's not satisfied. Since I'm the principal investor, I'm the one who is suffering from his continual attempts to funnel off large amounts of silver with his band of cutthroats. Do you understand?" His back was relaxed against the carriage seat across from Shelly, but his eyes held hers.

"Yes. He just sounds so sure of himself."

"Miss Young—" his voice remained soft and patiently controlled "—most thieves believe that what they are stealing rightfully belongs to them. It's easier that way."

"Oh. I thought that thieves just didn't care that what they wanted belonged to someone else." When she had picked Mr. Hill's flowers as a child she hadn't thought they belonged to her, she'd just wanted them.

"Don't let Mr. Ryder fool you. He's a dangerous, violent man. He takes what he wants by any means available to him. Don't for any reason become involved in a conversation with him."

"I don't intend to," she said, meeting his stare.

"Good. I don't want you to get hurt."

He had looked out the window of the moving carriage then, his words hanging in the space between them like a threat. Shelly had more questions she wanted to ask but doubted they'd be received well.

She wondered why she didn't feel reassured that Karl was concerned about her welfare. She lugged the pail to the next window. She felt caught in a precarious position between two men fighting over one mine. She didn't completely trust Karl, but she had no specific reason to doubt him, either. As for Ryder's gang, they were scoundrels in Shelly's opinion. Their meetings often ended with talk of the women at the whorehouse called Lacy's. Diego and Lloyd were especially vocal on the subject. Shelly had passed the tall brick building with the peach curtains a couple times. Once, she had tried to imagine what went on behind those pretty curtains. Her images of such things were formed from what she'd seen her mother's animals doing, and to think of grown men and women acting like that was embarrassing. She'd never had the nerve to ask her one female friend in Santa Cruz, who'd married at fourteen and already had three babies, about the details of making the babies.

Shelly could not wait to be finished with this job and escape these men.

Dillon strode down the street to Snelling's with an ugly sneer on his face. For the past two weeks he'd been growing more and more furious. The theft and sabotage of his mine seemed unrelenting; he was losing thousands in ore at every twist and turn of the road down from the Sierras. The highwaymen even found the alternate routes he and his men had used. Almost everyone had some losses due to robbery, but the Avalon was robbed too frequently. Someone was playing informant and damned if he knew who. Why had he become a target? Was it personal? Every trap he had set for the culprits had failed.

The men he employed were jittery, on guard against one another, not knowing who would turn out to be on the other side. Dillon had Parker and Lloyd followed, but they were innocent. His father had urged Dillon by letter to put a watch on Diego, but Dillon refused to do that to his friend. Diego was the one person he completely trusted. His other partner, Adam Jefferies, came close. Dillon had grown up next door to Jefferies in New York. The man was intelligent, decent and generous with his considerable wealth.

Lloyd had left San Francisco to help Jefferies in the mountains of Nevada. Dillon planned on leaving himself. He was nervous about his stolen silver being shipped out, but he had little chance of preventing that even if he was around. He had contacted all of his fellow shippers with whom he was on good terms to keep an eye out for any suspicious amount of large unsmelted ore whose owner had an unfamiliar name. The names of mine owners who had struck rich veins were public knowledge in this town.

The whole thing made him sick. He had sunk considerable time and money down his shaft in the hard rock of Sun

Mountain. His father must be laughing back in New York. He'd written him of his problems, hoping for some sound advice from a man who had been successful; all he'd gotten in return was the "I told you so" message and a strong suggestion to come back to New York and concentrate on Ryder Shipping. Dillon's hands were clenched tightly as he turned down the alley to Snelling's building.

He pushed the door open on its creaky hinges. He was very early, since he couldn't sleep more than a few hours these days. He wandered down the hall into the front office, glancing at the girl washing the windows. He welcomed the improvement in the offices. Gone were the dust piles, caked mud from men's boots, the odor of cigar butts and mold. Snelling was too busy to notice his surroundings but had acted on the complaints of men in his employ and those who rented space from him.

The girl turned and gave Dillon a cool, bored look, then swiveled back to the window. He'd never thought her worth much notice the few times he'd seen her, but this morning his agitated state was making him acutely aware of everything around him. All that he saw in her face were her incredible eyes. They were of an extraordinary hard, silver gray; they were the most intriguing thing he'd seen in weeks. Funny he'd never noticed, but he was like that, always so busy and preoccupied that he often missed what was going on right under his nose. And her expression while she regarded him was almost disdainful. Why should she feel that way about him? Had he offended her? Offended someone close to her? *Under his nose.* Hadn't she begun working here at the same time he'd started holding his early morning meetings? He remembered staring at her skirts under that desk the first morning he'd seen her. He'd asked Snelling about her the next day. The girl had approached Snelling about the position and his clerks had threatened to leave if he didn't hire her. Why had she come here of all places?

Dillon's breath slowed and then ceased. Realization ignited in his gut and flamed up to burn in his eyes. All fatigue left him and he reached her in three strides.

"You!" he accused furiously. He whirled her around to face him, his eyes blazing blackly down into hers.

"What?" cried Shelly. Waves of fear rose up like bile in her throat.

"What a fool I've been. Weeks of searching and here you are!"

"I don't know what you're talking about," she said, spinning away from him.

"You've been spying on us! God, what you've cost me." His eyes bored into her.

"I haven't done anything to you," she forced herself to say calmly, staring back.

"What's going on, Dillon?" asked a voice behind them.

Dillon turned to Parker, then pointed behind him at Shelly, who backed way. She stumbled over her pail, knocked it over and fell with a thud onto her hip and elbow.

"This is what is wrong—our little spy here, our little maid."

"Her?" Parker looked down at the sprawled girl pushing herself up, her skirts dripping wet. "Dillon, I can't believe that."

With arms crossed, Dillon looked at Parker in disgust. "It makes beautiful sense. The robberies picked up with the thaw, as we suspected they would, but they took a disastrous turn for the worse about four weeks ago, and that is when this—this maid," he stammered, "began *cleaning* here."

Diego walked forward from where he had been standing by the door, listening to Dillon's accusations. He looked at the girl slowly rising from the floor. "She looks pretty harmless."

"Of course, a perfect disguise on someone's part." He turned and glared at Shelly. "Who are you working for?"

Shelly stared at him silently, her mind a complete blank. Her bruised hip throbbed. Dillon Ryder was frightening in his anger. Karl's words came back: *dangerous, violent.* The three men stared at her as she faced Dillon. She held her chin

high and her back rigid, but her limbs shook. "I work for
Mr. Snelling. Ask him!"

"Who else?"

"No one else."

"You're lying!" He reached for her, but Diego stepped in
front of him.

"You don't know she lies."

"I know." He did not take his eyes off her pale face.

Shelly threw up her hands. "You see me clean here! Why
would I lie?" She had to talk fast. This dark-haired devil did
not look as if he would believe anything she said, although
the others might. "I'm in here washing windows, minding
my own business, wishing I was home in bed, and you come
in here and accuse me of I'm not sure what and make me
fall." She gingerly touched her burning elbow and stared at
the blood that came away on her fingers. "I'm bleeding,"
she said softly.

Parker and Diego turned to Dillon. "It's not my fault,"
he yelled. "She tripped over her own stupid pail!" He
brushed Diego aside and walked toward the girl, who
stepped backward until her legs bumped a chair. "Sit and
talk."

Shelly sat, glaring at him. Parker walked over and handed
her his white handkerchief. She smiled gratefully and gently held the cloth to her elbow. The room was silent as she
removed the cloth and looked at the red stain.

Dillon appeared unmoved. "All right, Miss...?"

"Young."

"Miss Young, let's begin, shall we? How long have you
worked here?"

"About four weeks."

Dillon looked meaningfully at his friends. Diego
shrugged. "Coincidence," he said.

Damn them, fumed Dillon. Why did they refuse to see the
connection? "Where are you during the day, Miss Young?"

"I work and live at the Faulding on Powell Street. It's a
boardinghouse." Just let me go, she pleaded inwardly, and
I'll never come back.

Dillon walked up to her and rested his hands on the arms of her chair as he leaned over her. His expression was fierce, but under the rigid lines of his mouth he had a soft cleft in his chin. In a quiet, coaxing voice that contrasted with the hardness of his eyes, he continued interrogating her. "Why would you need more work? I assume you get free board and they work you hard." The false friendliness dropped out of his voice. "What would entice you to get up at such an ungodly hour to scrub more floors?"

"Money," Shelly answered unflinchingly.

"Ah, yes, the money. How much?"

"None of your business!" She hated the way he had his face so close to hers and knew he was trying to frighten her. He was a brute. She would never confess, and there was no way they could find out about her spying, yet she couldn't stop trembling.

Dillon ran his hand through his dark hair as he turned away from her. "We can't prove anything."

"Let her go," Parker urged from the desk edge he had set his weight on. "She's always been gone before we finish. We're all a little on edge," he added, seeing Dillon's reluctance to give up.

Dillon whirled on Shelly, making her jump in her seat. "I have my eye on you." He pointed a finger at her. "If you're at all responsible for my troubles, you'll suffer the consequences. Now get out of here!"

Shelly did not wait to hear him say it twice. Without looking at any of them she stood up and walked stiffly to her cloak on one of the big oak desks. She could feel three pairs of eyes boring into her back. "Since you want me to leave now, I'll let you wipe up the spilled water." She pulled on her cloak and strode out of the building, slamming the door behind her.

She had to walk to the Faulding, since she'd left Snelling's before Karl arrived in his carriage. Besides, the last thing she needed was that man with the black eyes to see her getting into a handsome carriage that no maid could possibly afford. Her hands shook under the rough wool of her cloak.

They were still shaking as she opened the back door of the Faulding and stepped inside. Aggie was pouring herself a cup of coffee when she looked up to see Shelly come in. Her welcoming smile died on her lips.

"Why are you wet?"

Shelly looked down at the soggy wool of her skirt showing beneath the cloak. "I...tripped. Stupid of me, but I was washing the windows and I stepped without looking and fell over the pail."

Aggie shook her head. "You do too much, Shelly. Look at yourself! The hollows under your eyes grow darker every day."

"Oh, stop. It shouldn't be much longer anyway."

"Is it that important to get to New York? You won't know a soul there. Your family will be complete strangers to you. Maybe you won't like them."

"Family is family. It's where I belong. I won't serve strangers all my life."

"If you would just quit this morning job and put off going a little longer."

Shelly shook her head. She had to go back to Snelling's or Dillon would be confirmed in his suspicions. "I'll have enough saved soon. Don't worry about it. Now, I thought I'd make muffins this morning, apple muffins. I'll have the apples diced in minutes. You just sit down and drink your coffee."

Aggie did as she was told. She relied heavily on the girl and thought of her more and more as family; she was disappointed that Shelly was determined to leave as soon as possible.

It was early evening when Shelly came in from an errand Aggie had asked her to do. She had walked long in the damp, chill air of the windy April day. In Santa Cruz she'd often walked through the woods whenever the mood took her. Her face glowed now with color. She set the basket of oranges that she had purchased for tomorrow's breakfast on the table. Aggie stood quietly behind a chair and did not return Shelly's smile.

"I had a visitor while you were gone."

"Oh?"

"A man named Dillon Ryder." Aggie watched Shelly's face drain of color. "He asked about you."

"He gave me a difficult time at work this morning." Shelly pulled off her cloak and cast it over the back of a chair.

"Why didn't you mention it?"

"I didn't want to worry you. He accused me of spying on him. Ridiculous, isn't it?"

"Yes! But why would he suspect you? He wanted to make sure I knew where you went in the mornings. He wanted to know of your character."

Shelly dumped the oranges into a blue-and-white bowl. "What did you tell him?" She thought it was rather bold of him to come asking about her when he was the thief.

"I said you were a hard worker and I trusted you completely."

Shelly swallowed a lump of guilt. "Thank you."

Aggie shrugged. "It's the truth. I don't know why, but I feel that something terrible is going to happen. I worry all the time about Tom. I should have heard from him by now. And now this Dillon Ryder! He was very polite, but he seemed...dangerous." Aggie studied Shelly's blank face. "Please don't go back there."

"If I don't, he'll be convinced that I was the one spying on him and think I'm too scared to go back."

"You *should* be scared to go back there, whether you spied on him or not!"

"I'm going, Aggie."

"You're going crazy." Aggie picked up a dish towel and slapped it against the table.

Karl Booker opened his door at Shelly's quiet knock. She looked up and down the upstairs hallway and slipped inside his room.

"What happened? I waited in the carriage, but you didn't come."

Shelly faced his coal-black hair and tense white face. "He knows. Dillon Ryder knows I've been spying on him, though he can't prove it."

"Damn! I knew it had to happen sooner or later!" He slapped the stack of papers he'd been holding down on the table in his room. "You didn't hear anything today, then?"

She shook her head and quickly described the morning's events. "I thought I'd go back tomorrow and make like I'm innocent, but I don't know if they'll even be there, since he suspects me."

Karl scratched at his beard and appeared to be thinking about something else. Then his eyes turned on her, their paleness disturbing her, their alertness making her feel he'd been thinking about a great many things. "By all means, go back tomorrow, but only to clean. Now that Dillon's caught on he'll move fast."

Shelly cocked her head. "You know him well."

"I know him."

"Did you know him in New York?"

"What makes you think he's from New York?"

"I can hear it in his voice when he gets mad."

Karl ignored her comment and brusquely threw her a bag of coins. "You now have enough to get to New York. I thank you for your help. I couldn't have done it without you, Miss Young." He opened the door for her.

What had she done exactly? Wouldn't Dillon go on stealing from the mine? But Mr. Booker very much wanted her to leave, and she didn't want to be seen standing in his room by a passing boarder, so she left.

At five o'clock the next morning Shelly was finishing the window washing on the second floor at Snelling's. She was tired and knew she wouldn't serve breakfast with much grace. This would be her last day here. She'd return her key to Mr. Snelling this afternoon. Her mind was little on wiping out the streaks across the windowpanes and mainly on escaping the building before the men showed up. The thought of seeing Dillon Ryder frightened her. She had no doubt he'd make her suffer if he could prove his accusations. Shelly pictured him slowly strangling her while staring down at her with his black eyes. She jerked out of her imaginings to find herself standing in the middle of the room, wringing a cleaning cloth in her perspiring hands. Well, if he dared touch her she'd knee him so hard in the groin he'd scream in agony, just the way Mr. Hill had taught her after an older boy in town had accosted her in the woods.

She gathered up her cloths and the pail and blew out the lamp. She'd find her way downstairs in the dark because she'd already extinguished the lights below to speed her departure. She was making her way down the darkened hallway when she heard a key rattle in the back door. First, she just felt surprise, but when the door swung open and she heard the male voices, her throat constricted painfully. They were early!

She took two steps forward but became paralyzed when heavy footsteps started up the stairs. She urged herself to walk past them but did not move. What would he think of her here in the darkened building? Her conscience, tainted with guilt, colored her perceptions.

In a flood of dismay Shelly bolted for the office nearest her before the men rounded the corner at the landing. It was the room she always listened from. She closed the well-oiled door behind her and hid in one of the large cabinets bordering the thin wall. This was the place she'd eavesdropped from when their office window was closed. She sat holding her pail in her lap, cursing them, cursing herself and cursing Karl. She didn't want to do this anymore. She was scared. Her usual impulsiveness and bravado had carried her far, as they always did, but they'd fallen away when Dillon Ryder's hard hand had grasped her shoulder and spun her around. He was no drunk Grady Allen she could push over when he got out of hand. He was all big man, full of pulsing energy that was completely unfamiliar to her.

She leaned her head back, closed her eyes and listened to them offer up some ridiculous schemes to protect their silver. Who wouldn't question that many coffins coming down the mountain? She sat up straight when she heard her own name.

"Miss Young doesn't seem to be the culprit. The proprietress at the Faulding backed up everything the girl said and had great confidence in her. Snelling said he'd send a clerk to pick up the key from her if she'd been a problem. I think that's a good idea. We might have incurred her resentment because of our unfounded accusations. Enough about her. Here's a list of men that I want eliminated immediately. They're all suspected informants."

Shelly was shocked. Now she really knew what kind of crooks these were if they'd kill men not proven guilty. Had they spared her because she was female or because they really believed her innocent? Dillon Ryder said he was giving everyone a copy of the list and leaving one in the desk drawer for Lloyd when he returned this evening.

Shelly had to see that copy! She'd relay the information to Karl and he could warn those men. Diego talked Dillon and Parker into joining him for breakfast. They stomped down the stairs while Shelly's heart pumped furiously. She burst out of the cabinet as soon as the back door slammed behind the men. She ran into the office next door and went straight to the only desk. Never before had she taken anything material, but this was justified, she told herself. Her hand hesitated only for a moment before she yanked open the desk's top drawer. A newly folded piece of paper lay on top of some files. She grabbed it and ran to the window to see by dawn's light the names of the condemned men. But when she gazed down at the opened sheet, she gasped—the paper was blank!

"Well, well, well!"

Shelly spun around, clutching the paper to her breast, and gaped at the glittering eyes in Dillon Ryder's furious face. She groped for something to say, some defense, but there was no point.

He walked slowly, carefully, to her and snatched the paper out of her hand and slipped it inside his coat pocket. "You won't need this." His fingers closed on her arm. "Come with me."

She let him lead her through the office, but at the door she jerked her arm out of his grasp and bolted down the stairs. Dillon ran after her and at the back door his fingers clutched her skirt. He yanked her from the door of her escape and held her tightly.

"You'll never get away," he sneered. She flailed at him with her arms and legs in a frantic effort to break free; she was such a bundle of writhing motion that Dillon could not contain her, and she ran down the few steps of the building and through the alley toward Battery Street.

The big black carriage was waiting at the end of the alley. The door swung open when she was almost upon it. She thanked God that Karl had thought to come this last time. But instead of Karl's calm figure sitting coolly on the seat, there was another man, a Mexican. Shelly stopped in her tracks and cast one anguished look behind her. Dillon walked up with a satisfied, malevolent smile on his dark face. Shelly shuddered, the shaking extending to her hands and legs. Her one last attempt to flee was aborted by his strong hands, which gripped her waist and lifted her into the carriage.

Chapter Three

Shelly sat frozen across from Diego. He met her eyes and looked away, his mouth tight. Dillon Ryder climbed in and the carriage rolled off at a fast pace. He reached over and forced her head up, his fingers under her chin.

"Start talking."

Shelly drew back in her seat. Dillon growled and Diego grabbed his arm.

"Don't worry, I won't hurt her." He shook off Diego's hand.

Shelly lowered her eyes to the floor. The carriage came to an abrupt stop and Diego got out first and held the door. Dillon reached over and pulled Shelly out with him. They were in a deserted alley at the back entrance of a three-story building.

"Where are you taking me?" she asked hoarsely.

"No answers until *I* get some."

He yanked her toward a flight of wooden stairs, but Shelly, the desperation of her situation setting in, grasped the banister at the bottom of the steps and held on with fierce determination. Dillon tried jerking her away, his hands closing on her waist. Shelly locked her arms on the wooden pole and screamed.

At the top of the stairs Diego raised his hands. "Shut her up!"

Dillon clamped one hand over Shelly's mouth, wrapped his arm around her waist and pulled. Shelly clung. Dillon let go of her waist and wrenched one of Shelly's hands off the wood railing. Holding her wrist, he pulled her other hand off, then cinched his arm around her arms and waist and carried her up the stairs and into a long dark hallway, his hand still over her mouth. Diego held open the door to a room and Dillon deposited the squirming girl inside.

"Here, hold her hands while I tie her mouth." Dillon gagged Shelly's mouth with his bandanna, the cloth tied so tight at the back of her head that she was sure her mouth would split at the corners.

"Now what?" asked Diego, pushing Shelly's hands back to Dillon.

Dillon looked Shelly up and down. She twisted futilely in his grip and then stood still. "Give me your bandanna." Dillon bound her hands with the red scarf.

"Well, we're out of bandannas."

Dillon glanced at his friend. "Thank you for that observant piece of information." Diego grinned. Dillon looked back at the girl. *Yes, now what?* He wanted answers but didn't know how to get them. He wished he could hand the job to Diego, but his friend would probably take the girl out to breakfast and compliment her on her brilliant eyes, which were now narrowed on Dillon. Wearily, he reached for the worn gold drapery covering the window. He ripped off a strip.

"Sit." He nodded his head toward the small settee. She didn't budge. Dillon pressed her down, then jerked his hand from the burning warmth of her shoulder through her dress. Her damp heat reminded him she was scared, and young. He bound her feet together and to the leg of the settee. "That ought to keep her quiet," he muttered.

Shelly shivered as she stared up at the two men who towered above her. Dillon Ryder walked out into the hall with Diego. She could hear them having a hushed conversation but could not make out a word. In the short reprieve she had from that awful man's presence, she looked around the small, one-windowed room. A red carpet spread out under her feet. The furniture consisted of a settee upholstered in worn gold brocade, a low table in front of it and a taller table at the side. The tall table held a lamp, but the room was illuminated only by the early morning grayness pouring in between the open draperies.

Shelly pulled her gaze away from the window when Dillon returned.

"I have a busy day ahead of me, so don't take long to answer my questions when I remove that gag." He bent down to loosen the cloth. "If you raise your voice, I'll tighten this so tight you'll have a smile to your ears. Understand?"

Shelly nodded.

"I want to know who you're working for."

His body was tightly coiled, waiting for a name to drop from her lips. Shelly wished she could save herself by telling him, but she would not release this man on Karl.

"I can't tell you," she whispered.

Dillon's face clouded and his lips tightened into a rigid line. He pushed himself away from her. "You don't deny what you did?"

The silver gray eyes glittered up at him. "No, I spied on you."

"Why?"

Shelly gazed up at him in growing bewilderment. Why was he so slow to suspect the man he was stealing from?

"Never mind why. Who for? Whatever he's paying you, I'll pay more. I've already lost thousands—what's a hundred more? Just tell me the bastard's name!"

"Let me go and I won't bother you again."

Dillon stepped away and laughed. "You'll never get the chance!" He stood, hands on hips, looking down at her. Her gaze met his for a second before she averted her eyes nervously. Her face was pale and her bottom lip and chin had a slight tremor, but she was far from breaking. He chewed on the inside of his cheek for a full minute. "Are you so devoted to all of your friends?" he asked softly. "How about the blond woman at the Faulding?" Dillon's eyes glowed when she suddenly stiffened. He moved close, so close she had to tilt her head up to see him. "If you don't tell me what I want by evening, when I return, your blond friend is going to be very sorry she ever knew you."

"Aggie has nothing to do with this!"

Dillon snorted. "But you do, and you aren't talking." He reached down to her.

"No! Leave her alone!"

He retied the gag. "Think about who's more defenseless." One dark brow arched up as he listened to the muffled noises coming from behind Shelly's gag. "Don't make a hasty decision. You'll have plenty of time to sit here and consider it."

Shelly blinked dazedly at the white door when it closed behind him. She would not cry, she would be brave, but one silly, hopeless tear slid down her cheek anyway. When he came back she would give him what he wanted. Karl could protect himself better than Aggie could against Dillon's pack of thieves. None of the money was worth this, she thought.

The sun was fast declining in the sky when Dillon Ryder quietly slipped back into the purple-shadowed room. Shelly turned her head when she heard the door open. Her body was numb from the agony of sitting in one position all day. She shuddered under his scrutiny. He bent down and untied her gag.

"What's his name?"

"Karl Booker," she whispered, her voice barely audible.

Dillon remained expressionless. "I've never heard of him." He reached inside his coat and pulled out a small whiskey flask.

"What are you doing?"

"I want you to drink this."

"Why? I'm telling you the truth! That's his name." He unscrewed the top of the flask. "He's real tall and thin, he has black, black hair...he always wears black." He held the flask to her lips and Shelly twisted her head away.

"Remember the blond lady," he warned.

Shelly's eyes clung to his face. "His name is Karl Booker. He's staying at the Faulding! You can find him there." She was puzzled by how unenthused he was about the information. He again pressed the flask to her lips and Shelly choked as the burning liquid flowed down her throat. He forced her to drink until the flask was empty, then screwed the top on and went to stand at the window, his back to her.

"I'll tell you the same thing no matter how drunk you make me!"

She was not sure how long he was away from her side, but when he returned all of her bodily discomfort was gone. She felt limp and had a difficult time remembering why she was in this strange room.

Dillon lifted her to her feet. She swayed slightly but remained where he'd stood her. "Who have you been working for?" He tilted her head up and looked into her eyes, noting the dilation of the pupils. The laudanum had affected her quickly. She smiled vacantly at him. He shook her. "Who hired you to spy on me?"

"Spy?" She slurred the word. "So tired...sit down...shaking me..."

"Damn." Dillon pulled off her white cap and was surprised at the length and thickness of the coiled braids crowning her head. He threw her cloak, which he'd retrieved from Snelling's, about her shoulders, fastened the clasps down the front and pulled the hood over her head. He took her arm and walked her out the door, but she couldn't manage the stairs and he had to carry her down. He plopped her in the seat of the carriage waiting at the bottom. Diego held the door open.

"She gave me the name Karl Booker, not that I believe it's real. I've never heard the name. She says he's staying at the Faulding, not that I believe that, either, but check it out. Be quick. The boat leaves in an hour."

"You're taking her with us?" Diego's voice came close to squeaking.

"I don't have any choice," Dillon responded vehemently.

Diego rolled his eyes. "You could have a carriage take her to the Faulding, or you could just leave her here! Ah, *amigo*, I think you have gone *loco*. She can't do you any more harm."

"I want what she knows. I think I gave her too much laudanum, so I'll ask her again when it wears off. And she'll be more scared when she finds out she's not in San Francisco anymore. I'm going to make sure she never gets in my way again."

Diego threw his head back and laughed. "She is going to be in your way every minute of every day from now on. I tell you, leave her!"

A muscle in Dillon's right cheek jumped. "Just go check on this Karl Booker."

Diego turned away, shaking his head. "You'll see," he threw over his shoulder. "You'll regret this."

The deck of the riverboat to Sacramento was crowded with men anxious to discover what luck they would have finding silver in Nevada. In the darkness were small mountains of packages filled with food, blankets and miner's tools to be sold at exorbitant prices in the new mining towns.

Dillon sat under an overhang on a bench facing the boat railing. He had one arm wrapped tightly around the girl next to him. A blanket was draped about her and enveloped her face. Dillon pressed her head against his chest. Shielded like this, he felt sure no one would notice her drugged state. Parker sat on the other side of her.

The boat was ready to pull away when Diego bounded up the gangplank. He did not wait for Dillon to ask.

"A man named Karl Booker left last night. That was all Mrs. Thornton would tell me. She 'will not discuss' any of her boarders past or present. I bought one of her boarders a drink, a Mr. Klapper. He was more informative. This Karl Booker was tall, thin, had black hair, beard and mustache, and he was very polite and even more quiet, almost unfriendly. He did not socialize with any of the boarders. He'd been boarding there for eight months. He sold insurance for a company back East. He gave no reason for leaving. The end."

Dillon sighed. "Thanks, Diego. I knew he wouldn't be there. She worked there. I'm sure she knew he had left. He's the perfect person for her to accuse."

"There is the small possibility that she's not lying," Diego said.

"But it's damn small. How can I trust someone who was already involved in a deception?"

"I really didn't think it could be her," Parker commented, peering into her sleeping face. "She's so young, and so little."

"What do we do with her?" asked Diego.

"We'll let her know how much we enjoyed chatting with her blond friend, this very respectable Mrs. Thornton," replied Dillon.

Parker said nothing and Diego rolled his eyes.

Shelly became slowly aware of how her body bounced and rocked. She wanted to sleep but couldn't stop moving and jerking awake. Her head cracked against something hard and she whimpered and opened her eyes.

Diego. He sat across from her, his legs stretched across the stagecoach floor. His black hat was tipped low on his forehead, and he appeared to have his eyes closed, but she felt him watching her. Slowly she uncurled her legs from the seat and lifted her head from the side of the small coach. Pain throbbed behind her eyes. A snore at her side made her turn to see Parker lolling next to her. She straightened and scooted as far from the big man as the seat would allow. Any minute he was going to topple into her lap.

"Where are we going?" Her voice was a bare husk of its former self. Diego didn't answer. Shelly's eyes narrowed and she clenched her teeth against the urge to kick his booted feet. "Mrs. Thornton? Is she all right?"

He lifted his hat a fraction of an inch and met her gaze. "I have orders not to talk with the prisoner."

"I don't want a conversation! I'd just like to know about Aggie and where I am!"

He lowered his hat. Shelly snapped up the shade and looked out the window. "I've never been here," she muttered to herself. She couldn't recall much since she'd been trussed up like a hog in that room. Obviously some drug had been added to the whiskey. She vaguely remembered a body of water; that must have been the Sacramento River. She also remembered being held, arms often around her, warm and tight. She shuddered, assuming Dillon had touched her. At least he wasn't in the coach. She checked the braids on her head and repinned them. Her nerves stretched taut in the midst of the silent men. Had they done anything to harm Aggie, as that horrible man had implied? Her eyes narrowed and she glanced at the two near her. She could tell nothing from their lounging postures. She turned back to the window and stared out helplessly, longing for her sketchbook and a piece of charcoal to vent her frustration with.

Hours later, the stage stopped and the door was flung open from the outside. Diego stepped out smoothly and Parker groaned and stretched and climbed out. Shelly poked her head out the door and came face-to-face with Dillon's dark, well-chiseled visage. His eyes narrowed over a grimly set mouth.

"You don't plan on leaving, do you? Not after I've brought you so far." He pulled himself inside and closed the door. Sitting down across from her, he chewed thoughtfully on a piece of jerky.

Shelly's mouth watered when she smelled the spicy dried meat. Her last meal had been the night before last and she'd eaten little, due to nerves. She avoided staring at his food and looked into his eyes. Mistake. She turned to the dust-coated window but still saw those black, glimmering devil eyes. She pulled her arms across her chest.

"Where am I?" Her voice cracked with nervousness.

"You're not in San Francisco."

"I know that!"

"You're in Placerville. Destination, Virginia City."

Eyes huge, she stared at him. "Why?"

"It's a long trip. Maybe you'll feel like talking."

Shelly shook her head. "I don't have anything else . . . Aggie! Mrs. Thornton . . . What have you . . . ?"

"She'll recover."

Every muscle in Shelly's body went rigid with rage. She stared at him with more hate than she'd ever felt in her life, more hate than she'd ever had for Grady Allen and his threats and gropes, more hate than she'd had for Tommy

Larsen when he'd grabbed her in the woods when she was twelve and stuck his tongue in her mouth and shoved his hand between her thighs. This man just stared back at her, his eyes looking right through her. At least Tommy had run off when she'd started screaming and picked up a rock to bash his head in.

"I told you everything," she said in a low voice. "How could you harm that woman?"

His eyebrows rose almost imperceptibly. "I didn't think it would work on you. Was I wrong?"

She turned away. "No." She felt him staring at her in the silence that followed. His presence seemed to fill the coach. Never had she been so overwhelmed by someone. Her eyes filled with tears, but she would not let them spill, not until she was away from him. She chanced a look at him and for a second saw uncertainty in his dark eyes, then they narrowed and veiled all emotion.

"Karl Booker left the Faulding the night before last." His voice was expressionless.

Shelly's mouth gaped open. "But I talked to him that night... I told him... He must have left after I went to bed," she said wonderingly.

"Oh, that's very good."

"I went to bed early that night," she tried to explain.

"Shut up! Don't say anything if you can't tell the truth!"

"Then I guess I'll just keep talking my little head off!"

Dillon mashed his fists into his thighs and leaned forward. "You're coming with me to Virginia City, and you're going to die in Virginia City unless you tell me *everything*."

Shelly squeezed her trembling arms as tight as she could against herself. "Are you saying you're going to kill me?"

"I'm saying that you'll never leave Virginia City! You'll never go home!"

She swallowed convulsively. "You can't do that."

He was across the coach in an instant, his hands poised to circle her neck. "Who's stopping me from killing you right now? Who's stopping me from doing anything? Your friend told me you have no family in San Francisco. No one is going to come charging after us to rescue you."

Shelly's lips parted and her wide-eyed gaze locked with his dark, narrowed one. She lost her breath as his power flooded her body, filling her stomach, twisting in her guts, turning her legs numb.

Dillon looked down into eyes the color of his precious silver. Their brilliance was bewitching. His gaze dropped to her full, parted lips. Such loveliness and such threat. He felt a stab of lust and almost laughed at himself. God, he was stupid when it came to women. How like him to let his feelings get mixed up: anger and desire, wanting and hating. He couldn't trust himself and he certainly couldn't trust this young woman. Slowly he lowered his hands. Her breath came fast. He needed her scared and relished the small power he had over her, since she left him feeling helpless and frustrated.

A loud knock on the coach made Dillon and Shelly, only inches apart, turn with startled haste to the door. Dillon moved away from her and pushed open the door.

"Blackie's here," Diego announced, looking from Dillon's grim face to Shelly's nervous expression.

"Out," Dillon ordered Shelly, following right behind her into the blinding sunshine. He led Shelly across a street crowded with rattling wagons and buggies. Dillon nodded at the man with black hair and eyes who stood with elbows resting on the back of a saddled mule. Five more mules were strung out behind him.

"It's a good thing you've got money, Mr. Ryder. These animals were priced ten times what they should have been. I only paid it 'cause there was nothin' else available."

"Still no stages?"

"Nope. Stage office said the road—if you can call it that, more like some wild Indian trail—anyway, they said it was impossible for their stages."

"This will do then." Dillon dropped Shelly's elbow and left her standing in the dirt road between two mules.

"I wish I was goin' with you," Blackie continued. "Virginia City is all this town talks about."

Dillon grinned at the young man staring wistfully at a pack train winding its way out of town. "I need you back on ship, but here are some funds to keep you entertained until you head back to the city in the morning." He counted out some money and handed it to Blackie, who accepted graciously and then began to eye the young woman beside his boss. Dillon followed his gaze. "Get on the walk," he snapped irritably.

Shelly obeyed. Blackie continued to glance at her curiously as he scratched a mule behind its ears. Dillon scowled. That there would be men interested in his hostage hadn't crossed his mind.

"So, are you going to ride double or are we going to repack the mules?" asked Diego. Dillon stared at the three saddled mules and the three mules packed with the supplies they'd need. "Or would you like me to ride double?" Diego smiled.

Dillon glowered at the girl. She was looking up the street. He turned back to his grinning friend.

Diego's eyes glowed. "She might tell me something informative while wrapped in my arms."

"I'm sure it would be nothing I'd care to hear repeated. We'll repack the mules. Where's Parker?"

"Nearest saloon."

"Let's get started." Dillon turned around and saw nothing of the girl. "She's gone!"

Shelly felt faint from lack of food and water and the residue in her body of whatever drug he'd given her. She'd asked for the direction of the sheriff's office and had run a couple of blocks up the crowded walk, past curious expressions, until dizziness had caused her to lean against the side of a building for a moment's rest. As she fought a swirl of blackness she heard running footsteps stop suddenly behind her.

"You turn right around and start walking," Dillon demanded.

Shelly dug her fingernails into the wood siding. His hands clamped down on her right shoulder and left arm and swiveled her around. Shelly was so light on her feet she spun right into his chest, moaning as her nose banged into his sternum. "What is wrong with you?" Dillon pushed her away from him and then grabbed her under the arms to keep her from sinking to the plank walk. She clutched at his arms and closed her eyes.

"I need food...and water," she whispered. She kept her eyes closed against the pounding in her head.

Dillon carried her back and lowered her bottom to the walk. He took her hands from his shirt and put them on the wood post next to her. She clung to it.

Diego pulled the cigar out of his mouth. "She sick?"

"Hungry."

"Who is she?" asked Blackie.

"Nobody," answered Dillon.

"Trouble," Diego said simultaneously.

"Here." Dillon plopped a canteen and a handful of jerky in Shelly's lap. With arms that shook she grasped the canteen and struggled to twist off the cap. When she'd succeeded, she tilted the canteen forward, the stream of water missing her mouth by inches.

Dillon cursed and took two long strides to stand in front of her. "You're wasting it!" He pulled the canteen from her hands. Shelly grabbed for it and he raised it out of her reach. "I'll hold it!" He planted one booted foot on the walk next to her thigh and propped his free arm on his knee. "Open your mouth." She glared at him for three seconds and then parted her lips. Dillon carefully poured a manageable stream into her mouth until she lifted her chin, then he plucked the cap off her lap and twisted it back on.

Shelly picked up a piece of the dried meat and ripped off a chunk with her teeth. She chewed, staring at him silently. Dillon shook his head and turned to find Diego grinning like a fool, his cigar sticking out of his mouth.

The men repacked the mules, checked the girths and added a few supplies they'd brought with them. Shelly chewed and watched and soaked up the midday sun. Her eyes widened when she saw Dillon stash chocolate into a pack. His black slouch hat was pulled low over his eyes, a

red woolen shirt covered his broad shoulders, and his gray
trousers were tucked into coarse black boots. The other men
were dressed in similar fashion. Shelly looked down at her
own gray cotton dress and wool cloak and wondered what
she was in for. Parker returned with a bounce in his stride.
Minutes later Dillon motioned Shelly to a mule. "If you
can't ride, I'll tie you on."

"I can ride."

"I warn you, we have a few days' travel ahead of us.
Don't make it any more miserable than it'll already be."

Dillon nodded a farewell to Blackie, then started them off,
leading a packed, riderless mule alongside him. Shelly
smoothed her skirts and cloak over her straddled legs for
modesty's sake. She kicked the mule to follow Dillon and
resigned herself to being terribly sore by evening. Diego rode
behind her, and Parker brought up the rear, pulling along
the second packed mule.

They plodded along the Old Emigrant Trail from Placerville to the Carson Valley, joining wagons loaded with furniture and supplies bound for the mines, as well as whiskey
peddlers carting their bar fixtures and the profusion of
prospective miners and mules. The road was well marked
from all the recent travelers to Virginia City. Spring had
opened the doors again to the silver, and men had been
flocking in droves to Sun Mountain for the past month. The
ground was slightly damp, sparing them the dust of sum-
mer.

Rather than look at Dillon's tall back, she gazed up at the
towering pine trees, whose pure, heavy scent surrounded
her. To her left were green rolling hills scattered with large
rocks overhung with morning glory. On her right, the south
fork of the American River rushed by. She pulled up her
hood to prevent sunburn. From as far as she could see ahead
and behind, she was the only woman in this winding press
of humanity.

As they crested the first considerable elevation, Shelly
looked back at the scene of thick, forested foothills, open
valleys and blue winding streams. Diego followed her gaze

and smiled widely, his teeth large and white under his droopy mustache. "Nice, yes?" he asked.

Shelly wanted to ignore him, but he seemed so boyish and goodwilled. "Yes, very," she agreed. She faced forward again and met the annoyed, dark eyes of Dillon Ryder.

Chapter Four

They rode without stopping until the sun sank low in the sky. Dillon led the trio following him to the side of the road and a frame shanty. Here most of the travelers to Virginia City stopped to eat and even to sleep.

Shelly was numb in her nether regions and bone weary. In dismounting, her legs collapsed beneath her as her feet hit the ground, and she found herself squatting in the dirt. A warm hand clasped her arm and helped her up. She smiled thankfully at Diego.

"We're going to eat here?" she asked hopefully, smelling the tantalizing aroma of hot food from the shack. Since starting on the trail she'd eaten only some cheese and dried meat that Dillon had handed her.

"And sleep here, too," Diego answered.

Shelly wondered exactly what their sleeping arrangements would be. She followed the men into the building but stopped short behind Dillon when she saw the food. A big burly man was slapping pork, beans and fried potatoes on tin plates for a long line of men. There were a few rough benches to sit on, but many stood to shovel the food into their mouths. Their plates and utensils were then used for the next man with barely a wipe of a greasy cloth.

"Now we know why this place is named Dirty Mike's," muttered Dillon.

Shelly did not find the prospect of eating in such uncleanliness appetizing, but bodily needs demanded and she stood in line sandwiched between Dillon and Diego. The benches were full, but a woman in the place was unusual and a gray-shirted miner let her have his seat. Dillon stood next to her.

The hot food warmed Shelly and made her feel human again. She washed it down with a cup of coffee, included with the meal. Once her hunger was appeased, she looked about the room at the motley collection of menfolk; there were dapper, although rather wilted, gentlemen, probably from San Francisco, and gaunt, desperate men and young ones with boyish enthusiasm lighting their faces as they laughed and joked over their dinners. She heard several foreign languages.

Dillon and his men took places on Shelly's bench as the other diners finished. Shelly discreetly studied the group she was with to see where they fitted in this crowd. They were not like the men at the next table, who were filthy, talked in whispers and eyed her speculatively; they were not fashionable, yet they held themselves with calm assurance.

"I didn't expect so many of them," Parker said. "If your theory is right, Dillon, there's gonna be a lot of unhappy men."

Dillon shrugged. "There are enough taverns to dull the disappointment."

"They don't know what they're in for," said Diego, vividly remembering his own previous experiences in Virginia City.

"For most of them, Virginia is going to be just another way to earn a wage, not a fortune," Dillon mused. "They're still thinking like gold miners. They assume they can open a surface deposit, shovel dirt into a rocker or even use their picks to uncover the ore, but none of them can go deep enough that way to get the thick deposits of ore."

"At least you pay the men well who're working your mine. That should make for less discontent," said Parker.

"Good wages haven't stopped *someone* from stealing." Dillon stood. "Let's grab a place to sleep." Shelly followed him unresistingly into the next room, mulling over his conversation with Parker. Her spine tingled from the uncomfortable possibility that she'd made a mistake. Maybe Dillon was not the thief she'd been led to believe he was.

The sleeping room was wall-to-wall men. "No beds?" Shelly squeaked beside Dillon. He didn't answer. Parker and Diego left to get the blankets tied to the mules.

"Hey! What we got here?" exclaimed a hairy man, sitting up to watch Shelly lift her skirts as she stepped carefully over his legs. His hands snaked out and grabbed the edges of her dress and held them over his face.

"Stop it!" yelled Shelly, and tried to yank her skirts away.

"Whooo-wheee!" he hooted under the folds of material.

Dillon looked over his shoulder and stepped back over the men he'd already passed. He kicked the ribs of the man holding Shelly's skirts then he lifted her into his arms. Their eyes locked as she fell against his chest, hers frightened and his angry. The man on the floor groaned in pain. "You shouldna brung her here if ya didn't want us lookin'!"

"You can look, just don't get within twenty feet." Dillon set Shelly down in an empty space. She kept her eyes riveted on his chest to keep from seeing all the stares she felt focused on her. When Dillon sat on the hard floor, she sat beside him. She glanced at him and found him focused on the plank wall across the room. He was chewing on the inside of his cheek, his eyes narrowed. She doubted any men would bother her as long as she remained under his watchful eyes, but how did she fare with him?

The lanterns were dimmed shortly after Parker and Diego returned with the blankets. Dillon removed his hat, coat and boots, then stripped himself of shirt and trousers to stand in his long underwear. Shelly lowered her eyes immediately and removed her own boots, but that was all. She curled up in the blanket Diego had handed her and listened to the men settling themselves. She sighed miserably and shifted. When she lay on her back, the floorboards dug into her spine, but if she turned she would face Dillon or Diego. She remained on her back, willing herself to sleep.

* * *

Dillon awoke to the rustling, stretching sound of men moving about, gathering their clothes and grumbling about the hard floor. The remnants of a warm, soft dream faded as he opened his eyes to the warm girl he held in his arms. His bicep pillowed her temple, his arm embraced her waist, and his throbbing arousal pressed against her bottom. He abruptly pulled away from her, waking her. She rolled onto her back and opened eyes as gray as the morning light. Dillon looked away while she sat up and straightened her clothes in a dazed, sleepy way.

The men paid her little attention in the cold morning. Shelly cast quick glances around the room, careful not to rest her gaze on any dressing male. She saw Parker standing in front of a dirty mirror on the wall. Hanging by separate strings from a large nail next to the mirror was a comb, missing several teeth, and a communal toothbrush. Parker efficiently combed his hair over the bald spot in the middle of his scalp.

Shelly undid her two long braids, combed her fingers through the cascade of kinked hair as best she could and drew it back in one long braid. She pulled on her boots and then, following Dillon's example, rolled up her blanket.

Breakfast was a hurried plate of beans and a mug of warm coffee that did not brace Shelly for the cool outdoors. She lagged behind the men on their way to the tethered mules, walking a bit bowlegged and dreading the placement of her tender flesh on the bony animal. She stopped and eyed her ride with a pronounced twist in her lips. Dillon turned and stared at her with hands on hips and black coat hanging open. Shelly crossed her arms over her cloak and glared back. "Why? Why do I have to go?" He didn't answer, but she could see the muscles in his jaw tightening. Diego grinned, lit a cigar and leaned against a tree.

"Get on your mule," he finally said.

"No!"

"Lower your voice, damn it!"

"*No!* I want to know what you're going to do with me! And I don't want to get on that mule!"

Dillon strode forward, grasped her around the waist and heaved her onto the mule. Shelly cried out as she landed hard on the animal's back; in the next instant she reeled off a punch into Dillon's chin.

"Ouch!" He grabbed her wrists in each of his hands and shook her. Shelly went still but averted her eyes from his narrowed gaze and looked up at the deep green branches of a tall pine tree. "I don't know what the hell I'm going to do with you, but you're coming with us, because I won't rest until you tell me what you know." He threw her hands down. "Be gracious about it!"

Shelly made a strangled sound and picked up the reins to the animal whose every move tortured her lower torso. "Brute, animal, beast..." she called Dillon under her breath. "Slithering snake, rabid wolf," she added in a louder voice as they all moved out onto the trail. Diego laughed behind her and Dillon's spine stretched in front of her.

The ascent of the trail after Dirty Mike's was gradual but continuous. The ground was deeply furrowed by streamlets from melting snow and the wheels of freight wagons. As the day wore on, conditions grew messier, with the melting snow creating stretches of thick mud that severely impeded the traffic. Shelly watched in amazement as a wagon sank to its hubs in the dark, slushy earth. Travelers who did not get stuck picked their way through the abandoned packs of their less successful predecessors. The remains of broken stages, wagons, carts, even wheelbarrows, lined the trail. When Shelly saw bones, she recoiled and turned an alarmed face to Diego, who rode beside her.

"Men and mounts that got caught in a storm," he explained.

"Was this in the spring?" she asked worriedly.

"Some came too late in the fall and got caught in winter storms. Some got caught in a late spring storm. They were too hurried, too greedy."

Shelly thought of Aggie and the letter she was still waiting for from Tom since the middle of March. "When was this spring storm?"

Diego lifted his eyes from her white, blue-tinted hands. "Mid-March. Why?"

"I know someone who came up here about then."

"Who?" demanded Dillon, turning around.

Shelly should have been used to the roughness in his voice when he spoke to her by now. "Mrs. Thornton's husband! I'm sure you remember her!"

They were at a standstill in the trail. "Let's move," Dillon said.

Shelly kicked her mule after him, feeling depressed. There was no escape with Dillon ahead and Parker behind. To her left were trees upon trees. On her right was Diego, and beyond him the river crashed over rocks and boulders in a canyon that deepened as they climbed. The branches of the pine trees met over the trail and obscured the sky. The air grew colder, shielded from the sun, and Shelly bowed her head and watched the trail slowly inch by below her. She jumped when Diego touched her with his leather gloves, offering them to her.

"No," she said, shaking her head but smiling gratefully.

"*Si, si.*" He slapped them down in front of her. "If you don't wear them, I won't, either, and then we'll both have cold hands."

Shelly grinned. "All right, then. Thank you."

"It's nothing," he said with a wave of his hand.

Dillon looked over his shoulder in time to see Shelly about to pull on the warm gloves. "If you want her hands to be warm then she'll wear my gloves, not yours. I'm the one who wanted to bring her."

"I remember," groaned Diego. He took back his gloves and winked at Shelly.

She gingerly took the gloves Dillon held out, expecting at any second for him to backhand her across the face with the soft leather. Shelly preferred this arrangement over the previous one. She didn't care if Dillon's fingers grew stiff with cold. It was hard for her to believe that Diego, as nice as he was to her, or even Parker had hurt Aggie. She still had the handkerchief back at the Faulding that Parker had given her to wipe her bloody elbow. Surely they would have been rougher with her by now if they had really hurt Aggie. She puzzled over their characters until she saw a strange shack built of wagon bottoms, packing cases and burlap. Several men were peeling off the trail and heading toward the structure.

"What in the world is that?"

"A new saloon," answered Diego. "You'll be seeing many more."

She did. In every gully and small valley a saloon was in the process of being erected, if not already put together, with whatever supplies could be scrounged together. A few of them offered the standard fare of beans, bacon and potatoes.

They ate their evening meal at one of these shacks. There was no structure for sleeping in the near or far vicinity; Shelly suspected she'd be spending the night on the cold ground. Dillon tied up the mules in the woods and unpacked the things they needed for the night while Parker and Diego collected firewood. Shelly leaned against a tree, refusing to help them since she wasn't here of her own choosing. She could be at the Faulding taking a hot bath, lying on a mattress or sketching all the thoughts and sights of the day onto paper. She'd seen so much in the last couple of days that she'd love to be able to draw.

"We're going to need this fire," Diego said, squatting beside her. "It's freezing now and I can still see the edge of the sun."

"What will make Mr. Dillon Ryder believe me so I can go back to San Francisco and sit in a warm kitchen?"

Diego chuckled and looked up at her. "If I knew that I'd tell you."

"You would?"

He didn't answer, instead busying himself with arranging his wood for a fire.

"Diego?"

"Hmm?"

"I can't believe you really harmed Mrs. Thornton." He readjusted a branch that had been fine where it was. "I don't believe Parker did, either." Shelly's eyes were fastened on his face. She watched him glance at Dillon, who was throwing down the blankets. "And I don't even think Mr. Ryder hurt her."

"You can believe what you want." He struck a match and soon had the fire blazing. Shelly sank down and stared into the flames. She couldn't relax, since every way she sat or squatted hurt. The fires of the other travelers glowed, scatterings of gold through the trees. Various conversations droned around them. Dillon tossed her a blanket and she pulled it around her, resting her chin on her knees and sitting far back on her bottom. Parker pulled out a bottle of whiskey, took a long drink and passed the bottle to Dillon. Dillon drank and reached in front of her to pass the bottle to Diego. Shelly shot her arm up and grabbed the bottle's neck, her hand clasping part of Dillon's hand. He stiffened and tried to pull away with the bottle, but Shelly rose to her knees and hung on.

"I need this," she said softly.

Dillon released the bottle to her. "Go ahead."

Shelly took a swallow and choked. She took another and then one more. She handed the bottle to Diego. "So what am I going to do in Virginia City?"

Dillon didn't look at her. "Stay out of trouble."

"For how long?" He shrugged. "End of conversation," Shelly intoned wearily, and curled up on the ground.

Before she opened her eyes, Shelly heard morning birds. She smiled, relishing the cocoon of warmth in which she was wrapped. Only her face was cold. The first thing she saw when she opened her eyes was the large male hand a foot or so from her face. It was attached to an arm that lay beneath her cheek. Shelly realized the warmth she felt was from the body pressed tightly against her back and curling to follow her bent legs. His other arm was draped over her waist and under the blankets they were sharing. Shelly carefully picked up the arm with her thumb and forefinger and moved it off her, gently setting it down somewhere behind her.

"Good morning," whispered a deep, familiar voice in her ear. Shelly stiffened. "You were shivering last night."

"Really?" She sat up. A man walked past the spot where Parker lay, hands on his chest, snoring. His big frame was covered with two blankets, compared to the pile that Diego was curled under.

As if feeling her eyes on him, Parker snorted awake and sat up. His thin hair stood in tufts on his head. He yawned noisily. "'Mornin'." He nodded at Dillon, ignoring Shelly.

Diego got up without acknowledging anyone and walked a few trees away. Parker slowly followed. Shelly pushed herself up, but Dillon grabbed the end of her braid and stayed her. "How long are you going to hold out on me?"

Shelly was surprised by the softness of his voice. "I'm not." She turned to look at him. He lay on his back, clasping her hair in his hand. They each searched the pair of eyes opposite them, cool gray meeting dark, troubled brown.

"You've done a fine job with Diego. He believes you, but since he didn't believe you were spying on us in the first place, I can't really depend on his judgment, can I?"

"Why ask me?" She held still while he searched her face.

"You're not real timid, are you?"

"Are most of the women you push around frightened of you?"

He wasn't going to tell her that he avoided women whenever possible. "What will make you believe that I own the Avalon mine and I've been the one getting robbed?"

"Nothing." He frowned and released her hair, his gaze leaving her and going up to the sky above. "I already do believe you own that stupid mine," she added. He sat up in surprise, but Shelly was already up and walking to the trees.

After breakfast at the saloon they continued to ride up the rail. A trickle of men on the way down passed them by. Some were mule train drivers who stopped for no one. Their mules were loaded with ore from the Washoe mines and wore bells to warn of their approach. All travelers moved to the edge of the narrow trail at first sight or sound of them.

The men who stomped down the trail on foot were a weary, ragged lot. Some called out warnings that disappointment was ahead, but their words had little effect on the excited men who had yet to experience Virginia City for themselves.

They rode into a mist, and much of the ground they passed was covered with snow. Shelly was grateful for Dillon's gloves. He'd wrapped his hands in strips of wool blanket. The group of men that rode in front of them were a boisterous lot. They passed their bottle of whiskey and told ribald jokes that warmed Shelly's face even when she didn't understand them.

Conditions worsened and Shelly followed Dillon's example and dismounted, pulling her mule behind her. The slush was deep, but more inhibiting of their progress were the rocks covered by a layer of ice and then a layer of snow. Two mules had slipped after straying off the edge of the trail and tumbled down into the canyon, jarring Shelly's nerves with their unearthly screams.

She couldn't hold her skirts up and lead a mule, so her sodden dress slid around her feet. She perspired with the effort it took to walk through slush and step over smooth sheets of ice, if not gingerly on them, while pulling her mule behind her.

She carefully guided her animal around a deep hole of mud where a Mexican vaquero was trying to free two of his mules. His curses colored the air in a mixture of Spanish and English. His third mule skirted the mud and kept going, causing the vaquero to yell. Staring at him, Shelly walked into the hind end of Dillon's mule.

"Oh, sorry," she apologized automatically.

"Here, give me your mule," he said gruffly. He reached for the reins she held.

"Why?"

"You look like you're ready to fall over."

"I'm fine. I can handle the mule," Shelly insisted. Dillon shrugged and turned back around. Shelly regretted her stubbornness; he *should* do her work. She was too willful for her own good. Hadn't she always been told so? She sighed and imagined how dreadful she must look. Her braid and clothes were decorated with dried chunks of mud that had been thrown up by hooves and feet. She assumed her face was dirt-streaked like everyone else's.

Toward evening the mist turned to cold rain accompanied by a cruel wind. Shelly shook uncontrollably as she plodded along behind Dillon. At least, she consoled herself, the rain was washing off some of the dirt. Dillon looked back at her with greater frequency. "Just up a bit is Strawberry's, where we can bunk for the night," he called back. Shelly almost groaned in relief that the end was near.

"Is this one like a real hotel or like that Dirty Mike's?"

Dillon grinned and slowed down to walk beside her. "It's in between the two."

"I suppose there's little chance of getting a hot bath?"

"No. You'll just get dirty again anyway. It will be like this tomorrow, too."

Shelly did groan this time.

There were scattered groups of men standing outside the large log building that was Strawberry's, as if they enjoyed conversing in the rain. The water dripped off the brims of their hats as they related their adventures on the trail.

Shelly followed Dillon inside and joined the crowd in the front room. The bar along the left side was jammed full of men in varying stages of inebriation. The room rang with their laughter, shouts and curses. The smell of wet wool, rancid sweat and alcohol was overwhelming. Shelly made straight for the immense fire across from the bar. Logs five feet long blazed in the hearth. A noxious steam rose from a variety of socks, boots and coats that were laid out before the heat.

She took off her cloak and her shoes and set them near the fire, then turned around like meat on a spit, as near to the intense heat as she could get. She stopped and held up her skirts to midcalf to dry her stockings. Her eyelids sank in luscious enjoyment.

"Evenin'."

Shelly dropped her skirts and opened her eyes to see a very tall, bearded man next to her. "Hello," she said warily.

"You're the first woman I've seen going to Virginia City." His smile was friendly. "You with family."

"Not exactly." Shelly looked over her shoulder for Dillon and did not see him. She stepped close to the big man. "Actually, I'm being taken to Virginia City against my will." The man's eyes widened. "This man is making me go with him. I want to go back to San Francisco."

"You're joshin'?"

"No, it's the truth! I need someone to take me back to San Francisco."

"Well, I'm not goin' that way. And I don't get in the middle of folks' problems."

"This isn't a disagreement I'm having with a husband or a father. This man is a stranger."

The man took a step back and stuffed his hands into his pockets and eyed Shelly uneasily.

"There you are!" interrupted Dillon, seeing Shelly stiffen. He turned to the discomfited miner. "Has she been babbling to you about her wretched life?" Dillon shook his head and smiled ruefully. "I didn't want to bring her, but she begged to come. As soon as the trail got rough she wanted to turn around and run home. Just like a female, isn't it?"

The tall man smiled in obvious relief and nodded his head. Shelly wanted to punch them both. She spun away and marched through the room to the door, which she flung open. She stepped outside, realizing her mistake immediately when she stepped down into a puddle in her stockinged foot. She drew her skirts up and looked down at her foot, mired in mud. Over her shoulder came the voice she was tired of hearing. "Well, just look at you! No wonder that fellow doubted your story."

Shelly turned as best she could with one foot on the step and the other in the puddle. "You don't look so good yourself! You've even got mud on your nose."

"But I'm not trying to solicit help from strangers."

"I wasn't, either! We were having a friendly chat until you embarrassed me."

"Of course."

"I hardly feel remorseful for trying to get away from you and this—this place!" Rainwater dripped off her face. She was tired, cold, wet and sore. She'd never get to New York from here. She didn't have to hide her tears in the rain.

Dillon picked up her braid and tugged gently. "Let's go in and eat." She didn't move. "The food is better here than at Dirty Mike's."

"That's not saying much, and I don't want to eat with you."

He released her braid and it dropped heavy and wet against her back.

"Come have dinner—and then we'll talk."

Shelly regarded him thoughtfully; he seemed reasonable. She swept before him like a queen and Dillon shook his head in weary amusement.

Chapter Five

The dining room at Strawberry's was not big enough for everyone present to be seated at one time, so they were served in shifts. Shelly shifted her weight from one foot to the other impatiently. "Where are Parker and Diego?"

"At the bar," Dillon answered curtly.

If he'd rather be there than in line with her he shouldn't have taken her from San Francisco. They had to wait for two shifts to eat before it was their turn. When they got their chance to sit down at a table, waiters served them beans, pork, potatoes and bread. Shelly smiled at the food heaped on shining clean plates. She sipped her coffee, sweetened with molasses, and scraped up every crumb of food with her bread before she rose from the table.

Dillon staked out a place in a corner of the sleeping room right after dinner.

"Don't you want to join the others at the bar?" Shelly asked as Dillon rolled out his bedding. The room was littered with bedrolls but was empty of people except for two old men asleep against the far wall.

"No, I don't. But I suppose you'd like to join the fray yourself," he said wearily.

"What an excellent idea!"

Dillon stopped spreading his blanket and eyed her intently.

"I'm not serious, Mr. Ryder." She dropped to her knees and spread her blanket. "On second thought, a drink might make this hard floor bearable." She spread her cloak for extra padding and folded the hood for a pillow.

"Don't go to sleep," Dillon ordered when she lay down and pulled the blanket over her. "We're going to talk."

"My mouth moves even when I lie down." She rolled to her side and saw a full-blown scowl on Dillon's face. He sat straight against the wall, one long leg stretched out in front of him, the other bent at the knee and propping his arm. "You're the most irritable person I've ever met. Did your mama bite you every morning so you'd get off to a bad start?" The scowl cleared from his face and his rich brown eyes widened in surprise.

"You're a nervy girl."

Shelly frowned. "Yes, I suppose. My mama didn't teach me some things." From the other room a low, rumbling voice rose in song above the shouts of the miners.

"You can tell me what's missing from your education later." For the space of a few moments, Dillon pondered the questions he would ask Shelly, then he turned to her. Her eyes were closed. "Shelly?" He shook her shoulder and she moaned. He shook her harder. "Wake up!" She rolled onto her stomach and within seconds her breath was deep and even. "Damn!" He had to laugh. Nothing went the way it was supposed to with her. She was so different from any woman he'd ever met in drawing room or whorehouse. He'd never expected her to be so resilient on the trail; she insisted on leading her own mule, grabbed the whiskey bottle and didn't seem to have any problem digesting the god-awful beans they had to eat every day.

Shelly slept like Parker that night, deep and steady. She awoke, her nose an inch from the wall. She rolled over and saw only blankets where Dillon had lain. Sitting up, she struggled to make out faces in the dim light but heard only snoring men. She picked up her shoes and walked a weaving path between bodies to the door.

She found Dillon in the front room, leaning against the hearth and staring into the flames of a newly started fire. He held a tin mug of coffee in his hand. He looked up as Shelly walked toward him. When she was near he offered her his cup.

Shelly's eyes widened, but she accepted. The hot coffee washed the dryness from her mouth. "I missed our talk."

Dillon snorted. Shelly sat on a bench near the fire. Dillon followed and stood above her. "Where did you meet this Karl Booker whom I've never heard of?"

"At the Faulding. He'd been there over six months when I started working there. He'd sit with me in the front room sometimes when I did some mending. He confessed to having some business problems but asked me not to mention what he told me, since everyone else thought all he did was sell insurance and didn't know how well off he was, or would be, if he could stop the robberies at his mine."

"What does he look like?"

Shelly told him. "I have a picture I drew of him back at the Faulding."

"You drew him?"

"I draw everyone."

He wasn't going to ask if she had drawn him—as he knew she was waiting for him to do. "Can you think of some reason why he asked you to do the spying for him?"

Shelly shrugged. "He knew I needed the money to get to New York."

"New York! What do you want to go there for?"

"I have family there. There and nowhere else." She took another swallow of his coffee while he scrutinized her face. He began a barrage of questions, which she answered patiently, but he learned no more about his mysterious enemy.

"Did you ever think of the wrong you were doing?" he almost yelled at her when he'd exhausted his questions. "Any feebleminded person could have figured out that the Avalon was, and is, mine!"

Shelly looked up at him and frowned. "There is one strange thing. He did know you. He said so. I asked him once if he'd known you in New York and he didn't answer, but he spoke of you as being a man who just took what he wanted, that once you caught on to something you moved fast. He had to have at least observed you for a long time to say such a thing."

Dillon stared at her unseeingly; he agreed with her, this *was* strange, but still he couldn't make heads or tails of her information. He sat down beside her and held out his hand.

After a moment's confusion Shelly handed him the cup. He looked down into the empty mug and scowled.

"Well? Do you believe me?"

"Maybe. Maybe not."

"You believe me. And where does that leave me?"

"On your way to Virginia City. And if you don't try to escape and stay with me as long as I say, I'll pay you one hundred dollars on our return to San Francisco." Shelly's mouth dropped open. Dillon leaned close and looked her straight in the eyes. "You also have to promise to tell me anything else you think of that could help me find this man."

"And if I don't agree to this deal I can go back to the city?"

"No. You just don't get the one hundred dollars."

"So I have no choice about continuing with you."

Dillon didn't understand why she seemed angry. "A hundred dollars is plenty more money than you could make at the Faulding in a month. I can't spare the time to take you back. And if I could, or trusted someone to do it, wouldn't this Karl Booker be a menace to you since you've found out he's not what he claimed? Maybe he'd come back for more information in hopes you'd learned something from being with me."

"What am I supposed to do in Virginia City."

Dillon shrugged. "Do you like to read?"

"No."

He sighed and looked down at his boots. When he looked up he met her hard eyes. "I never hurt that landlady of yours. None of us even threatened her."

"I already figured that out! Was that confession supposed to mollify me?"

Dillon looked puzzled. "I thought it would make you happy."

"Give me two hundred dollars at the end of this fiasco and I'll be mildly content." Dillon's eyes widened. "And I want some of it up front. And you pay for all my food and lodgings and necessities." She almost started laughing at his incredulous expression.

"All right, if you swear you won't ever try to run away."

"For how long?"

"I need to be here about a month."

"It's a bargain." She extended her hand. Dillon took a long time to hold out his. They shook hands and she didn't feel at all like laughing anymore. With their skin touching and their eyes meeting, she felt as if she were giving her life away.

Dillon pulled his hand away first, feeling hot, perspiration breaking out on the back of his neck. Her skin was warm, a little rough, calloused, and her grip stronger than he'd expected; the feel of it made him want to touch more. He was relieved when a few men came out of the adjoining room and ended the intimacy between him and this strange girl.

The bitter cold night had frozen the previous day's slush. It was impossible for a vehicle of any kind to get up the mountains from Strawberry's. Those men with wagons had to stay behind, while the men on foot and mule started up in the crackling cold air.

Shelly sat bundled in a blanket on her mount.

"We've got a long hard hike ahead of us," warned Dillon.

The hooves of Shelly's mule slipped on the icy trail once they got moving. She scooted off the animal's back and walked beside it. Her boots did not do much better on the slippery surface, but she felt more in control. She dragged her mule by the reins and bent her head before the chilling gusts of wind that whipped down the mountain. Behind her she heard a slipping sound and looked back to see Diego's mule struggling up from where it had fallen on buckled forelegs.

"*¡Madre de Dios!*" shouted Diego, scrambling off the animal. "*¡Estúpido!* I hate this place! Horrible weather, horrible food!" His exclamations poured out as he jerked his mule along. Shelly heard Parker snicker. He seemed impervious to cold; at least she never heard him complain. He was not fat, but big and thick.

When they reached the crest of the mountain they had been climbing, Shelly looked down and saw a huge sapphire lake.

"Lake Bigler," Dillon said in answer to her questioning look.

"It's beautiful!" Snow-covered mountains surrounded the blue expanse of water.

"And downhill," added Diego happily.

The downhill portion was faster but not easier. The midday sun had melted the snow into slush. When they were not slipping, they were sinking. Shelly took each step cautiously, alarmed by Diego's curses behind her. Any moment she expected him to come crashing into her and send her flying down the mountain. Her cold skin and bones were no longer her primary concern as she struggled to remain upright.

She lifted her eyes from the trail in front of her to see how Dillon was doing. He placed his feet surely on the ground without complaint. She returned to watching her own feet but was too late, she'd stepped in the middle of an ice patch. Her feet slipped out from under her. Shrieking, she let go of the mule's reins and flailed her arms back and forth as she tried to regain her balance, but she only had the choice of falling on her hands and knees or her bottom. She opted for the former and slammed headfirst into Dillon, who could not move out of the way fast enough. His feet shot out from under him and he landed on his backside with his legs stretched across the trail. Shelly sprawled over him ungracefully, her chest across his thighs, one of her hands clawing at his boot and the other trying to push herself up.

"Get off of me!" he roared, shoving her aside.

"Gladly!" Shelly yelled back, picking herself up.

Dillon turned his back on her and retrieved the reins of his mule. Shelly glared at his broad back until Diego, grinning widely, pushed the reins of her mule into her hands.

Diego sighed when they had descended to the bottom of the decline and the Lake House was in view. "I can't wait for food, fire and rest."

"Food and fire, but little rest," warned Dillon. "I want to press on to Carson City."

Shelly shook her head. "Not going to stay here? I'm freezing. I'll be dead before we get anywhere else."

"You'll make it."

Diego said nothing.

After more beans and even more coffee they returned to the trail. Shelly alternately rode and walked in martyred silence to the top of the hill that rose from the Lake House saloon. She looked curiously over the summit. "It's horrible!"

"Isn't it?" agreed Diego.

The ground was covered unevenly with snow and dotted with sagebrush of a fairly uniform size and shape. There were no trees. The mountains rose sheer and bold. The sky was a dusty gray weight.

"It may not be a beautiful place, but the silver's not bad," commented Dillon.

"Is that all you think about?" snapped Shelly. Her temper worsened as they made their way down and then back up another rise. She was sick of ice and slush and muck and wind. She knew she was a muddy mess and sincerely hoped she offended Dillon Ryder every time he looked at her. They reached Carson City at nightfall. Shelly felt a supreme relief when she saw the lights of the town. Dillon got them all rooms at an inn and led Shelly to the door of the room he would share with her.

"I've ordered you a bath. I'll leave you alone for a while."

"A bath." Shelly sighed to herself, closing the door behind him. The room was warm, clean and luxurious compared to the other places they'd stayed. Thrown over the bed was a red patchwork quilt. A mirror hung above the pitcher and bowl on the unpainted wooden dresser. Shelly sneaked a peak at herself. Her hair was plastered to her head with mud and dried sweat; her face looked darkly tanned from dirt; and her eyes were bloodshot from exhaustion and the bright reflection of the sun off the snow.

Shelly answered a knock on the door and let in three blond, blue-eyed girls with little pug noses. They quickly dragged in a tin tub and filled it with hot water.

"Your husband was right, ma'am. You do need a bath," blurted out the youngest.

Shelly nodded. "Where is he—my 'husband'?"

"Washin' up downstairs."

When the girls were gone she stood a second trailing her fingers in the steaming water. "Oh, Lord, what a pleasure this will be." She shed her clothes and climbed into the tub. After vigorously scrubbing body and hair, Shelly simply lay back and relaxed till the water began to cool.

When she got out of the tub she realized she had to put those filthy clothes back on. She was wrapping a towel around herself just as Dillon walked in. She blushed and crossed her arms under her breasts to hold the towel securely in place. He stared at her. "Thank you for the bath." He did not respond. "I was just getting up my nerve to put on those clothes again." She pointed her toe at the mess on the floor, her pale leg exposed.

Dillon was boggled by the girl before him. She was different from the cleaning girl at Snelling's and the girl he'd dragged up the trail from Placerville. Her hair was incredibly long and thick and waved around her waist in wet tendrils. Her face was unblemished and fair. And her body... Why hadn't he noticed it before? He realized he was staring and looked away. "There's no need to put them on," he said, throwing a package on the bed. "I bought you some new clothes. Necessities. I thought you'd be finished by now. I'm sorry," he went on in a rush.

"Clean clothes?" Shelly said wonderingly.

He raised his hand. "They're men's. They'll be too big, but more appropriate."

"I don't mind!" She walked to the edge of the bed and pulled the bundle toward her while one hand still held her towel in place. She dumped the contents onto the bed, delighted to find long underwear, three pairs of woolen socks and black boots.

"I got the smallest pair they had," Dillon said.

There was also a red-and-gray-checked wool shirt and black trousers. The last item was a pair of gloves.

"Thank you for letting me wear yours."

"Sure." He handed her a gray felt hat and looked into her eyes, the same color as the hat, only more silver.

She flushed. Why was he regarding her so...intensely? Shelly sat on the bed, hoping Dillon would leave and she could put on her new clothes, but he stuck his hands in his pockets and rocked backed on his heels, still looking at her, up and down. "I should get dressed," she hinted.

"Of course. I'll go see what's taking our food so long."

As soon as the door closed behind him, Shelly flung down the towel and pulled on the long underwear and shirt. The trousers gaped open around her waist, but she fixed that with a strip of her cotton shift tied around her middle. Dillon returned with a tray when she was pulling on the socks. "I hope it's not beans."

"Picky, picky." He set the tray on the bed and Shelly saw beefsteak, beans, cabbage, biscuits, turnovers and a bottle of brandy. She sat cross-legged on the bed, her wet hair trailing down her back. As there were no chairs, Dillon, his own plate in hand, joined her on the bed, positioning himself a respectable distance from his captive. They silently satisfied their appetites. When stuffed, Shelly sat back against the pillow. She was drowsy from the warm bath and food. Dillon placed the tray on the floor and leaned back next to her, his brandy glass in hand.

Shelly looked him over out of the corner of her eye. His beard had grown in dark and thick in the four days since they'd left San Francisco. His hair was damp from bathing and waved glossy and dark on his head. He was handsome. The realization hit her like a board over her head. She was affected by his appearance in a way she'd never felt with anyone else. She wished she had her sketchbook so she could put him down in strong strokes. She got a knot in her stomach from looking too long and poured herself a glass of brandy. The unfamiliar liquid trickled down her throat like hot honey. She took another sip.

"Will we get to Virginia City tomorrow?"

"Yes, but don't expect lodgings like these. It's a primitive, uncomfortable, dirty and lawless town."

"Wonderful. Do you have a comb I could use? I forgot to pack mine," she added sarcastically. Dillon got up and pulled one out of his saddlebag for her, then stood watching, sipping his drink, as she brought the mane of hair over her shoulder and set to work on it. Her breasts bounced with each tug of the comb through her tangled hair. He grew warm and removed his shirt and boots before he sat down beside her in trousers and long underwear.

Shelly handed him the comb. "What am I going to do there?" she asked irritably.

"I can think of several things," Dillon muttered under his breath.

Shelly finished her brandy. "Name one!" she demanded, oblivious to his sarcasm.

Ever so slowly, Dillon moved his face close to hers, took her chin in his fingers and turned her mouth to meet his. He kissed her with the barest touch, his lips pressed against her closed mouth. Shelly's eyes widened and she stared into his, startled. She felt pierced to the core of her being when their eyes locked. He kissed her again, gently. His thumb caressed back and forth across her cheek and his lips moved to trace the line of her jaw. Shelly's eyes closed. His touch was so soft, comforting; a wisp of a sigh escaped her lips, which he had momentarily abandoned. She forgot what they'd been talking about; she was aware only of his mouth as it brushed her eyelids, and his hand as it caressed the column of her neck.

Her eyes and mouth opened when she felt the wet tip of his tongue in her ear. Dillon took that opportunity to confiscate her open lips. With more pressure now, he pressed his lips to hers and pushed his tongue inside. Shelly pulled back, but her head was stopped by the wall. Dillon pursued his unfair advantage and came against her more demandingly, moving close and drawing his leg up over hers.

After her initial surprise Shelly was overtaken by the pleasure of the wet, grainy feel of his tongue as it played in her mouth. Her tongue instinctively flicked to meet his and she was immediately aware of a tightening within Dillon's body. Her hands gripped the brandy glass in her lap as she was assaulted by a sweet, unfamiliar yearning. Following the dictates of her body, she let her tongue be drawn into the hotness of Dillon's mouth, where his teeth lightly scraped it. Shelly moaned softly when he sucked tightly on her tongue and created a pull of sensation throughout her body.

Dillon, greatly encouraged by her response, undid the buttons of her shirt and carefully folded the fabric away to reveal one temptingly full breast beneath the long underwear. He moved his mouth from her lips to her collarbone, then rubbed his cheek against her warm skin as his hand enclosed her breast.

Shelly felt a delicious warmth pervade her when his hand was on her, but the floating feeling was pierced abruptly when Dillon squeezed the tender flesh of her nipple between his thumb and forefinger. Sensation so intense slammed through her that she cried out. She was not sure if it was pleasure or pain, but it was foreign and jolting.

"No!" She pushed his hand away and scrambled off the bed.

Dillon stared up at her, his face flushed with arousal, his trousers uncomfortable. Before him stood the object of his desire, her thick hair coiling and falling in shining ripples about her body, her eyes pouring rich silver, her lips reddened from his kiss and her breasts heaving gently. And the lady said *no*.

"Don't touch me," she warned.

"I could make it worthwhile for you," he urged softly, unwilling to let these sensations come to an end.

"How? Money? Make me into the whore you want?"

Dillon shook his head in an attempt to clear the confusion of this ridiculous situation. He cursed himself for even succumbing to her pretty face and lush body. How could he be so stupid as to be charmed by a woman who had done him nothing but harm? He tried to be so careful about getting into uncomfortable situations with women. "Just forget it."

"Do that!" She buttoned her shirt and climbed back into the bed and under the covers. She wiggled close to the edge and lay stiffly on her side. It was so silent in the room that she thought she heard her eyes blink. She was embarrassed, angry and confused all at once. Her lips still felt the imprint of his. Her breasts ached and her nipples were erect, and she craved his touch again. The bed squeaked as Dillon rose and walked across the room to put out the lamp. Shelly tensed when he returned, but he made no move toward her. She felt like crying or screaming, but instead her exhausted mind and body dropped her into sleep within minutes.

Dillon listened to her breathing grow even and deep, and still his manhood throbbed. He could still feel Shelly's soft skin, hear her sweet gasp. He gritted his teeth, determined to make his lust dissolve and his common sense return.

Chapter Six

∽∽∽∽∽∽∽

They got off to a late start the next day due to Shelly's insistence on waiting for the general store to open so she could buy paper and pencils. She knew the delay irritated Dillon no end and she relished his irritation. She'd like to make him miserable for a month to pay him back for the awkwardness she now felt because of the previous night's entanglement. Her own quick response to his kiss galled her the most; he must have used some trick to get her to forget herself like that.

She and the men were quiet for most of the ride from Carson City to Virginia City. "My favorite place," muttered Diego, interrupting Shelly's brooding. She looked up at the gap that cut through the mountain in front of them. The sides of the mountain crowded in on both sides of the road, leaving barely enough room for two wagons to pass side by side. "It's called Devil's Gate," Diego informed her.

"I'd believe hell is on the other side," murmured Shelly.

"Just might be for you," Diego said, winking.

Once they'd passed through the eerie form of Devil's Gate, the road led up to what Diego told her was Gold Hill, and on either side of them, men toiled in the dirt. Shelly stared in openmouthed amazement as she looked from one side of the road to the other. These men were the dirtiest creatures she'd ever seen—and that was pretty filthy considering what she'd passed on the trail. Diego told her that many of these miners lived in holes dug into the side of the hill. Two miles farther they reached Gold Hill. The concentration of miners was thick both on the sides of the road and going in and out of the saloons.

A short time later Shelly realized that nothing Dillon had said had prepared her for the sight of Virginia City, not that he had said that much. She pushed back her hat and let her mule slow down and stop while she studied the scene in front of her. The men smiled at one another as they watched her expression turn from wonder to disbelief and then to a bleak resignation.

The most luxurious buildings in the town were rickety wood shacks that looked as if they might be saloons. Canvas tents dotted the hillside and, Shelly guessed, you'd be lucky to have one of them, since many of the abodes were made of a mix of burlap sacks, old shirts, crates and even sagebrush. Whiskey barrels served for chimneys. As in Gold Hill, men were living like animals in holes in the mountainside. And everywhere there was mud. Men had to wade through it among the jungle of tents and up and down the steep hill that the settlement took over. There was only one street to speak of, and it twisted down the middle of the community. A couple thousand men swarmed over the hill. Shelly heard the boom of dynamite from where they looked down at the town, and she watched the spray of dirt that accompanied the sound.

"Shall we go on?" asked Dillon.

She jerked, noticing that they were all watching her. "No, I don't think so," she said numbly. Dillon took her reins. Shelly didn't fight him; she hid her long braid under her hat. "Where will we be staying?" They were passing a tent of burlap and faded shirts with a pair of feet sticking out the end, the boots encrusted with mud.

"In a tent."

"A real tent?"

He turned and grinned at her. "Yes, a real tent with a cot to sleep on."

Relief flooded Shelly's face.

"I'll stop right here," Parker said as he dismounted and handed his reins to Diego. Shelly watched the big man disappear into one of the many saloons.

She followed Dillon between the makeshift living quarters and pulled her hat low over her eyes. She would prefer to go unrecognized as a woman. The sense of lawlessness that surrounded the town was intense.

Dillon stopped in front of what may have once been a white tent but was now spattered and speckled brown. Diego led the mules away while Dillon took Shelly's elbow and ushered her inside the tent. The noise of the dynamite, the picks, the talk and the laughter were muted inside the dim confines.

"Is this your tent?"

Dillon nodded. "And Diego's and Jefferies'."

"Who is Jefferies?" Shelly sat down on one neatly made cot, took off her hat and rubbed her scalp.

"My partner."

"Oh." She recognized the name. She set her hat on her knees and looked up quizzically. "What now?"

"I have to go find him." Finding Jefferies was not the problem; Shelly was. He didn't want to drag her around with him, yet he sensed her anger and resentment and did not trust her to stay put. And there were hundreds of men in this town who had probably not laid eyes on a woman—especially a pretty woman—for quite some time.

Shelly turned her gaze from his frowning stare and looked around her. She was surprised by how clean the interior of the tent was. The broom in the corner was silent testimony that someone swept the tent out. She wondered if it was Dillon who insisted on neatness. There were two other cots beside the one she was sitting on, both tucked tight with blankets. There were a couple of crates that could be used as tables or chairs. There was even a mirror hanging from the pole above her head. She grinned.

"What are you smiling about?"

Shelly sighed and faced Dillon. "I'm going to honor our bargain, so you can stop staring at me and go find your partner." Dillon nodded curtly and left. Bored, Shelly lay down and slipped into a dreamless oblivion.

She awoke to voices and opened her eyes. Looming above her were the tall figures of Dillon and another man. Shelly levered herself to a sitting position and saw the most gentlemanly-looking man she'd seen since she'd left San Francisco. He was clean. He sported an impeccably trimmed mustache and no beard, the waves of russet hair were shining softly, and his white shirt, buff trousers and green coat were all in one clean piece, unlike the tatters that many of the men were in. He looked to be in his midforties and his body was straight and clean.

"My name is Adam Jefferies."

Shelly nodded. "And I'm Shelly Young." She stood to stretch out her legs.

"She never even poked her head out of the tent," announced Diego, walking into the tent. Shelly glanced at Dillon and he shrugged.

"Please sit down, Miss Young."

Why was this man being so polite? She perched on the edge of the cot and tried unsuccessfully to stifle a yawn. "Excuse me." The last thing she wanted was them to think they were boring her.

"Quite all right," Jefferies said, sitting down on a crate in the middle of the tent. Dillon lounged on a cot behind Jefferies' back and when Shelly looked at the older man she had to see Dillon's long legs, wide chest and dark face. Diego sat down on the same cot and rested his elbows on his knees.

"You must excuse the furnishings here, Miss Young. I would have sent for something more comfortable, only I'm hoping I'll not be in this dreadful place much longer."

Shelly nodded. "I can understand that."

"Miss Young, I want to tell you about the Avalon, our mine."

"Go on, then."

"The Avalon is owned by Dillon, Diego and myself. Diego told us about the silver here. Dillon convinced me to throw my lot in with them. He really thought I would like the untamed wilderness of the West. He was wrong."

Shelly grinned. "Are you from New York, too?"

"Yes, that very cultivated city with good restaurants, roads and real buildings. Anyway, Miss Young, we struck our claim in the fall of '59 and we have been blessed and cursed ever since. In transporting our ore to San Francisco for refining we have been badly hit by highwaymen. The robberies abated during the height of winter, when the trail was impossible to pass on. As soon as the thaw came we suffered worse than before. Last week we lost another man, Lloyd Everett.''

Shelly flinched. "He's dead?" Jefferies nodded. "He was there in the beginning when I spied."

"You see why Dillon has been so upset with you. We need to know who the man is you've been relaying your messages to."

Shelly's chin lifted and Dillon grimaced. He'd told Adam that she'd said all she was going to, probably all she could.

"Mr. Jefferies, I understand the importance of finding this man. However, he played me for a fool, and I really don't have any information to help you. I've already told him—" she nodded her head at the man whose name she didn't want to speak "—everything I could. I know he doesn't believe me, but—"

"My dear, it was my idea to speak with you again about it. I feared perhaps Dillon had not made the best impression."

Shelly's chin lowered a bit. "You're right about that," she agreed as Parker came in and stood just inside the tent flap.

Jefferies looked away from her. "Now we have to decide what to do with you."

Shelly had a headache. He didn't have to look so annoyed; she hadn't invited herself along.

"Miss Young, you are a very attractive woman among many men. It concerns me."

Shelly looked down at herself and wanted to laugh, but then she remembered Dillon's reaction to her in these very same clothes and she sobered.

"It's not that the men around here would want to hurt you," Jefferies continued. "They just go after what they want in a rambunctious way, like oversize puppies. Maybe it's all the dreams of riches in their heads. We need some kind of arrangement so that you won't be bothered overly much by the miners.''

"Maybe she could be your wife," Diego suggested to Dillon, punching his leg. Shelly and Dillon stiffened simultaneously.

"Maybe she could pose as a family member to one of us," suggested Jefferies.

Shelly squirmed under four pairs of eyes.

"She doesn't look like any of you," observed Parker quietly.

Dillon turned to Parker. "No, she doesn't." He kept looking at Parker. Slowly, Diego and Jefferies followed the direction of his gaze.

Diego laughed. "She looks like you, *amigo!* I guess you got yourself a sister!"

Parker stuck his big hand out. "No!"

"Yes, that's an excellent idea," agreed Jefferies, eager to get the situation settled. Besides, what Diego said was true; Parker was fair skinned like the girl, his eyes were gray blue and his hair was brown, duller by far than Shelly's mahogany color but closer than anyone else's.

Shelly was uncomfortable with Parker's displeasure, though the men thought it amusing. Since Parker and Lloyd had shared a tent, it was decided that Shelly would take Lloyd's cot. "Couldn't I just stay in a tent by myself?" she asked.

"My dear, not only don't we have another tent, but you would hardly be safe or, for that matter, alone, for long. She's all yours, Parker—one new responsibility, a very pleasant one, I'm sure." Jefferies was unable to restrain his grin at the big man's scowl.

Shelly walked over to Parker. "I won't be any trouble, really." Diego and Dillon laughed behind her and she cast an infuriated glance over her shoulder.

Parker's smaller tent was next door. There was room for two cots inside and a crate that separated them. On top of the crate was a lantern. Under the cot that Parker threw his hat on was a large canvas bag. The other cot was scattered with clothes.

"It's like he left it," Parker stated flatly.

Shelly's stomach contracted as she looked at Lloyd's belongings, lying there as if dropped in a hurry. She was nervous about taking the bed of a dead man, and one she'd helped to murder. Shelly gingerly picked up the clothes and folded them into a neat pile.

"You might as well wear anything that comes close to fitting."

Shelly cringed. She didn't know if she could, but the sweater might be useful.

"I'm sorry about Lloyd," she whispered, her back to Parker.

"Me, too."

Shelly sat down on her unmade cot and faced him. This was going to be a long stay.

Shelly awoke to the explosion of dynamite and the clanging of picks on her second day in Virginia City. She was warm under a heavy load of blankets. Parker was gone and his blankets were thrown loosely over his cot. She stretched out her limbs and wondered why she had slept so well in a dead man's bed.

Her stomach grumbled as she sat up. She dragged Lloyd's comb through the long waves of her hair and then braided the length into one thick braid. Wishing she had some water to wash her face, she made do with a quick scrub using the edge of a blanket. She pulled on Lloyd's gray sweater, crammed on her hat and stepped outside.

By midafternoon Shelly was thoroughly miserable. Besides being bored, she was starving, and her money was in a saddlebag somewhere. Besides, Dillon was supposed to buy her food. She could not find Dillon or Diego or the others. She finally retreated to her tent to avoid explaining to one more man that she was up here with her brother and was not interested in any profitable situation they could devise for her. One week in this place and she would go crazy unless she found something to do. She jumped off her cot when Parker came into the tent.

"Figured you might be hungry," he said in a monotone with blank face.

"You figured right." She refrained from saying what a slow figurer he was.

Shelly followed him inside one of the wood shanties that lined the main road. There were no windows, but lanterns hung from nails in the walls. A wood stove burned hotly in the center of the room, and the place was toasty warm and greasy smelling. There were crates to sit on and a few real tables and chairs filled with card players. The bar consisted of a couple of wagon sides and was almost hidden by the men standing around it. Glasses and bottles lined the shelves behind it. The ceaseless din of conversation from the crowd bounced off the walls. The men closest to Shelly looked at her with blatant curiosity. The talk directly around her abated. Men made room for her at the bar, and Parker squeezed in beside her. Shelly tried not to betray her nervousness as she sensed dozens of eyes staring at her back.

She stared straight ahead—and met the fierce brown eyes of the large man behind the bar. Her gaze was drawn to his huge, bristly beard, its blackness broken only by two streaks of white down either side of his mouth. A bushy mustache curled down into the beard, and his hair ended three inches below his collar. The hugeness, the blackness of him, even his very stance behind the bar, one hand on his hip and the other palm down on the makeshift counter, intimidated her.

"I don't believe I've had the pleasure," boomed the big man. Many bodies in the room leaned forward to hear the girl's response.

"Shelly, this is Hank," said Parker, making the introductions. "Hank, my sister, Miss Harrington. We want some food."

Shelly was surprised to see the man named Hank smile. His dark eyes crinkled up and his lips lifted the ominous, drooping threat of his mustache. "I think I can manage that. Pleased to meet you, Miss Harrington."

Shelly had almost finished her plate of beans, pork and bread before she felt like talking. "You have quite a crowd in here. Is it always like this?'' she asked Hank, who stood near her and Parker after serving some of the men.

''Usually.''

''Seems like you could use some help in here,'' Shelly hinted. He looked at her speculatively while Parker's fork stopped midway to his mouth. ''I don't have anything to do since he—'' she jabbed Parker in the side with her elbow ''—dragged me up here. I can cook. Can you give me a job?''

''Now wait a minute—'' exclaimed Parker, but he was cut off by Hank.

''For how much?''

Shelly tilted her head to one side. ''Six dollars a week.''

''Six dollars!''

''Surely you can afford that. What do you say?''

''No sister of mine is going to work in a saloon!'' shouted Parker, finally able to get some words out. What a little scheming fox she was! Dillon would kill him.

''Don't listen to him,'' advised Shelly.

''Hey, Harrington, don't be selfish! We want female company, too, especially one that cooks,'' yelled a miner.

''You ain't gonna do nothin' but cook?'' asked a young man, leaning on the bar.

''Maybe I'll hand you a glass of whiskey once in a while.''

''Shelly!'' Parker warned.

Hank laughed. ''Maybe you can take care of yourself in here.''

''It's a fine idea, Hank,'' called out another voice. ''We need somethin' to look at besides your ugly mug.''

''Looks like if I don't hire you, some of these men'll make me regret it. All right, Miss Harrington, you got yourself a job.''

Shelly grinned. ''When do I start?''

''Now!''

A chorus of cheers went up, completely drowning out Parker's furious words.

Chapter Seven

Shelly's first day at Hank's whirled by in a talking, laughing, working frenzy. She felt herself expanding as she chatted with hundreds of friendly strangers who were very happy to have her around. She didn't notice when Parker left, after giving up on trying to get her out of the saloon. She worked long after dark, barely found her tent in the night and was asleep as soon as her body was prone.

Her second day at Hank's was a repeat of the first. She learned to pour whiskey and serve the slop of beans and bread that Hank called food faster than she could think. A few times she wondered if Dillon knew what she was up to.

"Hank, that does it for me. I can't stand any longer."

"Okay, tuck yourself on in."

She pulled her hat from under the bar and had almost made it to the door when a hand grasped her elbow. "You leavin' us?"

Shelly nodded. It was Luther. Golden-haired Luther and his half-witted friend, Tongue, were two of the meanest men in Virginia City. They enjoyed accusing men of cheating at cards so they could fight. Tongue had a disgusting habit of licking the face of the man he was brawling with, thereby earning himself the crude nickname.

"Now, that ain't real friendly of you."

"It's got nothing to do with friendliness."

"Well, I'll just escort you to your tent."

"That won't be necessary."

Luther grabbed his hat off the table and pushed it down on his head. "Why, I couldn't let a pretty thing like you walk to your tent alone, now could I?"

"You sure could!" yelled Hank.

Luther ignored him and pulled Shelly against his chest. "I'm glad you decided to join your brother. It's been real dull here with no ladies."

"Luther, it's your deal," the miner who'd been playing cards with him said softly.

"Hell," muttered Luther, "there ain't no men in here. You're all a bunch of women."

Shelly remained very still against Luther's body. This man was too dangerous to fight unless one was sure of winning. She waited for a chance to run.

Luther eyed the pile of coins in the center of the poker game. He shoved Shelly away and went back to his chair and his whiskey. Shelly walked quickly out of the saloon. Wrapped up in her blankets back in her tent, she lay on her cot, uneasy. Most of the men respected and liked her, but there were a few crazy ones like Luther. She was vulnerable in this town with nothing to protect herself. She could use a good frying pan under her bed. As she twisted about restlessly in the cold tent, her nose and ears icy, she decided she had to get something like a knife, which she could carry inconspicuously in her boot.

She bolted to a sitting position when the tent flap flew up. Her feet hit the floor before the large figure had come all the way in. "Get out!"

"You entertainin' someone?" asked Parker blandly.

"Oh, Parker!" Shelly laughed, sagging back down to the cot in relief. "I thought you were someone else!" She told him about Luther while he lighted the lamp. "You don't have an extra knife, do you?" she asked when she'd finished recounting her night.

"Nope."

Shelly sighed, as much at his answer as the blunt way he said it.

"Dillon should have Lloyd's knife. I'll try and get back earlier from now on."

Shelly looked up at him in surprise. He still looked expressionless as usual, although she detected a friendlier light in his eyes. "Thank you, Parker," she said softly. He nodded. "But that's not necessary. I don't want to get in your way."

"You're already in my way. You're living in my damn tent!"

Shelly flushed. Not knowing what else to say, she crawled back under her covers and turned on her side, facing away from him.

"I've been gettin' too tight anyways," he mumbled. "Won't hurt to come back earlier. A little earlier."

Shelly smiled.

The next evening, after Shelly finished working at Hank's, she went to see about Lloyd's knife. Outside her tent she viewed hundreds of campfires around her. The talk of the men was loud and she knew from previous nights that the activity went on until dawn.

Shelly called Dillon's name softly from outside his tent. She hadn't seen him since her first day in Virginia City and was nervous about talking with him. The tent flap flipped open and Dillon's tall body blocked the light from inside. "What, have you come visiting?" he asked mockingly.

"No!" She looked up at him from under the brim of her hat. Just the sight of his handsome face and sarcastic smile irritated her.

"What do you want?" He made no move to invite her in.

"Where's Diego?" she hedged, peering around his body into the tent.

"Oh, so it's him you've come to pay a call on." Dillon reentered the tent and sat down on his cot, where a mess of papers was spread out. "Well, you can stand there until he comes back if you want to." He was annoyed his friend had made such a good impression on her. He picked up a paper and ignored her.

Shelly stepped into the tent. "Did you know I'm working in Hank's saloon?"

This was another thing irritating Dillon. "An appropriate place for you. You were probably born and raised in one."

"Yes, didn't I mention it?"

"Then why didn't you just stay there? You'd do much better as an honest barmaid than as a scheming spy."

"Why, thank you for the compliment!" Shelly was furious with him and dismayed with herself for becoming engaged in this stupid argument. She spun around to leave and collided with Diego as he stomped into the tent.

"*¡Hola!*" Diego grasped Shelly by the shoulders. "How are you?"

"I was just leaving." She tried to walk by him, but he did not take his hands from her shoulders.

"That doesn't answer my question." He scanned her face. "I heard you almost had some trouble in Hank's place."

"You heard?" Shelly crammed her hands into her trouser pockets and wished Dillon would leave so she could talk to Diego about the knife.

"Everyone knows everything around here, or at least a version of it!"

"The reason I came over is because of what happened last night."

"What happened last night?" asked Dillon, annoyed no one had told him.

Shelly ignored him, but Diego didn't. "Luther wanted to get friendly with her. He got talked out of it, but I would be careful near him," he warned Shelly. "You working in that place is an invitation to some men."

"Maybe she knew that."

"What is eating you?" Shelly yelled.

Diego waved his hand toward the other man. "His insides. If he wasn't so stubborn he'd get it taken care of."

Shelly frowned. "Is he sick?" she whispered.

"Very."

"Will you two shut up? I'm fine!" he bellowed. "Let's get to what you want."

Shelly sniffed. "Parker said you have Lloyd's knife. Can I use it?" Dillon looked incredulous. "I need something to protect myself against some men."

"What men? Just the ones you don't like?"

Shelly rolled her eyes up to the ceiling. "I swear I won't use any weapon against you or your men unless..."

"Unless what?"

"Unless one of you gets, you know... too friendly."

"Don't worry!"

"Worry," contradicted Diego.

Dillon glared at Diego before his gaze returned to Shelly. "I bet you don't know how to hold a blade."

"I'm not some fancy city lady."

"I'm not talking about whacking up a piece of meat or cutting a chicken's head off. I mean holding a knife to kill or maim a man twice your size."

"No, I don't, but I bet you could show me." She returned Dillon's stare. When he stood she knew he'd accepted her challenge. He got the knife out of a small locked trunk and handed it to her.

"Don't hold it like that. Here, like this."

Shelly didn't budge as he moved behind her and stood close. She glanced at Diego, who was sitting on his cot pulling off his boots, a huge grin on his face. Dillon took her hand and positioned her fingers over the hilt. His skin was warm and rough with calluses. "You slash like this, stab like this." Shelly was distracted by the soft touch of his breath against her cheek. He guided her arm and she forced herself to concentrate on the movements he led her in.

Dillon stepped away and watched her practice what he'd shown her. "That's it." He was surprised at her quickness and disappointed it was unnecessary for him to show her again, while her soft, round backside pressed into his loins and sent heat blazing through him.

She looked up and smiled. "Thank you."

Dillon nodded, staring at her.

"Good night," she said to them both.

"*Buenas noches,* Shelly," Diego called from his cot. Dillon didn't speak.

She'd gone a few yards outside the tent when Dillon called her back. "Come here a minute."

"Your legs work."

"Impertinent girl. Halfway then."

They met and Shelly crossed her arms beneath her breasts. "What?"

"I thought you'd be wanting this." He hefted a saddlebag up. "You remember the things that were so important we had to wait for the store to open?"

"Oh, I do!" She dug her things out of the bag, the small sketchbook, the pencils, the envelopes, the hairbrush and some money.

"And I want to apologize for being rude back there in the tent."

Shelly's jaw almost hit her chest. "I accept your apology, until the next time."

"Next time?"

"You can't help yourself." She clasped her belongings in her arms. "You're socially graceless and rude as a general rule."

"Oh, forget this!" He strode back to his tent, telling himself she wasn't worth one kind word, the stubborn, willful little monkey.

Shelly wiped her hands on her trousers and sighed. This was her sixth day at Hank's. To see the men shovel up the food she had prepared was infinitely better than sitting lonely in her tent. Today she was making bread. She'd had a nasty surprise the first time she had measured out flour. Long black worms had fallen into the tin can she'd poured the flour in. She had dumped the whole mess outside and Hank had yelled at her. Now Shelly carefully strained the flour that she measured before she made bread out of it. Only the worms were thrown outside.

"You seem to be getting along very well, Miss Harrington," observed Jefferies, coming to stand at the bar. His shirt was white and clean.

Shelly poured him a cup of coffee. "I'm fine," she said. "Though I do want to get back to San Francisco as soon as possible," she assured him emphatically.

He smiled and raised the cup to his lips. "I understand. Dillon told me you took the job at Snelling's for the money. Don't you have any family to help you?"

"No, I don't, not yet. However, in your fair state I do. Have you heard of the Exeters? The Youngs?" He shook his head. "No matter. When I get there I'll find them."

"You're a very determined young woman, aren't you?"

"I suppose." She shrugged. "Mr. Jefferies, how do you get your clothes so clean here? There's no river nearby."

Adam Jefferies laughed. "I pay someone to take my laundry to Carson City."

"Ahhh." Shelly wished she had a spare set of clothes so she could do the same. She should have brought her muddied dress and petticoats, which she'd left in Carson City; instead, they'd probably got thrown out with the filthy bathwater.

Shelly had been in Virginia City for more than a week before she found out what happened to Aggie's husband, Tom. She'd asked almost every man she served if he knew of him until she was sick of hearing the question fall from her lips. She could hardly believe her ears when she heard a positive answer.

"Tall man? Gotta wife name of Abby?" asked the thin, bearded man.

"Aggie?" Shelly corrected hopefully.

"Yeah, Aggie."

"Does he have copper-colored hair and brown eyes?"

"He had. He died of pneumonia on the first of April. He took sick fast and died fast," he elaborated bluntly.

The excitement drained from Shelly and she felt weary. "Where is he buried?"

"Down the mountain where they're all buried in unmarked graves."

"Oh. How did you know him?"

"Met him here in this saloon. He got sick soon after that. Hey, he weren't no kin of yours, was he?" the miner asked, noticing Shelly's gray face.

"No, he was not related to me," she answered, moving away from him.

Shelly dragged through the rest of the day thinking of the sad news she had to pass on to Aggie. Back in her tent that night she lighted the lantern and pulled out the pages of the letter she'd already begun to compose to Aggie, explaining her whereabouts. Shelly didn't enjoy writing, the strokes of a picture expressed more of what she felt and wanted to say, but she struggled through the letter nevertheless. She folded the pages into the envelope.

"Anybody home?" she called out at Dillon's tent. Dillon opened the tent flap and Shelly thought it would be nice if just once he smiled when he saw her. "How do I go about sending this letter to San Francisco?"

He took the letter out of her hand. "I'll have to read it first."

"What?"

"I have to read it. I just thought I'd let you know." He turned back into his tent.

Shelly followed. "You will not! Give it back!"

He held the letter way above her head. "Listen, Shelly, you could easily pass on some information to Karl Booker in here, or God knows who else."

Shelly shook with hot, righteous anger. "Then handing it to you would be the dumbest thing I could do. I'd find someone else to send it."

"Maybe you were counting on me thinking that. Maybe you thought you had me all wrapped up in a blanket of trust and didn't have to worry anymore. And if there's nothing in here, why are you so upset?"

"Because it's private, you jackass!" she screamed.

"Maybe," Dillon continued, trying to reason with her, "this Karl would intercept it." He ripped open the envelope and held her off with one hand clenched in her sweater. He shook open the pages. He began to read and Shelly stood like stone, her hands bunched into fists at her sides.

He read about where she was and how her actions had precipitated the destination. He read about the death of Mrs. Thornton's husband, and in Shelly's attempts at comfort he learned about the death of her mother. There was no self-pity. There were no secret messages. He felt very small as he finished the letter and put it back in the torn envelope. He looked up to see Shelly glaring at him, silver fury flashing from her eyes. "I'll see it gets there," he said curtly, tossing the envelope onto his cot. He'd done what he had to do, he told himself.

Shelly saw no regret in his face. She strode back to her own tent, dashing a tear off her face. She was sick of the mistrust, the testing, the lack of privacy and the unfriendliness. She spent a good half hour lying on her back, knees drawn up and feet planted firmly on the blankets. She fiddled with her broken fingernails and examined her calluses and thought about the picture she was going to draw of Dillon, a truly ugly one. Her entire body stiffened when she heard Dillon's voice outside the tent.

"Shelly?" She did not respond but levered herself up on her elbows. "Shelly?" he called again, more insistently.

"What?" Her voice was harsh. He walked in, tin coffee cup in hand, and looked down at her. She sat up, bringing her feet to the floor and brushing a strand of hair off her cheek. "Well?"

"I'm sorry," he said. "But you would have done the same thing in my place," he offered in his defense.

Her hands squeezed the cot on either side of her legs while she studied the big toe of her right stockinged foot.

"I had to make sure. I won't read anything else you write."

Shelly looked up at him. "So, you trust me?" Their eyes met and a shock of warmth shot through her.

He sat beside her. "Yes," he said dismally. He bent forward, resting his elbows on his knees.

Shelly frowned. "Then what's wrong?"

"Believing you've told me everything means you don't know very much and therefore are not much help."

"Well, I'm sorry," she said sarcastically.

"Forget it," muttered Dillon. "Want some?" He offered her his tin mug, which still held steaming coffee. "If you can stand it. The water's so bad here you have to mix it with two parts alcohol and it still taints the whiskey."

Shelly smiled and reached for his cup. She wondered at this sharing of cups, which they'd done once before. Her thumb brushed his fingers as she clasped the handle. She took a few sips and handed the cup back to him.

Dillon placed his left hand over her hand that held the cup and pressed down until she touched his thigh. Shelly swayed toward him, pulled by the hand he held. Her lips parted in silent exclamation and she looked into Dillon's eyes, which were focused with hot purpose on her lips. "I'm going to kiss you," he said almost despairingly. He raised his eyes and Shelly's lids fell under the onslaught of his gaze. His lips softly grazed, pressed, then gently sucked at the fullness of her mouth. When he nipped her bottom lip a gush of heat spread outward from deep inside her belly. She opened her mouth fully, caressing his tongue with her own. The kiss grew hotter and deeper and Dillon smoothed his right hand up her back, drawing her closer to him. Shelly lifted her free hand to his shoulder and she felt hot, hard muscles through his shirt.

The swish of the tent flap opening and the brush of cool air that flooded in hit them at the same time. Dillon broke away from Shelly, his arm dropping from her back. Parker stood before them. He threw his hat onto his bed and scratched his head before he sat down on his cot with a loud groan.

Dillon strode out of the tent without a word. Shelly stared at her feet, but Parker still had a good view of her red face until she flung herself backward onto her cot. He rolled his big body down on the cot and, hands behind his head, stared at the canvas above his face. So much for returning earlier, he thought.

Six days passed and Shelly avoided Dillon. She'd never thought she had a lustful bone in her body until she met him. She didn't care for her reaction to him; she forgot

everything else but touching him when he was so darn close
to her. He ate his meals at Hank's and Shelly did well at
serving him without ever looking in his face or speaking to
him. She meant to anger him but instead he seemed amused,
and that made her feel self-conscious.

He came to her tent only once. It had been at night when
she got back from Hank's and before Parker returned. She
had smelled whiskey on him. He'd asked how she was and
had never stopped looking at her. Every nerve in her body
had rung out with warning, like the city bells when a fire
flamed. He'd left when she asked him to. She'd drawn for
hours that night to relieve her anxiety.

But at the end of this sixth day she was tired of her tent
and she wanted the friendly conversation of Diego and Jefferies. Of course, she'd have to tolerate Dillon's company,
as well, but as long as she was not alone with him she
thought she could endure him. And trust herself.

Diego greeted her enthusiastically. Dillon also seemed
pleased. The atmosphere had changed in their tent. Shelly
looked around while Diego pulled out a crate for her to sit
on. "What's different here?" she asked. Both men watched
her. She realized that the small trunk of clothes that had always been under Jefferies' cot was gone, as were all the
other little signs of his presence, the gloves, cravats and
books on his cot.

"Where is he?" asked Shelly in a hushed voice, sure
something terrible had happened to him. Two enormous
gray eyes rose to Dillon's face.

"He went back to San Francisco this morning."

Shelly gaped. "Back to San Francisco?" Dillon nodded.
"This morning?"

"That's what I said."

"Why couldn't I go with him?" she almost wailed.

"You have a bargain with me, Shelly. You'll go back
when I do."

"And when will that be?" she demanded, the hostility
spilling out of her.

"Soon. Maybe a few days, maybe a week."

"Maybe a month!" Shelly added.

He shrugged. "I thought you liked it here." He had the nerve to grin.

Shelly opened her mouth to say something but couldn't think of anything cutting enough. She snapped her mouth shut and left the tent.

"*Ay,* I told you she wouldn't like it." Diego crossed one leg over the other where he lay on his cot.

"I brought her here and I'll take her out." Dillon stood and unbuttoned his shirt.

"How noble, *amigo.* But you and I know that you want that *chica* in your bed. But I don't think—"

"I don't care what you think!" Dillon threw his shirt at Diego's face.

"*No tienes razón. Tienes que ser simpático para conseguir una mujer.*"

"If you're going to talk, talk in English!"

Diego grinned at his friend. "I said, you have to be nice to get a woman."

Dillon threw down the boot he had just pulled off. "Diego, I don't want her."

Diego laughed and laughed. "Are you lying to just me or to yourself, as well?"

Dillon blew out the lamp. "Go to sleep."

They settled in the darkness. Enough time had passed that Dillon was sure his friend was asleep, when Diego's voice came softly through the tent. "Just because your stepmother used you for a stud doesn't mean every woman is out only for her own."

"That's what I thought until I met Teresa. Remember her?"

"*Sí.* Two out of two. Go for twenty and then tell me about it."

"Women and me just don't mix, Diego. I don't understand them. And they sure aren't interested in giving me what I want."

Diego snorted. "You don't know what you want. And if you did, you'd hop the other way like a jackrabbit if it looked like a woman was going to give it to you."

Dillon didn't respond. He rolled onto his side and felt as confused as he had when he was sixteen and was having an affair with his stepmother. Cora. He'd been so young when he'd met her, only fifteen. His mother had died the year before, leaving him with a father who drank to dull his grief. Loretta Ryder had been a strikingly beautiful woman with deep blue eyes and black hair. She had loved husband and son fiercely, possessively. She devoted her all to both, would do anything for her husband but always seemed to side with him against Dillon, no matter how unfair, no matter how much his father beat him.

They came back so clearly, these hated memories. He'd been inside the bodice of a lovely, flirtatious kitchen maid at a neighbor's house. The live-in relation of the mistress of the house opened the pantry door on them. The widow Cora Lane was the most sensuously beautiful woman Dillon had ever seen, with her deep gold hair piled on her head, her dark green eyes and wide, red mouth. She took him to her sitting room and told him to sit next to her on the rust velvet divan. She'd been wearing a dark, walnut brown morning robe, embroidered in gold thread and fastened under her generous breasts. He'd sat stiffly and glanced about the room, noticing the drapes drawn against the sunny day. He jerked his gaze to her face when she told him to leave the maid alone. He expected a lecture, but she asked him why he didn't just go visit a brothel, and he'd blushed. Smiling, she asked if he'd ever seen a completely naked woman. Dillon had not answered. She'd unfastened her robe and pulled it off. She wore nothing underneath.

They met nearly every day for months. Dillon fell in love with her every word, her every move, her very presence.

Looking back, he could see the changes. There'd been increasingly frequent times when she'd been unable to see him. His father drank less, yelled less and made more of an appearance around the house. Dillon hadn't noticed at the time. All he thought of was Cora, her body and the things they did together.

When Dillon was sixteen John Ryder announced his plans to marry. Even now Dillon's fists clenched at the memory.

His father was a wealthy man with a beautiful home. Why should Cora be content with the son? The elder Ryder demanded his son's silence when Dillon protested the marriage. His father had laughed when Dillon admitted to being in love with Cora. Cora assured an incredulous Dillon that they would go on as before. He hated her then. With a bitterness new to his young heart he hated her.

Cora approached Dillon every time John Ryder was away. Dillon hated himself for still wanting her. The thought of her with his father, doing the things he'd done with her, enraged him, but the rage didn't prevent his lust. Cora knew. She went out of her way to brush against him, tormenting, tempting him to break his resolve and come to her. She hacked away at him until, finally, she felled him.

One afternoon when Dillon was deep into his father's whiskey and his father was at his office, Cora won her first victory. Dillon swore to her and himself that he would never touch her again, but he couldn't stop.

The sweat broke out on Dillon's face as he remembered the last time. They were in his father's bed, where Cora liked it best. That was how his father found them. Dillon's stomach roiled with the memory. He could still feel the hardness of the headboard as he sat up against it. The light from the fire had danced crazily about the room, alternately shading and illuminating his father's contorted face as he beat his naked son. Cora's screams had punctured the red mist of Dillon's pain. He had been thrown out that November night in 1846 and had stayed away nine years.

He had talked the captain of one of his father's ships into letting him board as a sailor. He'd had romantic visions of sea life, which were drowned under the rough personalities of the men he worked with and the harsher elements of wind, rain and ice as they sailed around the Horn. The men laughed at his uncalloused hands and gave him the lowliest jobs. Dillon worked hard to prove himself, and when he'd stepped onto the shore of California he'd felt years older. For a time he lived in a shack he'd found, eating fish from the streams and wild game, after he'd learned how to shoot and hit something. He abandoned his shack when he heard of the discovery of gold. He met Diego in a gold camp. They were both wild seventeen-year-olds ready for any risk. The two had stuck together like brothers ever since.

As for women... Dillon rolled on his back in the tent and grimaced. Diego was more interested and had better luck; he never wanted as much from them. When he was eighteen Dillon had fallen in love with Teresa Smith, a half-Mexican sixteen-year-old living with her parents. She said she returned his love and had tortured him with stolen hours of touching, never consummating their great love, never agreeing to marry him. She up and married an older widower in town who had a white house, no children and a nice bank job. That was when Dillon gave up.

When he returned to New York with Diego by his side, Cora was long gone. He and his father never referred to her or that time. His father pushed him into the Ryder Shipping business and took a third wife, a plain woman whom Dillon avoided. Diego abhorred the New York winter and returned to California with a long list of specific instructions from Dillon and his father on opening an office of Ryder Shipping in San Francisco. Within months Dillon followed Diego west. He made one trip back to New York, where he entangled himself in a bunch of commitments to his father and then got away as fast as he could back to California and claimed his mine, the only thing he had that didn't have his father's name on any of the papers.

Dillon sighed in the dark of the tent. All his memories had him wide-awake. "Diego?" No answer. Was Shelly asleep? He tried to imagine that picture. She didn't even like him, so why was he attracted to her? He was hopeless.

Chapter Eight

Dillon stepped out of his tent early the next morning and took a deep breath of the cold air. He liked this place in spite of its barrenness. Row after row of blue-gray mountain ranges rolled off below him to a great, flat valley in the distance. The only natural adornment was the sagebrush. And the silver.

These mountains were yielding up a fortune to him. The robberies had dwindled to almost nothing. He had a good crew who worked in shifts around the clock. The man he'd hired to take Lloyd's place, Bill Mitchell, was working out. Mitchell would stay in Virginia City when Dillon, Parker and Diego returned to San Francisco. Then Parker would come back and oversee the mine. Dillon had ordered lumber and furnishings to be freighted in to build the Avalon mine office and a residence for Parker.

Dillon stretched his arms above his head, arched his shoulders back and yawned wide. Out of the corner of his eye he saw Shelly step out of her tent. She pulled her hat down and flung her long braid behind her shoulder. Their eyes met briefly. She ignored his wave and made off for Hank's. So, she was still mad at him. He watched the motion of her round bottom as she made her way through the tents. He saw quite a few men smile and greet her as she passed. He had wanted her to be miserable here as a kind of punishment, but she had never come close. He was the one who was miserable. He didn't like her working at Hank's and being around all those men. He didn't know exactly what she did all day when he was at the mine. Parker had told him that she always came directly back to her tent after working and she'd never brought anyone with her. Dillon had felt foolish asking. Most of all, he was miserable for wanting her. The image of her mouth and eyes came often and without warning when he was down in the mine or trying to get to sleep or discussing plans with Adam. He was drawn to her now, even after last night's rehashing of his unpleasant history with women.

Was he demented or could there be a chance that she was different? Maybe if he just made her his mistress he'd be okay. The thought made him excited and nervous. He didn't think a relationship would be easy with Shelly, but the arrangement might work as long as he stayed in control and didn't get too involved. He could use her and enjoy her for just a little while. It was an idea.

"How much will ya charge me to cook this here rabbit?"

Shelly appraised the dirty, hairy miner holding up the skinny, dead animal. "One dollar."

"Done."

She took the animal by the ears and carried it outside to skin it. Her mouth was watering as she imagined succulent roasted rabbit meat. She was losing weight on her meager bean-and-pork diet. She squatted down at the side of the building near the back and pulled out the knife that had belonged to Lloyd.

"I thought we were gonna play cards?"

"Can't now. Got a message from Karl."

Shelly paused. That voice was Luther's.

"Who?"

"Karl! The man who's payin' us. We gotta leave, go back to the cabin. He wants us to get the silver out of there and take it to San Francisco."

"Aw, damn. I'm gonna get in a game first."

"You can find your own way then."

"Luther, just one game."

"Follow the Carson River."

"And which way is the damn river?"

"Tongue, I'm surprised you can find your own—"

"All right, I'm comin'. Slow down!"

Shelly remained still until she no longer heard their gushing footsteps in the mud as they walked away. She ran into Hank's and thrust the lifeless rabbit into the miner's chest. "Sorry, you're gonna have to cook it yourself!" She ran back out and headed for Dillon's tent. It had to be his Avalon silver they were talking about in that cabin.

No one was in Dillon's tent. She would have to ask directions to the Avalon, since she'd never been there. She ran up the path, slipped in the mud and went sliding down onto her backside. "Damn!"

"Temper, temper," said an amused voice behind her.

Shelly twisted around and extended her hand toward Dillon. "Oh, I found you!" She missed his openmouthed surprise. He gave her a hand up and she gritted her teeth against the cool mud seeping through her trousers and long underwear. "I know where your silver is!" She hopped up and down. "Luther's keeping it in a cabin by the Carson River, but they're going to move it!"

Dillon grasped her shoulders in his big hands. "What are you talking about?"

Shelly took a deep breath and explained exactly how and what she had overheard. Dillon's eyes hardened before she finished. His face grim, he turned to Diego standing behind him. "Let's go." They ran to saddle the two horses they'd gotten in trade for three sturdy mules. Shelly stood by, feeling proud she was of help, until Dillon rode up and lifted her in front of him. "You're coming."

"Why?"

"I don't know how long this will take."

Dillon led their horses out of town and the six miles toward the river at a fast run. Shelly held tight to the pommel of Dillon's saddle, glad for his arms braced on either side of her to keep her from tumbling off. He led the way to the right when they came to the tree-shaded banks of the river.

"Oh, look at all that water," groaned Shelly. "I want a bath."

"Later," promised Dillon distractedly. They slowed the horses when they saw the cabin ahead. "We're going to have to move in closer." Dillon kicked his horse ahead, keeping them shielded behind large cottonwood trees. When he had taken them as close as possible he dismounted and pulled his rifle out with one hand and Shelly off the horse with his other. She pointed excitedly to the side of the cabin where two large freight wagons stood under the trees. Canvas coverings were tied over large mounds that filled the wagons. A group of horses was tied to the same trees.

Dillon grasped her hand and tugged her after him as he crept up to the cabin. Shelly stiffened when she heard several voices from within. Dillon's brows rose as his eyes probed hers. Inside, several men were arguing about whose turn it was to cook. Someone complained about Mickey's cooking. Someone else asked, "How about a card game?"

Shelly recognized Tongue. "It's them," she mouthed soundlessly.

"Go see if they have a back window," Dillon whispered to Diego. He released Shelly's hand and set her away from him. "You stay here," he ordered in a whisper. He handed her a gun he pulled out of his boot. "Just in case." He waited for Diego's wave from around the corner. When it came he crept along the cabin wall.

Shelly's fingers tightened around the rough bark of a tree while she watched the events in front of her. She pictured Dillon taking a bullet in the gut and she broke out in a cold sweat. She kept her eyes on him as if that would protect him, and she realized it was very important to her that he not get hurt.

Dillon crawled to the cabin door and stood when he reached it. His shoulders rose slightly as if he were taking a deep breath. He threw his weight against the door and sent it crashing open. Shelly dug her nails into the tree at the screaming sound of splintering wood. She heard Dillon's voice, "Don't move!" before he disappeared inside. Shelly stepped back to the horses and nervously stroked the neck of Dillon's mare until her patience evaporated.

There were three men besides Luther and Tongue inside the cabin. All of them were armed. Dillon surprised them and Diego popped in through the back window at the same time. Dillon told the men to drop their guns and they slowly moved to obey, expressions of astonishment on their faces. They recovered quickly. Luther's gun belt hung from his hand, almost to the floor, when he suddenly reversed direction and swung the belt into Dillon's face, simultaneously drawing another gun hidden in the waistband of his trousers and aiming it at Diego. Three guns went off at once. Dillon and Diego both shot Luther in the chest while Luther's bullet lodged in the wall after grazing the shoulder of Diego's shirt. When Dillon and Diego had swung toward Luther, the other men dived for their guns, sensing it was their lucky last chance.

Shelly poked her head over the window and saw Tongue raise his gun against Dillon. Tongue's head was barely three feet from her. Without thinking she aimed her cocked pistol and pulled the trigger. The explosion echoed inside her head. Tongue fell to the floor but she stood paralyzed, the gun in her hand. She never even noticed the man who was taking aim at her—a second before Dillon shot and killed him.

The two remaining men were subdued. Dillon and Diego bound their wrists behind their backs and tied their ankles together. Diego shoved them outside, where they sprawled in the dirt. He reloaded his guns while Dillon went to Shelly. She was slumped against the cabin wall. Her knees and arms were unbearably weak. She tilted her head back when Dillon came to stand in front of her. "Are you all right?"

"Yes," she whispered, but she felt dizzy and nauseated and could not stand on her own. Dillon pulled her up and into his arms and held her against his chest. He was warm and hard and solid. She slowly brought her arms to rest about his waist.

"Thank you, Shelly." She drew back and looked up at him, and he ran a finger down the line of her cheek, softly brushing a strand of hair behind her ear. "When I handed you that gun I never thought you'd save my life with it."

The beginning of a smile pulled up the corners of her lips. Before the smile could grow, Dillon's lips were pressing into hers. She closed her eyes against his sweet assault, not thinking, just absorbing the warm comfort of his lips. Her hands gripped his sides, her fingers digging into the flesh and muscle at his waist. Just when she opened her mouth to him he pulled away. Her eyes flew open to lock with his hot gaze. She flushed, realizing that yet again she'd fallen into his arms. Was he aware of her steadily growing, uncontrollable feelings for him?

Dillon removed her hands from his waist, squeezing them gently before he dropped them to her sides. He pulled her hat down on her forehead and moved away, a little bemused as to why he had kissed her. There was no reason beyond how distressed and vulnerable her eyes had been and how soft her lips looked. He shook his head at himself, and behind him, Shelly wondered what he thought of her.

Dillon and Diego tied the two men to a tree and then examined the contents of the covered freight wagons. "Looks like Avalon ore," said Dillon. He clasped Diego's shoulder. "I don't expect much, but let's see if those men can tell us anything."

The men confessed nothing Dillon didn't already know. He saw how well this Karl had kept information from all those working for him. The desire to get his hands on the man was consuming.

"Where's Shelly?" Dillon asked Diego. His friend was tightening his saddle. He would ride to get Parker and their personal things.

"I saw her go in the cabin." Diego swung up on the horse. "She didn't answer me when I went in and talked to her. She's just staring at the gun."

Dillon looked toward the cabin and then up at the sun. "Hurry back."

Shelly was staring at the blood-spattered walls. The flies buzzed furiously in the pungent air. "He was a miserable human being, Shelly." Dillon pulled the gun from her sweaty hand. "He would have killed you if he'd had the chance."

"I know."

"Come on, let's go outside. It stinks in here."

He led her to a tree and she sat in the warm sun and watched the nearby river while he buried the three men in a common grave. She leaned her head back and closed her eyes while he wiped down the cabin with a blanket wet with river water. When the sun sank low, Dillon built a big, cheering fire and cooked up some of the potatoes and salt pork that the men inhabiting the cabin had left. "Shelly, come over here and eat."

"I'm not hungry."

"Come over here anyway."

Shelly plopped herself on a rock by the fire. Tongue deserved to die, she felt. It was just all that blood. She could not block the gory images from her mind. The falling darkness made her nervous and jumpy. "Dillon, what if they had friends? What if they come?" she whispered, her eyes flicking to where the two men were tied and gagged under the tree. Dillon, holding his plate of food, pointed with his free hand to the rifle by his thigh.

They heard the sound of horses at the same time. Dillon was ready with the rifle and a cocked pistol when the riders came into view. Shelly had flattened herself against the ground in panic. She heard Dillon chuckle. "I'm glad it's you," he said.

"I'm glad, too," groaned Diego as he slid off his horse and stretched his back in an arch. Parker followed close behind him.

"I made some food here." While Parker and Diego ate, Dillon dished up a plate for Shelly and held it under her nose where she sat cross-legged on the ground.

She shook her head and got up. "I'm going to sleep." She untied a couple of blankets from one of the pack mules and walked a short distance away.

Dillon tossed his own and Shelly's plate down in the dirt. "What about that bath you wanted?" he yelled after her.

Parker scooped more potatoes out of the frying pan and Diego watched Dillon.

"Forget about it," Shelly answered wearily, spreading her blankets out.

"No, I don't think I will. In fact, I'm going to make sure you do get one." He stood up. "You have blood splattered all over your face and clothes."

Shelly jerked her head up. She'd no idea that blood was on her, but now she could feel it. Unconsciously she lifted her hands to her face and rubbed her cheeks. She was so dirty she did not know what was blood and what was plain dirt. She looked down. It was dark and she was not close enough to the fire to see what was on her clothes. Suddenly, she had to have that bath. She jumped up and ran in the direction of the river.

"Got any soap?" Dillon asked the men.

Diego nodded toward the horses. "My saddlebags." Even Parker had stopped eating and was watching his boss. Dillon dug the soap out and disappeared after Shelly.

Chapter Nine

Shelly tore a button off her shirt in her haste to get the clothing off. Dillon walked up as she flung the garment on the ground. "Get out of here!"

"Don't you want the soap?"

"I want you to leave me alone!" She strode up to him. "I wouldn't be here if it weren't for you! I wouldn't need a bath or be covered with blood and dirt. And I wouldn't have killed a man!" she screeched.

"Whoa, now, just a minute."

Shelly shoved both her hands flat against his muscled chest. "I hate you. Do you hear me? I hate you!" She shoved him again.

He shoved back. "Don't blame me! You got yourself into this mess."

Shelly ran at him again, her mind a maelstrom of rage, and punched him in the stomach. Dillon grunted, grabbed her arm while she kicked and clawed and wrestled her to the ground. Pinning her with his body, he wrenched her arms above her head, stilling the frantic movements of her legs with his own. "Damn it, Shelly. Calm down!"

"Get off me!"

"So you can punch me again? No, thank you." Shelly spat in his face. Dillon stiffened, then wiped his face with the back of his hand. "That is enough," he ground out. "You're going to be still and listen to me or I'll tie and gag you like those men up there."

She stopped struggling but turned her face away from him, exposing the side of her neck where her pulse pounded. Dillon watched the frantic rhythm. His eyes moved down to her breasts, which were pushed up from the way he held her hands above her head. His face grew hot and he felt a tightening in his loins.

"I'm sorry you had to kill that man. It was a horrible thing to see. But, dammit, Shelly, you brought this on yourself by spying on me." The curve of her hips and her soft legs against him were doing wild things to his imagination.

"Get off me." Her voice was fierce.

Dillon meant to. He began to lift one leg off her and then lowered his body instead. His mouth closed on hers while she bucked in refusal beneath him. He pushed his tongue in her mouth and immediately withdrew it when she tried to bite it. He licked her lips, coaxing her, but Shelly strained every muscle of her body against him. Dillon groaned and rolled off her.

Shelly jumped to her feet. She couldn't take any more. The day had been too long, too hard. Her head was aching. If Dillon made one more move on her, one more demand of her, her head would split open. She backed away from him and walked to the bank of the river, where she yanked off her boots and pushed down her trousers.

"What are you doing?"

"I'm going to take a bath! That's what I came here for. What did you come here for? To watch?" She glared at him where he stood, arms crossed over his chest, his eyes fixed on her. She didn't know what he expected, but she was not going to give him a show. She resented the full moon above, which illuminated her. She plunged into the icy water in her long underwear and squealed from the shocking cold. With her back to him she removed the sodden garment with shaking fingers and threw it on the bank.

Dillon walked closer and extended his hand with the soap. "Take it."

Shelly debated. She inched forward and reached out. At the last minute Dillon raised his hand and Shelly automatically jumped up to grab the soap. She ducked back in the water, soap in hand, and knew that Dillon had seen her breasts fully exposed. He was being a brute. She turned her back on him and rubbed up a thick lather.

Dillon watched her stiff neck. God, he wanted her. He wanted to pull her out of that water and take her on the grass. What was wrong with him? Why had he teased her? He prided himself on being a man who did not need women overly much. Not for a long time had he felt so out of control.

Shelly turned to find him disrobing. He unbuttoned his shirt. He pulled down the top of his long underwear. The muscles rippled in his arms, his shoulders, his hair-covered chest and even his stomach. His hands worked on the buttons of his trousers. "You like watching?"

Shelly jerked her eyes up to his. She could recognize stark lust when she saw it. "No."

"Liar."

He jumped into the water, hooting and hollering at the cold. "Hurry up with that soap!" He waved his arms up and down and jumped around.

Shelly had never seen anyone look so ridiculous in her life. "I'm not exactly comfortable, either." She tried to undo her filthy braid with one hand holding the slippery soap. "Here, take it while I undo my hair."

Dillon avidly watched her crouching approach as she kept her breasts beneath the water. The water barely came to his hips. Hair trailed in a dark line down his belly, disappearing into a nest of curly hair that was cut off by the water. Instead of going any closer to the dark, naked man, Shelly threw the soap in his general direction. Her limbs were stiff and the throw was poor. Dillon almost fell trying to catch the glowing white bar.

By the time Shelly got the soap back from Dillon her teeth were chattering uncontrollably. Dillon climbed out while she soaped her hair. She held her breath and ducked under a few times to rinse off, coming up sputtering.

Fully dressed, Dillon watched Shelly come partially out of the water, her arms crossed to shield her breasts.

"W-w-will you h-h-hand me my shirt?"

He tossed it to her and Shelly caught it, but her hands were numb and her arms shaking so much that she dropped it in the water. "Oh, no." She looked at Dillon in dismay. Her only dry clothes were her trousers and her socks. She was freezing and she was scared of what he would do with her half-naked.

"Here." Dillon stood over her and removed his flannel shirt. He sensed she was at some kind of breaking point. He piled his shirt and her trousers within easy reach.

Shelly's eyes narrowed suspiciously. "What about you?"

"I'm comfortable in this," he said, pulling the undershirt away from his skin with thumb and forefinger.

"Thank you," she mumbled, disconcerted. He turned away without being asked, and Shelly scrambled out of the water in an ungraceful rush. "Okay," she said when she had the clothes on and buttoned.

His eyes raked her over when he turned around, but his large shirt hid her effectively. Her hair fell about her in a wild, tangled array and her eyes were enormous. Her teeth were still chattering so he grabbed her cold hand and pulled her back to the camp.

Shelly grabbed her blanket when they reached the campfire and wrapped it around her shoulders. "Brrr. I'm hungry!" She scraped the cold potatoes off her plate and back into the skillet, which she put over the fire. She stirred the hard, dry food.

Dillon sat on a big rock and watched her while he combed his fingers through his wet hair. He reached for the whiskey bottle propped against a nearby rock. He took a long swig.

Shelly looked around them, her eyes squinting to peer into the darkness that the fire did not reach. "Where are Parker and Diego?"

"Bedded down in the cabin."

Shelly looked past him at the dark cabin. Did it still reek of blood? She shuddered. When her food was marginally warm she dished it up and chewed contentedly for a few minutes. "I know you're right. It's partially my own fault I'm here."

"Why did you ever get mixed up with that Karl man anyway?"

"I told you."

"For the money."

"You don't understand," she said softly.

"No, I don't!"

Dillon threw a rock into the darkness and took another drink. His physical frustration was excruciating. "I'm glad we're going back to San Francisco, so I can unload you."

Shelly's fingers tightened on her fork. He spoke with such contempt. She was glad they were returning, too, she reminded herself, and she didn't care how he felt about her, but the bleak, lonely feeling did not go away.

"Hurry up so we can go in."

Shelly glanced in the direction of the cabin. "Don't wait for me."

Dillon looked at her tight features and then stood. "I won't." He scooped up his blankets, mashed his hat on his head and grabbed the bottle by the neck. He walked toward the cabin, hoping he could fall asleep with lust churning in his guts.

Shelly put her plate down and spread her blankets. She squeezed her eyes shut when she felt the tears burning to come out. Crying would not help, she told herself. One tear, golden in the firelight, slipped down her face. She brushed it away with the back of her hand, but the dam was broken and the tears flowed down her cheeks.

"Shelly?"

She jerked around to see Dillon, still holding everything he'd left with.

"I forgot to tell you to put out the fire."

"I'm sleeping by it." She smoothed out a wrinkle in her blanket.

"What's wrong?" he asked uncomfortably.

"Nothing."

"Come up to the cabin. You'll feel better in the morning." He felt guilty; it was his fault she was crying.

"I don't want to go in the cabin. I'm staying here." Her throat was choked with tears and she knew she sounded like a blubbering baby. Dillon dropped his gear and walked to her. Shelly stood up. "Go away, Dillon."

"Just tell me what's wrong." He gently touched her elbow.

"Don't touch me!"

"Sh! Lower your voice!" He looked over his shoulder at the cabin. "They're going to think I'm trying something with you."

Shelly's mouth gaped open. After all the things he had threatened her with to make her scared of him, and now he didn't want his friends to think he was "trying something" with her. She cried harder.

"Lord, now what?"

"Leave me alone. I'm fine."

"You're not fine. You're crying all over the place. I'm not leaving until you tell me what's wrong." He threw off his hat and stared at her, hands on hips.

Shelly swiped at her tears with the back of her hands. "Fine! I'll tell you, since you have to know everything. I've gone slightly insane from lack of privacy and comfort for the past six weeks. Try to imagine what it's like to have your every action questioned. Try to imagine what it's like to have your monthly in a dirty camp of men. I had to wash bits of someone's brain out of my hair tonight. I had to put up with your lust. And after I found out about this silver stashed here, you still hate me."

Dillon stood very still. "Shelly, I don't hate you."

"No? You sure fooled me."

He took a step closer so she had to look up. "What do you think that display of lust by the river was about? It certainly wasn't hate."

Shelly raised her chin. "Maybe you hate me because you lust after me."

Dillon shook his head. Her pained, tear-soaked face was irresistible to him. He lifted a finger and stroked her wet cheek. "I have to be mean to you," he whispered, "to keep us apart. I have to get rid of you," he said, his fingers slipping over the line of her jaw and down around her neck, "so I'll stop wanting you so bad. Every time I'm nice to you, I start kissing you.'' He moved so his body was flush against hers. Shelly's gaze was locked on his mouth as he spoke. "I don't hate you, I don't,'' he whispered, lowering his other hand to her bottom. He squeezed the rounded flesh tight and pulled her hard against him. "I want you like you wouldn't believe. You'd laugh if you knew how much.''

Shelly raised her hands to his waist. "Make me laugh,'' she whispered.

Dillon opened his lips over hers and lost his mind in her hot mouth. She must want him, too, or she wouldn't be rubbing against him like this, drawing her palms up his back, cinching him tight with her elbows. Dillon went to his knees on her blanket, pulling Shelly down with him.

His warm hand rubbed her belly while he kissed her. Shelly pulled her mouth away and watched his hand slide down to her hip and squeeze. In nervous fascination she watched his brown fingers slowly travel up her body, his fingers splayed and his thumb pointed up her middle. Shelly quivered when he was just under her breast. She jerked one of her hands from his back and grabbed his encroaching hand. As she held it away she pressed her lips to his mouth.

Even as Dillon eagerly responded to her lips, his hand settled back on her ribs and inched up and covered her breast. Shelly gasped and opened her eyes to see Dillon looking down her body. He wasn't kissing her anymore but was concentrating on making slow circles through her shirt over the tip of her breast, causing her nipple to grow taut beneath his fingers. Shelly flushed with heat. She should stop this, but every passing second brought such pleasure.

Dillon softly pinched her hard nipple and she flinched, then arched back into him. He quickly undid the buttons of her shirt, then peeled one side of the garment down over her shoulder. Her naked breast, heavy and white, the nipple dark pink and swollen, made his blood race. The same sight made Shelly try to pull her shirt back up.

"No." He caught her hand. "Let me look at you. I've imagined this...." He closed his hand over her naked breast, then rolled the nipple between his thumb and forefinger until Shelly moaned softly, helplessly, her eyes sinking shut.

He kissed her again, sucking on her tongue, then fed her his while he pushed the shirt off her other shoulder and down her arms. The cool night air rushed over her naked skin, tightening her nipples more. Dillon quickly unbuttoned her trousers and shoved them down her thighs so they bunched around her knees.

Shelly tackled the buttons on his undershirt, wanting skin for skin. She'd undone only one when she stopped because he was caressing her nipples again. Her head fell back until his hand rubbed over her belly and delved between her thighs. She snapped her head up as he insinuated one finger inside her. The pressure building there became suddenly unbearable. "No!" she cried out.

"Have you done this before?" he asked quietly.

"No."

"Oh, Shelly...don't be afraid," he murmured as he eased her back down on the blanket and gently pulled off her trousers. He dug his hands into her hair and slowly lowered his body over hers. His elbows ground into the blanket on either side of her shoulders as he urgently took her mouth with his. He blazed a trail down her neck with his lips while he held her head still. He kissed the top of a rounded breast, nudged her arms out of the way and brushed his bearded cheek against her nipples. She jerked when his wet tongue flicked over one. Her hands grabbed his head, fingers curling into his damp hair, and he closed his lips over a rigid peak and sucked.

Shelly whimpered while fiery heat swirled inside her, streaming down to a sweet rush between her legs. He moved up to kiss her mouth again, only to return to her breasts and then back to her mouth and down again to her breasts, until she lay gasping beneath him.

Dillon looked down at her heaving body, breasts palest golden in the firelight, the nipples still shining wet from his mouth. He lowered his gaze to her smooth stomach and to the dark brown curls at the juncture of her thighs. "You're so beautiful," he whispered hoarsely, his eyes meeting hers. He tried to move her knees apart, but Shelly sat up and grabbed his wrists.

"God, this is scaring me," she whispered.

"It's okay," Dillon said, kissing her fingers while he knelt before her drawn-up knees. He'd only been with a virgin once before. That woman had urged him on, yet he'd not felt this raging desire. He freed his hands and tried to push her down.

"No, it's not okay," she persisted. "I feel crazy, out-of-my-mind crazy."

"I know, so do I." He pushed her back down with his weight, opened his mouth over hers and drove his tongue into her. She wrapped her arms around him and her hips met his grinding pelvis. When both were panting he eased off her and unfastened his own trousers, holding her eyes the entire time. He pulled out his aching hardness and gently spread her legs apart.

Shelly closed her eyes. There was no resisting when she felt so hot, limp and longing.

Dillon covered her with his body. His breath was ragged above her. "Put your arms around me."

Shelly obeyed. He slipped inside easily. "Dillon," she sighed, arching up to meet him. She wanted this. She wasn't sure why, but the completion of this act with Dillon seemed immeasurably important at this moment. Her fingers dug into his back as he pushed a little farther.

Dillon met the barrier, pulled back and thrust. Shelly straightened like a board beneath him. She shoved at his chest, but her hands collapsed beneath his weight as he buried his face in her neck.

"It hurts!" she cried. Dillon raised himself so he was propped on his hands. He withdrew partially and penetrated her shallowly. "Hurry, okay?"

Dillon grimaced. He wouldn't take long, but he had to go deeper and move faster. He lowered his body and brushed his lips back and forth across hers. "I'm sorry," he whispered hoarsely. He tried to kiss her, but she was gritting her teeth. He buried his face between her breasts and a moment later his release came. He cried out and went limp for barely a moment before he rolled off her. "Are you all right?" Shelly slowly nodded and took a deep breath. "Are you

sure?'' She looked exhausted and very unhappy; she pushed
his hands away when he tried to help her on with her shirt.
He handed her the trousers and then fastened his own up.
''Shelly, there are things I could do... that wouldn't hurt,
that—''

Shelly cut him off with a narrowed look. She had no idea
what he was talking about, but she was through. She
throbbed with soreness and disappointment. Right now she
could barely believe that she had let this happen. She didn't
know what to expect next, but it felt good when Dillon
pulled a blanket over them both and wrapped his arm
around her. Maybe the next time would be better, not so
shocking. She wondered how Dillon felt about it all and
wished she was brave enough to ask. She was asleep in minutes, with Dillon pressed warm and comforting against her
back.

Chapter Ten

Dillon woke in the last gray before morning and was aware of warmth. He raised his head and looked down the length of his body. Shelly. He lifted the coarse blanket and stared at her molded against him. Her knee rested on his thighs and her arm lay over his stomach. He grew hot looking at her but eased her off his aroused body. He listened to her sleepy, disgruntled noises as she resettled herself on her side, facing away from him, her hip rising in a graceful arc under the blanket. This was not the first time he'd moved her away. Twice during the night he'd awakened, his body screaming for another release, but Shelly wasn't a whore he could roll over onto and take. He didn't know who or what she was. He lay with his hands clasped behind his head and wondered. Last night had been inevitable. Every time they were alone together he wanted to touch her and seemed to do just that, and she... Hell, she seemed to want it, too. But why? And what would she want now? They'd both be better off if he did hate her as she had accused. He looked over at her and felt miserable.

He got up and checked on the bound men behind the cabin. He had a headache and a long way to travel today. He'd just finished saddling his horse when Diego joined him. The grin on his friend's face was an arm long.

Dillon remained expressionless as he checked the cinch. "She was a virgin."

"Lucky you," Diego said, eyeing his friend thoughtfully. He did not understand why Dillon let his memories control him. Every day was a new beginning as far as he was concerned. "There's nothing wrong with a virgin. You should be flattered."

Dillon glared at him. "I'm not. Right now I'd feel better if she were a whore."

Diego smiled. "Ahhh, but you wouldn't want her again if she were a whore. Maybe she'll be your mistress, *amigo*. You need one and she must like you."

"I don't want her to like me. I want her to stay the hell away from me. She makes me crazy!"

Diego watched Shelly get up behind Dillon and walk toward the river. "Maybe she would like to be your wife. You could use one of them, too. She'd make a fine wife."

Dillon slipped the bridle into his horse's mouth. "You know I can't marry her."

"No, I don't know that. You just think that. Your father's got you so tied up in contracts and—"

"Dillon?" Shelly had returned with the long underwear she'd forgotten by the water and rolled it up in her blanket. Dillon's back tensed, but he did not turn around. She glanced at Diego and immediately saw the sober watchfulness of his eyes. *He told Diego what we did!* Diego smiled his usual gregarious grin, but it was too late. "Dillon!"

Dillon tossed down the rope he was tightening around the pack of one of the mules and turned. "What?"

Shelly's heart dropped like a rock. He was angry! If anything, she'd expected him to be overly friendly. She had probably made the biggest mistake of her life last night.

"Well?" he insisted.

"Nothing," she whispered.

"Hurry up and get ready to leave." He turned back to his rope.

Shelly saw Diego's eyes fill with pity. She stared him down until he looked away and walked off. Surely there was some misunderstanding here. Dillon turned and met her eyes. They were nothing like the lover's eyes of last night. He pushed his hat higher up on his forehead. "If you're not ready to go we leave without you."

Shelly spun around and stomped to where Parker was kicking out the coals in the fire. She clawed her tangled hair into a bulky braid. How dare he treat her like this, as though they had done nothing! She wished he was sore between the legs the way she was. Now that she knew what rampant desire felt like she could fight it off next time, not that Dillon was acting as if there'd ever be a next time.

The trip back to San Francisco was long and boring. The trail was easier to maneuver, but they had the two prisoners to take to Placerville and the freight wagons of silver ore to get to San Francisco. Dillon spoke to Shelly only when absolutely necessary and was never alone with her. In San Francisco he paid for a carriage to take her to the Faulding. He held the door open after she climbed in. Diego and Parker were out of sight for the first time in days.

"Here's your two hundred dollars minus the one advance." He held out the bills.

"I don't want it!" She pulled the door shut with a bang and sat straight, shaking and hot. She heard Dillon give the driver the address. What was she proving? She threw open the door as the carriage began to roll. "Wait!" Dillon turned and the driver braked. "Give it to me," she demanded. Dillon approached and again held out the money. Shelly snatched it out of his hand. "I just want you to know that I think you're a vile man. I'd never done that before and you made it a nightmare." His eyes were dark and enigmatic. "You had no consideration for my feelings, just like I was a whore. And I'm not!" Her voice went hoarse. "I wouldn't do that with you again for—for anything!" She slammed the door shut.

She let herself cry for a good two minutes and then wiped her face with her sleeve. She felt odd walking up the steps to the boardinghouse. Tom Thornton was dead, her virginity gone, and she was one hundred and ninety dollars richer. She lifted her hand to the doorknob and the door swung open before her.

"Shelly!" exclaimed Aggie. The older woman opened her arms and Shelly walked right into them. "Gosh girl, you've gotten skinny!"

"So would you if all you'd seen on your plate was beans."

Aggie squeezed her tight. "Come in and I'll feed you something besides beans." She pulled Shelly into the kitchen and pushed her into a chair.

"Aggie, I'm so sorry about Tom."

Aggie nodded. "I'm getting along. I have to. I'm pregnant." She laughed at Shelly's shocked face. "Must have been the night before he left. Some kind of man, huh? Goes off to never come back but leaves a little one growing behind. But I own this place," she said, waving a spoon around the room, "and it's all I got, but it's enough."

"A baby?" Shelly whispered incredulously.

"It happens."

Better not to me, Shelly thought to herself, glancing down at her belly. Aggie set a bowl of fish chowder in front of her. "You can talk with your mouth full, 'cuz I'm not waiting till you finish eating to tell me your adventure. Did this Dillon Ryder treat you all right?"

"He was very angry," Shelly said around a mouthful of thick broth and white fish.

"Of course! I can't believe you really spied on them. Start from the beginning."

Shelly told of everything except her intimacies with Dillon. She didn't know how to talk of such things and doubted Aggie would want to hear about it. When she was finished with soup and story, Aggie put water on for tea.

"Lord, girl, I can't believe you came back in one piece."

"Have you seen Karl Booker since he left?"

Aggie shook her head, standing at the stove waiting for her water to boil. "I never would have suspected him. He was so polite, if a bit chilly in manner."

Shelly rested her chin in her hands. "Do you still have a room for me, Aggie? I understand if you don't. I'll be leavin' for New York pretty soon, but I'll work around here until I do."

Aggie set the teapot on the table in front of Shelly and sat down across from her. "I will always have a room for you, Shelly."

Shelly sat up slowly and tried to get her heart to shrink back to its normal size.

Shelly sat on the back porch of the Faulding shelling peas for dinner. There was a little bit of sun shining on the mid-May day. Shelly admired how it shone on the backs of the Brewer's Blackbirds that squawked on the building eaves above her. She sighed. Life wasn't bad here, but she still had the nagging desire to get to New York. She had the money she needed but felt reluctant to go now that Aggie was pregnant. She felt somehow responsible but didn't understand why, since Aggie would be pregnant even if Shelly had never arrived at her doorstep.

"Hola, señorita." Diego stepped up to the porch.

"Hello there."

"You look very pretty in a dress."

Shelly glanced down at her pink calico. "I don't always wear trousers."

"May I join you?"

"Of course."

Diego leaned his arms on the low porch railing. "How have you been?"

"Fine. And yourself?"

He nodded. *"Bien."*

Shelly thought he looked fine, but anyone would in clean clothes and clean hair.

"My friend, he is not so good."

Shelly's brows rose. "Really?"

Diego nodded. "I think he misses you. You anger him, and I know he angers you, but you do like him, yes?"

"Not particularly."

"He is a good man, Shelly. He is just no good with women."

"Diego, what are you trying to do here?"

He smiled. "I'm trying to get you to be nice to my friend when you see him next."

"I don't believe I'll be seeing him again."

"You will."

"Tell me what makes you think so, because I got the distinct impression that he wasn't interested—not that I am, either."

"He's interested."

Shelly snapped open another pea pod. "Has he mentioned me?"

"No."

Shelly dropped her hands in her lap. "Diego!"

"I've known Dillon for many years. I know when he's thinking about a woman."

"Well, how do you know I'm the woman he's thinking about?"

Diego pushed off his hat and rubbed his forehead with his forearm. "Who else? You're the only woman he's spoken more than two words to in the last few months."

Shelly shrugged. "I'm hardly convinced, Diego."

"You'll see for yourself."

"Do you want a cup of coffee, Diego?"

"*Sí*, coffee would be good."

Shelly stood up holding the bowl of shelled peas. "But we have to talk about something or someone else besides your illustrious partner."

Diego grinned. "Sure, my pretty *señorita*."

Chapter Eleven

Three days later Shelly had just finished clearing the breakfast dishes off the table when the front door knocker sounded. Aggie was in the privy being sick, which she was every morning. Mary was crying because the cat had chewed her doll's arm. A boarder was dogging Shelly's steps to and from the kitchen demanding to know why he couldn't have clean sheets every day. Shelly strode down the hall and threw open the front door.

Dillon stood on the stoop. He doffed his hat. "Good morning." He did not smile.

Shelly said nothing. His handsomeness tightened her stomach. He appeared the gentleman, in black trousers and coat, a snowy white shirt under a soft gray waistcoat and maroon-and-gray striped tie. His hair and mustache were trimmed and his beard shaved, exposing the sensuous curve of his lips and his strong chin. She'd forgotten he had a slight cleft there.

"Miss Young. I'm willing to pay a small extra amount toward the cost of clean sheets. I do believe it is your responsibility to provide basic standards of cleanliness."

Shelly spun on her tormentor, leaving Dillon standing in the doorway. "Mr. Wilson, we change the sheets once a week or when a new boarder takes the room. If that is not satisfactory for you I suggest you find an establishment that meets your requirements."

The man wavered. "Three times a week?"

"Mr. Wilson, I don't have any time left to change your bedding after making sure your meals are prepared with no milk."

The man stiffened. "Very well, I will look elsewhere."

Shelly nodded her head and turned to Dillon. "Yes?"

A ghost of a smile played on his lips. "You mentioned that—"

"Mary, stop that bawling this instant," Shelly yelled at the little girl at her side, who was pulling on her skirts. "You wanted that cat, and cats will be cats!"

Mary dropped Shelly's skirt, pulled in her quivering lip, clasped her doll tight to her breast and marched out of the room.

Shelly raised her hand to her forehead. "Oh, Lord." She ran after the little girl and left Dillon standing in the doorway. He looked after her and wondered why he'd had a nervous stomach walking down here. Obviously, Miss Shelly Young was too busy to have been worrying about him this past week and a half.

She returned five minutes later and found him leaning against the door frame, arms folded across his chest, hat in hand. "Sorry," she said, and closed the front door. Every one of Diego's words came back to her while she stood facing him. "What can I do for you?"

Dillon stood straight. "You mentioned in Virginia City that you had drawn a picture of Karl Booker. I'd like to see that, if I may."

So formal, thought Shelly. If this was what Diego called missing her, he was sorely mistaken. "You may. It's the least I can do after your generosity to me," she quipped. No reaction but a slight tightening around his eyes. "Come into the kitchen." She led the way, turning suddenly inside the warm room and catching his eyes on the gray folds of cotton covering her hips. "Have a seat." He pulled out a chair. "How about some coffee?"

"Just the picture would be fine."

"The coffee's fresh and hot. I'm going to have to dump it out otherwise."

"Okay, fine, I'll take some."

"Want some pie to go with that?"

"No, thank you."

Shelly set the pie tin on the table in front of him. "It's really good and fresh. Try a piece." She set down a plate, a fork and a large cup of coffee.

"Shelly, I didn't come here to socialize. I just need to see that picture."

Around the corner of the table Shelly stood with hand on hip. "Well, you don't get a look without a little socializing first."

Dillon's eyes slowly ranged up her body, pausing at her strong, long-fingered hand resting on her hip, moving again over her generous bosom, the white collar brushing fair skin, up to her lips pink and full, then skipping quickly to her bright gray eyes. She was more impressive in real life than in his dreams. He held up his hands. "All right, have it your way." He shook his head and watched her slice him a big piece of cherry pie and plop it on his plate. He cut a piece off with his fork and glanced at her, perched on the table, her breasts level with his eyes. The cherries burst tart and sweet in his mouth. If he had woken her that night and shown her how good she could feel with him, and had been nice to her on the trip back to San Francisco, maybe he could reach out and squeeze her now. Maybe he'd have her in an apartment where he could visit whenever he wanted—which would be day and night, judging from the way he felt as he watched her bend slightly and pour him more coffee. He finished his pie.

"More?" Shelly asked.

"No, thank you." He clasped his coffee cup tightly.

Shelly noticed he was having a hard time looking at her for more than a split second. "Did you like it?"

"Very good," he replied with a nod, sipping his coffee.

Shelly sat next to him. "How've you been?"

"Just fine." He looked at her hard then, as if trying to convince her how fine he was.

Shelly tried to read his mind in his eyes and failed.

"How about those pictures?"

"I'll get them." Shelly returned with her sketchbooks. She set them on the table and stood next to him. "Let's see," she said, opening the first one in the middle. "This is my mother."

Dillon glanced at the blond, fine-featured woman who didn't look a bit like the girl standing too close to him. He could smell strong soap, bacon and some earthy scent particular to Shelly. She flipped through animals and birds and vegetables and a bunch of people he didn't know. It seemed she had moved closer to him somewhere in the lengthy assault of images, which he had to acknowledge were impressively well drawn, but her skirts were brushing his legs and now he could feel her heat and he'd begun to perspire. He thrust back his chair and stood. "What are you doing? Just get me the damn picture!"

Shelly jumped and stiffened. Diego had been wrong. This man had no more interest in her than a used, dirty rag. Embarrassed, she flipped through the book and stammered, "I-It's here somewhere." She thought she'd passed it and had to start over from the middle. Then some pages fell loose from their glue binding and fluttered to the floor. Shelly tried to slow down her agitated search so she could find the picture of Karl, and Dillon could go. She didn't dare look at him.

Dillon watched the sheets hit the ground with a quiet rustle. He bent down and picked up one. It was a portrait of the little girl he'd seen this morning. The likeness was incredible, more so in how Shelly had captured expression and emotion. He reached for another one and saw a picture of legs and dark boots, nothing else, his name printed across the bottom. He looked up at Shelly turning pages, oblivious to him. He picked up the other pages, all of people he didn't know. He set them on the table and picked up the smaller book, the one he'd seen her buy in Carson City. He opened it and the first picture was of him, needing a shave, glowering. He looked mean. He turned the pages quietly and saw himself literally foaming at the mouth, with horns on his head and his mouth open wide in a shout. There were other people he recognized, shacks that looked like shacks he'd seen, but no one and nothing had appeared to Shelly quite as negatively as he had. He slowly smiled.

"I found it!" Shelly looked up and saw Dillon engrossed in her other book. She dropped the book she was holding onto the table and planted her hand down on the page he was about to turn. "No."

Dillon grasped her wrist and pulled it off the book. She slammed her other hand down, her body softly bumping into his side.

"Why?" he asked.

"They're private."

"I want to see how you see me," he said, his eyes on her face.

"I'll tell you."

He shook his head. "It's not the same. The pictures are more honest. Not that you lie, but...I can't see your words."

She slowly lifted her hand, feeling his sincerity, his valuing of her work. Dillon turned the page and saw himself in a way he'd never seen before, but it was the way he felt when he was about to kiss Shelly. He saw her fidget out of the corner of his eye and turned the page before she snatched the book away. There were too many pictures of Diego for him to appreciate. There were a few of Adam Jefferies. And then he saw himself again, from the back, hands on hips, facing the mountain ranges of Nevada. Did he have that many muscles on him? She must have studied him to have drawn them. He turned and looked at her, his gaze sliding down her body. He could draw her in as much detail if he knew how. She sidled in and pulled the book away. "Are there more?"

She nodded her head and thrust the picture of Karl into his face. Dillon moved his hand up to push it away, but his fingers paused on the edge of the book. The man looked familiar. He stared and then pulled the book from her and set it on the table, where he leaned over it. "Karl, huh? He looks like my father's man, Oscar Herblock, but Oscar is a facially hairless blonde. He's got the same strange eyes and sharp nose, though."

''Maybe he's wearing a wig.''

''Nah. He wouldn't be out of New York. My father would have mentioned it. Oscar is his right hand.'' He shut the book and stood straight. ''Thanks, anyway.''

Shelly handed him another sketch of the same man. The cold, closed expression was so like Oscar that a chill traveled down Dillon's body. ''I'll write my father and ask him if Oscar is still working for him. I never cared for the man, but my father depends on him.''

He handed Shelly back the portrait and watched her stack the loose papers. Karl and Oscar fell out of his mind and he thought again of the drawings she'd taken the time to do of him. Her friendliness had dropped away since he'd yelled at her. She bent and reached for a paper under the table. She had to drop to her hands and knees and Dillon had a fleeting vivid image of the night they spent together. He was swamped with heat and slowly, woodenly, moved behind her.

Shelly stiffened when she felt his hands on her hips. She tried to back up but he was in the way. The table post was in front of her. She turned around so at least she could face him and sat cramped beneath the table. He had that look.

''So, you are still interested,'' she whispered in bewilderment.

He laughed, but the sound was strained. ''Hell, yes. Was that what all that pie and coffee was about? To find out?'' Shelly lifted her chin. ''What were you planning to do if I reacted?''

''I wasn't. I just wanted to know.''

''Well, now you can know and see and feel.''

He crawled over her and Shelly fell back, supporting herself with her elbows behind her on the floor. Her head hit the post. ''Ow!'' And then his hot mouth covered hers. His legs bracketed one of hers and his arms came down on either side of her shoulders. His kiss was devouring and greedy and overwhelming. She was shocked to her toes since he'd seemed so cold earlier. She rested her head against the post and let him plunder her mouth while heat swelled inside her.

"I want you more than I did by the river. How can that be?" He didn't wait for an answer, maybe he didn't really want one, but soldered his mouth back on hers. Shelly wanted to touch him but couldn't without falling flat on her back. He raised his hand and squeezed her breast tight and hard through the gray cotton dress and white shift. Shelly whimpered and Dillon buried his face in her neck, his fingers kneading her and his thumb rubbing back and forth over her puckered nipple. "Will you be my mistress? I'll set you up in your own apartment, buy you clothes and take you out." Shelly shook her head, definitely not wanting to be such, but oddly pleased nonetheless.

He sat back on his heels, pressing her leg down to the floor, and searched her eyes. "I can't offer you anything else," he said desperately, his hands cupping both breasts now, making her arch. He slid both hands up around her neck to her cheeks. "I can't marry you...agreements I made...not in the plan...and I don't want to marry...don't need a wife and all that, but you..." He leaned forward, kissing her again and again.

"Dillon, let me up. This is not comfortable. Dillon!"

He pulled away, his breath heavy. "This is insane!"

Shelly laughed and Dillon crawled out backward. Shelly carefully followed, feeling weak and limp. She sat down in a chair while Dillon straightened his tie. "Think about it," he said thickly.

Shelly looked at him. "It's not in *my* plan."

She watched him leave, mashing his hat on his head, his gait a little stiff. She smiled.

A week passed and Shelly did not see Dillon again. She hadn't expected to, but she wanted to. She couldn't leave for New York, not while Aggie was so indisposed every morning, so she bided her time, working hard and dreaming of the family she'd soon meet.

She was on her way to buy some produce for the day's dinner, her basket swinging from her arm, humming a nursery rhyme she'd listened to Mary sing over and over all morning. She rounded a corner and saw Karl Booker just stepping out of a hotel and hailing a carriage. Shelly flattened herself against the wall and heard him give an address. Her heart pounding, she watched him ride away in the carriage. Slowly, she eased herself off the wall and looked above her at the hotel sign. *Hotel Royal.* She stepped inside the small but plush hotel. The man at the desk was staring into space but jerked to attention when he saw Shelly.

Shelly made herself look very disappointed. "I just missed my brother! As I was running up I saw him leave here and get into a carriage."

"Mr. Clark?"

Shelly hesitated but a second. "Yes...Clark. The man with the black hair and beard."

"Yes, Joseph Clark. Was he expecting you?"

"Not until tomorrow. What a disappointment. Do you know when he'll be back?"

"No, ma'am, I surely don't. Would you like to leave a message for him?"

"You can tell him Tilde is here in the city. I'll be staying with our mother. What room is he in?"

"Let's see, Mr. Clark is in number eleven."

"Thank you so much." Shelly hightailed it out of the hotel and down the street to the wharf and Dillon's office. The shopping could wait. Dillon was not in, but Diego sat behind the new desk that had been added to the office since Shelly had been there. His feet were crossed on the desktop, his hat pushed back and a cigar smoking in his mouth.

"Well, well, the great man is not in," he greeted Shelly.

Shelly perched on the edge of the desk. "When will he be?"

"Any minute. I will leave so you can be alone when he returns."

Shelly put her hand on his arm to prevent his rising. "I found out where Karl Booker is staying, only he's calling himself Joseph Clark now. He's at the Hotel Royal in room eleven. He's not there right now, but I don't know how long he'll be gone. Oh, I did want the keys to his room from that desk clerk! I wonder what I could find among his things."

Diego swung his feet to the floor and stood. "Let's go find out."

Shelly gaped at him. "Really?"

They waited until the desk clerk was checking someone in and then walked quickly through the lobby, Shelly curled against Diego's ribs on the side of him where the desk clerk could not see her. Diego knocked briskly on the door to number eleven. When there was no answer he pulled his knife out of his boot and picked the lock in five seconds. Shelly followed him in and shut the door behind her. They searched through the drawers, under the bed and in the desk. "You look through those," Diego said. "I don't read so good in English."

Shelly looked through the neat stack of bills, stagecoach schedules and blank writing paper. On the very bottom was a letter addressed to Mr. Clark. The large scrawl slanted across the page. Shelly studied the unusual bold curls and flourishes before she could focus on the meaning of the words. When she did start to read she didn't get far before she gasped and drew Diego to her side. "Oh my God! This is it!" She excitedly slapped Diego in the chest with the paper. "Someone, there's no signature, with writing almost running off the page as if he were in a great hurry, instructed Mr. Clark to move the ore out of the tunnel beneath the cellar of the Persian Cat, wherever that is, and have it loaded on a Captain Darvey's ship on June 30!"

Diego snatched the paper out of her hands. "Let's go!"

"No!" Shelly grabbed the paper. "We have to put it back, so he won't know." She replaced everything as they found it while Diego stood at the door, his foot tapping. They walked quickly down to the wharf and burst into the office, surprising Dillon and Adam Jefferies. Adam immediately stood.

"Miss Young!" He pulled out the chair he'd been sitting on. "Please, have a seat."

"Is this yours?" Dillon held up the basket she'd left behind on Diego's desk. Shelly nodded and he handed it to her. "I didn't think it was Diego's. Where have you two come running from?"

"Someplace very interesting," Diego said. Dillon looked from his grin to Shelly's perfectly gloating, pink-cheeked face.

"Do tell."

"Karl Booker's hotel room," Shelly answered. "Only now it's Joseph Clark."

"Go on," he said stiffly. He watched Diego lean his hands on the back of Shelly's chair and wondered what was going on in that scheming Mexican brain.

"I saw Karl come out of a hotel, so I found out what room he was in. Diego picked the lock and we found a letter instructing him about what to do with your ore."

"What the devil! Do you mean you—" Adam spluttered, and Shelly waved her hand at him. She proceeded to tell him everything she'd read in the letter.

Dillon and Adam were speechless when she'd finished. Finally, Dillon stopped staring at her and shook his head. "I'd heard that there was a building with a tunnel to shore made by smugglers to smuggle contraband. I thought the story was a legend." He shook his head again. "I can't believe you actually—"

"I can't, either," Adam almost shouted. "Diego, how could you have endangered her like that? What if this man had walked in on you?"

Shelly and Diego looked at each other. "You would have held him at gunpoint, right, Diego? And I would have tied him up with the curtains," she said, glancing at Dillon pointedly. Dillon disguised his chuckle with a derisive snort.

"That's ridiculous!" responded Adam.

Shelly smiled. It was fun to dabble in danger. She met Dillon's eyes and his gaze possessed her until he broke it by standing up and running his hand through his hair. "What hotel?" he demanded. "What room number?" She told him. "June 30—two days away. I know Captain John Darvey. I wonder if he knows who he's aiding and abetting and who he's ruining?" He started to pace. "He must have been offered a lot of money to do this, because he's basically an honest man. I'll see if he's willing to deal with me for even more. Maybe he can sail away somewhere and open an inn or something. He's a lousy captain." He turned. "And then we'll load up one of my ships instead of his."

"Nice," said Diego.

"Come on," he told Diego, "let's go check out this room eleven again. I want to meet the man. Shelly, you go home and stay there until you hear otherwise from me." She stiffened.

"I think I'll take a stroll down to the Persian Cat," said Adam, standing and putting on his hat. "I'll walk you back to the Faulding first, my dear."

Shelly thanked Mr. Jefferies for walking her home, smiled graciously and left him at the door to the boardinghouse. She heard him whistling down the street as he walked away. Still holding her basket, Shelly waited a few minutes for his whistle to fade in the distance, then set out again to get the potatoes and greens Aggie needed for supper. This late in the day the selection was limited, and she picked through the potatoes to find a bunch of worthy ones. She picked the least worm-eaten greens she could find and hefted her heavy basket over her arm.

She was two long blocks from the Faulding when she stopped to switch the heavy basket to her other arm. She blew a strand of hair out of her face and adjusted the bodice of her rust gown, which was too tight. When she straightened she looked up into the pale, bloodless eyes of Karl Booker not three yards in front of her. Without thinking, Shelly screamed and ran across the street, dodging carriages, carts and horses. She ran down the plank walk, stopped when she was across from the Faulding and looked behind her. The man with the blue-black hair was not in sight. Shelly stepped off the walk and wended her way across Powell Street, avoiding potholes and traffic. He must have gotten his message about his visiting sister, Shelly thought. She ran inside and bolted the door behind her. She did the same with the back door and then set her heavy load on the kitchen table.

"Now what is happening?" asked Aggie, plopping a big beef roast in the roasting pan.

"I just saw Karl Booker in the street. And he was looking at me with evil intent, so I ran home, figuring he knew it was me at his hotel this morning pretending to be his sister. I hope he hasn't guessed that Diego and I were actually in his room." Shelly poured herself a glass of water, drank down every drop and didn't notice Aggie's horrified expression until she'd set the glass down on the counter.

"Girl, you're going to cause me to miscarry if you continue with these antics."

Shelly winced. "I'll stay here and peel potatoes."

Chapter Twelve

The early evening of June 30 found Shelly sitting at the kitchen table, fiddling with the paper Diego had left her days ago with the address of Dillon's apartment. Tonight was the night his silver ore was being moved and she wondered what he was planning. She hadn't left the Faulding since she'd seen Karl or Joseph or whoever he was. Aggie was preparing dinner. Shelly got her cloak out of her bedroom and drew it on over her pink dress. "I'm going out for just a little bit," she announced.

"Shelly, I don't think that's a good idea."

"No, probably not."

Aggie frowned over her chopped onion. "Just see you come back in one piece," she yelled after the younger woman.

Shelly made it safely and quickly to Dillon's apartment without seeing Karl. She knocked on Dillon's door and had a gun shoved in her face.

"Shelly? What are you doing here?" Dillon asked, opening the door wider.

"I should ask myself that," she whispered.

He pulled her in and took her cloak. "You look nice," he said, his eyes running over her upswept hair and down her pink dress.

"I can't say the same." Dillon was wearing baggy white sailor pants, a red-and-white striped shirt, no shoes and a black cap pulled low over his head.

He chuckled. "It's my disguise." He waved his hand behind him and Shelly saw Diego and Parker dressed in similar fashion. "My ship is waiting. Captain Darvey took double what this Booker-Clark paid him and has sailed away."

"Dillon's feeling very good, Shelly," Diego said, laughing.

She thought they all were. She'd never seen such high spirits among them. Even Parker was doing a jig in his sailor's clothes. Diego was loading pistols and Dillon sat on the edge of a table and sharpened his knife.

"What about Karl Booker? Won't he be there?"

Dillon kept sharpening. "I certainly hope so. He'd already packed himself out of the Hotel Royal by the time we got there. What brings you out of your ordered hiding?"

"I don't obey well."

He smiled. "No, you don't. Don't tell me you came here on foot and alone?"

"All right, I won't."

"We're ready," Diego announced. He handed Dillon a couple of pistols. "We'll be downstairs." He and Parker strode out of the room.

"Get Shelly a carriage," Dillon yelled after them. He handed her one of the pistols. "Until this is all over."

She watched him pull on socks and sturdy brown boots. He tucked the scabbard at the back of his belt and put the pistol in the shoulder holster under his shirt. Shelly savored her glimpse of skin and muscle.

"Be careful," she whispered.

Dillon flashed her a smile. Grabbing her arms, he sat back on the desk and pulled her between his legs. Shelly offered no resistance.

"I'm not feeling careful." He wrapped her arms around his neck and lowered his mouth to hers. He kissed her thoroughly, his tongue plunging and swirling inside her. "Wait for me here," he urged against her lips.

"Uh-uh," she said, shaking her head. He molded her closer and she felt his hard maleness press into her hip.

"Why not?" he persisted, licking her neck.

"Too dangerous. I shouldn't have come here at all." She started to pull her arms down, but he grabbed them and held them and kissed her again, wet, hard and hot.

"Why not?" he asked.

Shelly pulled away and shrugged. She put her cloak back on, covering her aching breasts.

"I have to go. There's a crew waiting for me. Come on, I'll see you get in that carriage." He held her arm down the stairs and out the door. Diego and Parker stood by the open carriage. Their presence didn't stop Dillon from kissing her again, a hard, quick, possessive kiss. He lifted her inside.

"Good luck," she called out to them all. Dillon shut the door on her and she sat back in the dark seat and touched her lips with her fingers.

Dillon felt ready for anything as he rowed a dinghy to shore in the darkness. Three quiet sailors sat with him. They remained steadily ahead of the four other boats, each with four men. In the darkness Dillon could see nothing of the cave he knew was there or the crates of silver ore that he hoped were there. Captain Darvey, who had given in suspiciously easily to Dillon's demands, had brought him by earlier the previous day and shown him where the place was. Dillon had tied a horse at the top of the cliff above the cave, if for any reason he had to leave the beach by land.

The only sounds in the cool night were the dip and splash of the oars in the water. All the men were silent. Any other time Dillon would have enjoyed the damp, dark air on his face and appreciated the milky white glow of the moonlight on the black water, but tonight his neck ached with tension. So far everything had gone so smoothly that he knew his luck couldn't last.

Their oars hit sand and the men jumped out and dragged the boat ashore. Minutes later the second boat also beached. Dillon led the seven men to the base of the cliff and up the short but steep incline to the small entrance of the cave. Parker set a lantern on the floor inside. Outside one was unnecessary due to the light of the moon. Dillon's heart raced at the beautiful sight of all those crates of his unrefined silver ore. It didn't look as if the whole load could have been stolen from him, but he was certain he owned at least a good portion. He took his place at the end of the line the men formed when all had beached. They heaved the heavy crates one by one down the line, swinging them from arm to arm.

Parker stood next to Dillon, while Diego stood at the head of the line and supervised. Dillon stole a look up the face of the cliff. His horse wasn't visible from where he stood. He saw no one but still turned to look several more times, his roving eyes scanning the cliff that jutted above the small stretch of sand they were on. It must have been the fourth time he looked that he saw a ghostly glimmer. They were already loading the second boat and would soon have to take both back to the ship to empty the cargo. There was enough ore for many more trips.

Dillon passed a crate automatically while his eyes remained fixed on the indistinct shape near the top of the cliff. He passed another crate while Parker glanced at him curiously. Should he stay here and load as fast as possible? Or should he investigate?

"Parker," he murmured, "I'm leaving. After you get back to the dock, stay on board and I'll meet you there." Dillon slipped out of line after an answering nod from Parker. He strode up the line of working men to the entrance of the cave and then past it. He walked a short way up the steep, winding path, the whole while his eyes peering up at the cliff above. There it was again, a man and a glimmer of some object, metallic perhaps, maybe a spyglass. Dillon headed up the path. The glimmer vanished and there was the sound of shifting sand as it fell tumbling down the cliff.

Dillon broke into a run up the rest of the path and pulled himself over the edge in time to see a man fleeing on horseback a few yards away. At Dillon's feet, rolling back and forth, was a spyglass. The man ahead pulled up his horse alongside Dillon's and with a quick slice of a knife severed the reins tying the animal to a low bush. Dillon sprinted forward, a chill going through his body as his horse was pulled along by the stranger. He reached under his shirt, yanked his pistol free and took unsteady aim while running.

His first shot was wild, but it did spook his horse and the stallion strained against his reins. The other man pulled out a gun and fired. The first bullet whizzed past Dillon's head and made him flinch. Furious, he stopped running, stood stock-still and took careful aim. The man jerked and his arm flailed uncontrollably. The reins of Dillon's horse slipped through his fingers and the animal ran in Dillon's direction to escape the commotion. Dillon stood to the side as his horse ran past, grabbed the pommel of his saddle and swung himself up. The horse sidestepped and bucked, but Dillon hung on.

By the time he had his horse turned back around, the man before him was far ahead. Dillon couldn't seem to close the gap between them and, frustrated, he fired his gun again, but the distance was too great for an accurate shot. He had only three bullets left and the man before him probably had five.

The stallion he had was a strong animal and slowly he gained on the man before him as they came close to the city. When Dillon was barely within firing range he shot again, his bullet coming so close to the horse's head that the animal reared, allowing Dillon to narrow the gap. The man remained seated, but his hat fell off. Dillon wanted his head to fall off. Yelling incoherently, Dillon urged his horse faster, his body bent low over the animal's neck. Closer, he shot at the man's back and missed, but his quarry turned his gun on Dillon and discharged the five shots he had left, one of them into Dillon's left shoulder. Dillon grabbed the pommel with his right hand to stay mounted. His gun pointed down to the dark earth that was rushing by below the horse's hooves, while pain like lightning ripped through him. He willed the pain to the back of his mind and pointed his gun and pulled the trigger. The bullet flew into the night and Dillon cursed.

With no bullets left in either man's gun and no chance for reloading it was purely a race of speed as they entered the city, the lather flying from their horses. They galloped down empty Jones Street, then Broadway, the man Dillon thought of as Karl still in the lead and taking them into the black heart of Old Sydney Town. There were few people on the main streets, but in Sydney Town resided a vile night population, and men and women scurried away screaming and laughing before the horses.

Karl squeezed a few pedestrians between him and Dillon and inched ahead. Dillon's eyes remained fixed on the dark head. Before one of the shabby buildings Karl pulled up and fell from his horse in a frantic dismount and ran down a narrow alley.

Dillon reined in his horse behind Karl's and threw himself off before the animal had come to a stop. He could not lose the man; he did not know his way around Sydney Town as Karl surely did.

Dillon was aware of little but the man running eight yards ahead of him in a corridor littered with drunks lying against the walls. Dillon had to jump over a dozen prostrate bodies of men and some women. Karl looked back repeatedly to see if Dillon was gaining, each time losing a foot to Dillon. Those feet added up and soon Dillon was only five yards behind the man. Encouraged, Dillon spurted forward in a burst of energy.

The corridor widened and Karl ran up a rickety staircase that shook with the force of his pounding feet. Dillon followed, taking the steps three at a time. With a beastly growl Dillon lunged forward. He caught Karl around the knees and both men grunted as they fell on the stairs. They rolled off, breaking the railing, and dropped to the dirt alley. The buildings on either side of them rose up like gigantic tombstones, threatening to cave in on their heads and bury them in the darkness. They landed on their sides, but Karl swung himself over and reached for Dillon's throat. Dillon wrestled Karl's arms off, rolled over and pinned the man to the ground, but he curled up in pain when Karl kneed him in the groin. Karl raised his knife, glistening silver in the black night, and Dillon rolled rapidly to the right, evading the swipe of the blade as he reached for his own knife behind his back. Both men stood, their breathing labored as they walked around each other.

They circled and the moonlight hit Karl's face; Dillon couldn't believe what he was seeing. "Oscar?" Dillon whispered hoarsely. The man's pale eyes gleamed in silent acknowledgment. A flustered rage pounded through Dillon. The other man's advantage was his lack of blinding emotion. Dillon lunged like a mad bull, his knife missing Oscar's stomach by inches and leaving himself open. Oscar struck into the available opening. He savagely stabbed down Dillon's torso, ripping Dillon's flesh from his right shoulder to his left hip.

Dillon felt searing heat as the blade passed through him. The blood immediately pooled from the gash. He took a deep, shaky breath and banished fear, pain and hate from his mind, setting into a deadly calm.

They stalked around each other, swiping and withdrawing, neither making another mark. Their limbs grew achingly weary, but still they circled. A crowd gathered around them, attracted by the smell of death and the amusement of a blood-drawing contest. The boisterous drunkards, the sleazy women in old gauzy gowns and the murderers, thieves and gamblers clustered together around the two. They heckled them and placed bets, mainly for Oscar, since the red blood soaking Dillon's clothes and dripping on the ground was dramatically obvious.

Dillon realized too late that Oscar had maneuvered him against the rough wood wall of a building. The people who had placed their bets on Oscar hooted and hollered, their shapes ghostly in the mist that was swirling down the alley. Dillon swallowed as Oscar's knife swooped down. He waited until the last possible second to jump to the side, barely missing the cold steel. He dodged two more violent digs and then curled out of his defensive position so quickly that Oscar never saw his blade coming.

Oscar crumpled to the ground, still breathing, his eyes open and blinking, his mouth moving soundlessly, his hand loosening its grasp on his long-bladed knife. His blood quickly spread a red stain on his white shirt. The crowd moaned and gasped as the outcome differed from expectations.

Sweat ran down Dillon's face as he watched the dying man. His life would be completely spilled soon. Dillon reached down and ripped off the black wig to expose the pale, almost white, thin blond hair. "Why?" he whispered, but the man did not answer. Dillon's shoulders slumped. His satisfaction at revenge was dulled by his confusion and the weakness of his body. He just wanted to lie down. His fingers loosened on his knife, but observing the milling crowd around him, the way they stared at him, he tightened his grasp on the hilt.

He looked down at the slash in his shirt and the way the blood had soaked onto his trousers and spotted the toes of his boots. The pain was building, a pulsing throb that pounded across the whole of his chest, up his neck and into his head. He pushed his way through the ring of people, ignoring the painted woman who wanted to take him with her for doctoring. He swayed up the alley, fighting the sickly dizziness that kept threatening to engulf him. He slowly made his way out of Sydney Town, often stopping to lean for a moment against the solid wall of a building.

Behind Dillon, the crowd pressed in around the man lying on the ground. Oscar's chest rose in quick shallow breaths and his eyes shifted back and forth across the faces of the people bending over him. Soundlessly, his lips shaped the words *Help me,* a moment before he took his last breath.

Chapter Thirteen

Diego pounded up the stairs of Dillon's apartment building. His friend had not returned to the ship. *"¡Caramba!"* Diego exclaimed when he saw the long bloody body lying on the floor before Dillon's door. Dillon lay on his back, his breath shallow, the blood still wet. Diego knelt beside him, cut open the sailor shirt with his knife and gritted his teeth at the sight of the long, ugly wound. He unlocked the door with his own key and lifted his friend and carried him to the bed. He stripped him and washed him, found the bullet wound and covered the unconscious man with a blanket.

Diego left for a doctor, locking the door behind him. Minutes later, when they returned, he assisted the white-haired man. Dillon mumbled and muttered, as the doctor worked; the only words coherent enough for Diego to understand were "Oscar" and "my father."

"He'll need a lot of rest, fresh bandages once a day or more often if needed, and some laudanum or whiskey and good food."

"I'll be lucky if I can keep him indoors," sighed Diego, exhausted.

"Come get me if he runs a fever."

Diego saw the doctor out, then pulled off his boots and belt and lay down on the sofa. He put his hands behind his head and stared off into space, frowning in thought until he fell asleep.

* * *

Shelly knocked on Dillon's door the next morning after she'd washed the last breakfast dish. Diego opened the door for her. "Hi! How did everything go?"

"We got the silver and Dillon got a fight. He's flat on his back in bed."

"Is he all right? Can I see him?"

"*Sí*, but don't pull his blankets off. He's natural underneath."

Diego opened Dillon's door for her and she stepped inside to dark and quiet. Dillon was asleep in the big bed and Shelly felt she was intruding. She glanced behind her but Diego had closed the bedroom door. She pulled a chair close to the bed and perched on the edge. Dillon's lashes were black against his cheek, his chin and face were peppered with stubble and his hair needed a wash and comb, but he looked beautiful to her. She peeled the blankets down from his neck and gasped at the length of white bandage reaching from one shoulder to hip. There was another white wrapping around his other shoulder. She looked for a long time at his rising and falling chest, at the dark hair that curled on his tanned skin, growing thick down where she held the blanket back. She swallowed and felt very warm. Softly she touched his skin, smoothing her palm over his unwounded ribs. He flinched under her touch and she glanced up to his face to see his eyes open and fastened on her. She pulled her hand away, blushing furiously, and covered him.

"Shelly?" he whispered.

"Yes?"

"It was Oscar. I killed him." His voice was hoarse, low.

"I'm glad it was him and not you. How do you feel?"

"Like if I move I'll split open."

Shelly grinned. "You just might at that, so you'd better stay put."

"Then hand me the whiskey."

Shelly poured a generous amount in the glass by his bed. She stood and slid her forearm beneath his neck and raised his head to drink. He winced and then drank all the whiskey while her breast brushed the line of his jaw. She eased him back down.

"Do that for me when I feel better, would you?" he asked, looking at her body until his lids closed in sleep again.

Shelly returned the next morning to find both Diego and Adam Jefferies keeping Dillon company. He was halfway sitting up, not as pale, but every move still obviously pained him.

"Have you eaten anything?" she asked.

Dillon grimaced. "Not hungry."

"He's only drinking whiskey and coffee," Diego volunteered. Shelly frowned and Adam Jefferies cocked his head in puzzlement that she seemed to care.

"Well, I brought you something." She took away his whiskey bottle and he shouted feebly after her. She came out of the kitchen a few minutes later with a mug and handed it to him.

"Do I dare?"

"You'll like it. You'll want more."

I like having you here, he thought, taking the mug from her. Her eyes brightened the room, her voice was music, her every stride a dance. He shook his head to clear his mind of ridiculous, half-drunken fancies.

"Go on," she urged.

He sipped, then swallowed and finally gulped. He drained the cup and handed it back to her. "Can I have some more?"

Shelly laughed.

"What the hell was it?" asked Diego.

"Just hot milk and whiskey with cinnamon and sugar."

"Ahhh," Jefferies said. "This young woman knows her remedies. You'll be better in no time," he told a content Dillon.

Shelly made Dillon a second mug and then pulled out her sketchbook while the men talked about the mine. Diego got up to make more coffee and glanced at the drawing that Shelly was finishing. He burst out laughing. "Show him!"

Shelly held the pad up for Dillon to see. He blinked. "I look that bad, do I? Rather rude of you to point it out." The picture showed him with hair standing on end and bristles rampant across his face.

Shelly shrugged. "Maybe your friends will clean you up."

"Hah! I've done enough for him," said Diego.

"I'd be happy to go get him a barber," responded Jefferies.

"No, thank you," said Dillon.

"Then I will do it," said Shelly, dropping her sketchbook on her chair as she got up. Dillon jerked back against his pillow. Diego grinned and winked at Adam, who was staring at Shelly's back incredulously.

With Diego's help Shelly gathered soap, towels and a pan. In no time she had a stiff, reluctant Dillon propped up on pillows with his head tilted back and over a pan. She soaked his hair with warm water, massaged the soap gently into his scalp and along each fiber of hair. Dillon's eyes closed, his neck relaxed. Diego left the room. Adam stared.

Shelly didn't speak as she memorized every ridge in his skull with her fingers. His sigh was like a caress.

Adam rose, feeling like an intruder. "I'm going to get some more coffee."

"Stay still," Shelly whispered to her patient. "I'll be back with more warm water." She rinsed his hair until the black strands shone and then she rinsed some more. His eyes flickered open when she encountered the first tangle with his comb. "Sorry." Gently she combed down from his forehead and up from under his neck, the teeth of the comb feeling delicious on his skin. He groaned.

"Why do you bother?" he asked, looking at her lips and nose and eyes, upside down above him.

"I like having you at my mercy," she answered, digging and curling her fingers into his hair. She smiled down at him, but his gaze was reaching into her soul for answers and a surge of feeling swamped her. Her grip in his hair tightened, she pulled his head down farther and lowered her lips to his. He responded instantly, like fire in dry brush. His mouth opened and his tongue came into play.

Diego walked in. "I think he's still a little weak for this."

Shelly jumped back two feet, shame turning her face bright red, her eyes bright silver. Shame, not that she was caught kissing but that she was caught kissing Dillon, a man who had no respectable want of her. She grabbed her sketchbook and ran past Diego, ignoring her name when he called.

Diego turned and watched his friend ease his head up. "You're drunk and she's in love."

Dillon closed his eyes. "Don't speak to me of love."

Shelly was sweeping the kitchen floor of the Faulding a week later when Adam Jefferies came to see her. She made some tea and piled a plate with shortbread.

"We couldn't have recovered the stolen ore without you, Miss Young. I want to thank you for your help."

Shelly tilted her head. "You wouldn't have needed my help if I hadn't spied on you to begin with."

"If not you, it would have been someone else, but not just anyone else would have risked themselves the way you have repeatedly to help us. And though in retrospect I can say how very grateful I am for your help, I'm also dismayed by your lack of caution. I do hope you won't endanger yourself further for anyone's account. It's entirely foolish for someone of your sex."

Shelly bit into a piece of shortbread, feeling no compulsion to respond, having heard variations of this speech all her life from teachers, churchmen and townfolk; she'd always known life was dangerous, especially for someone as alone in the world as herself. What would Adam think of her if he'd seen her whack Grady Allen with the fire poker? Was he like some men, who thought she should have let Grady take what he wanted and cried afterward? She sincerely hoped not.

Adam Jefferies sighed loudly and watched Shelly chew. "I don't feel I've moved you at all, my dear. It's like talking to Dillon when his mind's made up, or my sister."

"I must ask, Mr. Jefferies," Shelly said, wiping her fingers on a napkin, "why does my welfare so concern you?"

Adam smiled. She certainly wasn't a timid girl. Her manner always surprised him, delighted him and dismayed him. He saw her again bent over Dillon's head, her hands gentle and caressing. She was a match for that boy if he'd ever seen one, much more his style than Annette King, Dillon's father's choice. For a split second he envisioned his friend and Shelly together in New York, where he could have their company once in a while. His thoughts came back to the present when the girl asked him if he wanted more tea. He nodded. She had such strange eyes, something familiar about them, but he couldn't place it. "Do you still want to see your relations in New York?" he asked.

"Absolutely."

"Good! I have taken the liberty of securing you quarters on the ship we're sailing back to New York," he lied. "At no expense to you, of course." The girl looked positively shocked. Adam loved it. "You don't mind, do you? It's really the least we can do. You will not have that tedious journey to make alone. You'll be among friends."

"But it really isn't necessary. I can afford the fare myself now."

"Buy yourself some new clothes! Besides, the ship is Dillon's and you certainly don't owe him money. We're leaving in three days. Does that give you enough time?"

"I guess so," Shelly said numbly.

He sipped another cup of tea and chatted with her about the New York climate and about his house and life there. He found her to be a very good listener and he felt quite interesting while her silver gray eyes looked at him. As he was taking his leave, Shelly insisted on knowing what prompted his generous offer. "Dillon can be very poor company, my dear. But I think you and I shall get along quite well." Adam knew that this particular scheme was going to blow Dillon's temper, but he felt quite optimistic about the outcome.

Shelly turned about happily in the tiny, cramped quarters that were her own on Dillon's ship *The Gold Wind.* She threw her cloak on top of her bunk. Opposite the bed was a washstand with a small mirror nailed to the wall above it. Her trunk lay next to it. From the middle of the low ceiling hung a lantern, which she didn't need now with the morning light streaming in through the porthole. She glanced out at the deep blue-gray water that surrounded them. She was on her way!

Also on board was a middle-aged German couple returning to Philadelphia. The woman was very fat and looked comical standing next to her thin, wiry husband. The other passenger was a strikingly beautiful blond woman named Jessica Ellis, a widow who had been cool when Shelly introduced herself. Shelly wasn't surprised. Most gorgeous women in her experience were standoffish, but the contrast to warm Aggie Thornton pained Shelly. Leaving her friend had been harder than she'd anticipated. If Aggie hadn't been over her morning sickness and wasn't feeling robust and cheerful, she wouldn't have left at all.

She smoothed the beige linen of the one new dress she'd bought and poked her head out into the corridor. She saw no one. Was she the only curious one? The German couple had the room to the left of hers; next to them were Mrs. Ellis and her maid. To the right of Shelly's room was Adam's, and next to him, she'd been told, was Dillon's cabin, though she hadn't yet seen him. She walked up on deck and watched the crew set sails as they made ready to lift anchor. She stayed out of the men's way, admiring their energy as they hurried about and climbed the rigging.

"You look excited," commented Adam, joining her.

"I am!"

"I hope you brought plenty to read, for when the excitement wears off and the boredom sets in. That is, if you don't get sick. You won't feel like reading in that case."

Shelly did not get sick, just sleepy, and for the first time in her life she started taking a nap every day. The most severe sufferer of seasickness was Dillon. Shelly did not see him for a week. Adam told her he'd taken to his bed the first day. She wanted to visit him, but Adam shook his head. "Not a good idea. Leave the lion in his den." Shelly pulled out her sketchbook and drew and drew and drew.

One week after embarking, Shelly accepted Adam's invitation to a game of backgammon on the sunny, breezy deck. Adam had taught her the game the second day on board. She spent many hours in his company and he amused her with stories of New York life and had extended her an invitation to stay with him in the city while she looked for her family. She was concentrating on how to move her pieces when she heard Adam call a greeting to his partner.

"Well, it's about time you were feeling well enough to join us."

Shelly looked up quickly to see Dillon at the stairs, his face pale, his frame a little thinner and his eyes riveted on her face. She smiled brightly and he took a step forward, his mouth opening. Her smile faded. He looked shocked. She glanced at Adam, who was watching Dillon, and she understood. "He didn't know I was coming with you?" she whispered in a stricken voice.

Adam, still watching Dillon, reached blindly beside him and patted her shoulder as if that would be reassurance enough. Shelly shrugged his hand off. "I can't believe you did this to me!"

Dillon walked over and stood unsteadily on his feet in front of them. His expression was so disappointed that Shelly was torn between pushing him off his feet and shriveling up inside. She stood and faced him. "I was under the impression that you were aware I was on board, that in fact the invitation had been extended from you as well as from Adam." She jerked her head in the direction of the older man.

"You were wrong." Dillon looked past her. "Why did you do this?" His voice was almost agonized, and Shelly could not bear it.

She turned on them both. "How dare you lie to me and put me in this position!" she railed at Adam. "And how dare you be so rude and ungracious about my presence!" she snapped at Dillon. She stamped her foot, spun around and stomped down the stairs, slamming the door of her cabin behind her.

She heard raised voices and then a pounding on her door. "Shelly, let me in!"

"No!"

"You don't understand," Dillon bellowed. "You don't belong in New York and you especially don't belong on my ship!"

"Oh!" Shelly flung open the door. "Stop screaming at me! And you have no say as to where I belong!"

"It's my damned ship and I'll scream if I want to!" He walked inside her cabin, slammed the door and glared at her. She glared back.

He shook his head and ran a trembling hand through his hair. "You won't know a soul in New York. This is a ridiculous scheme!"

"Unfortunately, I'll know you and Adam."

"I'll be returning to California as soon as I can."

"Good!"

"Shelly, be reasonable. You don't know this 'family,' you don't know what part of town they live in, whether they're alive or dead, or if they want a poor relation descending on them. You're chasing a rainbow."

Shelly stiffened. She didn't like someone else voicing the fears that had passed through her mind. "So? What are you going to do? Turn the boat around?"

"I'm thinking about it."

"Oh! How dare you! You can't control my life like this! I never would have gotten on your ship if I'd known how you felt, but now that I'm here, you just have to make the best of it."

Dillon crossed his arms over his chest. "That's impossible. This is impossible. You can stay on my ship, but I don't like it."

"I'll pay you the full fare, but now get out of my cabin."

"I don't want your money," he spat. "I just don't want you here!" He jabbed a finger in her direction. A wave of dizziness washed over him and he knew he had to get out. He was taking this too far, but it seemed New York threatened like a noose around his neck. In California he was his own man; in New York he was his father's son, Edward

King's future partner, Annette King's fiancé, and everything was spelled out in the contract his father had drawn up and he had signed. He sighed miserably and looked at Shelly. She was in a state. Her eyes were silver fury and he'd never seen her chin so square. "I'm sorry," he whispered. He turned and left, knowing that this was just the beginning. How was he going to stay away from her, confined as they were on this ship and drawn to her as he was? But he wasn't a free man in New York and he didn't want Shelly to know about his life there.

Chapter Fourteen

For the next five weeks Shelly avoided Dillon. She ate in her room if he tried to join her and Adam for a meal. She moved her chair across deck if he sat near her. She would not meet his eyes, would not look at him and definitely never spoke to him, though she heard the other passengers whisper about how strange she was. She discreetly drew portraits of almost all the sailors and passengers but never did she draw a line of Dillon's features. Her withdrawal, however, was becoming difficult to maintain. She was tired of being so vigilant to make sure she avoided him. And a new feeling was making her lift her chin and glance at him more and more frequently: jealousy.

Today she sat on deck next to Adam, who had begged for forgiveness for putting her in this uncomfortable position. "Dillon cares for you much more than he lets on," he'd told her weeks ago. "That is why he resents your presence so much." Shelly had scoffed at that, but Adam had remained adamant. "I was hoping he'd be pleased by my machinations. The fact that he is so upset leads me to believe that his feelings for you are stronger than I had expected."

Shelly had laughed at him then. "Give it up, Adam. He just doesn't like anything happening that he doesn't make happen, especially if he senses any kind of deceit."

"You know him so well, then?" he'd asked, smiling.

Shelly had frowned him down. For the past weeks he'd taken his cue and avoided the subject of Dillon.

Shelly finished her sketch of Adam asleep over his book next to her and looked down the deck at Dillon and Jessica Ellis leaning over the railing. A frown puckered her forehead as she watched the two lean their heads together as they talked. The ocean breeze blew Dillon's dark curls back from his head and played with the wheat-colored tendrils escaping from the woman's chignon. Shelly couldn't help herself. She turned to a blank page and quickly captured the intimate moment of the two contrasting heads bent so close. She slapped the book closed when she finished and drew a deck of cards out of her pocket. They were Diego's farewell gift. Obviously, he also hadn't mentioned to Dillon that she would be sailing with him. She spread out a game of solitaire on an empty chair seat.

Adam woke from his nap and watched Shelly handle the cards. Her movements were stiff, angry. Since her altercation with Dillon, he'd noticed her spirits flag. He followed Shelly's quick, darting look to where Dillon stood at the railing with the widow. He watched the woman lean into Dillon and smile. She was attractive with large brown eyes and white teeth, but he was surprised Dillon was spending time with her. Dillon did not flirt, did not know how and saw no reason to.

Shelly disarranged her cards with an irritated flurry of her hands. Adam was a little sorry he'd arranged for Shelly to sail with them, but he still had hope that Dillon would wake up and see what was in front of him.

Another week dragged by and Shelly felt more dismal. She wished Dillon had turned the ship around and taken her back to San Francisco. She could be on a different vessel now, happily anticipating her arrival in New York instead of feeling so vehemently unwanted. She didn't understand the man. How could he want her for a mistress in California and not want her in the state of New York?

She turned over in her bunk, where she'd been lying sleeplessly for the past hour. Last night she'd had a nightmare, the reliving of Grady's attack on her in the cabin, only Grady had turned into Dillon when she struck him with the poker. She'd run after him, crying, scared, but couldn't find him outside in the dark. Did he truly fancy Jessica Ellis? Shelly's cottons, calicos and wools did not compare to the confections in which Jessica paraded. Every flounce, tier and tuck were placed to accentuate her tiny waist and graceful arms. Her jewelry was a queen's treasure. Maybe Dillon had wanted her so much in Virginia City because there hadn't been much choice in females.

Shelly let herself imagine him in bed with Jessica. What man could turn her away? The widow displayed her interest boldly enough. The memory of Dillon's mouth on hers, his hands on her breasts, stirred Shelly immeasurably. She tossed off her blankets and popped up to a sitting position. The cabin was stuffy, closing in on her. She needed a walk on deck in cold, salty air to clear her head. She pulled on her cloak and, barefoot, left the small room.

A few minutes on deck had the desired effect on her senses. The cold, damp air chilled her hot thoughts as she sat on a coil of rope not far from the stairs. Wrapping her bare feet up in her prim, white nightgown, she pulled her dark cloak about her. The sky was a bolt of black velvet studded with sparkles. Her lustful thoughts ebbed from her mind and she felt she might be able to sleep. She was untangling her feet from her gown when she heard voices coming up the stairs. Dillon and Jessica. Shelly rolled her eyes and cursed under her breath.

"This cold air won't help you sleep, Dillon."

"You'd be surprised how much cold air can help."

"Well, then, I'll join you." Jessica took his arm as he walked across the deck.

Walk fast, thought Shelly. She'd wait for them to pass, then she would scramble down the stairs. The pair strolled slowly, Jessica twitching her hip against Dillon.

"Brrr, it's cold out here," she said, stopping and pulling Dillon to a halt beside her.

"You should have worn more," muttered Dillon, looking down at her almost shoulderless royal blue gown.

"I didn't know you were coming up here when I saw you leave your room. I was coming over to invite you to share a nightcap with me. That's what helps *me* sleep."

They were both facing away from Shelly, looking out over the railing. She had to try to creep away now.

"Dillon, you do like me, don't you?" asked the sultry voice.

Shelly froze where she had risen on her knees. God forgive her, but she wanted to hear his answer.

"Yes, of course."

Shelly watched as the older woman turned into Dillon, giving Shelly a view of her body in profile. "Dillon, I've been very obvious. The journey is not getting any longer." She raised her mouth in the moonlight. Dillon met her halfway as Shelly sank back down to the ropes. Jessica's face was shielded by Dillon's dark head as he moved his mouth over hers. The irony, railed Shelly silently, to escape from her cabin and her imaginings, only to see what she feared.

"So, will you join me for that drink?" Jessica spoke against his mouth.

"Maybe."

Jessica pulled away. "I'll wait for you." She stepped gracefully across the deck.

Shelly was shivering. She decided to race for the stairs as soon as he turned his head. The moment came and Shelly stepped out of her rope nest. The few yards to the door were unprotected by any kind of cover. She glanced back at Dillon. He was staring out at sea. She gathered up her cloak and gown and scurried across the space. The moon shone brightly on her fleeing figure and the deck vibrated ever so gently with the hurried tread of her bare feet.

Shelly never heard him. Halfway down the stairs a steel grip clamped about her wrist. Her right foot was in midair, descending to a lower step. Caught off balance as he whipped her around to face him, Shelly twisted, then fell, landing hard on her knees on two separate steps. Other than her grunt of pain when her knees hit the wood, she was silent.

"Are you all right?" Dillon crouched beside her, taking her arm and searching the side of her face nearest him. Her eyes were closed and her lips tightly compressed. She nodded her head and stiffly stood up with his help. He noticed her bare feet, which were nearly blue from cold. Her hair was floating around her freely in a way he'd not seen for a very long time. Shelly started moving down the steps away from him and Dillon recaptured her arm. "Oh, no you don't. What were you doing up there?" he asked accusingly.

"Believe me, I had no intention of spying on you, if that's what's worrying you."

"Seems strange, you up there at the same time, in the cold and not dressed for it."

She shot the fist of her free hand into the shoulder of the arm that held her captive. "Your conceit is really incredible! I was out there before either of you because I couldn't sleep. I had a nightmare—a nightmare because you were in it. I wanted some fresh air." She was whispering fiercely, aware of the people behind the doors along the corridor. She tugged her arm out of Dillon's grasp, knowing that the only reason she was able to do so was that he let her. Her eyes blazed silver at him in the light of the single lamp illuminating the stairs. She was affronted by the smug smile on his face, and she resented his intimidating height as he stood on a step above her. She spun away and marched rigidly down the slightly swaying corridor toward her room.

"What are you doing?" she demanded when she stood in front of her door, her hand on the knob. Dillon stood directly behind her, towering over her, not touching but so close she could feel the heat of his body.

"I'm seeing you to your room," he answered casually.

Shelly's eyes narrowed on his face. She tried to decipher whether his intentions were friendly or not. She couldn't decide and turned the knob and stepped into her room. The lantern hanging from the ceiling was turned low and dimly illuminated the tiny room. Shelly stood riveted by what she saw. The German couple, Maria and Franz Weiss, were in her bed in the middle of a rather heated embrace. Shelly quickly took a step back as soundlessly as possible. She had just reached for the door when Maria opened her eyes, saw Shelly, with Dillon looming behind her, and screamed. Shelly jumped and slammed the door. Dillon grabbed Shelly's hand and pulled her after him, down to the end of the corridor where it was darkest.

Silently, Shelly looked up at Dillon's blank face. Her eyes were huge. She raised a hand to her mouth. "I'm so embarrassed," she whispered between her fingers.

Dillon cleared his throat. "An accident," he said, and choked.

Shelly moved her hand from her mouth to his arm. "Are you all right?"

He looked away from her, his face red. Shelly tugged on his arm until he looked back at her. When his eyes met hers, he doubled over choking, and she realized he was laughing, and loudly.

"Stop it!" she hissed, shoving him against the wall as she looked down the corridor in alarm. He only broke out in louder gales.

"You should have seen your face when you turned around!" he spluttered. "Or her face! Even his face!"

A smile trembled on Shelly's mouth as she shook his arm. "Sh, they'll hear you."

He tried to control himself, but as soon as he looked at her again, he laughed and held his forearm over his contracting stomach.

"What a scream she had," whispered Shelly. "I'm surprised everyone didn't come running out." She smothered her own nervous giggle with her hand. "They should have locked their door," she gasped, but sobered instantly when that same door opened and Franz Weiss stepped out in his burgundy silk dressing robe.

"How dare you! How dare you stand out here and laugh!" He strode furiously down the hall toward them.

"Oh, Lord," mumbled Shelly under her breath. "I'm really sorry. I got confused and I thought it was my room."

"My Maria is very upset," he continued, ignoring Shelly's apology.

Shelly heard Dillon choking behind her and she bit her bottom lip to keep a straight face. "I'm really very sorry. I don't know what else to say."

"Stupid Americans," he ranted. He wagged his skinny finger in Shelly's face, so close that she blinked rapidly. He scolded them a few more minutes, slowly inching back to his room. Finally, he retreated completely, his shoulders slumped.

"I guess old Maria won't give him a second chance," whispered Dillon in Shelly's ear. Shelly giggled, a delightful sound to Dillon, and his arms encircled her, pulling her back lightly against his chest.

Shelly twisted her head to look up into Dillon's face and the smile slowly faded on her lips. His eyes were so warm, the dark lashes framing the desire that Shelly felt transmitted to herself. She turned in his arms.

Dillon's lips came down and softly caressed Shelly's mouth, moving away before she wanted him to. Her face lifted, following his mouth, but he teased her with light, feathery kisses across her cheeks, nose and forehead. "I could use one of those second chances, Shelly." His voice was thick against her mouth.

"Second? Don't you mean sixth or seventh?" she whispered. Dillon's laughter rumbled in his chest and Shelly felt it shake her breasts. It was warm and happy and completely melted her. She pressed closer and raised her mouth, this time with lips parted. His lips met hers in a fiery kiss, his tongue sliding in to plunder her mouth relentlessly. Shelly clasped her hands about his neck, her nails digging into his skin as she arched up against him, the full fury of her desire sweeping over her. His invading tongue touched off acute sensations that shot down her body to her toes, only to vibrate back up again and explode between her thighs.

"Why?" she asked, pulling away. "Why didn't you want me to come?"

Dillon pressed his forehead against hers. "God, girl, I wanted you waiting for me in San Francisco—so I could do this to you when I got back." He kissed her again, his mouth hot and hungry. "I won't be in New York long. I hate it there. I can hardly compromise you if you're in the arms of your family.''

She evaded his seeking mouth. ''I don't want to be compromised again, anywhere.'' Dillon slid an arm behind her legs and swung her up in his arms. ''Dillon, I won't be your mistress.'' He carried her into his room and kissed her mouth quiet. He kicked the door shut and set Shelly on the bunk. Her eyes were huge, dazed, a dark smoky gray staring at him as he shrugged out of his overcoat.

''Your feet are like ice,'' he murmured, picking them up in his strong, warm hands. He rubbed them gently and then tucked them between his thighs, the soles of her feet pressing against his swelling loins.

Shelly closed her eyes for a moment as a wave of eroticism passed over her. She kept her feet completely motionless, scared to feel any more than she already did, scared to arouse him further, yet not wanting to pull away.

Dillon watched her face. Her lips trembled and he reached out one long brown finger and gently traced their dark pink outline. Shelly swallowed and looked down at her hands clasped tightly together in her lap. Her resistance was still strong and waging a battle with her desire. His fingers strayed down and lightly caressed her neck, sending quivers bounding across her flesh.

''Dillon, we don't get along,'' she mumbled.

He twined a lock of her hair about his finger. ''We could.'' He lay down next to her, where she sat leaning against the wall at the head of the bunk. He propped himself up on an elbow and turned her chin so they could see each other. He reached into her lap and pried loose one of her hands, dragged it to his mouth and pressed a kiss on the back of it, then turned the hand over and kissed the tip of each finger, nipping her middle one, before he kissed the center of her palm, lightly licking her skin.

Darts of pleasure from the tickling wetness shot up Shelly's arm and into her breasts, causing her nipples to tighten under the concealing folds of her gown and cloak. Her chest constricted painfully as she watched Dillon's dark face against her white skin. His shirtfront was partially open, revealing the corded muscles of his neck and dark curling chest hair that made Shelly hungry with deep, primitive longings.

Dillon hoped she'd weaken if he went slowly; he wanted her unprotesting and eager. The constriction of his pants was uncomfortable and urged him on. He placed her hand back in her lap and unhooked the three clasps of her cloak, all the while her eyes on his face. "Take it off," he said softly.

She frowned. She wanted him to do it, but she pushed the cloak off her shoulders, then raised her hips to pull it from under her. Dillon took the garment from her and dropped it to the floor. He stared at her and she squirmed.

In a defensive gesture Shelly crossed her arms over her breasts. Dillon smiled. He tugged her arms loose with one hand, still lying propped on his elbow. The gown had a high neckline and betrayed no skin. Dillon dragged his eyes from the two thrusting breasts and turned them to her stomach, beneath the white fabric. His hand slowly descended to rest on her belly and absorbed the quiver of her flesh. He caressed in a circle before moving his hand up in a direct line to her right breast.

Shelly stiffened when his hand cupped her. Her eyes slammed shut as he squeezed. She leaned back against the wall but did not stop him. Dillon lifted the breast in his hand and kneaded it gently, leaving untouched the nipple that poked through the folds of her gown in blatant arousal.

Then he grazed his fingertips over the hard nipples of both breasts, barely touching but causing Shelly to moan. He stopped. "Take off your gown," he whispered, his voice a husk of its usual strength.

She opened her eyes and stared at him. He was completely clothed. She licked her lips, which felt uncomfortably dry.

Her wet, pink tongue washing over her lips caused Dillon to grit out his request again. "Take off the gown." He closed his eyes briefly and took a deep breath. Then, in a softer voice, he spoke again. "I want you to do it." He picked up one of her hands and brought it to the neck of her gown.

Shelly unfastened the first button, her eyes locked with Dillon's. She hesitated between the first and second button for a few seconds, and Dillon impatiently shifted to his knees and looked down at her. He was ready to rip the gown off if she went any slower, but she proceeded to unfasten the next two buttons without delay.

The act of undressing cooled the hot flush of desire in her. If he had removed her gown between sweet, drugging kisses, she would not have grown cold with self-consciousness and doubt as she did now, while slowly parting the front of her gown.

Dillon was first startled and then exasperated when the woman in his bed suddenly slid out from under his eyes. He remained where he was and stared at her standing in the center of the cabin, one hand still at the last button near her waist. The gown gaped open to expose the inner curves of two beautifully formed breasts.

"I can't do this," she stated simply. He sat up, his eyes narrowing. Shelly shifted her feet. "I'm sorry," she whispered. "Neither of us should have gotten started in this." His silence was unnerving. He was poised on the edge of the bed, ready to pounce. Shelly took a step back. "Dillon, don't do anything," she warned uneasily.

Dillon chewed on the inside of his cheek. He jumped to the floor and took a step forward and the door swung open.

"Dil..." His name faded on Jessica's lips. She looked from one to the other, her hand tight on the doorknob. Her blond hair was loose down her back and she had changed her royal blue gown for a robe of ruby red silk. "Well, now I know what was taking you so long!"

"I was just leaving," muttered Shelly, buttoning her gown.

"So was I!" Jessica snapped indignantly.

"Excuse me." Shelly grabbed her cloak and pushed past Jessica and out the door.

Before following in the angry girl's wake, the widow offered wryly, "I suggest you make a habit of locking your door."

"I'll remember that next time." Dillon needed a drink. He wasn't going to be able to sleep in this state unless he got pretty tight.

Chapter Fifteen

Shelly lounged in the sun near Adam the next day. She hadn't fussed with her hair and it lay down her back in a thick braid. She wore her old, rust wool dress, not wanting to be attractive, but the tight bodice accentuated parts of her anatomy, while the color brought out the red highlights in her mahogany hair. She thumbed through her sketchbook, looking at the pictures of Karl, thinking she'd done well in capturing the cold menace of the man. "Here are some I did in Virginia City." She handed the book to Adam.

He chuckled at the miners with their mules, pickaxes and shovels, their beards scraggly and their clothes dirty. "These are good!"

Shelly leaned close and looked at the picture of a mule with head lowered, back feet in the air and pack flying off. "They were funny. I needed amusement there."

"Has he seen this?" asked Adam of the fierce representation of Dillon. His hair curled back wildly from his face, which was covered in a thick beard. His eyes were hard and furious. Over his shoulder he held a pick as though it were a weapon.

"He saw it." She leaned back in her chair and closed her eyes. She hadn't slept well after leaving Dillon. She'd felt restless and aroused and too curious about how long Jessica had stayed in his cabin. Would he have forced her if Jessica had not interrupted? The possibility made her nervous.

There was a rustling of paper and a familiar chuckle. "Where are her breasts?"

Shelly's eyes flew open. Dillon was sitting next to her, looking at the picture she'd made of a mermaid. "They're underneath her hair!"

Dillon slowly smiled at her. "Can't you give us a hint of them?"

Shelly scowled. She hadn't expected him to be so friendly after last night—unless Jessica had taken good care of him. "You can fill in that part."

"No, not me. I'm not much for drawing. Besides, it's been a while since I've seen a naked breast." Shelly pulled the book out of his hands.

"Shelly," Dillon said softly, "you were the one to run out on me last night, so why am I getting scowled at?"

Shelly jerked her finger to her lips and looked to see if Adam was listening. He was. She glared at Dillon until he excused himself.

All the passengers were to dine with the captain one evening a week later. Shelly wore her gray dress, which was sober, formal and appropriate. She brushed her hair into a simple chignon and opened her door. Up the hall Jessica Ellis came out of her cabin, her maid behind her, smoothing a fold on the bell of Jessica's black velvet dress. Her hair was curled and threaded with thin black ribbon. Glowing pearls hung from her ears and around her neck. Shelly popped back into her room and shut the door. She felt dressed to serve dinner, not eat it. I am a maid, she told herself. She felt no shame about her position in life, but she was going to fade right out beside the widow. She threw all her dresses on the bed. The brown one was a marketing-for-tomatoes dress, the rust was too worn, the beige was her only new one but looked too daytime. She held up the well-mended pink one, the one she'd been wearing when Diego told her she looked pretty. The dress was inappropriate for supper, but at least she'd add some color to the table.

Shelly was the last to arrive for the meal. She became jittery at the silence that fell in the room as all eyes turned on her, unaware of how the pink in her dress accentuated the pink that bloomed in her cheeks from running up to the captain's quarters. She scooted past the first mate and accepted the chair the captain pulled out between his own and Maria's, and directly across from Jessica. Next to the older woman sat Dillon, and he winked at her when she looked at him. She analyzed the why of his wink while Captain Holt filled her wineglass.

Throughout a delicious dinner of potato soup, biscuits, peas, carrots and chicken, Jessica did her best to keep both Dillon and Captain Holt occupied. Her topic was shipwrecks, and she seemed to have read every newspaper account, for she knew of many tragedies that made Shelly reach for her wine. The drink flowed generously during the meal; everyone felt the need to imbibe. They'd been eight weeks at sea and all were restless.

Shelly wished she'd been seated next to Adam so she'd have had someone to talk with. Maria, still angry and embarrassed about Shelly's intrusion, totally ignored her. Shelly watched Jessica lean her body too close to Dillon.

"Do you have family in San Francisco?" Shelly asked the captain, noting the gold band on his hand.

He turned to smile at her in what looked like relief. "In New York, Miss Young. My wife, Melissa, and our five children reside there. I'll be happy to see them again."

"How long have you been away?" She loved the way Jessica was scowling.

"About eight months."

Shelly's eyes widened. She was surprised he wasn't more interested in the widow. Her own father had been a seaman, but her mother always sailed with him until the fatal fire that had taken his life. All Shelly had of his was the engagement ring he'd given her mother, now packed in her trunk, and a portion of a letter signed by him, his last name burned away but for the *Y.*

The large consumption of wine had everyone relaxed and jolly. Captain Holt, Dillon and the first mate, Arthur Spiro, related tales of the sea. Mr. Spiro's eyes were riveted on Jessica, who had finally noticed and was beginning to redirect her attentions. Shelly liked Dillon's disinterest in the woman and happily drank more wine. The laughter and talk swirled in her head. She'd never had wine before. When the party disbanded, Shelly noticed Jessica stroll with Mr. Spiro away from the passengers' quarters.

Shelly realized she was drunk when she left the warmth and noise of the dining room. She giggled as she held on to Adam across the swaying deck in the darkness.

"I think you had too much wine."

She laughed at how stern and old he sounded. "I'll be fine when I get to my cabin."

"And I'll see to that."

Before they reached the stairs, Shelly heard a guitar and a plaintive voice. She stopped, jerking on Adam's arm. "Music!"

He pulled her along. "It's just a sailor."

"Let's go listen."

"It's not a concert, Shelly. It's just an out-of-tune guitar and the croaky voice of a crew member!" Shelly glared up at him. The tilt of her chin and the flash in her narrowed eyes struck a chord of familiarity in Adam. He gazed at her wordlessly.

"It sounds good to me."

Adam sighed in relief when Dillon approached. "Help me convince her to go to her cabin. She's had too much wine and has the fool notion of being serenaded by a sailor," he pleaded with his friend.

Dillon took note of Shelly's determined stance. She was pulling away from Adam like a stubborn mule. "No harm in a little music now, is there, Adam?" Dillon offered Shelly his arm, which she gladly accepted, and they walked away from Adam, an appalled expression on his face.

"Thank you, Dillon." Shelly giggled, smiling up into his face, missing the dark intent there. He led her to the ship railing. Across from them a lone sailor sat on a pile of canvas, singing to the night watch of love.

"What a beautiful night," sighed Shelly, looking up at the sky. Dillon slipped one arm over her shoulders as he followed her eyes to the stars. His solid warmth felt good against her. Their past quarrels faded into vague darkness. There was only the rocking ship below, the stars above and the man snug against her. When she lowered her gaze from the stars to Dillon, she saw raw desire. He barely touched her, his arm was light on her shoulders, his other hand clasped the railing behind him. It was she who molded the length of her body to his, she who raised a hand and slowly traced the outline of his lips with her finger. She pressed, testing their firmness, their softness.

Dillon took her hand from his face and lowered his mouth to hers. Shelly's eyes closed and she saw the image of a thousand stars in the darkness of her eyelids. She moved against him as his tongue pushed past her lips and slid wet and hot inside her mouth. Dillon broke the kiss with a violence that startled her. He looked at her long and hard and then grabbed her hand and pulled her across the deck and down the stairs.

Shelly stumbled after him as he dragged her along. Her world spun crazily by the time Dillon turned and scooped her up into his arms. Inside his cabin he released only the arm beneath her legs, so she slid slowly down the front of his body. He lighted the lamp by his bunk, closed and locked the door, then returned to her, taking both her hands in his and pulling her close. When they were chest to chest, Dillon bent and nuzzled her neck. Shelly's senses reeled and she closed her eyes. In the back of her brain a message was struggling to surface, but it was drowned in sweet pleasure and drugging wine. She was aware only of the virile man before her and the churning deep below her belly.

He cradled her face in his hands and kissed her. Shelly held on to his arms, needing an anchor to keep from washing away in this sea of feeling. His hands slipped down her back, caressing lightly, pulling her closer. She buried her fingers in the hair at the back of his head, the soft locks like silk in her hands, and she moaned.

Dillon knew there'd be no fight tonight. He realized he was taking unfair advantage of her drunkenness, but honorable thoughts were plowed under as he deepened the kiss and her tongue met his stroke for stroke. He wanted her in his bed tonight, no matter the price he'd pay tomorrow. He sank down on the bunk and pulled her onto his lap. He strewed kisses across her face as he pulled out the pins that held up her hair. In moments the curling mass tumbled down her back, the fresh, clean smell floating around him.

"Oh, Shelly." His hands tightened possessively on her waist. He took her mouth again, unable to appease his hunger for her lips. He slipped his hands down to her feet and slid off her shoes. When her slippers had fallen to the floor he gently massaged her feet, then slid his palms up her thighs and rolled down her stockings.

With an arm supporting her back, he left one hand under her dress, gently rubbing a leg while he kissed a path from her mouth to her neck. He took his hand from her thigh and unbuttoned her bodice to expose one hard-tipped breast. She clenched her fingers in his hair as his wet mouth surrounded her nipple.

"Let's take this dress off," he whispered hoarsely, meeting her dazed eyes. She nodded and he pushed her to her feet and shoved the gown off her shoulders, down her arms and over her hips until it fell to the floor. He wasn't making the same mistake twice by letting her undress herself.

Shelly stepped out of the pile at her feet, untied her crinoline and let it plunge to the floor. The chill of the boards beneath her feet was only a dull discomfort. There was a distant roaring in her ears as she raised her hands to loosen her stays. She tossed the corset to the floor and untied her petticoats, her eyes transfixed on Dillon's face as the white cotton material slid off her. He took a step toward her while Shelly slowly pulled at the ribbon of her camisole, aching to be touched by him.

Dillon stared at her nipples puckering in the cold room and easily visible through the thin material. He clenched his jaw and lowered his eyes to the triangle of dark curls he could see through her drawers. His heart pounding, he tugged the camisole over her head. Her breasts bounced free and he caught them, his palms and fingers running over the soft, firm flesh. Shelly grasped his forearms as he aroused her with electrifying swiftness. Dillon released her breasts and untied the white ribbon of her drawers. He crouched at her feet and pulled the garment down her legs while Shelly rested a hand on his shoulder and picked up one foot at a time. On his way back up, Dillon pressed a kiss against the curls between her thighs.

Shakily, he threw off his coat, unbuttoned his shirt and trousers, his eyes on Shelly the entire time. She was beautiful as she swayed unsteadily on her feet. Her hair draped over her shoulders, not completely hiding her lovely breasts; gooseflesh was breaking out over her smooth skin. He tore off the rest of his clothes except for his trousers. She lowered her eyes, following the trail of black hair down his stomach to where it grew thick, revealed by his unfastened trousers. He forgot that she was drunk as she stared boldly at what his pants were still barely concealing. He reached out and grasped her shoulders, yanking her to his mouth, which fastened hungrily on hers. He embraced her tightly, groaning as her breasts thrust into his chest, then pushed her to the bed, his mouth moving on hers urgently as he crushed her beneath him. This was what he'd been dreaming of for weeks, to feel her naked beneath him, to touch her everywhere.

Shelly arched her neck up and closed her eyes, awash in pleasure, all sensation and no thought as Dillon lay between her legs. She stretched her arms around him as he pressed himself against her, his breath rasping harshly against her cheek. She dug her fingers into his shoulders as he slid down and suckled her nipples. She relaxed on the sea of her intoxicated enjoyment, and slowly, little by little, it pulled her down into darkness. She sighed softly, just before her fingers fell off Dillon's shoulders.

Dillon knelt between her legs and pushed her thighs farther apart. Her lax limbs offered no resistance and he glanced up at her face. "Shelly?" He shook her by the shoulders and cursed. Poised above her, he looked down at her slack, open body. He hadn't realized she'd been drunk enough to pass out. He was going to have hell to pay tomorrow. His eyes flicked down her body again. What would she remember? She'd probably assume they had completed the act when she awoke naked in his bunk. It would be so easy now to relieve this throbbing need that was driving him mad.

With a lithe movement he jumped to the floor and stripped off his trousers. His sex jutted out full and furious, but as he looked down at her slumbering so peacefully, a streak of guilt flashed through him for even thinking about taking her unawares. He wouldn't be able to face her in the morning. He cursed again, looked down at himself and groaned. He turned down the lamp and climbed resignedly back into bed, pulling the blankets over them both. He pushed Shelly to the edge of the bunk, but the bed was too narrow to escape from the warm, torturous feel of her body. He turned on his side, facing away from her, and violently punched his pillow. He did not know how he would sleep in this state of arousal, so intense it was painful. The curve of her hip pressed into his buttocks. She was going to pay for this! This would be the last time she'd leave him on the brink while she went off to sweet dreams. In the morning he'd show her what torment really was!

Chapter Sixteen

Shelly's eyes popped open. She licked her parched lips while two conflicting needs made themselves known: she had to relieve herself and she needed a drink of water. She sat up, threw off the blankets and swung her legs across the bunk. She yelped when her legs landed on a warm body in her bed.

"What?" Dillon jerked up on his elbows.

"What are you doing in my bed?" demanded Shelly.

Dillon suddenly felt surly. "It's *my* bed," he growled, turning over and propping his pillow behind his back.

Shelly, oblivious to her nakedness, reached across him to the small table where she kept her matches.

"Looking for something?"

"My matches!"

He pushed her away, pulled out the drawer in his table and lighted the lamp with his matches. The light flared and Shelly grabbed for the sheet, clutching it around her breasts. She was very much aware of his body, also naked, only inches away. She covered her eyes with one palm and tried to remember the events that had led her to his bed. There had been all that wine with supper, and she dimly remembered being on deck with him. She must have been drunk out of her mind, but she was completely sober now.

"How could you?" she sputtered, looking at Dillon accusingly. "You took complete advantage of me. I didn't know what I was doing!"

Dillon crossed his arms over his bare chest and glared at her. She might look particularly desirable right now with her hair in wild disarray and her eyes flashing, but he was infuriated by her tone and accusations when he'd had such a restless night.

"Just what do you remember?" he asked ominously.

Her eyes glittered dangerously. "I don't want to remember any of it!"

"What is the *last* thing you remember?" he demanded.

She set her mind to the disgusting task of recalling their intimacies. "I remember," she said tightly, glaring at him, "you taking off my stockings...and my dress."

He nodded. "Then what?"

Shelly frowned and averted her eyes. "I took off my other things?" she whispered unbelievingly, looking to his eyes for confirmation.

"That's right. Then what?"

"We...I..." She remembered. It was like a fuzzy dream, but it had happened.

"Well?"

"I remember everything. There is no need to talk about it." She refused to look at him. She could not remember the completion of the act, but she was not going to admit it and then endure a gloating description of her wanton actions.

"Even the way you conveniently passed out?" he asked harshly.

Shelly's eyes flew to his. "You did it to me while I was asleep?"

Dillon looked at her with utter exasperation. She was itching to throw all blame on him when he was the one who'd been teased unmercilessly. "Do you really think so low of me?"

Shelly flushed hotly. She lowered her gaze to her lap and shifted her seat on the bed. Then she looked up. "No," she admitted. Suddenly, the fact that she had yet to relieve herself was her primary concern.

"I'm never drinking again," she swore vehemently as she gracelessly clambered over Dillon, pulling a blanket with her to shield her naked body. She still displayed an intriguing amount of skin for his perusal. "Turn around!" she ordered, her back to him as she yanked up her drawers, which she found on the floor. She was shivering uncontrollably from the damp chill in the cabin.

"What are you doing?" Dillon watched her hop from one bare foot to the other.

"I'm going to my room!"

"Oh, no you're not!"

Shelly finished pulling on her camisole and turned to face him. "I'm not going to stay with you, Dillon," she said rationally and calmly. "I'm sorry about earlier, but—"

"That's what you said last time."

Shelly spun around when he rose from the bed. She had no desire to see him naked. She quickly gathered up her clothes while Dillon positioned himself in front of the door.

"Why are you doing this?" She approached him, holding her clothes and not looking below his chin.

"We're going to finish what we started."

"No."

"Yes."

"Dillon, I have to go... You know..."

"No, what?" He leaned against the door, one hand resting on the door handle, the other on his hip, and watched her fret with the pile of clothes in her arms.

"I have to relieve myself!" she snapped, stomping one foot, furious with him.

Dillon's lips twitched in amusement. "Shelly, I have a chamber pot in here. You don't—"

"Shut up! If you think I'll go in here, in front of... Well, just forget it!"

"And you can forget about leaving," he said softly.

"I'll scream."

"I'll strangle you first."

Shelly turned away from him to ease the strain of keeping her eyes from dipping down his naked body.

Dillon admired her waist-length hair and her round bottom through her drawers while she fumed. "Shelly, go fetch me my trousers and I'll leave you alone for a minute."

"Get your own trousers!"

"I'm guarding the door."

"I want to go back to my room," she ground out.

"The only concession you get is a moment's privacy." He pushed himself off the door and bounced on the balls of his feet. "What's it going to be?"

Shelly slowly moved to get his trousers. She walked backward with her arm outstretched, hand holding the black garment.

"Thank you." He pulled them on. "You can turn around now." She did not. "The chamber pot's in the closet." He stepped out into the corridor and then popped his head back in. "Shelly, don't lock me out. I *will* break down the door and that will draw an audience."

Shelly let the clothes she was holding fall to the floor when the door closed behind him. Bastard! She pulled out the pot and used it, then got her drink of water from the pitcher.

"You can put it back in the closet," Dillon said when he returned and saw her holding the pot in the middle of the small room.

She shook her head and took off the top. She grimaced. "You let me go or I quietly throw this on you."

Dillon paled. "You wouldn't."

Shelly smiled.

Dillon's brows drew together. "I don't understand you. Sometimes you act as if you want me as much as I want you."

"Move out of the way."

Dillon sat down on the bunk and Shelly backed to the door, holding her defense carefully in front of her. "I wouldn't ever force you to make love to me."

"Right!" Shelly looked down at the garments she would have to leave behind.

"I could have done it when you were asleep, but I didn't want to."

She glanced up at him. He looked so damn serious. "I'm going to put this pot down and pick up my clothes. If you make one move toward me I'll throw it at you."

"I swear on my mother's grave that I'll never touch you when you don't want me to." She didn't respond. Dillon lay

down on his bunk, his face turned toward the wall, his arm
flung over his eyes. Shelly picked up her clothes, opened the
door and looked back at him. God, he was beautiful without a shirt on, all spread out and still against the wool blankets. She quietly closed the door. He had sworn and she
believed him; of the many things he was, a liar wasn't one
of them. She took a few silent steps forward, still holding
her bundle. "Would you swear on your precious mine?"

Dillon stiffened and rolled away from her to his side.
"Yes," he answered after a minute.

Her heart beating a fast, exciting rhythm, Shelly dropped
her clothes and trailed her fingers down the brown length of
his arm. His muscles jumped at her touch. With a muttered
curse he jerked his arm away and turned toward her. His
eyes, black and angry, bored into her face, skipping down
to her body and back up. "For God's sake, make up your
mind!"

Shelly felt like mush from the waist down. Out from under the cloud of duress she was free to feel all the feelings her
body and heart had for him. "I have." She pulled off her
camisole in one fluid motion and his eyes rounded. "I want
to stay. I want you to make love to me." She reached a
trembling hand to Dillon's chest and stroked the hard, hair-
roughened male breast, her fingers passing softly over the
red scarred wound.

He stared in amazement.

She let her fingers slide down to his stomach.

"Oh, Shell," he groaned, pulling her down to the mattress, reveling in her surrender, which allowed him to strip
off her drawers and leave her naked in his arms.

She wrapped her arms and legs around him and gave
herself up to the man and the moment. She protested when
he disengaged himself from her, but fell silent when she saw
him shed his pants. She saw his swollen flesh spring out of
its confines and grow bigger. She raised apprehensive eyes
to Dillon's face.

"I won't hurt you." His eyes glittered darkly as he lay
back beside her, studying her face. "I haven't given a damn

about what a woman felt in a long, long time, but I want to make you feel good.''

She tensed as he raised his thigh and settled it across hers. The heat of his skin was shocking. His hand moved to her shoulder and his thumb stroked her collarbone. Shelly could no longer endure his examination of her face and body and she raised her head off the pillow to bring her lips to his.

Dillon obliged with slow, light kisses, his tongue teasing her lips apart and creating a fire in her mouth. His hand moved from her shoulder in silken caresses to the proud thrust of bosom below. One of her hands tangled itself in the soft locks of his hair and the other rested on his shoulder. Her tense muscles relaxed as he continued to touch her without hurry. His hand smoothed down her stomach to the hair between her thighs. He deepened the kiss, his mouth more demanding as his fingers combed through the tight curls, dipped into the well of moisture and coated his fingers before he slid them everywhere over the soft flesh between her legs. Shelly closed her eyes and moaned against his mouth, her fingers clutching his shoulders.

Dillon's breath grew ragged when she spread her thighs under his caressing hand. He slipped two fingers inside her while his thumb softly rubbed higher. He brought her close to unfamiliar ecstasy, and she gripped his forearm, her nails digging in, and arched her hips to meet the plunge of his hand. When she seemed pained with pleasure, desperate and hot, he withdrew his hand.

Dillon looked into her face, his eyes blazing and his upper lip beaded with perspiration. She nervously slid her thighs farther apart as he laid his body onto hers. His chest flattened her breasts and made it hard to breathe. She looked into his face and felt more anxious at his half-shuttered eyes and his shallow breathing. Between her thighs she felt the insistent pressure of his hardness. She remembered the pain from last time. She held his shoulders and squeezed her eyes shut as he slid inside. Her muscles tightened against him involuntarily, but Dillon waited before pressing further. He kissed her neck, her cheek, and nibbled her earlobe. Then he pushed farther.

Shelly felt herself stretching. She opened her eyes and saw him poised motionless, braced on his elbows above her. "Okay?" he asked softly. She nodded, her eyes not leaving his. She smoothed her hands down the damp skin of his back while he nuzzled her neck. She was ready for more and slid her palms down to his buttocks and gently pressed the tightly muscled flesh into her arching hips. Dillon groaned and thrust.

Shelly's mouth dropped open and her eyes shut. She hadn't realized he had so much farther to go. She squirmed under him, feeling sensations so intense they scared her. Her arms gripped him as the lower portion of her body felt out of control.

"Easy, easy," Dillon whispered. He brushed his hand across her cheek, smiled briefly, barely, then closed his eyes as he surged over her.

Shelly could see that it felt very good to him. She tried to relax and fought the urge to tighten and move. Then his mouth came down on hers, his hands on her hips, pulling her to meet his every thrust as they increased in tempo. She gave of her mouth until he buried himself in her with one final thrust.

His panting, sweating body lay heavily on her, his face buried in her hair. Between her thighs she throbbed with an unsatisfied ache. Even as he tenderly kissed her neck she felt like a failure. To her utter vexation she began to cry. Was it supposed to be like this? She doubted Jessica Ellis had this overwhelming desire to claw her nails down Dillon's back in frustration. Dillon eased his replete body off Shelly and saw her tears. She tried to brush them off, but he stayed her hand.

"What's this?"

"Nothing."

"Did I hurt you?"

Shelly could not abide the concern in his voice. She wanted to get away.

"Did I?"

"No!"

"What, then?" He kissed the tears from her cheeks so gently that she cried more.

"I want to go back to my room." She sat up and swung her bare legs off the bunk.

"Shelly, tell me what's wrong." She jumped off the bed and grabbed her dress. Dillon jumped after her and held her arms down so she couldn't pull the dress over her head. "I deserve to know what happened!" His voice had lost its patient concern. "Are you just mad because you finally let me make love to you again?" He jerked the dress out of her hands. "It was your choice. You came to me!"

She stood shivering and shaking like a sail in a high wind. "It's not that. I'm not blaming you." She dashed the tears off her face and refused to meet his eyes. "Don't yell at me anymore."

"Let me know what I did."

She chanced a look at his face. His eyes snapped with exasperation and something akin to hurt bewilderment. She opened and shut her mouth.

"Yes?"

"I'm miserable at that!" she burst out. "I don't know how to do it. I feel awful and like an idiot!"

Dillon's face relaxed as he looked down at her bowed head. "Yes, you're hopelessly miserable." He barely masked the amusement in his voice. Shelly glared at him, her chin quivering. "Come here, you twit." He scooped her up in his arms, plopped her back in the bed and sat right beside her. He settled the covers over them both and then his arms around her. "I'm the one who was miserable at it," he said softly. "I was too fast. You were wonderful. And you probably feel awful because we're not finished."

Shelly looked warily up at him. *What else was there to do?* "What about Jessica? Was it better with her?"

Dillon was admiring Shelly's breasts, which were barely covered by the blankets; one little tug and he'd expose her nipples. "I never made love to Jessica."

"But she stayed in your room the night I left."

"For a few minutes." Dillon looked into her eyes. "It's you I want," he said hoarsely. "And I'm more interested in doing some things that don't involve talking about your jealousy." He captured her mouth with his own before she could respond and he pulled down the covers that shielded her breasts. Her nipples hardened instantly between his fingers, causing a low groan of pleasure to escape him.

His hands swirled like fire over her skin and she felt the caress of cool air as he pushed the blanket down to her knees. His hard thigh nudged its way between her legs, keeping them slightly open. All the while his lips were fused with hers. Shelly's mouth grew acutely sensitive beneath his, like a receptacle of pleasure that he filled over and over.

He slid one arm beneath her neck and lay half on her and half beside her. The fingers that had thrilled her breasts dipped lower and lower in caressing circles until he reached the part of her that was waiting. Swallowing her moans, he gently teased her with vibrating fingers. They glided into her swollen flesh and tapped her very core.

Shelly's legs tightened around his thigh. The soft, tantalizing brush of his chest hair on her unbearably sensitive breasts made her gasp. She gripped his rhythmically moving arm with one hand, and the other lay bunched in a fist by her pillow. The tension in her body became unbearable and heat flushed outward from beneath his hand. She kept her eyes glued to his as his fingers played her on and on until there was no turning back. She closed her eyes and gave herself up to more sensation than she'd ever felt in her life. It was a wild, sweet pulsing that surged from the center of her, washing away all the frustration and fear. She rode senselessly on the waves of it until they ebbed and were gone.

Softly panting and sweaty, Shelly opened her eyes and gazed at Dillon. He smiled. "Feel better?" Shelly groaned. He laughed and brushed her lips with his and pulled his fingers from deep between her legs. She whimpered at the withdrawal and Dillon swallowed, eyes flaring hotly at her incoherent sound. His hand returned, stroking her with a gentleness that was strained.

Shelly turned to her side and twined her arms around his neck. She offered him everything. He kissed her passionately while his body trembled with need. He pulled her knee up over his hip and caressed her bottom briefly before he buried himself deep within her. His mouth twisted away from Shelly's as her flesh closed around him.

She crooned against his cheek as he throbbed inside her. Her body was swollen and sensitive. He moved against her slowly and her pleasure flared anew. Suddenly, he rolled to his back, holding her close. He pushed her thighs between his and pulled her hips tight against him as he thrust inside her. Shelly braced her elbows on his chest and looked at him distrustfully. His eyes were closed, his lips parted. His eyes flickered open when she remained stiff on him.

"It's all right," he whispered. His hands smoothed up along her body to capture and hold her breasts. Shelly's arms turned to jelly as he pinched her nipples. She fell on him and opened her mouth over his. Her hair fell around them, creating a steaming enclosure for their kisses. She could not get enough of his mouth and tongue. She rose up on her hands and began to pant above him, tensing and untensing her body as she rocked back against him.

"Oh, Shell." Dillon stared at her face, suffused with pleasure, and her breasts bouncing above him. His fingers tightened on her hips and he arched his body up and over, rolling Shelly under him and pounding into her, one of his thighs between her legs and his mouth sucking hard on a nipple.

At the first wet touch of his mouth on her breast, Shelly felt waves of shock down to her toes. She gripped his back and arched beneath him in a shuddering climax, dimly aware of Dillon's own release. Drained, almost numb, she held him to her, his heavy body a warm pleasure. She listened as his harsh breathing returned to normal. She'd never guessed that the physical union between a man and a woman harbored such mutual feelings of pleasure. Why hadn't anyone mentioned it? She felt a part of him. Surely no bad

feeling could slither between them ever again, not after
they'd shared so finely.

Dillon raised his head from the warm alcove of her neck.
He traced her lips with a fingertip while her eyes shone silver. "Did you lock the door?" he asked.

Shelly smiled. "No."

"Weren't we lucky to be uninterrupted, then?"

"Not necessarily. I was definitely too preoccupied to notice an intrusion."

Dillon laughed, hugged her tight and rolled next to her.
Shelly nestled against him. They were both asleep in minutes.

Chapter Seventeen

Shelly awakened to the gray light of an early ocean morning coming in through the porthole. Dillon was asleep, lying with his head pillowed on her hair, his hand resting on her belly and his knee bent over her legs. Shelly gazed at his peacefully slumbering face. His lashes were black against the brown skin of his cheeks. During the hours they'd slept his face had grown black stubble. She scraped her fingernail against the roughness of his cheek. His lips twitched. She stretched and felt like liquid sunshine from the top of her head to her pointed toes.

She slid the sheet down, baring Dillon's brown shoulder, his arm that so possessively lay across her stomach, under her breasts. He was a beautiful man and her heart quickened at the sight of his muscled torso as she drew the sheet down to his waist. Enough was enough. She had to get back to her room before everyone was up and about. She slid out from under his arm and leg and placed her feet on the other side of the bunk, over his body.

Dillon woke and rolled to his back. "What are you doing?" he asked groggily. His eyes were bleary as he squinted at the naked nymph with tousled hair perched on his legs.

Shelly stared at him a heart-stopping moment before she turned away. "I have to go back to my room now." She pushed herself off the bed.

Dillon's arm whipped around her waist before her feet hit the floor. "That's what you're always telling me," he groaned, pulling her down so she lay with her nude back against his bare chest. The sheet rode just over his hips, separating them but not shielding her from the heat and hardness of him.

He pushed her to the mattress and Shelly looked up at him incredulously. "You just woke up! And it's morning!"

Dillon flashed her a broad smile. "What does that have to do with it?" He ripped the sheet off his body.

Shelly flushed scarlet at the bold display of his readiness. It seemed indecent in the light of morning. "I have to get back before anyone knows that—"

"Oh, hush." His mouth and body came down over hers. He spread her legs with his knees while Shelly bubbled over in protestations beneath his hungry mouth. By the time Dillon had his fingers between her thighs she was clinging wordlessly to him.

Dillon rode her exultantly, lasting until she trembled in release beneath him. He helped her gather her clothing and made sure the way was clear before she ran back to her room. She let the underclothing she carried sink to the floor. She'd only put on her dress to make the mad dash down the hall. Now she pulled it off and crawled naked into her own bed, wanting nothing against the skin that was still warmed by Dillon. She dozed until breakfast.

Dillon stood with his back to the ship railing and watched Shelly start down the steps to her cabin. She was sleepy and Dillon understood why. He was still seeing the soft smile that had graced her face just for him when they'd taken a walk around the deck after breakfast.

"So, you're not ignoring each other anymore." Adam stepped up beside Dillon at the railing and looked searchingly into his partner's face, which had gone completely blank. "Oh, really, Dillon, you of all people, being owner of this ship, know how thin these cabin walls are!"

A grin broke across Dillon's face. "I didn't realize that we were so loud."

"Loud enough. And unmistakable. I imagine that was the first time?"

"Why so curious?"

Adam leaned close and looked Dillon directly in the eyes, not put off by the younger man's sharp tone. "She's young and alone and I feel responsible for her. I did put her on this ship, in your path."

Dillon nodded emphatically. "Why did you do such a stupid thing?"

Adam looked out to sea. "She's a special young woman. I wanted to make sure she got to New York all right." Half the truth was good enough for now, he thought to himself. "I'm rather fond of her—not," he was quick to add, "in the way you seem to be. What happens when we reach New York?"

"I don't know."

"Well, how do you feel about her?"

Dillon shuddered. "I don't want to talk about it."

Adam snorted. "That's wonderful! You're going straight home to a marriage with Annette King. I'm sure you haven't mentioned that to Shelly."

"No, I haven't. But I don't love Annette."

"Is that supposed to make Shelly feel better?"

"What am I supposed to do," Dillon demanded, rounding on Adam, "turn to her in bed and say, 'Listen, I'm engaged to be married, but I don't want you to worry about it'?"

Adam ignored Dillon's absurd question. "How is she going to feel when we reach New York? It'll be worse then. I'll tell her myself."

"Not a good idea," warned Dillon. "I've put off my marriage this long and it can be avoided longer still."

Adam would jeopardize their friendship if he spoke to Shelly. Besides, it would be best for Dillon to tell her himself, if he only would. "I pray that you tell her soon," Adam muttered, hoping that Dillon wouldn't be able to do it, would damn his father and marry the woman who was right for him. He strode off down the deck, scowling.

Dillon waited until everyone was behind their cabin doors for the night before he knocked on Shelly's door. She opened it a crack, after asking who was there. She was in her nightgown, her hair falling loosely over her shoulders. "May I come in?"

Shelly hesitated. Her eyes met his. She knew that she could refuse and he would go away, but he looked devastatingly handsome in his black boots, gray trousers and partially unbuttoned white shirt, which revealed the crisp curl of dark chest hair. Shelly stepped aside and Dillon locked the door behind him.

There was a seriousness about them both tonight. Gone was the violence of their repressed passion, which blocked out more rational thought. Now they were very much aware of the choices they were making, and the chances they were taking.

Shelly's eyes darted to the bed she had already turned down. She shifted nervously on her bare feet, the nightgown brushing softly across the tops of her toes. It was obvious they'd soon be in that bed; she felt awkward now because the other times it had just seemed to happen without such premeditation. She felt silly and uncertain of how to proceed from where her feet were glued to the floor. She sincerely hoped Dillon would soon do something to ease her discomfort.

Instead, he worked on quenching his thirst as he poured himself a second glass of water from the pitcher on her little table. She admired the pull of his linen shirt as his back muscles stretched in the act of pouring. When he turned and caught her staring at him he smiled. Shelly didn't respond; she was thinking how handsome he was, as she'd been doing all day, and remembering every touch they'd exchanged.

He walked to her bunk, passing her on the way, and sat down and tugged off his boots, dropping the leather footwear to the floor with a loud plunk in the otherwise silent room. He leaned forward, hands on either side of him on the dark blankets of the bed. "Come sit down."

Shelly complied, a little slowly. She avoided his face as he unbuttoned the rest of his shirt. His fingers moved deliberately as she watched. He pulled the shirt off, shoulder muscles rippling. The stiffness in Shelly's body was loosened by swiftly flowing currents of hot blood. This darkly handsome man was Dillon. Dillon. He made her feel good, wild and reckless. Giddily, she reached out her hand and placed it on his warm chest, just over his heart. Her palm pressed against the strong, steady beat and she looked into his eyes.

What Dillon saw in those gray silvered depths frightened him. Simple lust he could easily deal with, but he saw more, like loving and longing. His immediate thought was to pick up his boots and run. Every second they wove themselves tighter into the tapestry of a story that was ill-fated, but he could no more stop himself than he could have caused the ocean to disappear.

He took the hand she held against him. Together they watched his long brown fingers twine between her smaller, whiter ones. He kissed each of her knuckles, his breath whispering warmly against her skin. He lay back on the bed and pulled her down beside him by tugging with their joined hands.

On their sides they faced each other, not touching but for their hands. They looked at each other leisurely, admiringly, in a way that they had always been too rushed for before. Shelly's eyes ran over the rugged lines of Dillon's face, the curling locks of his hair and his square jaw. The scent of brandy wafted from him, a fine, pleasant smell. Shelly thought brandy would forever remind her of him. His chest loomed large next to her, brown, warm, hairy. She took an unhurried look at his manhood swelling beneath his trousers, as yet undemanding.

Dillon admired the sheen of Shelly's hair as it cascaded about her face and over her shoulders. The pink color was high in her cheeks, her eyes were glinting with mysterious lights. Her waist dipped dramatically low before the rise of her hips. She smelled of sunshine and her hand was warm in his, gently holding, squeezing lightly.

Shelly shivered all the way down to her toes when Dillon moved to unbutton her gown. He propped himself up on his elbow, not releasing the hand he still held between them, and unbuttoned her to just below her breasts. Her eyes fastened on his face as he looked down the length of her body. He ran the palm of his hand up her legs, pushing her gown to the middle of her thigh. He raised dark eyes to her face. "I love to look at you."

Shelly's breath caught in her throat. She touched his chest, smoothing her fingers over his male nipples, intrigued when they stiffened under her fingers. Her lips ached to be kissed and she wondered why he took so long to get to it. He lay down on his back as Shelly smoothed her hand over his stomach. She raised herself up and bent over him. Surely he would kiss her now, but he was still, his eyes sparkling with dark fires as they fastened on her mouth. His lips curved with a wicked sensuousness. Swiftly, Shelly pressed her lips to his, blotting out his smile.

They kissed until their lips were swollen, their bodies pressed tightly together. Dillon shifted, tangling her legs with his own until she lay completely on top of him. He took the hand that lay on his stomach and threaded it through his own, so both her hands were caught and held down on either side of his face. It was sweet torture to lie against each other with hands bound together, unable to explore, adding to the anticipation of their desire.

Dillon rolled Shelly off him, and with one pair of joined hands he raised her gown above her waist. He pulled her hand down with his to unfasten his trousers. Shelly giggled at the awkwardness of the feat, but the laughter died in her throat when she felt the hardening length of him against the back of her own hand. He was velvety smooth and hot. Shelly laid her head back on the pillow and accommodated Dillon's welcoming weight as he covered her with his body, placing their hands on either side of her shoulders.

His trousers abraded her legs and her gown shielded her breasts from contact with his chest. It was only their most intimate parts and their bellies that rubbed together naked. Shelly felt as if she were smothering with desire.

Dillon's hands tightened over hers. He ran torrid kisses along her cheek and over the bridge of her nose. "I want you now," he said against her mouth.

"Yes," urged Shelly. Her body tensed as he poised above her. She raised her hips in welcome and then he was inside, sliding in and out with long strokes. Shelly crooned softly and Dillon covered her mouth in a kiss, drinking all of her cries so no one would hear them through the thin cabin walls. They rocked together wildly until Dillon tore his mouth from Shelly and thudded violently into her body. His breath was harsh and rasping in her ear. Shelly strained beneath him and at the moment she felt his sex erupt within her she reached her own pinnacle.

When his racing heart had slowed to normal Dillon freed her hands for the first time and eased off her, pulling her gown back down over her legs. Shelly trailed her fingers down Dillon's cheek and pressed the pad of her forefinger into the cleft in his chin. She brushed his mustache with a feather-light stroke. Dillon pulled her into his arms, his hands running down her back, pressing her closer at her hip, squeezing her shoulder, all the gentle touches of a lover. Shelly grew drowsy in the warm circle of his arms. She didn't remember Dillon turning the lamp out and pulling the covers over them both. Later, when he made love to her again, it was like a sweet, satisfying dream as his hands and mouth spread pleasure over her body.

They had almost two weeks of passion and the luxury of indulging it. Dillon came to her room every night, but by afternoon Shelly would be quivering inside with wanting him. There was little else to do but remember the pleasure of the night before and thereby arouse herself with the memories.

"Why don't we go down now?" she asked him on deck one foggy afternoon.

He chuckled. "What? And end the anticipation?" She nodded vigorously.

He'd made her wait. He loved the sweet building torture of getting through the day without touching her and then going crazy when the sun had set. She was so eager for him, and yet it was nothing shameful. She liked sex and she liked it with him. There was no pretension about it with her and he couldn't get enough of her affections.

"Was there a special woman in your past?" she'd wanted to know one lazy evening.

Abruptly, he'd gotten out of her bed without answering her. He couldn't talk about Cora with her, so he'd thought it best to leave. But other than that one night he was in bliss and refused to worry about anything beyond the present.

Chapter Eighteen

"She's a far cry from the girl you brought up the trail to Virginia City, isn't she?" said Adam, leaning against the railing and nodding toward Shelly, where she sat on deck.

Dillon continued looking out at the sea. "I guess so."

"She's a woman now. What if she's carrying your child?"

Dillon winced and turned to face the man at his side, as much because of what he'd said as the pained, pleading way he'd said it. "I'll take care of her."

"But not the way she deserves."

Dillon's jaw tightened, but he said nothing. The noose was getting tight. They'd be in New York in two days.

Adam slammed his fist on the railing and shook his head. "She's not a whore!" His voice trembled with the anger he held in check to keep his voice from carrying across the ship. "I know you've been ill-used in the past, but that's no excuse for this. That girl loves you!"

"Keep my past out of this! For your information she's not even mentioned love."

"Oh, don't be a fool! Anyone who looks can see that she positively glows when you come near her."

Dillon snorted and shifted his feet. His hand clenched the railing in front of him, but his face was casual, impassive, as he looked at Adam.

"I don't see how you can look her in the eyes. Or maybe I'm wrong and you really don't care about her. Or maybe you're scared of what your father would say—"

"My father can go to hell. And everyone else can follow right behind," Dillon snapped. "I don't want to be married. Not to anyone."

"What is so bad about marriage?"

"Obviously something, since you've never married."

"Your father's first marriage was a good one," Adam said softly.

"No one sees what goes on between two people behind closed doors," he responded, leaving Adam puzzled. Dillon walked down the deck, passing Shelly without acknowledging her and going down the stairs. She stared after him and wondered. She hadn't seen him looking so troubled in a long time, but then maybe the preceding dreamy weeks had distorted her memory. She was on the greatest journey of her life, to be reunited with a family she'd never seen, and traveling by her side was the man she loved. Yes, she loved him. She hadn't been able to tell him but surely he knew. She'd never have gotten this involved if she hadn't felt so strongly. They had yet to speak of their future, but Shelly was sure they had one. This couldn't just end. She'd stay with Adam in New York, she'd find her family, and she'd act very respectable and wouldn't let Dillon touch her until he married her. So, she'd finally admitted it to herself. He'd better agree. She'd better go down and tell him what the plan was. She put her sketchbook aside to follow him downstairs.

"We should be in New York in two days," Adam said, sitting down next to her. Shelly nodded and moved her feet to stand up. Adam looked at her out of the corner of his eye. "I'm sure Dillon can't wait to see his father and stepmother," he added sarcastically.

Shelly frowned. "Does he not like his family?" she asked softly.

"My dear, Dillon hates his father and is indifferent to his stepmother, yet for some inexplicable reason he still tries to please that sire of his. The man's mercenary, more difficult than Dillon is. It's a good thing you're staying with me and not with the Ryders. There's usually a nasty fight brewing at some end of that house."

Shelly sat back. "If Dillon's father is as stubborn as Dillon I can see why."

"He is. He wants Dillon to stay in New York. He wants Dillon to marry and to take more control of Ryder Shipping."

"And Dillon objects to all of these things?" she asked quietly.

Adam shrugged. "Maybe he just likes California. He's been successful out there. The mine is something his father has no control over, unlike Ryder Shipping. You'd think his father would be proud of his son's success on his own."

"Yes, you'd think so." What would Dillon's father think of her, she wondered. If she could keep the restless Dillon in New York, that would be a point in her favor. But, if the elder Ryder took a liking to her, then Dillon might, out of sheer rebelliousness, turn against her. She sighed and stood up.

"And now John Ryder is really going to be furious."

"Why?"

Adam's green eyes met hers. "Because of Annette."

Shelly blinked.

"Dillon is engaged to Annette King, the daughter of his father's best friend. But now, with you...well, Dillon is hardly going to marry her, is he?"

Shelly shook her head as if to clear it. He was still looking at her. "No, of course not," she whispered, and walked away from him while he stared after her.

"Go away!" yelled Dillon from the other side of the door.

Shelly opened his door and stepped inside. He glared up at her from where he lay on his bunk, coatless and hands behind his head. She shut the door and leaned back against it, her hands clenched into fists and pressed into the small of her back. She stared at him, not realizing she was staring, as she tried to tell herself that there was nothing to worry about.

Unnerved by her scrutiny, Dillon felt his mood darken.

"What are you upset about?" she asked calmly. Dillon sat up and Shelly saw awful things in his eyes: worry, guilt, fear. She tried to hold on to the feeling of security she had in her love for him, but it was rapidly slipping away. "Is it Annette? Did I get the name right?"

He was silent—a silence deadly and confirming.

Shelly started to tremble. "God, I let you... I loved you... I..." Her hoarse voice died and she stared at him, horrified. She felt she was looking down a long tunnel at him, seeing nothing but blackness on either side, and Dillon looking away from her. She turned to open the door.

Dillon shot off the bed and slammed the door shut when she had opened it a couple of inches. His hands flattened against the door on either side of her head and he looked down at her. He was as close to touching her back as he could get without contact.

"I'm sorry." His voice was harsh, self-condemning. She shook her head. "Shelly, it doesn't have to change anything." He pressed against her bottom as if the feel of him would comfort her.

She flinched. "Get away from me!"

"I don't love Annette. She doesn't matter!"

A bitter, vile taste sprang into Shelly's mouth at the sound of the other woman's name on his lips. She could not breathe and was going to suffocate if she didn't get out of this room and away from him.

"I want you to come back to San Francisco with me. I won't be in New York long. I... You're important to me. I don't want—"

Shelly did not hear any more. She slapped her palms over her ears and refused to look at him when he spun her around to face him. Her temples pounded and nausea crept up her throat. "Let me go, let me go..." she chanted over and over. She saw black spots in her vision and she strained away from him.

"I won't marry her!" Dillon yelled, shaking her, his body sweating scared.

"*Let me go!*" Shelly screamed.

Shocked, Dillon stared at the pale, shaking woman in front of him. He removed his hands from her shoulders and held them up, then stepped away from her while she watched him with such hate in her eyes that he felt ugly. It took all his control to just stand there and watch her wrench the door open and flee when he felt like killing her for leaving. When he was alone, he wanted to kill himself.

Adam came to her cabin later that day to give his sincere apologies for the way things had worked out with Dillon. "I'd hoped he'd come to his senses and drop this plan to marry Annette and marry you instead."

"So, you planned this little matchmaking. That's why you arranged for my passage on his ship."

"Yes, and I did want to make sure you got to New York safely."

"Why didn't you warn me about him?" Her tone was furious.

"I had hoped I wouldn't have to. And I'm surprised I did." He looked down at her where she sat stiff and straight on her bunk.

"How long have you known that we were . . . involved?"

"I've always noticed the interest you two have held for each other," he answered, not wanting her to know that he had heard through the walls, as well.

"This is all humiliating and maddening and I'll never forgive either of you!"

"Shelly, I truly meant no harm. I thought your love would change his mind about a lot of things."

Shelly burst into tears. "He didn't want my love!"

Adam knelt before her. "Oh, but he does! He just doesn't know what to do with it, how to honor it."

She buried her face in her hands. "Go away."

"Not until you promise me you're going to stay with me in New York until we find your family."

"No!" He sat down on her trunk. "I'm never leaving this cabin," she added.

"Me, either."

Shelly groaned. "All right, but go now." He did and she wept. She wasted an entire day and night crying. Her last day on the ship, when the tears were spent, she thought of ways to kill Dillon if he ever came near her again. It felt good to hate him.

Adam studied Shelly in the afternoon light inside the carriage. He hadn't seen her again on ship after he got her promise to come stay with him. She'd taken all meals alone in her room. Now she sat pale and quiet across from him, watching the busyness of the streets outside the window.

"We're almost there," he announced quietly. Shelly turned to him and smiled absently. "I want you to rest at my home for a few days before you start worrying about finding your family."

"Funny, a ten-week ship's passage seemed like rest enough to me."

Silence grew between them as the carriage rolled up Broadway toward Adam's Fifth Avenue house. Shelly stared out her window at the tall buildings lining the street filled with crowds of people, horses and carriages. It didn't look safe to walk. They turned off Broadway and made their way to Fifth Avenue. The street grew quieter and less crowded block by block.

"I mean it, Shelly. I want you to get your bearings before you meet your family."

"I don't know if I can wait." She wanted to find her relations and put this sordid mess behind her.

"I'll help you find them. I'll get someone on it."

"Thank you, Adam." She tilted her head to one side. "Why are you trying to take care of me?"

Adam thought it was obvious. He'd botched things for her pretty well with Dillon, but he wasn't going to bring that name up. "I make a habit of taking in penniless orphans. It gives me a sense of accomplishment."

The corners of Shelly's mouth twitched and she chuckled softly. "And here I was thinking I was doing you a favor by keeping an old man company."

"Old man!" he roared.

Shelly's chuckle bubbled into laughter.

Chapter Nineteen

A week flew by at Adam's house. Adam treated her like the daughter he'd never had, and Shelly looked on him as the father she could not remember. She felt terribly pampered, yet she knew she gave Adam pleasure. He dragged her daily from one shop to another, buying her a parasol, hair ribbons, a pair of kid gloves, a hat or a dress. He took her to elegant restaurants for lunch and supper. At night there was the ballet, the opera, the theater.

"What about my family?" she cried once as he rushed her out of the house.

"I have someone locating them," he answered, shutting the door behind them.

If this was what he called "rest," Shelly feared what he considered being social. He left her little time to dwell on Dillon, and Shelly knew that was his intent. Their second day in New York, Adam's friends had begun to descend on them. He introduced Shelly as a cousin, and although there were wagging tongues about that claim, his friends accepted her.

One young friend of Adam's more than accepted Shelly; he was undeniably interested in her, and he had Adam's approval. Peter Benson was tall, blue-eyed and blond. His family owned a factory, was wealthy, and, Adam assured Shelly, Peter was single and very much a gentleman. Adam had introduced them at the ballet their second night in New York. Peter was captivated by Shelly in her pink tulle dress and had managed to get himself included in their plans every

evening since. Shelly found him sitting next to her at every
dinner and was amused by his persistence. She thought him
charming with his easy smile and engaging conversation.
She appreciated his solicitousness when he brought her re-
freshments or found her a chair, but her heart never tripped
over itself.

Alone in her room every night, after Belle, the maid
Adam had hired for her, retired to her own chamber, Shelly
lay in darkness, overwhelmed with memories of Dillon. If
she'd known he had a woman waiting for him she would
have summoned the extra strength necessary to resist him.
He'd had no right to her attentions when he could give her
no future, but that was the way of the world. Men took
without scruples and women were left to suffer the consequences.

She stared at the canopy above her head. In the darkness
it looked indigo blue, but when the morning sun rose, the
fabric turned a misty blue, like Peter's eyes. He would never
have treated her so heartlessly. He was so considerate that
she took him for granted. Whereas Dillon made her so angry. She remembered the way his eyes glowed with a disturbing light whenever he felt strongly about something. His
brusque manner made his kinder moments more exciting.
Shelly smashed her pillow over her face to quell the thoughts
of Dillon.

She was staying in Adam's beautiful home. The bedroom she had was the paradise of a princess with its huge
bed, oriental carpet, writing desk, vanity and wardrobe. She
had her own lady's maid to fuss over her hair and clothes.
Adam wanted her to stay as long as possible, even after she
met her family. She suspected he was lonely in this big
house, in spite of his social life, which was too much for
Shelly. The past couple of days she'd been remembering the
quiet of drifting fog through tall pine trees. She'd sent Belle
away more often than not so she could do her own hair and
put on her own clothes, though the ones Adam had bought
her were harder to put on by herself.

Shelly could make some decisions about her future on the
morrow, for her relatives, the Exeters, had been located. She

curled her toes in nervous excitement. It was hard to believe the moment was almost upon her after waiting so long. She fell to sleep imagining a house filled with warmth and lovely, loving people.

Shelly had insisted she go alone to her aunts' apartment, so Adam climbed out of the carriage at a friend's office. In her lap she held a gift of chocolates she had purchased, Adam's idea. The carriage stopped in front of a brownstone. Adam's coachman helped Shelly out and told her he would wait. She looked up at the front of the building in trepidation and took one of the longest walks of her life up the stairs to apartment G. She carried the chocolates in her gloved hands like a shield in front of her.

Before the door she raised her hand to knock and then lowered it. She was dismayed by how clammy and afraid she felt. She pressed her lips together and knocked firmly. Voices tittered behind the door before a small voice asked who was there.

"It's Michelle Young."

"It's a Michelle Young. I don't know her, do you?"

"No, you don't know me," Shelly cried through the door. "I'm Sarah's daughter from California."

"Sarah's daughter?" the voice gasped.

"Sarah's?" echoed a shriller voice.

The locks on the door rattled as they were unlatched and the door opened a crack. A plump face peered out at Shelly. The woman looked her up and down and then opened the door farther. "Sarah's daughter?" she whispered in an awestruck voice.

"Let her in, Sylvie," screeched an old woman from where she sat in a rocking chair.

"Sylvie? You must be my Aunt Sylvia." Shelly smiled.

The woman smiled back tentatively. There was little resemblance between Sarah and her sister. Sylvia's eyes were a bright brown instead of blue and she was a graying brunette rather than a blonde. Whereas Sarah had been very thin, her sister was plump.

"My, my, we didn't know Sarah had a child, did we, Aunt Becky?"

"Come here, girl!" ordered the old woman from the chair.

Shelly approached nervously. She hadn't been prepared for how old they were. She had pictured Sylvia the way her mother had described her when she'd last seen her, but that was almost nineteen years ago. And her mother's aunt looked ancient. Her face was heavily wrinkled and her lips had thinned, pulling into her largely toothless mouth. Her drab brown dress hung on her and she wore a white cap with weary gray ringlets of hair framing each cheek. Her eyes were a vivid blue, jumping lively in her face as they made their own inspection of Shelly. "Sarah never wrote of any children or marriage. She never wrote at all, for that matter."

"Mama couldn't write well," explained Shelly uncomfortably.

"So, where is Sarah?" demanded the old crone. "Is she dead?"

Shelly winced. "Yes, she died a few months ago."

"Where is your father, dear?" asked Sylvia.

"He died many years ago."

"I'm sorry. Sarah mentioned us, did she?"

"Oh, yes."

"Then you know there was little love lost when she left," Becky said.

"Aunt Becky, the poor girl did not come all this way to hear that about her mother!"

"It's the truth!" Becky struck the floor with her cane.

"Please sit down, Michelle." Sylvia pointed to a chair with badly frayed upholstery. "Whom did Sarah marry?" she asked, sitting in a chair next to Shelly. "I never married, but that was all Sarah thought on. She was a dreamer, my sister. She could—"

"Will you be quiet and let the girl answer! Whom did she marry?"

"She married Captain James Young."

"A captain, was he?"

"Yes, ma'am," replied Shelly, acutely uncomfortable with this less than ideal reception. "Don't you remember?" Her voice wavered in the room.

"The last thing she told us was that she had accepted a position as a lady's maid for a sea captain's wife," explained Sylvia. "We never heard from her after she sailed away."

Shelly pulled the pearl-and-diamond ring out of her pouch. "Here is her engagement ring." Shelly handed it to Sylvia. "She said she showed it to you both and that you didn't want her to marry my father because he was a rogue, and that when she left you were both angry with her. Surely you've forgiven her by now?"

"Never saw it," announced Becky.

"I'm afraid I haven't, either." Sylvia handed the ring back to Shelly. "Sarah had a habit of making things up, just harmless stories, but we could never completely trust her. She was a sweet girl, though."

"Ungrateful and lazy would be more like it!" snorted Becky.

"My mother was neither lazy nor ungrateful, and I can't explain why you don't remember her ring." Shelly's face was hot as she glared at Becky.

"My, my," the old lady crooned, "she doesn't look a thing like the Exeters, but she sure sounds like Sarah in one of her tiffs."

"Would you like a cup of tea, my dear?" asked Sylvia.

Shelly swallowed, but the lump in her throat remained. "Yes, that would be nice," she answered softly. There was silence in the room while Sylvia set up the teapot and cups and Becky glowered at Shelly.

Shelly had taken her first sip of tea when Becky smiled at her, the gleam in her eyes unsettling. "Do you remember your father?"

Shelly stared at her. She wanted to lie, but there was nothing except a blinding void when she tried to conjure up his face. "No."

Sylvia held her cup rigidly as she watched Becky.

"How can you be sure that your mother *really* married?"

"Because she told me she did," Shelly answered with quiet dignity, "and I have the ring he gave her." She held it up as if it were the final proof.

"She could have stolen that!" declared Becky with a dismissive flap of her thin hand.

Shelly gasped. Sylvia laid her hand on Shelly's stiff arm. "Michelle, dear, I can't excuse Aunt Becky's harsh words, but we were familiar with Sarah's behavior. It's possible that she never married and simply left for California to hide that deplorable fact. It's not uncommon for a woman to claim to be a widow in a new community and live well."

"You believe that is what she did, don't you?" demanded Shelly, shocked. "You think she lied to me!" Sylvia squirmed uncomfortably while Becky nodded. "Why?"

Sylvia spoke softly. "We never saw the ring, she never told us of an engagement or even that she was seeing someone. As I said before, she was a dreamer."

"You mean liar," whispered Shelly.

Sylvia set her cup and saucer down. "You say my sister died recently, but to us it's as if she died long ago. For so many years to pass and to hear nothing of a person, well, you just remember them as they were. Maybe Sarah did marry, but that is not as important as the fact that you came all this way to see us. It's delightful to find out I have such a pretty niece! Our family is so small now. How old are you, Michelle?"

Shelly was grateful for an easy question. "I'll be nineteen on February ninth." She glanced down at her lap, lost for words. The blue ribbon of the box of chocolates curled by her dress. "I brought some chocolates!" She handed them to Sylvia.

"Oh, Aunt Becky, look at these," she gushed, stripping the bow off the box and opening it. The two women helped themselves to several pieces of candy.

"Where are you staying?" asked Becky between mouthfuls.

Shelly explained, very carefully, that she was staying with a gentleman she had met in San Francisco. "He is very much older than me and treats me like a daughter."

The two women looked at her appraisingly. "Well, a girlie with the looks you have could surely have him for more than a father," Becky said slyly.

"Aunt Becky!" Sylvia choked.

"Let me finish! But I believe you," she stated grandly. "You have a certain dignity about you."

"Thank you." Shelly had to smile.

Becky curtailed her rudeness and told Shelly that they took in sewing and her fingers were still nimble enough and her eyes strong enough for the tedious work. The trouble, she informed Shelly, was the stairs of the building. In spite of this happy chatter, the information about her mother hung like a waiting noose in Shelly's mind. Her aunts were sincere, and if they were not wrong, her mother *was* a liar.

"What about your brother, Ben, Aunt Sylvia? My uncle?"

"Ben? That fool is very much around! Would you like to see him, too?"

"Yes, very much."

"How long are you going to be in New York?"

That depended on them. "I don't know for sure. It should be a while."

"Aunt Becky, let's have Ben over for dinner!" Becky nodded her head. "How about this Thursday?"

"Could I come and visit you both before that?" asked Shelly.

"What do you want to sit around with two old women for?" asked Becky sharply.

Shelly smiled. "You're not just two old women, you're my aunts, and I've come a long way to sit and talk with you."

Sylvia's chuckle sounded like a pleased purr, while Becky looked flustered.

Shelly weighed the ring in her hand on her way to pick up Adam. *Was there a James Young?*

Adam immediately noticed the strain at the corners of Shelly's eyes and the paleness of her face. "How did it go?" he asked, after stepping into the carriage.

"Fine. They were older than I expected, but very nice."

"Did they receive you well?"

"They were surprised, of course, but delighted."

He watched her carefully. "Shelly, do you feel all right?"

"Yes, why?" Her eyes met his.

"You look peaked, a little pale."

"I am tired. I've been looking forward to this day for so long and now I'm drained." She had no desire to tell him of the darker aspects bothering her. She didn't want him feeling any more responsible for her than he already did. He didn't ask her any more questions and in the silence she thought of her mother. Could she have met a sailor while working as a lady's maid for the captain's wife? Maybe there had been more than one man and she would never know who had fathered her.

Waiting in the parlor at Adam's house was Peter. If it had been anyone else Shelly would have excused herself, but Peter was easy to be with. He sat next to her and Adam poured them sherry. Shelly banished her troubled thoughts and enjoyed the late, golden afternoon. Adam shuffled through the messages that had collected while they were out.

"That looks like an invitation to Maxine Obercamp's ball," observed Peter. Adam cocked an eyebrow at him. "I received mine today," he quickly explained. "You are going, aren't you?"

Shelly sighed. "A ball?" She couldn't keep the weariness out of her voice.

"Maxine is famous for her parties. We'll go if you want," Adam said.

Shelly smiled at Peter. "How about a stroll in the park instead?" Peter looked sublimely disappointed. Shelly hid her grin in her glass of sherry. "Maybe a game of cards?" she suggested cheerfully, but that didn't clear his frown. After Peter left, Shelly pleaded tiredness and they ate supper at home for the first time that week. Later, she joined Adam in his study, where he read a newspaper. She selected a chair near the fire, opened her sketchbook and began drawing her Aunt Becky.

She finished her drawing of the cranky woman and lolled back her head. Above the mantel hung a portrait Shelly had admired before. She gazed at the slight, redheaded woman with bright green eyes. She looked very much like Adam. Her hair was curled elegantly on her head, exposing tiny ears and a slim, white neck. Her gown was corn yellow and trimmed with blond lace. "Who is that woman?" she asked.

"My sister," Adam answered tensely, without looking up.

"She's beautiful." Shelly slipped her sketchbook down into the side of the chair and stood up, moving about the room. Wherever she stood the green eyes gazed at her. Usually, Shelly found this to be an unnerving occurrence in portraits, but these eyes were so gentle, even twinkling with a soft amusement. "Where does she live?"

There was silence behind her. Shelly turned and saw Adam looking at the portrait with a great sadness in his eyes that warned Shelly before she heard his words.

"She's dead." He looked back down at his paper.

She wanted to ask how she had died, but Adam's bent head did not encourage conversation. In a whispered question she asked the woman's name.

"Marianna."

Shelly sat back in the chair and looked up at the woman who crowned the room.

Chapter Twenty

Around the dinner table at the Ryder household in Tarrytown that same night sat Dillon, his father and stepmother and Annette King and her father, Edward. Annette sat across from Dillon and often stretched her leg out so she could touch Dillon's leg with her foot. At those secret caresses Dillon looked across at her and smiled so distractedly that Annette wanted to kick him, which she did. Dillon made no sign that he felt it.

He compared her to Shelly. Annette's hair and eyes were as dark as his own and people often remarked that they looked more like siblings than a couple betrothed. Her lips were her most expressive feature, changing quickly from a pleading pout to a cajoling smile to a thin, displeased line. She was taller, slighter and smaller breasted than Shelly. She was poised and sophisticated, very social and horribly spoiled, sometimes mean and petty and often fun and charming. And she didn't do a thing to his pulse rate.

This was the third evening that the Kings had come for dinner since Dillon had come home. Unlike the Ryders, who lived north of the city, the Kings had a large home on Fifth Avenue near Adam Jefferies. Often the visits to the Ryder house included sleeping over, since they visited until late. Tonight was no exception.

"We went to Tillie's ball Friday night, Dillon. You should have come. Everyone was there." Annette pushed her food around with her silver fork and looked up at him.

"He's been a recluse ever since he arrived home," muttered his father, sitting at the head of the table, an older, more lined replica of Dillon.

"It must be the California sun," Annette said. She could pick on Dillon, but if anyone else criticized him she flew to his defense. "I've heard it makes men crazy."

"That's ridiculous," John Ryder said. "Dillon has always been crazy."

Jane Ryder smiled at her husband, her soft blue eyes adoring.

"I don't enjoy your parties, Annette," Dillon said, ignoring his father. "Wearing tight clothes and getting dizzy and sweaty trying to dance in a crowded room is, at the very least, boring."

"It wouldn't be if you spoke to someone."

"And have to listen to their vicious gossip?"

"Talk about California! Everyone wants to know about the place and it's all you have on your mind, anyway."

"If I wanted to stand around and discuss the place I never would have gotten there!"

"We're all very proud of your adventures, Dillon," his stepmother chimed in, "but it would be so nice if you picked up your life back here. This is where your responsibilities and future lie."

Dillon rolled his eyes.

"So, have you two set a date yet?" asked Edward King. He was a kind, overweight man, ruled by his hardheaded daughter and more than he knew by his clever friend. He and his wife, Abigail, dead nineteen years now, had been close friends with the Ryders. It had long been the desire of the two fathers to meld King's shipbuilding business with Ryder's shipping business. Their wives had seen romantic possibilities when nine-year-old Dillon had reluctantly taken two-year-old Annette for a ride in front of him on his pony. By the time Annette was seven she told everyone that she was going to be Mrs. Dillon Ryder. Dillon had accepted his fate. Annette was not a bad sort; she seldom cried and she was braver than most girls. Besides, marriage was something far away, and he never thought about it—until recently, when no one seemed to leave him alone about it.

"It would be nice if you picked a month, or even a year!" added his father.

Dillon looked around the table, all eyes focused on him in various degrees of expectancy. He pushed his plate away from him, the tender roast beef suddenly unappetizing. "I'll be returning to California soon."

John Ryder stared furiously down the table at Dillon. Annette leaned forward. "That will be perfect," she said. "We can have a winter wedding and I'll go back with you as your new bride."

"I don't think you'd like it there much, Annette."

"That hardly matters if my husband is going to be living there. I'll have to get used to it. Maybe you've avoided the best of society up until now, but that will change when I get there. I'm sure there are some decent, well-educated people there besides miners, gamblers and women of dubious reputations."

"I won't be here long enough for a wedding," Dillon said.

Annette opened her mouth and then snapped it shut. The color was high in her cheeks as she busied herself with her wineglass.

"So, you won't grace this house with your presence for long, will you?" his father demanded.

"No."

"I suppose you have to get back to your precious mine?"

"That's about it," Dillon answered lightly.

"And what about the business here? The merger? The contract? You've a long way to go before you fulfill the obligations of the contract. Maybe I should cut you off from Ryder Shipping, let you starve yourself digging in the dirt in that mine of yours."

Dillon crumpled the napkin in his lap. "You could do that."

John Ryder leaned forward, almost knocking his wineglass over, and opened his mouth to speak. Jane stood up. "Annette, let's go into the drawing room while the gentlemen discuss business."

Annette glanced at her hostess, reluctantly taking her eyes off Dillon's face. The ladies left, the men stood, and Edward coughed. "Feeling a bit too full. I believe I'll take a walk around the grounds."

Alone, father and son slowly turned to face each other again. John Ryder sat and Dillon followed.

"I don't need your mighty capital, Father. I don't need your ships or your advice or your connections. There are shipyards in San Francisco, there's money in my account and brains in my head."

His father pushed his plate out of the way. "Yes, but you want what I have. That's why you put your name on the contract. You want the mighty empire on both coasts. And you know damn well how little you know about the business. And that mine of yours could run out any day. You can't count on it."

"Don't believe everything Oscar told you," Dillon said softly. "He did betray you."

John Ryder waved his hand. "He just got carried away, thought he could bleed you and still work for me."

Dillon threw his napkin on the table. "Just like you to defend him even though he tried to kill me." His father had been shocked when Dillon had told him he'd killed Oscar in San Francisco and that the man had been stealing from him. Dillon had been offended to learn his father had sent Oscar to check up on him, make sure he was working the shipping business and not just "playing in his mine."

"Don't get waspish, Dillon. It doesn't become a man. Oscar got greedy, happens to the best of us. Twenty years I had him at my side. I'll never be able to replace him."

Dillon pushed his chair back. "I'm sorry I didn't bring his body back so you could cry over it."

He left the dining room, passed the drawing room and escaped outside. He walked the grounds of the house his father had built for Jane when they'd married five years ago. He didn't know why they'd built one so large unless it was for all the grandchildren they expected him and Annette to produce. He walked until the stiffness in his body began to fade. Rage was a common feeling when he was in the same room with his father. He strode up the hill to the gazebo and sat on the railing and looked out over the Hudson River flowing blackly in the night. He remembered vividly the pale blue eyes of Oscar as the man stabbed him. His father's lackey had always been mysterious to Dillon and a little frightening. He couldn't understand a mind that could work for the father and steal from the son, try to kill the son. But it had been so long since Dillon had felt like a son. He felt like another employee, a very disappointing one. He knew he wouldn't uphold the contract. He had agreed to marry Annette, whereupon King Shipbuilding and Ryder Shipping would merge. Dillon would manage Ryder and King Associates in the West, have unlimited access to funds to expand, though his father would have all controlling interest until his death. King agreed to the merger only if the marriage took place. Dillon had once liked the power and money that he had seen in his future. That was before Diego had heard of Virginia City. That was before he'd met Shelly. Now he really didn't care for Ryder Shipping except as a responsibility he had promised to undertake. When the cool October night had chilled him he returned to the house, pulling off his coat and unbuttoning his shirt on the way up the stairs. He kicked his bedroom door closed behind him and lighted the lamp on his wardrobe.

"Annette!" Dillon gasped when he saw her sitting calmly in the chair by his bed.

"Dillon."

"What are you doing here?"

"I'm sitting in a chair in my fiancé's room waiting for him. Where were you?"

"Out walking." He smiled. Annette often amused him. He stretched out on his bed, his hand idly rubbing his chest. There was a companionable silence between them for a moment.

"Dillon?"

"Hmm?"

"I don't care what you did in California, but here in New York you're mine." She slipped off her black slippers and rested her feet on the bed near his thighs. "I don't want anyone thinking I can't keep you interested."

Dillon looked at her curiously. Annette had never before sounded unsure of herself. He realized he'd never actually proposed to her. Nine years ago when he'd returned to New York after a long absence, he'd signed the contract. He'd bought her the engagement ring she'd picked out. He'd had to pay his father back for it. Looking at it now he figured she was tired of waiting. He wondered how upset she'd be when he told her he wasn't ever going to marry her. She snared his attention back to the present by reaching behind her and unfastening the hooks of her gown. "Annette!"

"We're going to be married, and if anyone catches us they'll make you marry me now."

"They're not going to catch us, because I'm not going to make love to you. Stop it!" he ordered as he saw the gown begin to gape at her breasts.

He sat up. "Annette, I don't love you," he stated bluntly.

She winced. She'd known that when he took her virginity more than two years ago, but she had teased him, gotten him alone, and they'd done it. The second time had hurt almost as much as the first, and she'd been unable to hide her disgust. "I love you," she said matter-of-factly. "You'll grow to love me."

He gently clasped her stockinged feet. "Annette, I like you, but I can't—"

"Annette! What are you doing in there?" Jane Ryder's voice was very perturbed on the other side of the door.

Dillon's jaw clenched and Annette sighed, bounced off the bed and opened the door. Jane was a tall figure in the doorway.

"Spying, Stepmother?"

"I clearly heard her voice from the hall."

"I bet."

"Don't worry, Jane, I tried to seduce my beloved fiancé, but he wants to wait until the wedding," Annette said flippantly. "Stodgy, isn't he?"

Dillon chuckled and Jane frowned.

"Go to your own room now." Her voice was kind but firm. Annette retrieved her shoes and slipped them on. "And, Dillon?"

"What?" he snapped, all amusement gone from his face as he turned toward his stepmother. He'd been cold to her since he'd met her, and watched her very carefully. She was like Cora and his mother, adoring his father and always agreeing with him.

"I just want to tell you, if Annette hasn't already, that Maxine Obercamp's ball is next Friday night. I thought you might like to attend."

"You were wrong."

"Oh, Dillon," cried Annette, now standing by the door with Jane. "You haven't attended a single party since you've come back. People are feeling sorry for me."

He scowled as he saw her eyes actually fill with tears. "Is there anything more important to you than a damn dance?"

"Yes, and you know what it is."

He shook his head. "Damn!" He picked the lesser of two evils. "All right," he said resignedly.

Before Jane could stop her, Annette ran across the room and bent down and gave him a hug. "Thank you!"

"You're welcome. Now get out of here." Annette sashayed out, holding up her loose gown, quite pleased with the end of the evening, at least.

Jane stayed in the doorway. "I thank you, too, Dillon. I'm sure this will make your father happy, also."

"I sure as hell am not going for your sake or his, so don't thank me!"

Jane sighed and shut his door.

Dillon pulled a bottle of brandy out of his cabinet and poured himself a drink. "Lord," he muttered. He sat in the chair Annette had occupied and propped his legs on the bed. When was he going to tell her she wasn't going to be Mrs. Ryder? There used to be good reasons for marrying her. Besides the merger, he used to consider his lack of love for Annette to be an advantage. He felt he could control her, and he could especially control himself. The marriage would have been comfortable, unconfining, hardly like a marriage at all. He didn't want for better or worse, because he might get stuck with worse. He didn't want to worry about trusting someone with forever and ever stretching out before them.

He just wanted to get back to California, work his mine, build the house south of San Francisco that Diego had the plans for and was supposed to start, and visit Shelly in warm lodgings whenever the mood struck him. He tossed back his brandy. If she truly loved him he could make her soften. He'd see her before he left.

Chapter Twenty-One

Shelly knocked on the door of her aunts' apartment for her third visit. Her uncle opened the door. Shelly knew because he looked like her mother, except he was plump, and his graying blond hair was thinning on the top of his head. She just stood there, staring, smiling, with tears in her eyes. The rosy-cheeked man smiled and held out his arms to her. Shelly walked into his embrace with an ease that surprised her.

"My, my, what big gray eyes you have," he teased, pulling away from her to get a better look, keeping his hands on her shoulders. "So, you are Michelle?" Shelly nodded, happier than she had been in a while. This had been her mother's favorite member of the family and Shelly could see why; everything about him was jolly.

"Well, it looks like you two don't need any introducin'," chortled Becky.

"Isn't this nice?" cried Sylvia, clapping her white hands together.

After a simple and filling dinner they went into the sitting room, crowded with knickknacks and odds and ends of furniture that the elder aunt and her niece had salvaged from their lives. Her three relatives told stories about a past Shelly was hungry for.

"Remember the pack of cats Sarah had?" said Ben.

"How could we forget those mangy critters?" Sylvia asked, sipping her tea.

Ben turned to Shelly. "She didn't like letting them sleep in the barn like she was told to," he explained, grinning. "She brought them in at night when Mother and Father were asleep and put all six, eight or ten, however many, in bed with her."

"It was my bed, too," added Sylvia. "No matter how much I complained she brought them in. I even told Mother, but she got tired of fighting Sarah about it."

"Filthy habit," scolded Becky, clucking her tongue.

Sylvia glanced at Shelly's face. "She just needed something to love."

"What was worse," continued Ben, "was when they had kittens and the house was overrun with them. Father threatened to drown them all and Sarah ran away. He said not to go looking for her since all the cats left with her!" Ben laughed and slapped his thigh. "Poor Sarah, never did get along with Pa."

Shelly leaned forward. "She told me how you tortured her with spiders."

"What spiders?" demanded Becky, pounding her cane on the floor.

"I used to find big, harmless spiders and pull their legs off. The legs still wriggled and I'd stick them in Sarah's hair. She liked to wear it down because she thought it was romantic. Anyway, all of them spider legs would be a-twisting in her hair and she'd run around the yard screaming, trying to get away from her own head!" Ben started choking on his words as laughter overtook him. "She looked like this." He stood up with arms outstretched in front of him, mouth gaping and eyes wide in terror, then he fell back to his chair. "She chased herself right into the river."

They told stories until both Becky and Sylvia were unable to hold their heads up. Shelly told Ben about her childhood in Santa Cruz and the animals that Sarah had been devoted to, which Shelly had sold or given away when her mother died. For a little while she was very happy.

Dillon kept looking around the ballroom, hoping he'd see Shelly. Adam always came to Maxine Obercamp's parties, but he hadn't tonight. Dillon drained the punch in his glass and gagged on the sweetness. Annette, laughing gaily, finished a waltz with Peter Benson and walked up to Dillon and tapped him on the shoulder with her fan. She looked regal in dark purple trimmed with black lace and gathered with silver bows.

"Oh, the things Peter's been telling me," she said.

Dillon shook hands with the man he'd known casually most of his life.

"Such a pretty girl he thinks this Shelly is who came to New York with you," continued Annette.

Dillon stiffened and looked again at Peter. "You've met her?" he asked quietly.

"Yes. And I'm quite enchanted. She's very refreshing. Though I'm disappointed that she did not want to attend tonight."

"Maybe she's not much for high society," said Annette, looking at Dillon all the while, not missing the tense jaw. "I'll have to call on Adam and meet her, since she's been such a close companion of yours. Imagine, going to Virginia City with you, a place you said is like one large mudhole in spring. How did a young lady manage to live in such a place, in a tent no less? I'm sure she can tell me many interesting things."

"Yes, she's full of stories," agreed Peter brightly. "How does it feel to be back in New York, Dillon? Are you going to stay this time? Everyone's laying bets that you'll marry within the month or murder most foul will be committed."

"Indeed," agreed Annette.

"I'm going to get something to drink." Dillon didn't excuse himself.

"Think you could manage to make yourself a little more enticing to my son?" asked John Ryder, speaking softly next to Annette while smiling down at her. Annette stiffened, a sick smile frozen on her face. Peter had gone to get her some punch. "I'm sure Dillon will want to leave soon. I'll make sure your father stays late. You get that boy of mine into your bed, give him something pleasant to associate with New York. At least get yourself pregnant. He's got a streak of honor running through him that would prevent him turning his back on his own bastard.''

''I'll do my best,'' she whispered.

Annette never got Dillon over the threshold of her house. He sat across from her in the dark carriage, took off his hat and loosened his cravat.

''I never wanted to hurt you.''

Annette looked out the window.

''I can't marry you. I'd make you miserable. I couldn't promise to be faithful. What kind of marriage would that be? We listened too much to our parents, our fathers.''

''I didn't. I wanted to marry you! You've been in my plans for years.''

Dillon looked out the window, too. ''I'm sorry.''

''Here's your ring.'' She slapped the diamond into his palm.

''You're bright, beautiful and rich, Annette. You'll find someone else soon.''

''Please do me a favor? Keep up appearances with me until you leave—for our fathers.''

Dillon cocked his head. ''I should have known they'd be pressuring you, too. By all means, let's keep up appearances.''

Dillon threw the diamond ring off the dock at the harbor. He didn't mind that it had cost a small fortune. He'd throw out ten huge fortunes if that's what it took to disentangle himself from his father's net.

The next morning Annette held Dillon's arm, her ringless hand hidden in gloves as they strolled through Central Park with John and Jane Ryder and another couple, friends of Annette's. Dillon was relieved to see Annette smiling and gay. He'd yet to have a private moment to ask her about her high spirits. His father looked approvingly at them, patted Dillon on the back once after Annette had hugged his arm close. Dillon wanted to laugh.

He was smiling at his new freedom when he looked up and saw silver eyes. He jerked uncontrollably. ''Shelly,'' he whispered.

She was standing about fifteen yards away, with that damned Peter Benson, and she was staring right at him. He pulled away from Annette.

"Dillon, where are you going!" Annette called.

"Dillon!" demanded his father.

Dillon barely recognized her. She was dressed in something frilly and white, and on her head was a little feminine hat, but those eyes that were narrowed on him were unmistakable. She turned and pulled Peter with her.

"Shelly!" called Dillon. He started running and so did she, Peter laughing as if it were a game, never having seen Dillon. "Shelly!" yelled Dillon.

Peter started to turn, but Shelly grabbed his arm. They disappeared in a double line of carriages. Dillon followed and ran after a carriage that was pulling away. He ran down the middle of the street, coming abreast of the vehicle when it stopped in traffic. He yanked open the door and saw an older man and two women. No Shelly. "What are you doing?" demanded the man.

Dillon slammed the door and looked around. Hundreds of carriages. "Damn!"

Shelly burst into the house, pulling out hat pins on her way through the entry, and strode right down to the library, where she'd left Adam for her jaunt in the park.

"Where's Peter?" asked Adam from his favorite chair.

"I sent him home." Shelly pulled off her hat, tossed it onto a chair and poured herself a glass of sherry. She was getting to like the drink.

"What happened?"

"I saw Dillon. With *her*."

"I see."

Shelly drained the glass. "I panicked and ran away like a fool when he started coming toward me. I challenged Peter to a race to the carriage. This city is too small for the both of us. I wish he'd go away."

The knocker on the door sounded. Shelly flinched and Adam sighed. "It's him," Shelly whispered, as if he could hear her through the door. "I do not want to see him!" The knocker was abandoned and a fist started pounding. "He might break the door down. He would." She poured herself another glass of sherry.

Adam patted her forearm as he walked by her. He swung the door open and had to step out of the way to avoid Dillon's fist in the process of pounding again. Dillon straightened and looked at the older man.

"I want to see Shelly."

"Did you run all the way?" Dillon was flushed, his hair mussed, his cravat hanging loose, his top shirt buttons undone and his breath a soft pant.

"Yes. I have to see her."

"I'm sorry, Dillon. She does not want to see you."

Dillon swore softly. He looked past Adam down the empty foyer, back at Adam standing casually, as if he weren't worried that Dillon was going to charge right past him. Dillon thought about it. "I just want to talk to her," he coaxed. Adam's brows soared and he did not move away from the door. "Damn it, Adam, let me in! I could just push you out of the way."

"That would make a very good impression on her," Adam said softly.

Dillon looked sharply at him. Over Adam's shoulder he yelled, "Shelly? I have to talk to you. Shelly, please!"

Silence.

"Maybe you could write her a letter."

"Shelly!" he yelled again. "Shelly!"

"Goodbye, Dillon." Adam closed the door.

"I can't believe he didn't just storm right past you!" Shelly said when Adam rejoined her. "Maybe he's more civilized on this coast. I wonder what he wanted to say."

"I'm sure it was a repeat of what he's said before," Adam remarked, grinning from behind the paper he'd begun reading.

"Yes, like wanting me to be his mistress. So, did he just go away?"

"I don't know. I closed the door in his face."

"I imagine that made him angry."

"I imagine. What would you like for supper, young lady?"

After Adam had retired, Shelly returned to the library. She was exhausted but keyed up with nervous energy. She kept picturing Dillon's intended as she'd seen her in the park, laughing and holding on to the man that Shelly had once loved, once held on to both clothed and naked. Her feelings didn't die the way they were supposed to. When she'd first seen him looking so handsome in the sunshine she'd felt her heart leap. She pulled her chair closer to the dying fire, which was leaving the room in darkening shadows. Above the hearth the portrait of Adam's sister, Marianna, was just as beautiful in this light—so unearthly.

Shelly stood up close beneath the painting. She slowly raised her hand and lightly touched the fingers holding the white rose on the lap of the painted woman. The bumpy texture of dried oil paint startled her more than if she had felt the warm skin of a living woman. She drew away and cocked her head, puzzled over her response.

She undressed in her beautiful room and felt lonely. Adam was content to have her stay here forever, taking her shopping, to supper and to parties. Shelly missed working hard, missed falling into bed tired in mind and body. Buttoning up her nightgown, she frowned at the big bed. In San Francisco she'd imagined moving in with her relatives and working among them as a member of the family. She didn't want to move into her aunts' tiny, cluttered apartment and take in sewing with them, or work as a domestic or in a factory and come home to them each evening. She didn't have a plan anymore.

She tossed restlessly for hours. She got up once to draw Annette King's face in an effort to dispel the woman's image from her mind. Memories of San Francisco and Santa Cruz played through her head. She wondered how Aggie was doing with her pregnancy. She remembered her mother graciously eating the first apple pie Shelly had baked, the one with too much salt in the crust. She remembered rain, dripping from tall pine trees and cold on her nose; the soft carpet of pine needles outside her cabin; the lights of

Grady's cabin through the trees if there was no fog; Grady's body outside her door.

Dawn was bursting in the sky when Shelly jerked awake, dripping with perspiration, her head full of mad dreams. Grady had been pounding on the cabin door while Sarah rocked insanely in her chair, prattling on and on about James Young, the fine and handsome man, the kind father. Shakily, she got out of bed, glanced at the drawing she'd done of Annette King. Lord, she'd made the woman look like a witch with that black hair and toothy smile. She slipped on her dressing gown and went downstairs. Maybe breakfast and coffee would straighten her out.

Chapter Twenty-Two

Dillon did not return home until the second evening after the day he'd seen Shelly in the park. His family was almost finished eating dinner when he took his seat, offering no excuse for his absence. He ignored his stepmother's inquiring eyes and his father's scowl. He piled his plate high with chicken; just thinking about the journey ahead made him ravenous. "I'm leaving for California tonight," he said casually, stuffing a forkful of chicken into his mouth.

"You're what?" exploded his father.

"Tonight?" cried Jane.

Dillon downed the glass of wine by his plate, then dug back into his food.

"What about the building of that new ship? You were going to look over the plans with Edward!" His father's voice was a barely controlled growl.

"I did that this afternoon."

John Ryder threw his fork down on the table. The silver utensil clattered and slid near Dillon's plate. "What about the wedding?"

"There won't be one."

"Dillon," protested Jane, "this is hardly fair to Annette. You know how she—"

"It's none of your damn business!"

John Ryder's fist hit the table, rattling all the china and slopping wine over the edge of the glasses. "Don't talk to my wife like that!"

"John, it's all right," murmured Jane, looking in alarm at her husband's purple face.

Dillon remembered all the times Cora had soothed fights between father and son at the table, only to breed them again when she had each man separately.

"It's none of your business," Dillon heard himself sneering again.

John Ryder stood. "Shut your mouth!"

Dillon stood. "Make me." His father took a step toward him. "I'm full grown now. You're past your prime. The fight will be more interesting." He heard Jane gasp.

"If you leave this house, you will get nothing. I will cut you off. You can say goodbye to Ryder Shipping."

"Goodbye."

Dillon took the stairs two at a time to his room. He threw some clothes and a comb into his saddlebags and pulled on his coat, then he left without saying a word.

St. Joe, Missouri, where he would catch the Overland Stage, was a long, cold ride away. He bypassed the inns where he could have stayed and made camp off the road. He sat by his fire and chewed on a stick. The hard ride and the cold air had cleared the temper out of his mind. He'd be back in San Francisco in a month, since he was taking the Overland Mail Express. He'd write Shelly, let her know he wasn't marrying Annette, let her know he'd be in California and if she came back... He'd stopped by Annette's earlier in the day and found out why she'd been so happy the day before. She'd told her father she wasn't going to marry and he was taking her to Europe, where she had always wanted to go. Keeping up appearances must have been solely for the benefit of his own father. Dillon tossed his stick into the fire and went to sleep listening to the crackle of burning wood.

Shelly looked out the drawing room window and sighed. The sun was shining on the naked trees, the colorful leaves having fallen. The wide sidewalks of Fifth Avenue were as she had pictured back in San Francisco. That seemed a long time ago. She leaned her forehead against the cool window glass and watched some of the most fashionable women in the city walk by. Garbed in the clothes Adam had bought her, she fitted in with these women, yet she felt like an impostor.

In the past few weeks since Dillon had pounded on Adam's door, she'd been depressed, an unusual mood for her. When she used to feel blue she'd draw, but there was no one she wanted to draw anymore. There were not enough trees to sit still under and watch the wildlife. Adam didn't have a garden for her to work in and watch things grow.

She turned from the window and sat in a chair to contemplate her latest problem. Yesterday, Aunt Sylvia mentioned that Sarah had left New York in the year 1843. If so, Shelly wondered how her aunts and uncle had not known of her, since she would have been a year old. She'd come to accept the fact that she might be a bastard. Her relatives were people too sincere to doubt, as much as it did hurt and bewilder her that Sarah had brought her up with a lie. But this new twist in the story of her past confused her. Unless Sarah had somehow, over the years, mixed up Shelly's birthdate and she was a year younger, but that was farfetched. She didn't feel a day younger than her eighteen years and nine months.

The likely explanation was that Aunt Sylvia had miscalculated the date as to when Sarah left New York. She'd clear it up today when Uncle Ben came to take her for a ride in Central Park. She ran to the door at the first knock and flung it open.

"Ready?" Ben asked.

"Yes!" She swept up her cloak and threw it over the shoulders of her long-sleeved gold dress and followed him down the front steps to the buggy at the curb.

"How do you like this rig I rented for the day?"

"Very nice." He helped her in and then hopped up beside her. They took a leisurely clip-clopping ride through the park, talking sporadically and amiably. At the first sight of her uncle, Shelly's head cleared of its wistful longing for California, and she temporarily forgot about the question she needed to ask him; however, the question was uppermost in her mind upon their return for the lunch Shelly had invited him to share with her. She put off asking it like an unpleasant duty. The cool, fresh air had given them both an appetite for the chicken, cheese, bread and cider that Shelly laid out. She watched in amusement as Uncle Ben went for his third piece of her apple pie. When he was swallowing his last bite, Shelly decided to take the plunge.

"Uncle Ben, yesterday Aunt Sylvia said that my mother left New York in 1843, but she really left before that, didn't she? In 1842 or even 1841?" He studiously brushed some crumbs off his shirtfront. "Uncle Ben?"

He looked up at her, his mouth turned down. He sighed and glanced out the window of the glass-enclosed room they sat in. "She didn't leave before that."

"But that's impossible! It would mean that either I am a year younger or my mother had me before she left New York. I don't think my mother confused my age."

"No."

"Is that all you have to say?"

Ben pushed his plate away and threw his napkin on top of it. "Sarah did leave New York in 1843." His voice sounded weary, old. "I know that because she lived with Sylvia and Becky until that time."

"Then why were you all so surprised to learn I existed? Was that some kind of revenge against Sarah that you took out on me? You all knew me until I was a year old!"

Ben shifted in his seat and flicked a crumb across the table with his forefinger. "No, we didn't. Sarah never was with child while she lived with us." He shrugged as if it did not mean anything.

Shelly raised a tight fist to her breast. "But...I don't understand. I'm really trying to, but I don't."

"Maybe Sarah was not your mother." His voice was very soft, the words spoken gently, but Shelly heard each word as if shouted. A minute passed and she stared at him.

"Of course she was. How can you suggest she wasn't?" she whispered hoarsely.

"She raised you. I believe that."

Shelly looked at him incredulously.

"I'm sorry." His voice was gruff. "I didn't want to tell you, and maybe I shouldn't have." She continued to gaze at him, her face pale. "Are you going to be all right?"

She nodded slowly. "Did you know as soon as you met me?"

He winced. "Sylvia and Becky told me. They realized it when you told them how old you were. We didn't know whether to tell you or not. Sarah raised you even if she wasn't your real mother and we like you. We want you to be part of our family."

Shelly managed a thin smile. "Thank you. You've all been very kind. But I think I need to be alone right now."

When she walked him to the door, he stopped and faced her. "You came all the way from California to see us and we found you to be a charming, lovable girl. We weren't kind at all, but maybe we were selfish."

"Is there anything else I don't know? I don't want any more surprises."

"Not that I know of," he answered solemnly.

She nodded and opened the door for him. "No wonder I don't look at all like her." She laughed bitterly. "She always said that I looked like my father. I wonder if she even knew who he was, or who my mother was. I wonder where she found me!"

She plucked at the fringe of her shawl and Ben watched warily, alarmed by the bitter way she was dealing with the shock. Tears he knew how to comfort. "Sarah is dead and we don't know why she lied. There must have been some reason," Ben assured her.

"Not one good enough." She looked at him miserably and then out the door.

He knew she wanted to be alone, but he felt as if he were abandoning her if he left now. "You come by and see Sylvia and Becky in a day or two." She nodded dutifully. Impulsively, he placed his hands on her shoulders and kissed her cheek. "It doesn't matter, Michelle. You feel like family to me."

Shelly watched him climb into his rented buggy before she turned back into the house. She climbed the stairs to her room, her shawl slipping off one shoulder and trailing to the floor behind her. Her hand rested heavily on the banister. She was thankful Adam wasn't home. She couldn't face anyone now. She shut the door to her room behind her, walked shakily to the washstand and regarded her pale face solemnly before splashing cool water on it.

First she was a bastard; now she was connected to no one. Who was Shelly Young, *really?* She went to her dresser and pulled open the bottom drawer, where she kept her money. She scooped up the velvet pouch and dumped the contents on the bed. Out fell coins, some bills and the ring. She held the ring up to the light that streamed in through her windows. "Maybe you're a fake, too," she murmured. "Where on earth did she get you?" She walked back to the dresser with the ring. The crack of the gold band hitting the wood of the bottom drawer was like a slap across her face. She kicked the drawer shut and turned back to the bed and counted her money. There was enough to buy herself a passage back to California. She had to leave this place that had been filled with one disappointment after another.

The gold dress she was wearing was sturdy and practical. She grabbed two more dresses from her wardrobe for the long sea journey back to San Francisco. In minutes she'd gathered what else she needed. She threw her cloak over her arm, picked up her valise and left the room without looking back. She walked down the stairs without even noticing the housekeeper, who passed her on the steps.

"Miss Young?" the older woman called, stopping and turning to look at the descending girl. "Are you leaving?" Shelly reached the bottom of the stairs. "What shall I tell Mr. Jefferies?" Shelly walked out the front door as if in a trance and shut it behind her.

She walked briskly down the sidewalk, her valise banging against her legs. She felt as if she had just awakened. Falling in love with Dillon, living with Adam, meeting her family were all part of a nice dream that had turned into a nightmare.

"Did Miss Young return from her outing with her uncle all right?" Adam asked Claire, his housekeeper, a few minutes after he arrived home.

"She and her uncle had lunch here and then she left a few minutes after he did."

"Oh? Where did she go?"

"I don't know, but she walked out with a valise. I asked if she were leaving, but she didn't seem to hear me."

"She left no note?"

"No, sir."

"She didn't say *anything?*"

"Nothing."

"Something must have happened. She wouldn't just run off. It must have been her uncle! Tell Rogers I want the carriage brought back around immediately!"

Claire hurried out and Adam looked angrily at the clock on the mantel. "Midnight. Well, Ben Exeter will lose some sleep tonight," he muttered to himself. He looked out the window into the darkness. If something happened, why wouldn't she wait for me? he asked himself. He would have held Dillon entirely responsible if he hadn't known the scoundrel had already left town. If that uncle of hers was responsible, then he would soon discover what kind of damage wealth could wreak.

Chapter Twenty-Three

Dillon and Diego crept up the shabby back stairs of Lacy's and eased open the door to the fourth floor. They both had days of trail dust and some honest mud caking their skin and clothes; never would they have been admitted through the front room.

"I don't know if this was such a good idea," muttered Dillon.

"It was this or go straight to the apartment." The latter was unacceptable to Diego. Visions of black-haired, blue-eyed Mary Lou had been haunting him for the length of a long ride. He hadn't seen her delightful face and form for the two and a half months they'd been out of San Francisco. He and Dillon had gone south to oversee the house Dillon was having built in San Mateo. The residence was almost finished. After checking out the construction the two men rode down to Durango, Mexico, where Diego's family lived. They'd spent a couple of weeks lazing in the sun and eating his mother's tortillas, but now Diego and Dillon were back in San Francisco to see about business.

They slunk down the peach-carpeted hallway. Dillon stopped at Virginia's door and Diego continued ahead to Mary Lou's. Dillon glanced behind him and rolled his eyes when he saw the trail of dirt they had left. He looked down at himself. Dried mud clung tenaciously to his boots and even to the trousers tucked into them. A thick layer of dust coated his shirt and he could feel the itch of it everywhere on his skin. In the still air of the hall he smelled something rank. It had to be himself; Diego was too far ahead.

"Just where do you think you boys are going?" demanded a huge voice.

Both men cringed. At the head of the hall stood fat Lizzie, Lacy's mulatto cook.

"Evenin', Lizzie," Diego said good-naturedly. "We just thought we'd pay a little visit." He removed his hat, ignoring the shower of dust that fell from it.

"Is that you, Diego? Where on earth did you get so dirty?"

"Riding."

"What makes you think these girls are gonna accept you into their rooms like that? Besides, Mary Lou ain't feelin' good. I just brought her some soup."

Dillon smiled at the crestfallen expression on his friend's face. Just then the door Diego stood by cracked open and a dark head peered around it.

"Diego?"

"Hi, Mary Lou."

"It's all right, Lizzie," she said to the large, scowling woman, "he can come visit me. Maybe he'll make me feel better. But don't tell Lace."

Diego strutted past the cook.

"I'm sure he can do things my soup can't," she muttered. "Well, Mr. Ryder . . ." Her eyes narrowed on Dillon. She hadn't seen this one near as much as the Mexican, but she never forgot a man in this house. "Might as well go on in and spread the dirt around. I'll go ask Virginia if she wants to handle you as you are." She stomped down the hall and Dillon let himself into the strawberry blonde's room. He'd been in but a few minutes when a small contingent of chambermaids entered carrying buckets of hot water. He watched appreciatively as they filled a brass tub. He had to remember to see Lizzie got thanked properly for this, even though she was only worried about him dirtying the sheets.

Standing, afraid to cake the chairs with dust, he removed his boots. He stretched his feet out and curled his toes under, sighing when they cracked. He dropped his hat on top of his boots and unbuttoned his shirt and trousers. Naked and alone, he slid into the hot water and dunked himself, shaking his head like a sea lion when he popped up. He did not have a razor, so the beard stayed. He made a rich lather with the perfumed soap.

"Well, well, well." Virginia laughed as she stepped into the room.

"Lizzie is more than kind."

"The way I heard it, you were fit for neither woman nor beast."

"True," he admitted, pointing at the pile of his clothes. Virginia daintily picked up her turquoise silk skirts and kicked the pile. The shirt and trousers moved stiffly. She wrinkled her nose. "Maybe you better move them out of the bedroom."

"I don't have a shovel, and if you think I'm going to touch them with my bare hands, you're crazy." Blue-eyed Virginia was the most dignified whore at Lacy's. Dillon always partook of her pleasures when his need became too insistent to ignore. Still, she was a whore and she sat on the bed and watched him step from the bath with frank appraisal; he had an attack of modesty and wrapped the towel around his waist. He'd been five months without a woman and his need had seemed pretty great during those hot Mexican days, but he wasn't going to rise to the occasion. His blood was so tepid it barely moved through his veins. His greatest desire was not the beauty in front of him but getting to his office to see if Shelly had responded to his letter.

"I've got to go." He dropped the towel and pulled on his filthy clothes.

"You just got here!"

"Yeah, I'm sorry. I've had a long ride, and then the hot bath . . . I need to go home and sleep." He glanced at her. A red flush stained her cheeks, but she was too well trained to loose her anger. "I'll pay the full amount, of course."

"Of course. We're not a bathing service."

Dillon pulled on his boots, paid extra, apologized for the dirt and left by the back.

Silver Fury

Later, dressed in clean clothes and shaved, Dillon sat at his office down at the docks. He reluctantly eyed the stack of correspondence piled high on his desk, proof of his long absence. He sighed and took another sip of coffee his employee Lamb had brought him and leaned back in his chair and propped his feet on the desk. He looked about his office with pride and pleasure.

He had moved from the small, cramped, upstairs office in Snelling's building when he returned from New York to take over two larger downstairs offices. Diego and Dillon shared one; the other, Lamb used along with several other men who worked for him.

His business enterprises were flourishing. The Avalon continued to offer up her rich silver ore while the robberies had ceased. Strange, but his father had not made a move against him, so he continued to run Ryder Shipping and make money, any day expecting the business to be taken from him. With success came the tedious responsibility of dealing with a large amount of correspondence that required his personal attention.

He shuffled through the pile and saw an envelope with a New York return address. He reached for it, very curious as to what Adam had to say. Dillon sat up straight when he read that Shelly had left Adam's house. Her aunts were not really her aunts and her mother was not truly her mother. Dillon could imagine how devastated Shelly must have been. She'd thought she was going to some great, glorious family. He laid the letter on his desk and brought his feet to the floor. This meant she'd never received his letter. For months now she'd been thinking of him as engaged still, maybe married. Did she even know he had left New York?

Adam had tracked down the shipping line Shelly had purchased her ticket from. She had returned to California. Dillon guessed she was in the city by now. He knew the first place to look. He walked with a light and hurried step to the Faulding. He was relieved that Shelly had not stayed in New York and sought comfort in Peter Benson's arms. The lovesick look on the younger man's face had made Dillon writhe. He climbed the familiar steps, annoyed to feel his heart pounding, and knocked on the door, expecting it to be thrown open by Shelly herself.

"Mrs. Thornton," Dillon greeted, tipping his hat and hiding his disappointment.

"Mr. Ryder!"

He came immediately to the point. "Is Shelly here?"

"Why, no! I thought she was in New York. Has something happened?"

Dillon frowned. "She left New York suddenly and Adam Jefferies, with whom she was staying, is worried about her."

"Oh, no. I haven't seen her, though."

Dillon glanced past her to the interior of the house. He did not see Shelly lurking in any corner. "Maybe she hasn't arrived yet. We don't know for certain that she'll return to San Francisco, maybe she'll go to Santa Cruz. If she shows up, please tell her I want to see her."

Aggie smiled. "I'll do that."

She firmly closed the door after saying goodbye. Dillon stood there, facing the wood door, a mystified expression on his face. She'd been in a bit of a hurry. She hadn't appeared very curious about the circumstances of Shelly's leaving New York when she had seemed so close to her a few months ago. Maybe her affections had cooled, or maybe she knew very well how her friend fared. Dillon turned away. It should have occurred to him that Shelly might hide from him.

Shelly had known that Dillon would look for her. She had thought much about him and Sarah's lies in her three months of near solitude on board ship. She had ventured little from her cabin and had been queasy for a good month while the ship had battled its way through tropical storms. Christmas and her birthday had passed unacknowledged. In this black mood she'd gone directly to the Faulding on disembarking at San Francisco, two weeks before Dillon knew of her possible presence in the city. Aggie had answered the door with a dish towel in her hand and had looked at Shelly in disbelief. They had stared soundlessly at each other for a full ten seconds....

"Shelly!" Aggie shrieked after regaining her senses, and jumped forward, wrapping her arms around the bulky figure of Shelly in her cloak. Shelly dropped her valise and embraced her friend, her eyes closing in silent gratitude that she was finally here and that Aggie still cared. Aggie was the first to break away. She picked up Shelly's valise and pulled her friend into the sitting room, closing the door behind them. She took Shelly's cloak and pushed her into the sofa.

"Did you just get here?"

Shelly laughed. "I just walked off the ship."

"Are you all right? You don't look so good."

"I'm fine."

"That's what you always say. You are also pale and thin. Maybe that's what those ocean voyages do to people. I'll get you some tea. I can't believe you're here!" She ran out and returned moments later with a tray of cups and a teapot. "What happened in New York? Your one letter said you found your aunts. Why are you back? Not that I'm not thrilled, I'm just so surprised!" Aggie sat down next to her and waited impatiently.

Shelly took a sip of tea and then another. "I didn't like it there. I got homesick."

"I know there's more than that. Out with it." Aggie frowned and Shelly sighed. "Stop keeping secrets. What happened that was so horrible?"

"I don't know where to begin." Shelly took another sip of her tea and then set the cup and saucer down as if they were a great source of annoyance. "I found my family, but I also found out that the woman who raised me, whom I thought was my mother, wasn't. And the man she described as my father was probably just her own wishful thinking." Shelly gritted her teeth. "She lied. Can you believe it? And why? I could have grown up knowing I was a foundling. People thought we were strange anyway." She bunched her fists in her lap. "I don't even know what my real name is!"

"I'm so sorry, Shelly." Aggie sensed the pain lurking under the surface of Shelly's angry words. She moved close and slipped an arm around the younger woman.

"I don't know where to go or what to do anymore."

"You'll stay here with me," Aggie told her. "Life has a way of working out when you think it's about to end. Wait and see."

"I haven't told you everything." Shelly took a deep breath. "Dillon and I . . . on the ship . . . we became lovers." She felt her face flame as she rushed to a finish. "And he had a fiancée waiting for him in New York, a real society lady."

"Oh, Lord."

"Oh, yes."

"At least you aren't with child." Aggie choked. "And at least he's across the continent so he won't be coming around."

"He's not. He's here. Adam told me he returned to California." Shelly turned to her friend and clasped her hand. "Oh, Aggie, I would like to stay here, work here again."

Aggie nodded. "But if he comes looking for me, you must tell him you haven't seen me."

"All right. Did he return with his wife?"

"No."

Aggie's brown eyebrows arched up speculatively. "That's interesting."

"No, it isn't."

"You can't hide forever."

"He won't be interested forever."

Aggie studied her young friend closely. She was weary and hurt, disillusioned, even listless, but not broken. Aggie slowly smiled. "I'm so very glad you're back. Are you hungry?"

Shelly smiled. "Starved!"

"You know, if you had listened to me," Aggie admonished, leading the way to her warm kitchen, "you never would have left and met all this grief!"

Shelly stopped dead in the doorway and stared at the baby asleep in the cradle. "Oh, my God! The baby! You had the baby! Well, of course you had the baby. Ohh." Shelly knelt by the child. "Oh, he's beautiful. It is a he, isn't it?"

Aggie laughed. "Yes. And I had that monster thre months ago."

Shelly looked up at her friend. "How have you man aged? Here I've been prattling on about my disappoint ments and you've given birth and run a boardinghouse."

Aggie shrugged. "I had some girls in and out, but no on as helpful as you."

"Oh, please, wake him up." Shelly was looking ador ingly again at Aggie's child.

"I will not!"

"I want to hold him."

"You will have many opportunities."

"What's his name?"

"Thomas Jacob Thornton."

"I'm impressed."

Chapter Twenty-Four

Dillon crumpled up the letter he'd been trying to write and threw the ball of paper at Diego's bent head, where his friend sat comparing two long columns of figures. Diego marked his place with his finger before he looked up.

"Let's go get a drink," Dillon urged.

Diego looked slightly shocked. He glanced out the window. The sun was still in the sky. "I won't argue with you." He put a check mark by the row he'd stopped at.

In the saloon Dillon got in an argument with a table of men about the Chinese and whether they should be burned out of their densely packed area of town. Dillon thought not, but was in the minority. Then they started on the slavery question while Diego ordered and paid for more drinks. Dillon and Diego stumbled out after two hours.

"No sense going back to the office," muttered Dillon. They weaved their way home in the five o'clock light, and as always they walked up Powell Street, and like always Dillon stood across the street and leaned against the wall of a building and stared at the white boardinghouse. Five minutes turned to ten.

"This is fun," Diego said.

"I know she's in there," Dillon said softly.

"So, go in and get her."

"She wouldn't—" Dillon stood straight. "Look!"

Shelly came out of the door and down the steps of the Faulding, pulling her hood over her hair.

"I knew it," he whispered. He waited until she reached the end of the block and then began to follow.

"Buena suerte, amigo," Diego called softly after him. Dillon was going to need all the good luck he could get with a woman as strong as Shelly. Diego grinned and walked home alone.

Shelly needed a walk, to feel the cold air on her cheeks and to rest her eyes looking at the ocean. Three weeks had sped by since she'd been at the Faulding. She loved Aggie and Mary and especially baby Thomas, but she couldn't stay cooped up in the house one more minute. Twice Dillon had come by the Faulding and Aggie had lied for her. She knew this was no way to live and was ready to give it up. She walked down to the docks, not the safest place, but the sky was a beautiful purple streaked with pink clouds. The fog would soon billow in and drown the color in gray. She listened to the wind that blew across her face, then looked down and watched the water undulate beyond the pier, a gray-green expanse.

Dillon stayed back until the sun had almost disappeared behind the sea and the creeping fog. She was near the end of the pier. His insides coiled tight as he walked toward her.

Shelly's eyes lifted when a sea gull screeched above her head, and she saw the form of a tall man not six feet from her. She gasped and turned to face him.

"Shelly," he said.

Shelly backed up to the end of the pier and Dillon frowned. "What...?"

"I knew you were there." Excitement quickened in him at seeing those large, familiar eyes again. He reached out to touch her face and she slapped his hand away.

"Don't touch me." She could smell the alcohol on him and it made her nervous.

They stared at each other. "How are you?" he asked politely, unnerved by how cold her gaze was.

"I'm fine."

"Do you always walk out at night?"

"That's none of your business."

"It's not very safe."

Shelly turned away and walked down the pier. "I was just leaving!"

He strode after her. "Adam's been worried about you. That was pretty rude of you to leave him without notice."

"I wrote to explain as soon as I got here!" She kept walking. Dillon grabbed her shoulder and spun her to face him. Shelly shoved him away. "Dillon, I don't want to talk to you! I don't want to see you! I don't want to hear you or smell you or feel you! I wish you'd jump off the pier." Hands on hips she stared at him, then turned away and started walking again.

Dillon looked at the water, dark gray now in the fading light. "I'd do a lot of things for you, Shelly, but jumping into that water isn't one of them. How about dinner?" He caught up with her. "No? What about a quiet evening in your parlor?" Shelly walked faster. "All right, my rooms?"

"Go away!"

"Diego will leave for the evening. That doesn't appeal to you, either? Let's go for a leisurely carriage ride."

A block from the Faulding Dillon grabbed her. Shelly shoved his shoulders, but he cinched his arms around her back and lowered his mouth to hers. Shelly gagged on the taste of whiskey.

"You're drunk!" She twisted away.

"No, Shelly..." He stared at her, eyes glittering, and Shelly felt scared and excited and didn't like either feeling. She spun around and ran.

"I'm not engaged anymore!" he yelled after her.

"I'm not interested!" she yelled back, reaching the boardinghouse. She slammed the door in his face and threw the bolt. Aggie came out of the kitchen.

"Dillon," Shelly explained, motioning her head to the door. "He's drunk."

"Got friendly, did he?"

"If that's what you want to call it." Shelly followed Aggie back into the kitchen. "At least the pretense is over. I was sick of hiding, but I'm going to carry a paring knife around with me when I leave the house from now on."

"If there is a house. I found a hole the size of a fist in Mr. Grodin's blankets this afternoon when I changed the sheets. I've told him not to smoke in bed, but he doesn't give a hoot what I say." Aggie attacked a potato with her peeler.

Shelly set the table and thought of a few succinct phrases to tell Mr. Grodin about his filthy cigar and a few choice words to plug Dillon's ears with. Why had he come back to San Francisco when he had so much in New York? Why didn't he bring Annette with him if he needed female companionship? Why was he still interested? Why was *she?*

Shelly was bouncing baby Thomas on her hip up and down the hallway the next morning after breakfast. She answered the door automatically when someone knocked.

Dillon's chin went lax when he saw her with the child. "Whose baby is that?"

Shelly lifted Thomas on her hip. "Whose do you think he is? Yours?"

Dillon shook his head to clear it. "Of course not!" he snapped, although for one fraction of a second the thought had flashed in his mind. "I came here to apologize for last night," he said abruptly.

"That's nice." Shelly shut the door in his face.

Outside, Dillon flushed. She had made her point. She didn't want anything to do with him. Fine then! He stomped down the steps and up the street.

Inside, Shelly shook. She leaned against the door and ordered her stomach to be still. Damn him for being so persistent! She would not let him charm her.

Shelly woke from a nightmare, sweating. She sat up and wiped a hand across her damp forehead. She felt headachy, scared and thirsty. The smoke from the fire in her dream seemed so real she thought she could still smell it. The woman's cries still rang in her ears. She swung her legs out of bed and walked to her dresser, where her pitcher was. She drank a glass of water and her throat cleared, but not her head. The floor seemed warm against her bare feet. She took another step, avoiding the rug, placing her foot on the wood floor. Very warm. Her sleepy mind came alert. The glass slid out of her hand unheeded and broke in two on the floor. Shelly ran to her door, flung it open and stepped into the hall. Black smoke billowed up the stairs from the lower floor. Shelly gaped, then coughed when she took a breath. She ran to the nearest bedroom, threw open the door and shouted, "Fire!"

Some doors were locked and she pounded on them and screamed. Aggie's door was unlocked, the children sound asleep. Shelly snatched up Thomas from his cradle and shook Aggie awake. The floors everywhere were warm, the crack of the fire below was getting louder. In minutes all the upstairs occupants were roused and huddled outside on Aggie's balcony, since fire was already eating the stairs. Shelly didn't want to think what was happening to the downstairs boarders. Two men scrambled off the edge of the balcony in their long underwear and dropped to the ground. One of the men remaining on the balcony held Mary over the side to the two men below. The women followed, Aggie clutching a crying Thomas. They were all safely on the ground when the fire department arrived.

Shelly held an awed Mary and stared from the street at the flaming building. Aggie clutched Shelly's arm while she held the baby in the other.

"I don't think Mr. Grodin and Mr. Jacobs got out," Aggie said in an agonized voice. "I told the firemen there were boarders downstairs."

The roof collapsed in a roar, but the fire fighters kept the flames from spreading to other buildings.

"Oh, Aggie. I'm so sorry."

"It's not your fault," Aggie said while tears ran down her face.

"But I forgot to tell Mr. Grodin not to smoke in bed."

"It wouldn't have made a bit of difference."

Shelly saw Aggie and the children settled in a nearby hotel that took in the victims of the fire for no charge. "Do you need anything else?" Shelly asked her friend, now snuggled in bed with both children.

"Why? Are you going somewhere?"

Shelly nodded and drew a blanket around her.

"Shelly, don't be crazy! My God, it's not even dawn yet. And you have no clothes on but a nightgown!"

Shelly smiled. "That's why I'm going before dawn. No one will see how I look."

"Where are you going?"

"I'm going to get us some help." She ignored the rest of Aggie's questions. She had enough doubts about what she was planning without letting her distraught friend talk her out of it. She alternately walked and ran barefoot to Dillon's Russian Hill apartment.

Her second spate of knocking got her a response. "Who is it?" demanded Diego.

The door opened slowly when she gave her name. Diego, in long underwear, stared at her. Beyond him in the door of the bedroom stood Dillon, shirtless, wearing only long underwear. She'd never seen him look so amazed. And so handsome, his strong chest looking as if it could shoulder her every problem.

"May I come in?" she asked when they said nothing.

"Of course," Diego said, ushering her in, shutting the door behind her.

Dillon came across the room, looking her up and down from her filthy bare feet to her blanket wrapper to her hair falling out of her braid and her dirty face. "What happened?" he asked hoarsely.

"The Faulding burned down. Aggie lost everything."

"Sit down, sit down." Diego brought her a chair. A minute later he was back with a full glass of brandy.

Dillon crossed his arms over his chest. "So, you ran over here in the middle of the night, barefoot, undressed, to tell me about it."

Shelly's heart tightened. "I preferred to come like this when it was dark out." *And I needed someone to help us,* she thought. *I need someone now.*

Dillon rocked back on his heels. "Okay, I understand that. So, you've told me."

Shelly felt her face flush. She hadn't thought she'd have to beg. In fact, she'd thought the first words out of his mouth would express his desire to help. She slowly stood and set the brandy glass down on the nearest table. She lifted her chin. "Aggie and the children have nowhere to stay. Her savings will not last long. I came to ask you for a... a...donation."

Dillon laughed. Behind Shelly, so she couldn't see, Diego drew a line across his throat and pointed at Dillon. He sobered. "Excuse me, but this request is coming from a woman who can't stand me to talk to her, who shuts doors in my face."

Shelly strode over to him and glared up in his face. "You owe me this!"

"For what?" he shouted.

"For everything! For lying to me! For using me!"

"I never lied to you. I just didn't tell you some things."

"Things I had a right to know!"

"Shelly, this is ridiculous. I don't owe Aggie money to rebuild her boardinghouse because I took advantage of you, which I admit I did."

"I lived at the Faulding, too, Dillon. That place was my home. Aggie and Mary and Thomas are my family," she almost sobbed. "And you owe me!" She did start crying then, but she managed to glare at him at the same time.

Dillon, arms still crossed, standing like a redwood tree in front of her, got a strange glint in his eye. "All right," he said softly. "I owe you. I offer you, not Aggie, a loan."

Shelly's mouth tightened. "You know I can never pay you back the kind of money we're talking about."

"Oh, but you can, Shelly." He smiled and dropped his hands to his hips. "The loan will have to be repaid by your person. Your person in my house, cooking my meals and cleaning my floors."

Diego, sitting on the back of the sofa, squinched his eyes shut and shook his head.

The blood drained from Shelly's face. She pulled her blanket around her and turned to the door.

"Don't want to work for my help?" he called after her.

Shelly flared at him. "I've never turned up my nose at working, but I'll work in a factory before I'll be your whore!"

"Did I say anything about you in my bed? Do you think because of one drunken night and several nights with too few choices in the ladies that I can't keep my hands off you?"

Shelly stiffened. "What, then? You just want to humble me? Use me as a maid because I insulted you by not wanting to be your mistress?"

"Three months as my live-in housekeeper, at my house in San Mateo, for lodgings for Aggie while the Faulding is rebuilt and for the construction of the new building. Is that too much for you to handle on behalf of your new family?"

"No," she whispered, though she foresaw great torments ahead, for she was still madly attracted to the man. "If you promise not to touch me, I'll agree to this."

Dillon hesitated. "I promise."

They looked at each other. "I'll go tell Aggie now."

Dillon shook his head. "You can tell her in the morning—after we get you something to wear. Go in the kitchen and wash up."

Shelly walked stiffly into the adjoining room. When the door closed behind her, Dillon slapped his head with his palms. "I can't believe I promised I wouldn't touch her!"

"You said many stupid things," Diego agreed from the sofa.

Inside the kitchen Shelly filled a pot with water, lighted the stove and warmed the water. She waited, staring at the pan until little bubbles formed on the bottom. She shed her nightgown and dipped a rag in the warm water. She felt nothing, as if she were floating above herself. She scrubbed her face, passed the cloth over her body, under her arms, and then soaped her black feet. She was rinsing her toes when a knock sounded at the door. "Don't come in," she yelled, crouching naked on the floor.

"Here's a clean shirt," Dillon said. "I'll hang it on the doorknob."

Shelly willed herself to relax, but she couldn't. She wrapped her arms around her bent knees and bit her lip. She was again going to leave the safety of Aggie and go with this man to a place she'd never been, stay in his house with him, be his slave. Three months wasn't that long and the reward was worth it, but she felt so scared and alone. She was sure Dillon felt something for her, but she didn't know what. She realized she wanted him to care about her, wanted him to want her, to want her body and her presence, her ideas. And this wanting of hers scared her the most, because she knew she could get very hurt again.

She slipped her arm out the door and pulled in the clean shirt. It was fine and white and fell long on her. Through it she could see the darker points of her nipples, so she wrapped the blanket around her again when she came out of the kitchen.

Dillon stared when he saw the blanket slip. He should have given her a thick, red flannel shirt, but he had thought the white looked crisp and clean when he pulled it out. Mistake. "There's about two hours till dawn yet," he said tersely. "I'm going back to sleep. You can have the bed."

"To myself?"

"Yes, unless you want to share. I'll keep my promise and Diego's got the only sofa." He looked at his friend, already asleep.

She walked into his bedroom and shut the door behind her. Shelly's stomach dropped when she looked at the mussed bed and the place he'd lain. She dropped her blanket and climbed in under his covers. She felt dizzy with exhaustion and anxiety as her head fell back to the pillow. She closed her eyes and wondered how many other women had lain in this bed, but not so innocently.

Chapter Twenty-Five

In the wee hours of the morning, when there was just a glimmer of light glowing on the horizon, the phantoms in Shelly's mind congregated and took hold. As she twisted about in the big bed, Grady Allen slid into the room and glided up to her. She watched as if in a trance as his hands reached out for the blankets at the foot of the bed. Slowly, hand over hand, he reeled in the covers, pulling them off Shelly's body. His mouth opened in a soundless laugh. His face was bleeding profusely from the blow Shelly had dealt him with the poker. She watched in horrified fascination as the blood dropped rhythmically onto the white bed sheet at her feet. She slowly moved her hand until she touched Dillon's side. He slept soundly on his stomach. She whispered his name, then called it out loudly, but he didn't stir. Grady's head bobbed in silent laughter. He dropped down on the bed, resting his arms on either side of Shelly's calves, and inched his way forward as she lay there, unable to move, frozen by terror. He crawled up the length of her legs, his leering face looming closer...

Dillon woke to someone calling him. He sat up on the rug in his front room and threw off his blanket. He listened and then ran into the bedroom.

"Shelly, wake up." He shook her briefly before he lighted the lamp by his bed. She trembled fiercely as he pulled her into his arms. "It's just a bad dream," he soothed when she opened her eyes.

Her voice quaked. "He was right here on the bed with me."

"Who was?"

"Grady. He pulled the covers down like that," she said, pointing to the bottom of the bed where the blankets were bunched.

Dillon looked at her, a frown creasing his brow. "You just kicked them off in your sleep." He let her go and threw the covers back up, admiring the length of her bare legs. "Now, who is Grady?"

"Look under the bed," she pleaded.

He gave her an exasperated look but bent down and did as she asked. "No one there."

"Go check the other room."

"Shelly, it was just a dream."

"Please, Dillon."

He looked down at her big eyes and her hands clenched around the sheet in her lap and walked into the other room. "Grady?" he called. "Oh, Grady, where are you?"

"Qué pasa?" muttered Diego.

"I'm just looking for a spook, go back to sleep." He peered under the table, glanced at the corners of the room, stuck his head into the kitchen and even checked to make sure the hall door was locked. "Nothing and no one," he said, coming back into the bedroom.

"Thank you. I know I'm being silly."

"You're welcome." He blew out the lamp.

"No, leave it lit!"

"I can't sleep with the light on."

"You're not sleeping in here."

"You try sleeping on that floor! I won't touch you. I won't even get under the sheet, just the blankets. Who's Grady?" He lay on his side, propped up on an elbow.

Shelly sighed. "Grady was my landlord in Santa Cruz. He owned a saloon in town and was his own best customer. As far back as I can remember he looked at me," she said softly, glancing at Dillon, but she couldn't see his expression in the dark. "He touched me now and again, but he was easy to push away. I didn't want to make a big to-do about it, because he might've raised the rent and my mama would've been all upset, not that she could've done a thing to stop him. She wasn't real good with people. But after Mama died he got more...interested. Right before I left Santa Cruz he came over and I thought he was going to rape me. I hit him with the fire poker. When I left he was unconscious outside my door, but I heard he's none the worse, just has a long scar to talk about. I don't know why I dream about him now and again. He didn't really hurt me.''

"No, but he would have." Dillon felt an overwhelming desire to protect her. He wanted to wrap her in his arms and smother her with kisses and tell her he'd never let anyone get that close to threaten her again. "Damned bastard.''

Shelly wished she could see his face. She felt safe with him in bed with her. She liked having him close. "Aggie might be worried about me,'' she said softly.

Dillon lay back on his pillow. "Serves her right for not telling me you were there when I asked.''

"I didn't want her to.''

"I figured that. Yet here we are.''

"Yes,'' she whispered, and fell asleep.

Dillon listened to her breathe until a thin gray light shone through the window. He rolled to his side and watched her sleep. It was going to be hell to have her close for three months and not touch her. He got out of bed and dressed.

After visiting with Dillon a store that sold ready-made clothes, Shelly knocked on Aggie's hotel door. She wore a new pink cotton dress and new underthings, shoes and cloak. Dillon had bought her five other dresses and she'd added to the pile hair ribbons, hairbrush and pencils and paper. He didn't begrudge her a thing, and Shelly found herself disappointed that he didn't fight with her. How was she going to keep him at arm's length if he was going to be nice?

Aggie opened the door and cocked her head at Shelly's appearance. "Do tell me.''

"I made a deal with Dillon," she said, walking in and shutting the door. "For three months I'll be his maid and in return he gives us the money to rebuild the Faulding and to pay for your lodgings in the meantime. He's already opened an account for you."

Aggie sat on the bed and Mary crawled into her lap. "Are you going to be his mistress?"

"No. That's not part of the deal." Shelly sat beside her friend.

Aggie nodded. "I just don't want you to do anything you don't want to, Shelly."

"Well," Shelly said softly, "I don't want to go with him, but we want the money to rebuild."

Aggie clasped Shelly's hand. "This is generous of the both of you, but if you change your mind you come right back and we'll think of something else."

Shelly shook her head. "It will be okay. It's myself I have to worry about most. I still have feelings for him, you know?"

Aggie nodded and then smiled. "Maybe this will work out very well."

Shelly did not like the look in her friend's eyes.

Dillon looked at Shelly and smiled to himself. They were nearing his house now. Would she be impressed? So often when he'd gone over the plans or walked through the empty rooms or picked out furnishings, he'd thought of her coming down the stairs, sitting in the dining room, lying in the bedroom. "We're almost there."

Shelly's eyes darted briefly to his before they once again looked out the window. The carriage veered off the hard-packed dirt road and turned down a narrower, bumpier lane. The descending darkness made seeing anything difficult. Shelly admitted to herself that her curiosity grew as they came closer. The carriage turned one more time and there stood the south-facing, two-story house. Shelly let Dillon help her down while she tried in vain to make out the details of his home.

The carriage driver had the front door open for them by the time they walked up the steps. Dillon lighted a couple of lamps inside the entry. "I'll show you around," he offered, pleased by Shelly's curious expression. To the right of the entry was the dining room and beyond that a large kitchen. The wood floors throughout the ground floor were all scattered with rugs. The downstairs ceiling had exposed, unpainted wood beams. "I didn't plan that," Dillon explained. "Diego liked it and left it that way when I was in New York."

"I like it, too." She could sense Dillon's pride in his home a mile away. She was surprised by how much she instantly liked the house. It was just waiting to absorb people within it, offering a place of refuge—but she was a visitor who would soon be on her way.

Dillon had combined his study and library into one long room. It was decorated in deep olive green, gold and brown. Leather chairs and sofa dominated the room, along with his large desk. Bookshelves lined the walls, and over the fireplace hung a picture of an exquisite, dark-haired woman. Shelly looked from it to Dillon. "My mother," he said, following her eyes back to the portrait.

A long length of green carpet stretched along the upstairs hallway. The door to the master bedroom was directly at the end of the hall to the left of the stairs. Dillon did not show it. The two bedrooms to the immediate left of the stairs and the two to the right were still unfurnished, but the two at the end of the hall were finished. Dillon took Shelly to her room and then left to get her trunk.

Shelly's room was yellow. All over. The large canopied bed had a yellow flounced coverlet, the curtains were lemon yellow, and the rug, the wallpaper and the furniture upholstery were in patterns with yellow dominating. Shelly felt like a prisoner inside the sun. She was in the mood for something more somber, more mist and moon. A door opened onto a large balcony where there was a chair and a view of trees in the moonlight. She heard Dillon whistling as he came back up the stairs and she shuddered. He sounded so happy.

Chapter Twenty-Six

Shelly was up early and had breakfast made by the time Dillon came down the stairs. She served him without speaking and then returned to the kitchen.

Dillon ate alone for a few minutes, expecting her to return. When he realized he was going to eat alone like the grand master, he put down his fork and walked into the kitchen. Shelly was buttering a piece of bread at the kitchen table.

"You don't have to eat in the kitchen."

"But I'm the maid," she said with wide eyes.

Dillon's jaw bunched. "Damn it, Shelly. Bring your food into the dining room."

"Yes, sir!" She hopped up and joined him at the big table. There was still no conversation. After breakfast, Shelly dusted and swept downstairs. She made lunch. Then she made supper. They were quiet meals as breakfast had been. Shelly noticed that each meal seemed to get eaten in a shorter amount of time. She didn't see Dillon after supper. She cleaned the dishes and walked past his closed study door on the way to her room. She was definitely keeping enough distance between them.

The second day at Dillon's home passed much like the first, only Shelly cooked a roast beef instead of chicken, and she spent the afternoon walking around the grounds instead of cleaning. She took her first good look at the exterior of the house. The wood siding was stained dark brown, and the green painted sashes of the casement windows were a bright contrast. The roof overhang shielded the wide porch from sun and rain. The second story was not as wide as the bottom floor, and the extra space on both sides of the house was used for balconies. A large stone urn, overflowing with red geraniums, stood on each side of the front steps. Shelly liked it.

She walked behind the house and noticed a small octagonal building about thirty yards away. There were large square windows in every other side. Shelly walked over and peered in one of the windows. She smiled with her hands cupped around her eyes and pressed to the glass. This must be Diego's, she thought. There were four pictures hanging on the walls without windows. They were all nudes, one blonde, one redhead, one brunette and one black-haired. There was a wood stove in the center of the large room, a big brass bed pushed against the wall under one of the windows and a bear rug on the floor.

She was in a good mood during dinner. Dillon looked embarrassed when she told him she'd found Diego's room.

"What, doesn't he want a home as big as yours?"

"Diego's not interested in settling."

"And you are?" He flushed, ate a bite of beef with too much horseradish and choked. Shelly looked down at her plate and counted the bedrooms in this house of his. Was he expecting many visitors? Big ones that came for a short stay or little ones that arrived tiny and wrinkled and stayed a very long time? She didn't look at him but listened to her heartbeat and wondered about what Dillon really wanted.

Dillon excused himself as soon as he finished eating and went back into his study. He poured himself a big brandy and sat on the sofa. This arrangement wasn't working out well for him. Shelly acted as if she wanted nothing to do with him, which made him angry, but when she started talking or looking at him he felt swamped with something heavy. He had to disguise his passionate interest in her, because she didn't want that, but it was hard to be casual around her, so he had to avoid her. He swallowed some brandy and called himself an idiot for bringing her to his house if he had to avoid her. She was probably laughing at him and his big, empty house. He *was* ready to settle, at least he wanted a permanent residence, something comfortable and private that he could always come home to. He refused to think about what else he wanted. He looked into the blue eyes of the beautiful woman above the fire. Her expression looked so knowing of his every secret want. He squirmed. Right at this moment his wants were pretty basic.

Shelly stood over Dillon with a pan of hotcakes at breakfast the next morning. "What's that?" she asked of the sketch of logs arranged in squares that Dillon had brought to the table with him. He'd brought a stack of papers with him. Did this mean he wanted conversation as little as she did?

Dillon turned to her to answer, but he came face-to-face with Shelly's bosom instead. He swallowed uncomfortably.

"Is it beneath you to discuss this with me?" Shelly snapped.

"No! I... This is what Deideshiemer's square-set timbering looks like," Dillon managed to say. "Parker sent it to me. We're having a problem with crumbling walls in the Avalon. We've gone so deep that we're also having water seepage." He looked at Shelly, who had sat across from him, to see if she even cared. Her eyes were on him, eyes that had turned a gray blue from the dress she wore.

"This Deide—something is supposed to support the walls?"

"Yes. We're trying it now."

Shelly nodded. "How is Parker?"

"Fine. We built a house for him. He still likes it there. The place has a few more amenities and permanent structures since you were there."

Shelly's heart lightened as they talked more and, elbows on the table, she disregarded her self-imposed avoidance of him. "When did you come to California?"

"When I was seventeen."

"I can't imagine you at seventeen," she said. "What were you like?"

Dillon met her eyes, liking them too much. "I was…" He closed his eyes a moment. "It's hard to remember, hard to separate myself from what was happening around me, the Gold Rush, being on my own for the first time, being so far from civilization as I had known it. I think I was slightly crazy, very impressionable and idealistic, and very naive. And you? What were you like at seventeen?"

Shelly blushed. "Dillon, that was only two years ago. I'm much younger than you."

"I know," he said softly, almost regretfully. He got up from the table then but Shelly stayed seated, wanting more.

She cleaned the dishes quickly and knocked on his study door. "Can you spare time for a walk?" she asked him when he opened the door.

Dillon looked pointedly at the pile of papers on his desk. "I've two businesses."

"I know, but—"

"I haven't even finished reading the mail yet that I brought from San Francisco." He motioned to a sack on the floor.

Shelly stepped back and held up her hands. "Don't worry, I won't force you!" She spun away feeling hurt and mad at him, and mad at herself for wanting to be with him at all. She went outside and sat on the steps in the sun. She buried her face in the crook of her arm. She smelled like maple syrup. She hadn't had a daytime bath since she'd lived in Santa Cruz. There'd been no time for daytime bathing at Aggie's or Adam's.

She ran inside, heated water and lugged pail after pail up to her room. When she had enough she locked the door and then checked the lock. Shedding all her clothes, she slowly walked to the full-length mirror and took a good long look. She shrugged. Not bad, if she were to compare herself to the pictures on Diego's walls. Shelly sighed and got into the tub.

Later she made dinner in a kitchen hot from baking and boiling food. Her hair was rolled into a low chignon, but little tendrils fell loose and curled around her face. She unbuttoned her gray dress to midway between her breasts and rolled up her sleeves. The ham and the cake were due out any minute. The green beans were just about tender. Shelly finished the raspberry sauce she'd made for the cake and stretched. She'd been in the kitchen for hours and felt silly. She ate a couple spoonfuls of raspberry sauce, turning her lips red, then poured the rest into a bowl. Some sloshed accidentally onto the table covered with flour. Shelly moved the bowl and pan aside and studied the mess. She dipped her fingers in it. The texture was like a paste and easily spread across the wood table. She poured a little more sauce and dumped a little more flour. Her fingers played, swirled and spread. She could make flowing hair with her fingertips. She traced the outline of a face, her face, and went on to draw lines for neck, chest, breasts, belly and hips. She laughed at the representation of herself as she'd looked in the mirror today. She added two plump raspberries at the tip of each breast. A dot of sauce made a belly button. She poured a handful of cloves between her thighs and chuckled. Out of the corner of her eye she saw movement and looked up. Dillon stood, staring at the table, hands at his side, mouth open.

Shelly dumped the contents of the container of flour across her picture while Dillon stomped to the stove. "The beans are burning!" he yelled.

Shelly jumped. "You don't have to scream at me!" She turned and glared at him.

"Well, look!" He motioned to the pot.

Shelly grabbed a pot holder and lifted the vegetables off the stove. The water was gone. She turned the pot upside down and nothing fell out. "Oh, well," she said softly.

He yanked open the stove door. "This looks done, or are you planning on burning it, too?"

Shelly pulled the overbrowned cake out, almost sizzling his skin on the edge of the pan as she whipped it by him. She pulled out the pan with ham and potatoes. "There, your supper is rescued." She set the food down at the end of the table. Dillon was staring at the heap of flour covering the drawing, the outline of hips still visible.

"What the hell were you doing?"

"Trying to burn your food, obviously," she snapped.

Dillon lifted his eyes from the cluster of cloves to the cleavage showing in her unbuttoned dress. "For God's sake, make yourself decent!" Shelly's face flamed and he wondered why her lips were so damn red. "You look like... You're in here drawing dirty pictures... What's got into you?"

"That wasn't dirty," she almost growled. "That was just me! Your dinner is done. Serve yourself!" She grabbed up a fresh loaf of bread and the bottle of wine she'd used in cooking and left the kitchen.

Chapter Twenty-Seven

Shelly awoke with a start several hours after she'd gone to sleep. She pushed off her blankets and left the bed to pour herself a glass of water. The house was still. She opened her door and peered into the hall. She looked toward Dillon's closed door and then stepped down the stairs. The white glow of the moon illuminated Dillon's study. She walked behind his desk and rested her hand on the back of his chair. A brandy snifter sat to the side and papers and ledgers were in stacks. She wondered if he'd been even half as embarrassed at seeing her picture as she'd been by him seeing it; maybe that was why he'd yelled and blustered so. She climbed back upstairs and looked toward his room again, her heart pounding in her ears. She walked down the hall and opened his door and tiptoed inside. Like his study, his bedroom was touched with moonlight. She could make out sparse furnishings and bare wood floors. To her right was the large bed. He lay on his side, facing away from her. The sheets dipped down, exposing his broad, naked back. She felt a rush of warmth and fear. Maybe he'd been slightly crazy and naive at seventeen, but she was definitely full-blown crazy and stupid at nineteen.

Dillon rose up on his elbow and turned his head. He watched her approach, hair floating around her, eyes large and shining silver in the moon's light. He turned away and lay back down. "What do you want?" he asked hoarsely, trying to sound surly.

Shelly pressed her hips against the mattress and laid her palms on the cool sheet.

"Shelly, go back to your room."

"Dillon? Remember on the ship when you said I was important to you?" She saw the tensing of his body above the sheet. "Did you mean it?"

"That hardly matters now."

"It does to me. I need to know."

"Why?" He turned just enough to look at her over his shoulder.

"I need to know the truth. I've been fed too many lies in my not-so-long life."

"Yes, I meant it. Now get out of here."

Shelly released the breath she'd been holding. "And I love you still," she whispered, undaunted by his brusqueness. "I've been going crazy trying to deny it to myself."

This time he turned over and propped himself up on his elbows, his palms flat on the bed near his hips. The sheet fell below his navel, revealing the wealth of his chest and stomach, ridged with muscle and covered with curling black hair. "You're saying things you're going to regret come morning," he warned roughly.

"I'm saying things I can't hold in any longer." She lifted one knee to the bed.

"What are you doing?" he asked as she moved her other knee to the bed so she was on all fours before him, then sat back on her feet. His face grew hot when she moved her fingers to the buttons of her gown. His sex stirred under the sheets and blankets. "Shelly, don't do this." She continued unbuttoning. Her fingers trembled. Dillon snatched her arm from her clothing and held on to it. "You drank too much wine!"

"I did drink plenty."

"I promised not to touch you!" he whispered fiercely.

"I release you from that promise."

"And you'll condemn me in the morning." She pulled her arm from his grasp. Through her white gown Dillon could see the mounds of her breasts pushing against the material. He closed his eyes and saw the raspberries peaking her breasts on the kitchen table. "You'll hate me," he warned, opening his eyes.

"I won't. I couldn't."

His stomach flipped as the gown opened to just below her breasts. He almost laughed at himself for trying to talk her out of what he wanted.

Shelly looked him in the eyes as his body strained away from her. "Don't you want me anymore?" she asked quietly.

Dillon clenched his teeth and looked away. He could tell her no and that would stop this, but she'd be hurt and humiliated. He'd be crazy with frustration. His forehead broke out in perspiration. The brush of cool air flowing over his groin made him jerk his face to her. A groan of defeat fell from him when he saw her holding back the sheet, exposing his hardness. He pulled the covers out of her hand and back over himself.

"You want me." She picked up his hand that lay on his blanket-covered thigh and brought it to her breast, pressing it over her heart.

Dillon wrenched his hand away and Shelly gasped, but he didn't give her time to speak. He rose to his knees and pulled her up by her shoulders. He ripped her gown down to her thighs, yanked her body next to his and rubbed the soft skin of her belly against him. "Don't blame me in the morning," he ground out as he buried his face into the hair that flowed around her neck. His mouth took hers then, demanding and impatient. He hoped he wasn't damaging their fragile relationship, believing she was coming to him out of loneliness and need but unable to hold himself back.

Shelly wrapped her arms around his neck and squeezed. Her mouth melted into his. Slowly she slid her hands down the planes of his back and held his waist as their tongues clashed. She lowered her hands and cupped his hard buttocks, feeling a rush of pleasure when he groaned into her mouth. She brushed her fingertips against the back and sides of his thighs as he drew the torn nightgown away from her breasts so that their naked peaks could brush his chest.

"Did you really think my picture was dirty?" she asked in a whisper against his ear.

"No, but it made me want to rip your dress off." He pushed her down on the bed, following her. Their hands moved unceasingly over each other and their legs lay entwined, twitching occasionally as sensation rippled down their bodies. Shelly arched her head back as Dillon's mouth closed over a breast. He slid beyond her grasp, down across her abdomen, and lay between her open legs. Pushing the gown up around her waist, he lowered his head.

"Dillon!" Shelly rose up on her elbows and saw his lips descending to her triangle of dark hair. She jerked her legs up and snapped them together. He met her eyes as he pried her knees apart and pulled her legs back down. "Dillon, no."

"Let me, Shell," he whispered as his thumbs stroked her inner thighs. She shook her head, but Dillon bent to her anyway. She jumped at the first touch of his lips on her mound of curling hair. "Easy," he murmured, "I won't hurt you."

Shelly remained propped on her elbows, watching him warily. His hands on her thighs held firm as she strained her legs against them. His head bent again and dropped light kisses up the softness of one thigh. His tongue dipped to taste her and Shelly sucked in her breath. Her stomach heaved with the unexpected pleasure of it and then his head nestled firmly between her thighs. His dark hair was midnight black against her white skin. Her face flamed with embarrassment as she lay exposed and open to him. His tongue entered her like a spear, causing her to cry out and her elbows give way as she sank down to lie flat on the bed, her hands clenched at her sides. His tongue created pleasure like some strange magic, and she covered her mouth with her hand to stifle the hoarse cries she couldn't stop. Her legs fell lax and wide. Dillon placed one hand on her pelvis as his mouth moved up to gently suck the tight bud of pleasure. With his other hand he trailed teasing caresses along her thighs, slowly sliding his hand up until he slipped two fingers inside her and dipped them in and out.

Shelly forgot to repress her cries and grabbed his hand that lay flat below her belly. Squeezing it, she raised her hips, a fine quivering in all her limbs as the sensations he was sending through her intensified. Her whimpering broke across the stillness of the room as she drew her knees up and let the fulfillment of her need crash over her. Not until the white light of her climax was fading did she lower her legs, feeling depleted and weak.

Dillon slid his body up along hers, his hand cupping her still pulsing flesh. Her face was turned away from him, her eyes closed and her breathing shallow. She tightened her thighs about his hand, holding it there even as she pushed her gown down to cover herself. He nuzzled her throat where the pulse beat strong. "Shelly, look at me."

She refused to. What she'd thought would be his humiliation of her had become a branding upon her body that sealed his ownership of her love. It was impossible to imagine any other man ever doing to her what Dillon had just done, and difficult to believe that even he had.

Dillon removed his hand from between her thighs and grasped her chin, pulling her around to face him. Instead of wasting words to dispel her embarrassment, he settled his mouth on hers in a warm, undemanding kiss, even though he ached to take her.

Then he kissed her cheeks and her nose. His desire was raging, and Shelly lay with her gown all twisted around her to conceal what he needed.

Shelly followed his gaze down her body and saw the evidence of his arousal. She rocked her hips seductively and pulled the gown out from under her, smiling at the flash of passion that flared in Dillon's eyes as her round hips were uncovered. She pulled the torn gown over her head and turned toward the man she loved. He pulled her on top of him, sighing deeply at the touch of her warm fingers clasping him. He took her hips in hand and arched his body beneath her.

"No." Shelly pried off his fingers and placed his hands so they lay palm up near his neck. She slowly lowered herself down on him. When only half of him filled her she stopped and gyrated around his rigidness. Dillon's eyes closed as she moved up and down, eventually bringing all of him inside her. He repeatedly tried to grasp her hips to bring her against him in quick, hard moves to eliminate this slow torture, but every time she pushed him away. She wanted him to remember this night forever.

"Oh God, Shelly," he groaned, drawing his knees up behind her. He caught her heavy breasts in his hands and thumbed the nipples to sensitive hardness as she rose and sank on him, again and again. She watched the sweat break out on his face. Then she sank deeply on him and was still. Dillon choked, and with a strength she couldn't escape he pulled her down, crushing her soft breasts against his chest, and threw his legs over hers, pulling hers far apart. He rolled her to her back and pumped urgently into her body. Shelly clamped her arms around his back as her own body began convulsively quaking, and then Dillon buried his hot face in her neck and groaned as he found release.

Shelly held Dillon tight and didn't plan on ever letting go.

Chapter Twenty-Eight

"Shelly, wake up."

The lump under the covers jerked and then flattened in a stretch. Shelly pulled the covers off her head and saw Dillon standing by the bed, dressed and holding an envelope. He looked so serious. She smiled. "Is it late?"

"Almost lunchtime."

She scooted over, making room for him next to her, but he remained where he was.

"This was in my mail." He held up the envelope.

Shelly sat up, holding the sheet high against her nakedness. "What is it?"

"A letter to me from Adam."

He held it out and Shelly reached for it uneasily. She doubted her letter of explanation and apology for leaving without saying goodbye had even reached Adam yet. Why did this letter cause Dillon to behave so coolly? Dillon sat on the foot of the bed and watched as she pulled the paper from the envelope.

Dear Dillon:

I was relieved to hear that you are fairly certain of Shelly's presence in San Francisco, and I only hope that by the time you receive this letter you will have seen her for yourself.

Though in my first letter I was deeply worried about her simply because of the fondness that I felt for her, I

now have an even greater reason for concern. I have
discovered that Shelly Young, as we know her, is really
Michelle York, my niece!

Shelly raised her eyes from the page and stared at Dillon
in amazement. "His niece?"
"Keep reading."

I know it sounds crazy, but it is the truth. It was several weeks after Shelly's departure that my housekeeper came to me with a diamond ring that she had
found among the maid's possessions. She did not believe the maid's claim of ownership and neither did I,
for I recognized the ring. It was Marianna's engagement ring! How on earth it ever got in this house I did
not know. It seemed only logical that it would have
been on Marianna's hand or among her possessions at
the time of the fire that took her life. The maid admitted, under my furious questioning, that she found the
ring in a drawer of a dresser in the room Shelly had
used.

I felt positive that Marianna did not leave the ring
behind, especially in a guest room. I asked myself how
Shelly could have had it? Had it been stolen many years
ago to fall eventually into Shelly's hand? Had it sur-
vived the fire? Was Shelly who she claimed to be?

I remembered those large gray eyes of hers, that dark
hair and that infuriatingly stubborn look she gets on
her face, of which I'm sure you are familiar, and that
she inherited directly from her father—James York.
The similarity is uncanny and I suppose I never noticed it because I was so maddened about Marianna's
marriage to the rogue and his responsibility for her
death that I put him as far out of my mind as possible.

I had been told that the little girl, Michelle, died in
the fire with her father, mother and mother's lady's
maid. I had no idea who the maid was, but going on a
hunch I visited the Exeters, those supposed relatives of
Shelly's. They did not remember the name of the man

that Sarah Exeter worked for, but he was a sea captain like James York, and this Sarah was his wife's maid. The story fits. We can but guess as to why Sarah tried to pass off Michelle as her own for all those years. Only God can judge her for what she did, but it seems horribly cruel to me. I'm only glad that the truth is uncovered.

I implore you, Dillon, to seek out Shelly and tell her of all this in spite of whatever differences the two of you have. I want her taken care of until I can get out there. The wretched journey is worth it to see my niece again. I have enclosed a bank draft for you to open an account for her so she will not need to depend on you for anything she wants or needs. I want her to have full power over the account.

I must say, Dillon, if I had known before what I know now, I never would have allowed you to end things the way you did with her. I want you to look after her, but do not interfere with her person again at the risk of our association and friendship. Besides, Annette is chomping at the bit and threatening to corner you in California. I guarantee you will not be a free man for long.

My best to you and mine. I will see you soon.

Sincerely, Adam

Shelly's hands slowly lowered to her lap, the pages of the letter held limply between her fingers. "My God," she whispered, staring straight ahead, oblivious to Dillon. Rushing into her mind came the image of the portrait that hung in Adam's study. Marianna. Her mother. That beautiful woman whom she'd admired was really her mother. And Sarah? A sinking sense of betrayal enveloped her for the lie she'd been brought up with. And Adam, that kind, generous man, was her uncle. It was too shocking.

Shelly looked up at Dillon and a chill ran down her spine at the peculiarly blank expression on his face. She understood his stiffness toward her. He was tense with this new knowledge. "You said you were no longer engaged," she said coldly.

"I'm not. Annette is keeping up the pretense until she leaves for Europe." The mistrust in her eyes chilled him. She could afford to be as suspicious as she liked now. Adam had been ridiculously generous in his bank draft. He watched Shelly's fingers slip up and down the edge of the draft. "Your journey to New York was not in vain after all."

"No, it wasn't," Shelly replied woodenly, responding to the harshness of his tone and the awareness of how she'd gushed her love all over him last night and he'd never responded in kind.

"You're a real lady now."

"And just what was I before? Does a rich family and legitimacy of birth make fornication ladylike? I would have thought you'd be happy for me."

"Oh, I'm delighted, Michelle."

She winced at the formality and strangeness of her full name on his lips.

"You have everything you want now, don't you?"

His challenging tone confused and angered her. She lifted her chin and nodded. "I suppose so."

Dillon watched her spread the pages of the letter back out and begin reading again. A tightness slowly constricted his chest. Obviously, he was no longer needed. "I assume you're not planning on making lunch, since the amount of that draft enables you to help Aggie build a palace all by yourself."

Shelly drew her knees up and wrapped her arms around them, the letter dangling from her fingers. She studied Dillon's face. "Sorry to lose your slave?" she asked softly.

His eyes blazed madly for a second. "I know what money does to most people."

"What does it do, Dillon?" He didn't answer her. "It does buy some freedom, especially for a woman. I admit I like the possibilities. Imagine, I may never have to be anyone's maid again!" She met his dark, glittering eyes. "And yes, I'm not planning on making your lunch. I'm not hungry."

Dillon stood. He couldn't speak. He wanted to tell her she couldn't be like this, but he didn't have anything to offer her now. He wanted to ask what last night had been. He'd been right to worry that her professed love was merely lonely need, mixed with straight physical lust. He slammed the door behind him and stomped down the stairs. Should he blame her? He'd been completely without family and funds when banished from his father's house; only his rage had sustained him, and being a man made getting by so much easier. He ripped off half a loaf of bread and cut a hunk of cheese for lunch. He wanted his maid back.

The sound of the slamming door reverberated in the room, then faded, and the quietness grew and intensified until it was unnerving. Shelly cleared her throat to interrupt the silence but was quickly enveloped by it again. She stared at the door, hurt and bemused as to why Dillon should be so angry and unfriendly. She turned to the last page of the letter and reread the warning written there to Dillon. She fought the idea that had taken shape in her mind, but it was stronger than any faith she had in Dillon. She was sure his desire for her had cooled considerably when he learned who she was; she was no longer the poor, unprotected orphan. She was his friend's—his associate's—niece, and he did not want to jeopardize that relationship, though he might be angry that it was no longer convenient for him to have her in his bed. She was dismayed that he could toss her off so easily, but he'd never promised her anything.

Shelly set the letter down. She glared malevolently at the closed door. Better she discover now how weak his feelings were for her, but what did she do about her feelings, which were deep and strong?

Shelly rose and went back to her own room. She was furious with Dillon for being a dark cloud over her happiness. As she dressed she tried to remember back into her childhood for some glimpse of her real parents, however faint, but there was nothing. Her first memory was with Sarah, and a flood of resentment toward the woman surged through her. Why did Sarah have Marianna's ring? Why would Marianna have taken it off? Where was she while her parents burned to death? At least Sarah had told that part of the history correctly. She'd always said James Young had died in a fire on his ship. Shelly assumed she changed her name from York to Young to make sure no one would destroy the fantasy life Sarah set up for them in Santa Cruz. Shelly rubbed her temples where a headache grew. Did anyone have any answers? Mr. Hill. Sarah had been friendly with her employer as she was with few people. Maybe he knew something.

Shelly went downstairs and made herself a thick ham sandwich, then knocked on Dillon's study door. The door was ajar and her knuckles pushed it open, causing Dillon to turn quickly from one of the windows, where he appeared to be doing nothing but staring out. She stood in the doorway and watched his tall, strong body walk around the desk and stand behind it. She was assaulted by the memory of that body against hers last night. She wanted him like that again, and forever, without having always to feel scared about losing him. She swallowed a bite of her sandwich. "I'm going back to Santa Cruz."

Dillon tapped his fingers on his desk. "How long will you stay?"

Shelly licked the mustard off a finger. "I'm not sure."

"I have some things to do in the city and then I'll take you there."

"There's no need for you to accompany me."

Dillon sat down behind his desk and leaned back in his chair. "Shelly, I realize that you didn't have anybody before, but Adam is your uncle, and he did ask in his letter that I look out for you." He did not want her out of his sight, not when their relationship was so shaky.

"Don't patronize me, Dillon." Shelly mashed the rest of the sandwich into a ball inside her napkin. "I left Santa Cruz alone. I'll go back alone. Tomorrow."

Their eyes locked. "Do you plan on coming back?" he asked.

If you beg me to. "I don't know."

He sat up and pulled some papers in front of him. "We'll leave for the city in the morning. From there you can take a ship."

"Thank you," she said stiffly. She shut his door behind her and tossed her uneaten food outside for the birds.

Chapter Twenty-Nine

Shelly sat on the porch of Mr. Hill's house and let the soft spring sunshine soak into her. She reached her hands to the sky and stretched. She was at home here in this white cottage with this kind man. Mr. Hill sat in a chair near her, only the little table with tea separating them. He'd been delighted to see her and assured her she was welcome as long as she liked.

Shelly gazed out at the two rows of roses that lined the walkway to the cottage. Rosebushes also clustered against the front of the house, the flowers growing up above the porch. Their fragrance wafted to Shelly and she sighed. The last week had been one of frustration. She hadn't found out anything about Sarah. Every secret had been buried with her. Shelly looked resentfully in the direction of the cemetery, the one place she'd avoided. Her little two-room cabin was now inhabited by a Mexican family of five, so Shelly couldn't very well tear apart the walls looking for clues to Sarah's motivations.

Mr. Hill had been surprised to hear that Sarah was not her real mother. Sarah had never been closer to anyone else, so Shelly had no place else to turn. With Mr. Hill she had sifted through every remembered conversation that he'd held with Sarah during the many years she'd cooked and cleaned for him, searching for some little phrase or spoken wish that would shed light on the mystery.

Mr. Hill thought it obvious. "She was in love with your father, and when he and Marianna died she kept you and pretended you were the daughter of James York and herself. It seems she believed her own fantasy."

"I know that's what happened," Shelly had groaned. "But why? *Why?*" She wanted an explanation for the explanation. She wanted to know if James York had ever shown a romantic interest in Sarah, and why she had no memory of her real parents. Had Sarah tried to banish them from her mind? Had she been so devastated at losing them in such a terrible way, burning to death, that she had struck them from her mind herself when she was just a child?

Now, after being in Santa Cruz a week, she was still asking herself the same questions, driving herself crazy, while Mr. Hill looked at her sadly over his spectacles. Hearing her low sigh caused him to frown, his gray mustache drooping down into his trimmed, gray beard.

"Shelly?" She turned to him and he glanced down at the stick he was stripping of bark with his fingernails. "No matter what she did, she loved you."

"Did she? Or did she love that I was part of *him?*"

Shelly stood outside admiring the morning dewdrops on the rose petals. She ran up the porch steps and snatched the clippers off the table and cut a bunch of the flowers.

"Why don't you take those to her grave?" came a quiet voice.

Shelly froze, her eyes like gray ice as she looked up at Mr. Hill in his morning robe in the front doorway. "Why should I?"

He shrugged. "A peace offering?"

"You mean forgive her?" she asked incredulously.

"Maybe then you could stop tormenting yourself." He moved back into the house.

Shelly followed him inside with the flowers, her joy in them gone.

Shelly leaned against the doorjamb, looking out at the layered violet-and-pink sunset. Mr. Hill sat in his rocking chair on the white porch, which glowed ghostly in the twilight. The squeak of his chair filled the silence as the birds settled down for the night. Shelly drew the warm cashmere shawl tight about her shoulders and crossed her arms under her breasts.

"There is a man in San Francisco," she confided softly. The fragrant smoke of Mr. Hill's pipe surrounded her. "I love him." She closed her eyes against the powerful beauty of the sunset. A warmth enveloped her as she spoke of Dillon, but underneath lay a painful loneliness. The tears burned behind her eyelids. She opened her eyes and looked ahead at the violet streaks sinking lower. "But he makes me angry so much of the time."

Mr. Hill's lips curved around his pipe as he smiled. "Love is not a smooth road, Shelly. You just have to bump along."

"Yes, but I don't know what he feels. There was another woman, who he says is no longer important to him, but I know how I felt about her, and her and him together. I would never want a child of his and hers! My moth—Sarah must have been insane!"

Mr. Hill rose slowly to his feet and walked to where she stood. His head blocked out the sunset and his face was in dark shadow. "Ask yourself if Sarah did so badly by you. Take a long, hard look at yourself. Are you an ignorant, illiterate, slovenly, mannerless, insensitive, immoral fool?"

Shelly stared speechlessly up into his shadowed face. He stepped past her into the house, and she caught the last streak of violet before it sank out of sight.

Shelly had been with Mr. Hill almost three weeks and felt it was time to leave. There was nothing for her to learn in Santa Cruz. She'd visited her only female friend, Amanda Phillips, and had sat in the kitchen drinking coffee while Amanda's three children ran or crawled in and out and Amanda sat hugely pregnant with her fourth. Shelly missed baby Thomas with a pang. She'd asked Dillon to check on Aggie when he was in San Francisco. That was about the only thing she'd said to him before they parted ways.

She pushed open the front door and stood gazing out at the cloudy afternoon sky. It smelled of rain. The wind picked up and bobbed the pink roses on their bushes, and twigs blew across the walk that led up to the house. Shelly leaned her head against the door frame and watched the approach of the heavy clouds.

On stormy days Sarah had tried to hurry home, at least for a visit, from her work here. She often rushed in with something baked that day—some pie or cinnamon rolls. She'd hug Shelly close, build up the fire, chattering away, and put on a pot of tea. They'd stand in the window and watch the rain, Shelly standing on a chair until she was taller. They drank their tea and munched their food, occasionally their hands darting out to catch the droplets, but mostly they squeezed together, enjoying each other's warmth as the cold wind hit their faces, blowing the sweet-smelling rain against their cheeks.

Shelly abruptly turned back inside, banishing her memories, but sitting on the table was the large vase of pink roses that she had picked the day before. Her fingers fluttered nervously at the fringes of her shawl. The soft pink petals glowed in the gray light. She walked close and touched a petal with her finger, and felt the velvet softness down to her soul. She snatched the flowers out of the glass vase, heedless of the water that dripped down her arms and on her dress. She went out the door and down the steps, breaking into a run as she went out the gate.

Grass had grown over the grave she hadn't seen in a year, covering the raw, bare mound she remembered. Shelly stepped cautiously among the rows of dead. She felt their presence, watching and judging. She laid her flowers under the crude wood cross that she had erected. A big drop of rain splattered on her nose and was followed by more.

"I've avoided this," she whispered. "I didn't want to come here." Her eyes burned and she couldn't tell if it was rain or tears running down her face. "I can't call you *Mama* anymore, but you're the only mother I remember." She squeezed shut her eyes, bowed her head and clenched her fists. "How could you do this to me?" she wailed, and the answer appeared in her mind. *Because it was the only way you could have me.* It was a lie for a life. The truth would have meant a loss. Shelly reached out and rested one hand

and then both on the mound of earth, drawing sustenance from the alive, springy feel of the wet grass under her fingers. "Did you love me?" she asked in a broken whisper. She saw before her a childhood spent running and laughing, a girlhood spent drawing and dreaming, and a young womanhood spent learning the rhythm of work. "I loved you." She laid her head on her hands and the tears came hot and fast. Her hair, pulled back in a ribbon, fell over her shoulder and shielded her face from the sting of the rain.

She stayed until she was soaked and cold, her hair hanging heavy and wet, but deep inside her glowed Sarah's love, however misguided or self-serving, like a mellow sun in her breast. She trudged back to the cottage, dragging her sodden skirts behind her, drained and exhausted. She focused only on the walk in front of her as she made her way through the gate and to the house. Her stiff fingers pulled at her heavy skirts to move them out of the way of her feet. She placed one foot on the first step, her eyes ranging up the rest of them. Her gaze rose up the legs and torso of the tall figure standing on the top step, and her eyes grew enormous. Warm, strong arms closed around her, drawing her against solidness and strength. Shelly's eyes closed as she clung to Dillon's shoulders.

"God, you're soaked." He slipped his arm under her knees and lifted her up while Shelly twisted her arms around his neck and buried her cheek into his shoulder.

"Gertie, get a bath for Miss York," ordered Mr. Hill to his maid. The girl jumped where she'd been standing and staring. Mr. Hill winked at Shelly. "The man you mentioned?"

Shelly nodded and a tinge of embarrassment colored her face when Dillon looked down at her, one eyebrow winging up in question.

"Well, go get those wet things off!" Mr. Hill waved them toward the room where Shelly was staying.

In the bedroom Dillon dropped his hand from behind her knees so she slid to the floor, her body pressing against his. "I've missed you," he whispered in a low growl. He kissed her cold lips.

"Is that why you're here?"

His hands tightened on her arms and he shook her. "What do you think?" he demanded. He pushed his fingers into her wet hair along her scalp, too roughly, but desperately. "Three weeks!" He clasped her cheeks. "I thought you might not come back."

"You were wrong."

He searched her eyes, still bloodshot from tears, but sincere. He kissed her again. And again. His lips opened and his mouth warmed hers until the wetness of her dress seeped through his shirt, reminding him of her soggy, cold body. "Turn around," he ordered. He unhooked her dress and pushed it down about her ankles.

"Dillon, I can do this," she said, stepping out of her garments.

"I'm sure you can." He untied the ribbon of her camisole and pulled it over her head. Her hank of wet hair slapped against her naked back and she yelped.

"Dillon, really! Go sit with Mr. Hill so he doesn't think—"

"I don't give a damn what he thinks." He yanked her so close her gooseflesh-dotted breasts were mashed against his chest. He cinched his arms around her and kissed her mouth. She was compliant in his arms until the door swung open and Gertie came in with steaming water. With cheeks scarlet, Shelly faced the wall until the tub was filled and Gertie was gone.

"You can turn around now."

She did, with arms crossed. "And you can leave now."

The grin fell from his face. "Shelly, my ship is in the harbor. I want to take you back with me as soon as you get out of this bath and get dressed."

"Fine."

"I'm serious, Shelly."

"I hope so."

He studied her distrustfully and Shelly almost broke out smiling, enjoying his worry, even though there was no need for it; she'd give him every chance to return her love. "But

I won't be going anywhere if you don't have the decency to go sit with Mr. Hill.''

He nodded, still puzzled by her lack of protest about leaving with him. "Here," he said, handing her a mug. "The girl brought in a hot toddy." Shelly took it gratefully. "And hurry up so we can get on that ship!" he added gruffly.

Her eyes shone. "I will, Dillon."

He was almost out the door when he turned back, hand on the knob. "Has that man, that landlord, bothered you at all?"

Shelly grinned. "He's scared of me."

Dillon nodded and left her with her privacy.

Chapter Thirty

Dillon carried a sleeping Shelly down the ramp of the ship the next morning. She stirred, her head lifting from his chest. "Where are we?"

"San Francisco."

"San Francisco!" She squirmed until he let her down. "I slept the whole way?"

He led her down the ramp to the waiting carriage. "I found it hard to believe myself, but we'll be at the house soon enough and you can make up every lost minute."

"We'll see about that." Shelly settled back into the carriage seat. She must have been exhausted to sleep when first reunited with Dillon. She had lain down as soon as she got on the ship, assuring Dillon it was only for a few minutes. She did feel refreshed.

Dillon closed the carriage door and regarded Shelly's satisfied expression across from him. He had spent a frustrating night watching her sleep in the bunk for which he'd had such different ideas. He would have awakened her, but she looked so pale. "On second thought, no time like the present." He pulled her to his lap and buried his face in the soft skin of her neck.

"Dillon!" He unbuttoned her dress and tugged it down one shoulder. "Not here!"

"Kiss me."

"You're crazy."

"Come on. Mmm...again...again. You feel so soft."

"The windows!"

"Who cares?"

"Ouch!"

"I'm sorry. Lie back."

"No! You can just wait." Shelly extracted herself from his arms and sat back across from him. She straightened her clothing while he devoured her with his eyes. She blushed. He leered. She looked out the window. "How's Aggie?"

"*Very* well, I'm sure."

"Very? How so? She hasn't missed me?"

Dillon laughed. "She's been too busy. Seems the foreman of the crew rebuilding the Faulding likes blondes with children. The way they're bossing each other around I expect a wedding announcement real soon."

"She didn't waste any time," Shelly said wonderingly.

"As we seem to do."

Shelly tilted her head. "Through no fault of mine."

Dillon leaned forward. "I disagree." He put his hand on her knee and slid it slowly down her calf, catching the bottom of her dress in his fingers.

Shelly kicked his arm away. "I was speaking of the holy state of matrimony, not a physical display of lust."

Dillon sat back and endured the long ride with his hands to himself. He had a sinking feeling in the pit of his stomach that the afternoon was not going to go as he wanted. Why was she coming with him if she didn't want a physical display of their mutual desire?

"Last room on the left." Dillon gave Shelly a push up the stairs before he ran to the kitchen and pulled a bottle of champagne off the ice. He gave his driver instructions not to disturb them before he rushed up to his room. He kicked the door shut behind him, his fingers tight around the neck of the cold bottle. Shelly stood by the window.

"You forgot glasses." Her silver eyes sparkled.

Dillon glanced down. "So I did." He set the champagne on the table by the side of the bed and came to stand before her. She gave no sign of unwillingness as he bent close. He brushed his lips against her cheek, her nose and the corners of her mouth.

"About Adam's letter," she said softly.

Dillon stiffened, then straightened. "Yes?"

"Explain your reaction to it."

He sighed. "Well, I admit it was a shock to learn that the woman I have compromised is my friend's niece." He saw by her patient eyes that she waited for more. "You no longer need me, Shelly. I thought I'd step back and let you see what you wanted."

"Oh! Don't make yourself sound so generous and so...so reasonable. You were downright rude, as if I weren't going to be available for your pleasure anymore!"

Dillon scowled. "I remember you being on the cool side in *your* attentions. It seemed likely you were planning on disentangling yourself from involvement with me."

She turned away from him and crossed her arms beneath her breasts, her back rigid. Dillon moved behind her, his arms aching to hold her, but his hands stayed at his side. "Shelly, you can't deny you were remote that day. What was I supposed to think?"

"Do you think my love is so fickle?" She faced him. "When I came to your room that night I told you how I felt. Nothing changed that—not money, not family, nothing! But I didn't know how you felt *before* the letter, or after reading Adam's writing, or even now!" She stalked past him and sat in the only chair in Dillon's bedroom.

Dillon stood pensively where she had left him. "You don't know me very well if you think Adam could deter me from taking you if I want you." He moved to stand in front of her, so close she had to tilt her head back to meet his eyes.

"*Taking* me? Sounds lovely. Undeniably romantic. Absolutely honorable."

"That will do." He dropped to his knees before her and grasped her chin. Her eyes blazed madly, but she moaned with the first soft touch of his lips on hers. He began gently, his tongue wetly tracing her lips before warmly insinuating itself within. Shelly's heart quickened and she gripped his forearm. She sought his tongue with hers while her lips throbbed with heat. His neck was hot under her hand; his thick curls were silk in her fingers.

He lifted her and took over the seat in the chair, pulling her to his lap, her feet dangling over the arm of the chair. He pressed her close to his chest, one arm about her waist and the other beneath her knees. His mouth moved over hers ravenously and Shelly clasped her hands around his neck and returned the fervor of his kiss. Beneath her bottom she felt his muscled thighs and the hard bulge of his confined flesh.

Dillon slid a hand up and down her ribs. He unbuttoned her bodice and pulled the sleeves down over her shoulders, down her arms to her wrists. He tugged down the front of her camisole and slid his hand over a full breast. The blood pounded in Shelly's head as she watched his brown fingers squeeze her. He rolled the hardening tip between his thumb and forefinger, his eyes flicking from what he held in his hand to the growing cloudiness of her gray eyes.

"I want you so much," he mumbled. He wanted her as he had never wanted a woman before. An aching tenderness was overcoming him. He wanted to make her happy, to show her how much he loved her, because he did. Oh God, he did. The feeling rose inside him so strong that he almost cried out with it.

Shelly squirmed on his lap as his mouth lowered and enclosed her nipple. A flash of heat ignited her insides as he slowly sucked. Her voice fell about his ears like a soft caress. "Did you want Annette like this?" He raised his mouth and flicked the wet, pointed peak of her nipple with his finger. "Did you?" she asked breathlessly.

He focused his eyes on her face as his hand brushed her ankle and removed her slippers. "No. Never."

He slid his hand up under her dress and petticoats. She grasped the fingers that were inching up her thigh. "Have you been with another woman...like this...since we made love by the Carson River?" she asked in a whisper. Her eyes locked with his and her grip tightened on his fingers when he tried to shake her off. He removed his arm supporting her back, pushed her down on the arm of the chair and pried her fingers loose.

Shelly wriggled onto her elbows and watched his slow, creeping hand move under her dress. She was not going to be able to talk soon. "Dillon, have you?" Then his hand found her. He cupped her swelling flesh and bent his body over hers so he could nuzzle her neck. Shelly shuddered with pleasure at his wet kisses on her throat and his gentle touch between her legs. The moisture seeped through her drawers. Dillon groaned deep in his throat, his lips covering hers urgently as his fingers became wet and slick.

With a supreme effort of will and physical strength, Shelly twisted away from Dillon and rolled herself off his lap, landing on the floor at his feet. He sat up and reached for her. She brought the flat of her palms over his hands and pushed them down so they lay on the chair to the sides of his thighs. She rested her own hands on his hard thighs and caressed him with smooth strokes. Coyly, she looked up at him. "Have you touched a woman's body since I let you touch mine?"

Dillon's eyes blazed madly. "What difference does it make?"

Shelly dug her fingers into his thighs. "I want to know how important I am. I want to know how important this is!"

"Very important," Dillon whispered, cupping her exposed breast in his hand. Shelly quivered as his thumb teased around her nipple. She bit down on her bottom lip and raised her hand. Dillon went still as Shelly traced the outline of the ridge in his trousers.

"How important?" she coaxed.

He groaned. "I never touched a woman since I touched you," he rasped.

"That's very good." She stroked a little more, waiting for him to ask the same of her. He didn't. She lifted her hand. "You assume I haven't been with anyone else?"

"Yes," he said, reaching for her, but she pushed his hands away. He sighed. "You love me," he explained. "And I hurt you. I didn't think you'd turn to someone else to make the pain I caused cease. It was more likely you'd try to hurt me." Dillon could have said more, but the woman was unfastening his trousers. He held his breath as she spread the edges of cloth apart. She reached in and pulled out his swelling manhood. Freed from the trousers it grew larger and stood at attention in her hand. Her fingers tightened around the base. "Shell," groaned Dillon, his hands motionless at his sides.

"Are you going to marry me?" she asked softly, sliding her hand up and using her thumb to caress the tip of him in slow circles. A pleased smile lighted her face as a convulsive shudder shook his body. He looked up from where he was watching her hand. His tortured pleasure glowed in his eyes. "Are you?" she prodded.

"Yes," he moaned softly.

"Good." And she kissed him where he was dying for it. His fingers curled in her hair, not forcing her down or pulling her up, just staying, every muscle in his body tense. This was not difficult, she thought, not if the barest touch of her lips was any indication.

Shelly raised her head and met his eyes. "When?" His eyes flared angrily and Shelly knew he resented being forced, but she was determined their fate be sealed. Her hand tightened convulsively about his hard length as her eyes remained locked with his.

He tugged on her hair now, trying to pull her up toward his mouth. Shelly winced but did not budge. His arms were trembling. Shelly arched her brows questioningly. Dillon rolled his eyes heavenward. "Whenever you want!" he roared, shaking her head.

Shelly smiled in triumph and began feathering light kisses up Dillon's stomach and ribs.

"Enough, enough!" Dillon pulled her off him. He cradled her face in his hands, her eyes huge with desire. Dillon took her mouth with his own in a possessive kiss. "Oh, Shelly," he whispered hoarsely against her cheek. He pushed her away. "Get in the bed!"

Shelly backed to the bed as Dillon got up stiffly. Her dress and petticoats were lying in a puddle around her feet when he joined her. Dillon's boots hit the floor when Shelly's camisole fluttered down. His eyes were on her breasts as he tore off his shirt, losing a couple of buttons in the process. Shelly turned sideways to him as she bent to pull down her drawers, showing him the temptation of round, lush breasts. He pushed his trousers off and cursed as he came to her, unable to wait for her to roll her stockings off.

Dillon pushed her down on the bed and swiftly rolled between her thighs. Shelly closed her eyes, her neck arching up as she prepared for a quick entry. Her eyes fluttered open when there was nothing. He was watching her, waiting for her. He gently eased into her and slid back and forth in a growing fever of sensation. Every crooning cry that fell from her lips caused him to plunge deeper. She ran her hands through the sweaty, curling hair on his chest as he struggled above her, his hands pressing into the mattress on either side of her face. Her hands dropped to his hips, which churned against hers, and she dug her nails into them, causing him to groan and bang against her violently.

He dropped from his hands to press his body close to hers. He felt her trembling, her body on the brink of climax. Her hands clasped his buttocks. "Oh, Dillon," she breathed over and over.

He buried his face in her neck. "God, I love you."

"Ohh!" Shelly's head arched off the bed. She clutched him as spasms of pleasure rocked through her; Dillon lost control immediately and gasped as he joined her a moment later.

They clung together until their breathing was normal. Dillon rolled off her and sat up, grinning boyishly. He bounced to the balls of his feet and stretched his arms high above his head and then up behind his shoulders. Shelly wondered how he could be so energetic when she wanted to take a nap. She crawled under the covers to preserve a little modesty in the daylight that illuminated the room.

"I have something for you." Dillon walked naked to the large wardrobe and pulled out a small box. He placed it in her hands. "Open it."

Shelly lifted the lid off and saw an opal necklace and earrings. "They're beautiful!"

"They were my mother's."

"What are you doing with them?" She lightly touched them.

"She left her jewels to me. I tried them on, but they didn't look nice with the hair on my chest."

"So... these are for me?"

"Yes." He fastened the necklace around her neck and the earrings on her ears. He leaned back and surveyed her. "You're beautiful." Shelly giggled and pulled him to her and gave him a dozen kisses. He grabbed the sweating bottle of champagne, uncorked it with a loud pop and raised it. "To us." He took a swig and handed it to her. "This room needs something, don't you think?"

Shelly looked around the bare room and nodded. "Some paintings and rugs would help. This floor is cold. A table with flowers right under that window," she said, pointing. "And a big chair to sketch in next to the table. And of course, another wardrobe for my clothes. This room is light, but a lamp... Why are you looking at me like that?"

"You have many ideas. I like your ideas."

Shelly blushed and took another drink of cold, fizzy liquid. Dillon drew his fingers down her arched throat as she swallowed. He cupped a breast and bent close, his lips parting. A knock on the door made him curse. "I said we didn't want to be disturbed," he yelled.

He was turning his attention back to Shelly when the maid he'd hired in Shelly's absence spoke nervously at the door. "I'm sorry, but you have guests."

"I don't—"

"They're from New York," she added quickly. Dillon's body stiffened and his eyes met Shelly's. "One is your father and the other is a Mr. Jefferies."

Chapter Thirty-One

"So, where is my niece staying? In San Francisco?" Excitement surged through Shelly's veins as she descended the stairs and heard Adam's voice in the drawing room.

"No, actually she is—"

"Here!" announced Shelly, stepping into the room. Adam looked delighted and she ran across the room and into his open arms.

"Would anyone care for some sherry?" asked Dillon. "No? Well, don't mind me if I do." He poured himself a healthy amount of the whiskey that was also on the table.

"I'll take one of those," his father said, stepping forward.

Shelly moved out of Adam's embrace only to stay by his side.

"John, I'd like you to meet my niece, Miss Shelly York."

Shelly took her first good look at Dillon's father. She remembered seeing him in the park that terrible day Annette King had been hanging on Dillon. The older man was incredibly handsome and looked so much like Dillon it was disconcerting. His brown eyes snapped with more intensity than his son's and his smile was cold, though it came easily. She preferred Dillon's rarer, warm smiles. John Ryder's gaze dropped to the opals around her neck. Shelly felt a nervous flutter in her stomach as the older man's features tightened, but he looked up smiling. She cast an apprehensive glance at Dillon, who was stonily sipping his drink and did not look happy. Her hands shook as she sat down next to

Adam. Dillon claimed to love her, so why was she so worried that he was ashamed of his father seeing her here? She made her voice sound calm. "How was the journey?"

"Long," groaned Adam. "I had hoped never to make it again, but I must admit seeing your face has made it worthwhile."

Shelly blushed.

"So, Dillon," broke in John Ryder, "Edward told us of the broken engagement. We've come to new terms."

"You came all this way to explain them to me?"

"Yes, I have," his father said, his eyes hard on his son's face. "I think you'll find them more appealing."

Dillon shrugged and the silence that followed made Shelly squirm. "Have your things been brought in?" The men nodded. "Well—" she stood "—I need to see about dinner. Dillon, why don't you show your father and Adam around the house?"

Shelly escaped to the kitchen, relieved to be away from the strange tension between father and son. She tried to remember what Adam had told her so long ago on board the ship about Dillon and his father, but she couldn't recall anything specific. She whipped up a cake while the maid prepared the meal.

Dillon, happy to do something like walk around his house instead of sitting with his father, led a tour. He was surprised he was more uncomfortable having his father in his house than he was being in his father's house. In the study he watched his father look silently at the portrait of Loretta Ryder above the fireplace. The portrait had hung in his father's house until Cora had moved in. Dillon had never asked permission to take it.

As they climbed up the stairs, John Ryder said, "Nice, Dillon. A bit remote and rustic, though, isn't it?"

"I wanted a home, not a showplace," Dillon said expressionlessly.

"Many bedrooms, Dillon," Adam commented upstairs. "Are you planing on having a large family?"

A vision of pregnant Shelly with a couple of toddlers clinging to her skirts filled his head. Yes, he wanted several children, but he'd never pictured it so vividly before. The idea terrified him and delighted him.

Shelly took a sponge bath after making her cake. She threw all her clean dresses on the bed and crossed her arms. She had picked out dresses for Dillon to buy her that were appropriate for a maid, not to entertain her future husband's father. Her one impractical addition was the white dress, which she'd yet to wear. She'd always wanted a white dress and, since Dillon was paying and she'd been mad at him that day, she'd thrown it on the heap. She couldn't wear it now; she had other plans for it. She put on a clean gray dress, brushed her hair and rolled it into a chignon. She removed the jewels and put them carefully away in the black box. They looked odd against gray cotton. She felt the need to impress Dillon's father and simultaneously had the sinking feeling that the task was impossible. The man seemed difficult, maybe even mean. Shelly shook her head. She shouldn't think that way about him. She could at least give him a fair chance.

She went downstairs and heard Dillon and his father behind the closed study door. Their voices sounded full of business. Shelly thought it odd to come so far and get to business right away. She'd ask Adam about Dillon's father. Adam. Her uncle. She was scared to believe the title was real. He was downstairs in the drawing room, fingering a fern that grew profusely in one of the windows. He turned at the sound of her footsteps and greeted her with a warm smile. "Dillon told me you were in the kitchen?"

Shelly grinned and sat in a chair near him. "I made us a cake."

"You seem happy here." He regarded her carefully as he sat down next to her.

"I am."

"I see that Dillon disregarded my . . . uh . . . advice in the letter I sent."

Shelly met his eyes. "I love him."

"I know that! How does *he* feel?"

"You needn't worry. He's going to marry me."

Adam chuckled. "It's about time that boy got it right. When's the event?"

"Soon," she said. "Unless his father has come for a long visit," she mumbled. "Dillon seems hostile around him. Do you know why they don't seem to like each other?"

"I think that is something you should ask Dillon. I'm finished telling his secrets. I brought you some things that might distract you."

"Oh?"

"Some of your mother's things, letters from your father, jewelry she left at the house. They lived with me when they weren't on that ship of his, which was seldom."

"Oh, Adam! Where are they?"

Her eyes were shining so brightly that Adam was touched by her excitement. "I loved my sister very much and it's a great gift to be able to make her daughter smile."

"Don't go getting sentimental."

"I wouldn't do such a thing."

"You always get what you want," Dillon stated blandly, throwing down the new contracts on his desk.

His father turned from looking at the picture of his first wife. "Usually. Or damn close," he said confidently. "She was a beautiful woman, my Loretta. I didn't want her to die. I've never found a woman as perfectly pleasing as her."

"Well, Cora tried her damnedest, she just spread her resources a little thin." John Ryder looked scathingly down at his son and Dillon blinked. "Why did Edward agree to merge without the marriage?" Dillon asked, changing the subject.

John sat down in a chair across from Dillon's desk. "He didn't want to sacrifice his only child's happiness and make her marry you since she did not love you and could not foresee spending a lifetime with someone she found so incomprehensible to her. Pretty good. Did you coach her?"

Dillon shook his head.

"She told Daddy how she wanted a gentle man who would not take her so far from her home. Of course, Edward liked that, the silly old fool. He felt quite contrite about disappointing you and me. I told him that it really didn't matter if our children were going to be difficult—we didn't need them. We could still have a solid partnership without being tied by marriage, hence this agreement. Fifty percent of control and profit goes to Edward and fifty percent for us. You need to sign the papers detailing the breakdown of the interests between ourselves. Thirty-five percent is in my control and fifteen percent is in yours."

"I'll read them closely after dinner."

"Annette wants no part of the business, so the contract specifies a generous yearly allowance be paid her after Edward's death. We'll have ourselves a Ryder empire one day, Dillon."

"Lovely to hear you looking forward to your friend's death, Father."

John's eyes pierced his son's. "I see an advantage when it's in front of me."

"What if I don't sign?" Dillon asked softly.

His father shrugged. "You'll miss out on a fortune. I hope your mine can support you. I'll take control of Ryder Shipping on the west coast. Maybe I'll shut it down or sell it—a shame after all the work you've put into it."

Dillon shuffled through the papers his father had so carefully drawn up. There was sure to be no disadvantage for his father in the pages.

Shelly announced dinner as Dillon was reading the papers. "I'm starving!" she said enthusiastically, standing beside him. "What have you got there?" she asked, looking over his shoulder.

"A new contract," Dillon said, rising.

"Such unusual writing," she said.

"My father's."

"Well, I hope it's better than the last contract! Come eat." She left the room. John Ryder rose slowly.

"This is the woman you chose over Annette King," he said dismally. "Annette is such a gracious young woman who knows her place."

"Don't you mean *your* place?" Dillon led his father toward the dining room and wondered if he should sign the contract, since it meant dealing with his father. He could survive just fine without the shipping and shipbuilding business.

Dinner was civilized due largely to the fact that Adam and Shelly did most of the talking while John and Dillon Ryder avoided being drawn into conversation. Everyone ate well of the soup, roast, bread and vegetables that the maid had prepared. Shelly brought the cake out and set it in the middle of the table. John Ryder and Adam stared at Dillon when he began chuckling and then burst out in loud laughter.

"Dillon, whatever is the matter with you?" asked Shelly innocently. "It's a fine-looking cake." She looked back at the cake piled with mounds of whipped cream, each round mound peaked with a bright red raspberry.

"It's a luscious-looking cake," Dillon agreed, still chuckling.

After dinner Dillon and his father returned to the study and Shelly closeted herself in Adam's bedroom. "Where are they?" she burst out as soon as she closed the door behind her.

Adam laughed. "In that trunk." He lifted it to the bed and opened it for her. On top were the letters. They were tied in two bundles with faded yellow ribbon. Shelly's eyes shone as she weighed the bundles in her hands. Her fingers lightly traced her mother's name on the outside of an envelope. She shivered and put them aside, planning to read them in private and at her leisure. She pulled out a pillow Adam said was embroidered by her mother. It was a burst of yellow and white roses on a green background. "She liked roses, too." Shelly smiled.

"Her favorites were the yellow ones."

"Mine are the pink."

She pulled out handkerchiefs embroidered with the initials *MJY,* some simply *MJ;* several of her mother's favorite books, flowers that James had given her pressed between the pages; beautiful brooches, earrings and necklaces, many of which had been passed down from Shelly's grandmother. After the small things were lifted out Shelly picked up the tissue-wrapped item. She brushed the leaves of tissue away and sucked in her breath as she held a delicately embroidered child's christening gown.

"Mine? I wore this?" Adam nodded. She wanted to cry, but there was still one more thing. She reached for the black box nestled in the corner. Inside was a heart-shaped locked of gold against black velvet.

"He gave her that before they were engaged and she wore it constantly while he was at sea." Shelly laid it in her palm. "Open it."

There was a lock of hair inside, a rich mahogany brown. Her fingers trembled as she unpinned a strand of her own hair and held the locket close. The same. She swallowed and could not look at Adam. "My father's?"

"Yes."

"Oh, my." Her fingers tightened around the locket and she cried.

When Shelly had dried her tears she slipped down to the study and sat in a big leather chair with her sketchbook. She missed her books that had burned in the fire. First, her parents had died in a fire. Then she lost all her drawn memories in one. The first drawing in the one she had now was of Dillon at his desk, the place he'd been so much of the time when she first came to his house. There were pictures of Mr. Hill, and one of roses and trees and birds and the front of Dillon's house. Now, she surreptitiously glanced at Dillon's father and put him down on paper. She had trouble with the eyes, which were so much like Dillon's in shape and color but very different in how hard they glittered. The man was watching Dillon read, his foot tapping always. Shelly wondered why he didn't pick up a book or a newspaper, but he only raised and lowered his glass of brandy as if the strength of his gaze would keep Dillon reading.

Shelly tossed her sketchbook down and stood behind Dillon and massaged his shoulders. He grunted appreciatively while his father frowned. She read over his shoulder of terms and conditions. His father's writing was difficult to read. No wonder Dillon was taking so long. The writing was messy, but not in a cramped way; it was a bold scrawl, as if the writer liked moving with much flourish and speed across the page. For some reason it looked familiar, as if she had seen it before. Bored, she sat back down. She picked up her sketchbook and drew Dillon, lingering with love on his neck, his jaw. She wanted to go to bed with him now, hear him say he loved her again.

She turned back to his father's picture and made his eyes as hard as she saw them. He looked very mean when she had added a few more lines. She duplicated his writing, which she found interesting. She pictured the word *ship* and she wrote it just as he had in the contract Dillon held. Why did she know this scrawl? She wrote words again, trying to duplicate the writing, almost running off the page. *Almost running off the page like he was in a great hurry.* She'd said that to Diego in Karl's room, the man who wasn't really Karl, as she held that letter that told of Dillon's silver. She couldn't look up. She stared transfixed at the writing she'd been playing with.

"Well, it's about time."

Shelly jerked her head up, saw Dillon lifting his pen to sign the papers. "No!" She flew across the room, shoving his arm away and knocking his inkwell over, making a great spreading black mess. He looked up at her in openmouthed amazement.

"What the hell?" yelled his father, jumping up.

Her hands trembling violently, Shelly picked up the papers, some of the edges soaked with ink, and studied the writing. "It is. I know it is," she whispered.

"What are you doing?" demanded John Ryder.

Shelly still couldn't look at him but held the paper and turned to Dillon, even her lips trembling now. "I recognize this writing, Dillon. It was . . . it was . . . the same writing on the letter to Karl, telling what to do with your silver."

Dillon's eyes narrowed on her face and she shuddered. Oh, sweet Lord, what if I'm wrong? she asked herself. He'll never forgive me.

"What is she babbling about? Has she gone crazy? Is she trying to ruin your life?" John Ryder grabbed the papers in Shelly's hands and pulled, but Shelly wouldn't let go. "Give them over!" he roared.

Dillon sat still and watched the tug-of-war over his desk. His father suddenly released his hold and Shelly fell back against a bookshelf.

"This is ridiculous!" John Ryder said, and threw up his hands.

"His writing is very distinct," Shelly said, not looking at either of them but down at the pages she held in front of her, shaking like a banner in the wind. "I'm sure it's the same. I wouldn't say such a thing otherwise."

"Bring the papers back," Dillon said unemotionally. Shelly obeyed and laid them on his desk, her eyes filling with tears. "Leave the room." She turned and kept the tears from falling until she was through the door.

His father shuddered. "Slightly insane girl, accusing me of that." He sat down, a slight tremor in his hands. Dillon lifted his gaze from his father's hands and blotted at the spilled ink with a newspaper. "As if I need to steal from my own son." His father laughed.

"No, you just needed to get me back on track," Dillon said quietly.

John Ryder studied Dillon's knowing eyes.

"You knew it was in my best interest to expand Ryder Shipping. You needed to keep me focused on my responsibilities, coming back to New York and marrying Annette so we could merge with Edward. Unfortunately, I didn't want Annette anymore, but I did need to spend time with Edward and learn about the building of our ships, didn't I? And if a little frustration on my part was what it took, then it had to be done. You could have told Oscar to keep his hands off my person, though, Father." Dillon smiled coldly.

His father just looked at him.

"It was close there, Father. I'd prefer a partner who had his men under better control. Oscar had too much power. But the Ryder blood was just too damn strong for that German." Dillon met his father's gaze, no cloud of confusion in his eyes.

John Ryder looked at Dillon uncertainly. "He was just trying to defend himself," he muttered.

"He did a damn good job. I should show you my scars!"

"I'm sorry about that, Dillon. If I'd realized it was just Annette that was such an impediment I wouldn't have had to go to such lengths. I truly thought you were only interested in playing with this unreliable mine. It's fine for a sideline, but you need to keep straight what will be most profitable for us. I've had the ore you didn't recover refined. I'll send you a statement on it. I put the money into building a ship. Sign the contract, Son, and we'll be in business."

Dillon looked at his father. "Do you want to know what Cora said she liked most about you?" His father looked surprised. "She liked your talent for getting what you wanted no matter the means." Dillon picked up the contract and slowly ripped it in half.

His father sat still, one ankle resting on his knee. "I'm sorry Oscar died before killing Shelly the way he was supposed to." He smiled.

With a bellow of rage, Dillon shoved his massive oak desk over and lunged for his father. The older man stood prepared and cool and caught Dillon on the chin with his fist. The blow slowed Dillon. The one his father belted into his stomach was worse. He doubled over, clutching his arms against him. He looked up to see his father before him, fists ready for the next punch, and the last fourteen years evaporated. He was sixteen again and naked. A surge of hate propelled him forward. He circled his father, looking for an opening. His father was good. Dillon ended up shoving his blocking arms until he had him slammed against the paneled wood wall. Dillon got his hands around his father's throat. John Ryder pulled at the tightening fingers and knifed one knee into the softness of Dillon's groin. Dillon yelled in pure animal rage and pain, collapsing to his knees but bringing his father down with him. Dillon, with slightly more weight on him, forced his father beneath him, and his hands tightened on the older man's throat.

Shelly had been sitting on the stairs with her head in her hands when she heard the crash. She jumped and then walked slowly down the stairs. She heard a grunt of pain when she was just outside the study. The door swung open noiselessly under her hand. In the yellow light of wall lamps Shelly saw them on the floor. They were both red-faced and slowly writhing, trying to strangle each other.

"Stop it! Stop it!" She spun around frantically and saw Adam standing shocked and speechless in the doorway. She grabbed the whiskey and brandy decanters off the table with shaking hands and splashed the contents into the faces of both men. Instantly, they broke apart, choking, gasping and rubbing their eyes.

Through a blur Dillon saw Shelly standing above him, an empty glass decanter in each hand. He rose stiffly, spared a brief glance at his father and felt a wave of disgust for the man, and a little for himself for rising to the bait and almost killing him.

John Ryder rose and ran a shaking hand through his dark, gray-streaked hair, now damp with alcohol. "You almost killed me, you idiot!"

Dillon stumbled to his overturned desk and leaned his hands on it, his back to his father. "Get out of my house. I don't want any part of Ryder Shipping, and if you ever interfere in any way with me or anything I care about—I will kill you."

"I will have my driver gather your things," Shelly said woodenly, unable to look for longer than a second at the man who stood so haughty. Adam backed out of the room, John Ryder followed, and Shelly came last, shutting the door on Dillon. She stood within four feet of John Ryder, like a guard, while the driver loaded his belongings into the carriage.

"How could you steal from him and lie to him?" she asked quietly.

He laughed bitterly. "You don't know the half of it."

"He's your only son," she said, as if that should have stopped him.

He faced her. "You think so?"

Shelly drew back.

John Ryder grasped her shoulders and held her at arm's length. Shelly, shocked and curious, did not struggle. "You're not bad, Shelly York. Oscar wrote you were a strident peasant, but you've got the body of Cora and a fair enough face. I guess that's enough for Dillon. Such low ambitions that boy has."

He released her and climbed into the carriage. Shelly stood a long time watching the road after she could no longer see the carriage.

"Dillon?"

He turned slowly from where he leaned against his desk to stare at the woman in front of him. He hadn't heard the door open. He'd been staring at his reflection in the black window and remembering the role his father had played throughout his life. The man had never been very interested in him, until he was fullgrown and able to be used for profit. Dillon felt weary in his soul and wanted Shelly to leave him alone; he couldn't bear just yet to answer the many questions she probably had for him.

"He's gone," she said.

Dillon nodded.

She held out her hand. "Come with me."

He stared at her hand, his own folded under his arms, which were crossed against his chest. She tugged one loose and gently pulled him after her to the kitchen. She had tea on the table and a steaming bath in front of the hot stove. The lamp on the table gave off a yellow glow. She stood before him and unbuttoned his shirt and pulled it off his arms. "You reek of whiskey. I hope it doesn't still burn."

Dillon let her unbutton his trousers and pull them down, along with his drawers. He braced his hands on her shoulders while she pulled off his boots.

"Get in."

The water was hot. He sucked in his breath and slowly leaned back against the tin tub. Shelly wet and soaped his hair. He groaned as her fingers pressed into his skull and down the base of his head. She rinsed him off and poured him a mug of steaming dark tea, then pushed him forward. He sipped the liquid while she soaped his back, her thumbs massaging along the sides of his spine. "Lean back."

She washed his scarred chest, his legs, her hands pressing into muscles he didn't know he had. She took the tea out of his hand and he realized he'd been about to drop the empty mug. She washed his feet and Dillon thought he could die now and be happy.

"Stand up." She dried him off and held out his robe. She picked up the lamp and he followed her upstairs. It was so nice not to think, just to do as she said. He realized as she closed the bedroom door behind them how much he trusted her. He climbed into bed in his robe and watched as she undressed. She left her underclothes on. He reached for her and pulled her close.

"Talk to me first," she whispered as his hand slid under her camisole.

"No, Shelly." He buried his face in the curve of her neck.

"Please. Tell me who Cora is. Your father said I looked like her."

Dillon rolled on his back and slipped an arm under Shelly's neck. "Cora was the first woman I loved. She married my father and slept with both of us, only my father didn't know that for a while." He felt Shelly stiffen beside him. "My story is not pretty."

She rolled to her side and smoothed her hand over his stomach beneath the gaping robe. "That's okay."

"You may share some physical characteristics with her, but that's not why I love you," he said softly.

"I believe you. Tell me more."

"My father almost killed me when he found me with Cora. I was sixteen. He threw me out. I got on one of his ships and worked my passage out to California. I didn't much like the sea and I'm not sorry he's going to close me out of the shipping business. I like my mine. And there's timber up north that's worth a fortune."

"Tell me more about your father."

Dillon sighed. "I came back after nine years and he treated me like an interesting possibility." Shelly caressed his belly and his chest and Dillon told her about the plans his father had had for him and all the ways Dillon had disappointed him. Shelly reached up and kissed a tear off his face when he spoke about his father's final betrayal.

Embarrassed by his tears, Dillon cursed his father's name.

"Outside he implied to me that he had another son."

"Not that I know of. My mother died after childbirth. That son lived a week and my father never picked him up. Can we kick the man out of our bed now?"

Shelly laughed and moved her hand down from his belly.

"Yes," Dillon gasped. He took the solace she offered with her warm body and generous lips and hands.

Shelly woke to a warm hand moving on her back. She groaned as the hand massaged the muscles of her lower back and then worked up her spine.

"I have something for you downstairs," Dillon said.

Shelly rolled over lazily and smiled up at Dillon. He looked wide-awake and handsome despite the puffy, discolored bruises on his chin from his father's fist. "How long have you been up?" she asked, yawning.

"Hours."

Something suspicious was going on. "What's downstairs?"

Dillon smiled. "Come down and see." He gave her a quick kiss on her collarbone and then bounced off the bed and walked to the door. "Put on some clothes first. You can't get married like that." He walked out and shut the door and Shelly screamed.

"Dillon, come back here!" She beat her fist on the bed. "Married!" she repeated to herself.

He poked his head back in. "Shelly, don't be so difficult. I know I agreed to marry you when you wanted, but would it kill you to marry me this morning?"

Shelly blinked, her mouth hanging open. "You beast," she whispered.

"What kind of answer is that?"

"It's a yes, yes, yes, *yes!*" She scrambled off the bed and ran toward him, clutching a blanket around her. He laughed and caught her and swung her around. She kissed him ten quick times and then pushed him away and ran down the hall to her yellow room, where all her clothes were.

Dillon was waiting at the bottom of the stairs for her. "Shelly," he breathed when he saw her at the top. She was wearing the white dress he'd bought her, the opals he'd given her, and a rainbow of ribbons in her long, loose hair. The ribbons were left streaming, tied in bows and threaded through a few small braids. "You look beautiful," he said when she reached the bottom step. He clasped her hand and pulled her toward the drawing room, where Adam and the minister waited.

"It's about time you two got this part done!" announced Adam.

Shelly flushed crimson. "Adam," she warned, looking at the minister. The tall, lanky man smiled at her. The ceremony was short and simple and Shelly was half-dazed throughout. Dillon slipped on her finger her mother's pearl-and-diamond ring, which Adam had brought with him. "I thought you'd like it back," her uncle said.

"I now pronounce you man and wife. You may kiss the bride."

Warm lips against warm lips. Shelly thought she was going to burst with happiness. Dillon was her husband. She had a home in this house.

Adam pointed to two large flat packages tied up in brown paper and string. "Your wedding presents!"

"How did you know?" asked Shelly.

Adam winked. "How could you both be in California and it not happen?"

Shelly ripped the paper off until she saw the oil-painted surface beneath. "My mother?" she whispered. Adam nodded. She slowly pulled out the portrait that had hung in

Adam's study. "How could you part with it?" she asked in an awed voice.

"It was easy, knowing that you'd have it. The other one," he said brusquely, not wanting her to dissolve into emotion and take him along.

She carefully unwrapped the package. "My father," she said simply when she looked into the gray eyes in the portrait. Her eyes, her hair and even her strong jaw. She touched his cheek. "He's really handsome, isn't he? And a bit reckless looking...with a touch of arrogance," she stated proudly.

"Shares a few similarities with your husband, doesn't he?" said Adam with a laugh.

Dillon grinned and stepped behind her, his arms circling her waist and holding her tight. "But I'm going to be around a long, long time to love you," he whispered against her ear.

Chapter Thirty-Two

Shelly crept down the stairs, holding her nightgown over her ankles with one hand.

"Sneaking away?"

Shelly dropped her gown and stood straight. "I thought you were asleep!" She turned to face her husband, who stood at the top of the stairs. He was barefoot and wearing a pair of loose, comfortable trousers with no shirt. They'd been married two days and not been fully dressed since her uncle had left shortly after the ceremony for a two-week stay in the most luxurious San Francisco hotel he could find.

"Sleep?" Dillon idly scratched his chest and came down the steps. "Without you?"

"You don't do it *with* me!"

He reached his wife, shared her step and cinched his arms around her waist. "I can't." He nuzzled her neck and squeezed her bottom, gripping her hard against him. "We haven't tried the stairs yet."

"I'm hungry!" She tugged his hands off her backside and laughed at his forlorn expression.

Dillon followed her into the kitchen, looking over her shoulder as she searched the pantry. "That looks good," he said, his stomach rumbling when Shelly pulled the cover off half a cherry pie. She plopped the pie on the kitchen table. Dillon got them each a fork and they sat across from each other and ate. Shelly satisfied her immediate hunger and sat back to watch Dillon devour his side of the pan. His hair was tangled and his unshaven face rough with bristles. She

lifted her bare feet off the cool kitchen floor to rest on his.
Dillon looked up and winked at her.

"Do you know when I fell in love with you?" she asked.
"Not that I admitted it."

"Let's see," he mused, his fork poised between pan and
mouth, a juicy cherry stabbed on the end. "Was it when I
tied you up in that meeting room and left you after threatening Aggie with harm? No?"

"No. It started when you apologized for reading my letter to Aggie. You really cared that I felt wronged. And then
you kissed me so soft." Dillon looked uncomfortable and
shoved another forkful of pie into his mouth. Shelly kicked
him, gently, with her big toe. "Your turn."

Dillon rolled his eyes. "I fell in love with you after your
bath in Carson City when I saw what you really looked
like."

"That was lust, not love. Be serious!"

"I seriously fell in lust then. When you were so damned
independent and surprising on the trail and in Virginia City
I began to teeter. When you came to visit after that bastard
Oscar stabbed me, I was falling. When I made love to you
on the ship to New York I'd almost hit bottom, and when I
thought I'd lost you in New York I knew I'd crashed." His
eyes were shining on her face while a tear slipped down her
cheek. "Is that enough? Do you wonder if I still love you?
Maybe I should show you?"

"I want some more pie," Shelly sniffed.

"Bring it up with you." His voice was low and throaty
and caressed her nerve endings.

"I can't do two things at once," she retorted with feigned
disinterest. Her face turned hot from the way he was looking at her.

"You don't have to." He picked up the pie pan in one
hand and came around the table and pulled Shelly up with
the other. "You eat your pie and I'll show you my love." He
draped an arm around her shoulders and walked her out of
the kitchen and back up the stairs, describing all the forms
his love would take.

Shelly shook her head, trying to suppress a smile, but when he suggested a particularly wild form of pleasure, she burst out laughing. "I'm supposed to eat while you do that? We'll make a mess!"

He pulled her into the bedroom. "The bed is already a mess from last night."

Shelly grimaced while remembering how she had spilled her soup in bed and then Dillon had spilled the wine, on purpose, all over her.

She sighed. She never would have guessed she'd be so blessedly happy with the man that had terrified her in the office of Snelling's Shipping a year before. Dillon shut the door behind them—and locked it.

* * * * *

presents
MARCH MADNESS!

Come March, we're lining up four wonderful stories by four dazzling newcomers—and we guarantee you won't be disappointed! From the stark beauty of Medieval Wales to marauding *bandidos* in Chihuahua, Mexico, return to the days of enchantment and high adventure with characters who will touch your heart.

LOOK FOR
> **STEAL THE STARS** (HH #115) by *Miranda Jarrett*
> **THE BANDIT'S BRIDE** (HH #116) by *Ana Seymour*
> **ARABESQUE** (HH #117) by *Kit Gardner*
> **A WARRIOR'S HEART** (HH #118) by *Margaret Moore*

So rev up for spring with a bit of March Madness...only from
Harlequin Historicals!

MM92

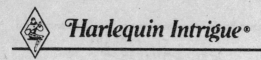

Harlequin Regency Romance™

WHO SAYS ROMANCE IS A THING OF THE PAST?

We do! At Harlequin Regency Romance, we offer you romance the way it was always meant to be.

What could be more romantic than to follow the adventures of a duchess or duke through the glittering assembly rooms of Regency England? Or to eavesdrop on their witty conversations or romantic interludes? The music, the costumes, the ballrooms and the dance will sweep you away to a time when pleasure was a priority and privilege a prerequisite.

If you are longing for the good old days when falling in love still meant something very special, then come to Harlequin Regency Romance—romance with a touch of class.

RRG

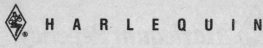

A Calendar of Romance

Be a part of American Romance's year-long celebration of love and the holidays of 1992. Experience all the passion of falling in love during the excitement of each month's holiday. Some of your favorite authors will help you celebrate those special times of the year, like the revelry of New Year's Eve, the romance of Valentine's Day, the magic of St. Patrick's Day.

Start counting down to the new year with

#421 HAPPY NEW YEAR, DARLING
by Margaret St. George

Read all the books in *A Calendar of Romance*, coming to you one each month, all year, from Harlequin American Romance.

American Romance®

COR1